ELIJAH N. MEKWUNYE

IS *Silence* REALLY GOLDEN?

In a Bully Infested World,
IS SILENCE REALLY GOLDEN?

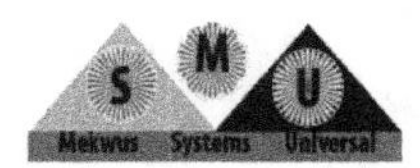

Is Silence Really Golden?
In A Bully Infested World, Is Silence Really Golden?
All Rights Reserved.
Copyright © 2017 Elijah N. Mekwunye
V4.0 R3.9

This is a work of fiction. The events and characters described herein are imaginary and are not intended to refer to specific places or living persons. The opinions expressed in this manuscript are solely the opinions of the author and do not represent the opinions or thoughts of the publisher. The author has represented and warranted full ownership and/or legal right to publish all the materials in this book.

This book may not be reproduced, transmitted, or stored in whole or in part by any means, including graphic, electronic, or mechanical without the express written consent of the publisher except in the case of brief quotations embodied in critical articles and reviews.

Mekwus Systems Universal Corp., Inc.

Paperback ISBN: 978-0-9979230-0-1

Cover Photo © 2017 thinkstockphotos.com. All rights reserved - used with permission.

PRINTED IN THE UNITED STATES OF AMERICA

*To my dearest Family and to the Disabled Community
who are constantly bombarded with Bully-like challenges*

The Oxford Advanced Learner's dictionary defines bully as someone who "frightens or hurts a weaker person..." The Merriam-webster dictionary defines a bully as "someone who frightens, hurts, or threatens smaller or weaker people." Another dictionary defines bully as someone who "seeks to harm, intimidate, or coerce another person who is perceived as vulnerable" or gullible. Perhaps you could relate to children who are bullied or often picked on, and sometimes beaten after school.

.... Bullying is a global problem that can only be solved globally.

Repudiate the Normalization of Bullying

The impact of bullying is felt universally and can be seen in all aspects of life. When one country invades another country, they often resort to bullying to control the natural resources and wealth of the invaded country. A leader of a country holding fellow countrymen as hostages for selfish gain is another example of bullying. Another example occurs in a family where a family member decides to be a vicious and vindictive dictator by bullying family members and squandering family's resources without accountability or consequences.

The impact of bullying is felt in a community setting when children are too afraid to go to school or too afraid to play outside due to their fear of bullies. Let us not forget the impact it has on a young lady who desires to sight see her community but too afraid of venturing out due to her fear of being bullied and mugged. Cases where a nonsmoker is subjected to secondhand smoke, on purpose, as a threat of annoyance and bullying, which sadly has led to some nonsmokers being diagnosed with lung cancer. This book offers encouragement to all those who at one point in their life suffered from the tyranny of bullies. What can you do to help mitigate this global problem? Repudiate the normalization of bullying.

TABLE OF CONTENTS

There is no doubt that when a given society is plagued with bullies, human existence in such a given society is usually threatened or under threat until that society fights back to reclaim its own. The world is becoming smaller and smaller each day, such that it seems that your problem is becoming my problem and my problem is becoming your problem. Consider a household that is being robbed at gun point for example, would your thought be one that lacks concern for the wellbeing of that household because you want to "mind your own business"? Or would you extend a helping hand by calling the law enforcers to that household for who knows, the next unfortunate door may be yours? Bully is nearly as old as man on the Earth. Scripturally, Cain literally bullied his brother Abel to death[20]. For just a little while the world that survived the great flood of Noah's day was happy to see an end to the Nephilim's[22] brutal era.

Bullying is a global problem that can only be solved globally.

Yes, bullying is a global problem that can only be solved globally. It typifies the fact that while no country is an island, no man can be an island even if he wants to. We all have survival instinct that is characterized by the embedded will not to die, but to live.[21] Since bullying is a global problem that can only be solved by the Supreme being, the Highest of the Highest, the designer of life as we know it, the priceless question is, what can you do to help mitigate this global problem that has plagued mankind from time immemorial?

The intention of this play is to provide a formidable answer to the question of whether or not silence can indeed be golden most of the time, if not all of the time with respect to dealing with bullies. You will soon find out in this play that bullies present themselves in different forms and shapes and are not limited to trusted ones in the name of family members. I will tell my story through the eyes of animated characters. Some of these characters will see through the human eyes and learn from their track records – the human behavior under certain conditions at a given time. Regardless of the unorthodox behavior of the animal world, mankind can learn a lesson or two from them about how the powerless can be made powerful and thus, curb if not completely eradicate the tyranny of bullies.

Some of my characters are a family of Fox, which includes Mamma Fox named Sassy her two sons, Zack and Sean. Zach is older. A family of Chickens with six little Chicks Ikem, Fuza, Nebum, Osey, Osan, and Mel. Chuwawa is the name of Mamma Chicken; and a family of Ducks. Cassandra is the name of Mamma Duck and she has four little Ducklings, the oldest one being Kazzy, followed by Mooney, Zaffy, and Akuna. The story begins when the Fox family decides to make a feast from both the families of Chickens and Ducks, but the Fox family is indecisive respecting which family they should devour first. Sassy sent her two boys with a message to both Mamma Chicken and Mamma Duck. The message is that at five o'clock PM today, both families (Chicken and Duck) will become dinner to the Fox Family.

The result? Understandably, Mamma Chicken does not take the news too kindly as she rumbles with unkind words all over the little Foxes. What about Mamma Duck? She does not say a word. She occasionally quacks as she aimlessly walks about with her neck in constant forward and backward motion as though in expectation of something great. So, the little Foxes mistake Mamma Duck's quacking for silence. They could not make a word out of her quacks. When these little Foxes tell Mamma Fox of the outcome, Mamma Fox decides to leave the Duck's family alone since Mamma Duck said practically nothing nor insult her little ones. We will soon however, find out how the Foxes feel about the Chicken's family.

What is the moral of this story and how can you apply it in your life? What can you do to help mitigate this global problem of bullying?

Mamma Fox	--	Sassy
Sassy's older son	--	Zach
Sassy's younger son	--	Sean
Mamma Duck	--	Cassandra
Cassandra's Ducklings	--	Kazzy, Mooney, Zaffy, and Akuna.
Mamma Chicken	--	Chuwawa
Chuwawa's Chicks	--	Ikem, Fuza, Nebum, Osey, Osan, Mel
Papa Ape	--	Francesco
Mamma Ape	--	Fiorina
Francesco's son	--	Rawlings
Porcupine 1	--	Oteetota
Porcupine 2	--	Pamimpao
Papa Tiger	--	Jeunkoku
Mamma Tiger	--	Kotito
Papa Slow Loris	--	Rindi
Mamma Slow Loris	--	Gunmi
Slow Loris' first son	--	Juba

Slow Loris' second son	--	Motepori
Slow Loris' daughter Papa	--	Motayori Zuka
Lion	--	Shelly Mokere
Mamma Lion	--	Magun
Lioness 1	--	
Lioness 2	--	

Human Characters:

Chiyem Chizom	--	Chiyem
Florence Chizom Pamela	--	Florence Pamela
Chizom Elizabeth Chizom	--	Lizzy
Onyekachi Chimebelem	--	Kachi
	--	
Board Certified Behavior Analyst		Gershom

The Play

PILOT – THE INTENTIONS OF A BULLY

In Sassy's den. Returning from the market, Sassy walks in. 'Zach! Sean!' she calls on her two sons. 'Yes, Mamma, here we are' Zach and Sean answer as they come running in to meet Sassy, Mamma Fox. 'Now, what are we going to have for dinner tonight since the market has nothing good to offer at the moment?' Sassy jovially asks as she is in a good mood. Let us listen to their conversation, shall we?

Zach: No idea Mamma, but you are the Mother and shine. The den mother. I'm sure you'll figure something out for us.

Sean: But Mamma, whatever it is you'll be figuring out, please let it be something we all can enjoy. Would you?

Sassy: [Keeping her jovial mood, she sarcastically asks] Yeah, yeah, yeah! Since when has Mamma come up with something you could not enjoy? Huh Sean?

Sean is silent with a fading smile as he anticipates what his Mamma has got cooking up her sleeves.

Sassy: Well, kids we are going to have for dinner either Chicken or Duck or both. But first, we are going to laugh at their misery as they both beg for their lives. So, this is what you boys are going to do. I'm sending the both of you to go and tell Chuwawa (Mamma Chicken) and Cassandra (Mamma Duck) that come five o'clock PM today, they will be our dinner. Got it?

Zach & Sean: Yes, Mamma, we got it.

Sassy: Good. Now you can leave, and I bid you well.

Zach & Sean: Bye Mamma. [Exit Zach and Sean]

[On their way to Chuwawa's den]

Sean: Hey Zach, which part of Chuwawa would you like to devour?

Zach: Well, I think I will enjoy Chuwawa's head and drumstick better than any other part of her body.

Sean: I think Chuwawa's head has already been spoken for.

Zach: Spoken for by whom?

Sean: Mamma of course. Who else?

Zach: We'll see about that won't we?

Sean: O yes! We certainly will! I'll like to see how you would talk Mamma into letting you have Chuwawa's head.

Zach: Ok you'll see. Now, what about Cassandra?

Sean: What do you mean what about Cassandra? Zach: What part of her would you like to eat the most?

Sean: Well, I am shooting for the head and her breasts?

Zach: Not even in your dreams will that happen. But keep dreaming. The breast certainly belongs to Mamma as you know how she likes to eat white meat only.

Sean: Alright, alright. But what is white meat?

Zach: White meat includes the breasts and wings of Chickens and Ducks which Mamma will go for. You can, however, settle for dark meat. I said that nicely because that is the only parts you are going to get after Mamma and I are done choosing. So, go figure.

Sean: Hey! Wait a minute Zach. What is "dark meat" and what do you mean by "go figure" and why should I always be the one settling for dark meat or whatever it is?

Zach: Good Sean, dark meat is any part of a bird that's not white meat. Dark meat includes the legs or drumstick of the bird and it's usually the fatty parts of a bird. When I say, "go figure," I mean go and figure it out. What I'm saying is that you should go and figure out the reason why you can only get the dark meat of the bird. I am in no way trying to be mean to you, I just want you to know that after Mamma chooses most of the white meat, there will practically be nothing left for you and I to share. Can you understand that Sean?

Sean: OK. Zach, I understand. I promise you Zach, a day is coming in which I will have my own family. I will eat nothing short of white meat since I can't have it now.

Zach: Sean, is not that you can't have white meat now. It's just that you are long way down the royal lineage. Be patient my brother. Remember, endurance can be golden, and patience is a virtue.

Sean: Zach, what is a virtue?

Zach: A virtue is something of quality that you must have to succeed in life. A virtue is moral excellence, or a positive trait or quality deemed to be morally good and thus is valued as a foundation of principle and good moral being. So, patience is one of the few qualities you need to succeed in anything you set your mind to do.

Sean: Wow! Zach that is deep stuff. How did you come to know all of that?

Zach: Good question Sean, I studied well. When I come across a word that I'm not familiar with, I pick up a dictionary and look for the meaning of that word. I like dictionaries that explain the etymology of a specific word.

Sean: Zach, did I hear you right? Did you just say etymology?

Zach: Yes, Sean. I did.

Sean: What on Earth is etymology? It's like I can't even say it right.

Zach: Sean paraphrasing a dictionary, etymology is simply the study of the origin of words and the way in which their meanings have changed from one generation and culture to another. It can also be the study of formation and development of words throughout history.

Sean: Wow! That is even deeper. Please Zach, tell me more.

Zach: Sure Sean. You know how Mom always tell you to set a concrete goal so that you can accomplish your tasks, especially the tasks of cleaning after you've had your meal?

Sean: Tell me about it Zach. I don't even know the meaning to the word "concrete" let alone what it does.

Zach: Sean, concrete is something simple, something small, and something achievable. So, concrete is something simple, small and achievable. Little by little is how the pig's nose enters the yard.

Sean: What? Zach, what do you mean?

Zach: Well, the statement that little by little is how a pig's nose enters the yard simply mean that you should attend to a small problem before it becomes uncontrollable. Having said that, Mom is asking you not to let your chores pile up to where they become so big in your eyes that you feel too tired to get them done. But if you divide those chores into smaller chores, it will become simple for you to complete one smaller chore at a time. Before you know it, you'll be done with the rest of your chores. That is how I handle my chores.

Sean: So, are you saying that it would be easier for me to do my chores as they come in than to wait for them to pile up?

Zach: Yes! Sean, you got the point and that is concrete. Yes, you have the chore small, simple, and as a result, achievable. That is, you can accomplish it in no time, and you'll be happy.

Sean: Thanks Zach.

Zach: Hey Sean, that is what big brothers are for. I am glad I can help.

Zach and Sean at Chuwawa's den

Chuwawa: What are you princes of the world doing here and to whom shall I send my gratitude for this August[1] visit? [Chuwawa sarcastically asks since there is no way she will welcome a visit from any Fox or deal with anyone possessing the behavior that remotely resembles the Fox's caliber[8].]

Zach: Sean, would you stop shivering? Are you afraid? You are going to make Chuwawa think we are afraid of her. [Addressing his little brother Sean who seems to be at the mercy of Chuwawa and shaking profusely at the frightening sight of Chuwawa's madness]

Sean: Of course, I am afraid! I am trying my best not to show it. She's acting as though she's out of her mind. Any pointers?

[Sean asks his brother for help on how not to express his fear in Chuwawa's presence.]

Zach: Just stop! Would you? Why are you terrified at Chuwawa's sight anyway?

Sean: I'm terrified because Chuwawa is hysterically insane!

Zach: Chuwawa may be hysterically insane, but, the bottom line is that she is afraid of us.

Sean: Seriously? Is she, really?

Zach: Yes, Sean! She is terrified of us. Haven't you heard about the sayings?

Sean: Zach, what sayings are you talking about?

Zach: The saying that let it be seven years that the carcass of a Fox lay bare on the ground, the great grandmother of a rooster or a hen is not well delivered to go there for a view.

Sean: Wow! That is so deep, Zach.

Zach: You see my dear brother, Chuwawa is not only afraid of you as you are standing there, she is even more afraid of your carcass! So, suit up yourself and act like a mean machine that you are.

Sean: Ok! Yes! I'm a mean machine! [Sean composes himself like he's getting ready to hurt someone.]

Zach: [Turning his attention to Chuwawa, Zach confidently says] We are here to deliver a message to you from our mother.

Chuwawa: Really?

Zach: Yes, really Chuwawa.

Chuwawa: Now, what message of doom does Mamma Fox have for me?

Zach: My Mamma said come five o'clock this evening you are going to be our dinner.

Chuwawa: Really? She said that?

Zach: Yes, Chuwawa. She surely did.

[Chuwawa is so distraught, hopping up and down, ready to fight.]

Chuwawa: Well, you go tell your sniffling no good for nothing Mamma that I will be right here waiting for her and her little army. Tell your Mamma that I will be here waiting for her rotten teeth and smelling little nose.

Then Chuwawa starts rapping – some of which you could make sense out of and others, not so much.

Chuwawa: ...if I didn't tell you then another Mamma would.
Look at your head with them slick looking scary
curl reaping where you do not sow
eating where you do not work

Sticking your nose where it does not belong
Hence, your nose is so short
because it's been chopped up
so many times, being where it should not be Cut
your coat according to your size
You've been sharking all them sweet a-pop-a
licking all them sweet a-pop-a
sweet-a, sweet-a, sweet a-pop-a pop-a sweet-a,
sweet a-pop-a

Zach: Are you serious?

Chuwawa: Go and tell your Mamma that a hunter has finally kill a Cougar in my farm. Shame onto your witch doctor who had scornfully prophesied that in my farm, a hunter cannot kill a mouse. Tell your Mamma that I said no matter how large the size of a goat may be, yes, he may even be larger than the size of an elephant, but when he faces the wolf, he will perish! A Jaguar that sleeps like a lazy one is only thinking about where his next meal will come from. Tear drops are not raindrops. We are not gullible. We surely are not gullible; patience is our virtue.

Sean: Zach, can we remember all that?

Chuwawa: You better! Hey boys, what do you call that hair dude on your knuckled heads, Jerry curl? That's not jerry curl, that's scary curl! Now, you get out of my little castle and go give my message to your Mamma! I am not going anywhere. I will be right here waiting for her!

As Zach and Sean exit Chuwawa's presence in disbelief of her theatrical display, Chuwawa ends the scene with the following soliloquy and her chicks' contributions.

Chuwawa: Talking about how they are going to make dinner out of my family and I, tell your Mamma to bring it on! I'll show her why they call me Chuwawa, the boom, boom destroyer! I'll be waiting for her right here! Talking about how she's going to turn me and my little ones into dinner. The beast can try; she is going to find out what I am made of. A tropical yam rules over pounded yam. Yes, a potato rules over matched potato. May there not come to be someone who rules over the practice of wickedness. The world is big enough for everyone. Live and let live.

Ikem: Tell them Mom. While the rats are away, the mice will play. May the rats stay farther away, just so the mice can play even longer. Those boys do not recognize who they are messing with. For in an imperfect world, the unwise think everyone but self is insane. The one person that is truly insane is the unwise lone star in the mirror.

Fuza: Yes, they must have confused us with Ducks and speechless Ducklings. Indeed, they are about to find out that the silence of a cat does not constitute her lazy, she's only exercising one of her enduring prowess – patience.

Nebum: Those boys thought that they can just walk in here and run over us as if they own the world. They thought we are afraid of them. Fear not, my people. The guts of a pig reside inside the pig; no one can kill us except if we let fear get the best of us. Let us join hands together to fight the fine fight for survival.

Osey: Nebum, don't worry about a thing. We'll show those hooligans that we certainly do not take insults from any beast. In a layman's terminology, we take nothing from nobody!

Fuza: Situation like this reminds me of one of my songs entitled "We Are Not Gullible" and it goes this way.

> Fending for its food
> A cat plays possum
> Eluding its predators
> A possum plays dead
> We are not gullible
> Patience is our virtue
> Eluding its predator
> The Hognose snake plays dead
> Trapping its prey
> The Rinkhals snake plays dead
> Tear drop is not raindrop
> Toad stool is not mushroom
> We are not gullible
> Patience is our virtue
> We are not gullible
> Bravery is our virtue
> Tear drop is not raindrop
> Toad stool is not mushroom
> We are not gullible
> Courteousness is our virtue
> We are not gullible
> Bravery is our virtue
> We are not gullible
> Patience is our virtue

Osan: Fuzza, that sounds great! Gone are those days when we let those boys walk all over us as if we are some defenseless family. We are going to show those hooligans that we are not grasses they stump[2] all over.

Mel: Fuzza, you are a good song writer and a singer. I cannot wait to get my foot on those scavengers. They are going to regret making mouth at my Mom. We were minding our business without disrupting the peace of others and out of the blue moon they want to come and eat us up just like that? Can someone please ask the evildoers, yes ask the wicked ones for me; what benefit is there to gain from the practice of wickedness? The greed of having it all just so others will have none, pursues the greedy one all about.

Chuwawa: That's alright chicks. Let's get ready for those goons. A lepidopteran moth or butterfly attempting to quench an open flame lamp with its wings will end up destroying itself. All you enemies of progress, get behind me! Billy the killer emphatically said he was going to kill Sammy the killer. A warning to Billy the killer: desists from such a horrible thought or else you will end up killing yourself. All you enemies of progress, get away from me. A lepidopteran moth attempting to quench an open flame lamp with its wings will end up destroying itself. All haters of humanity, yes, you traitors and backbiters, get behind me! Yes, stay away from me! Billy the killer vowed to kill Sammy the killer. A stern warning to Billy the killer: desists from such a wicked thought or else you will end up killing yourself. All you closet enemies of progress; you better keep hiding from me. All you secret and public enemies of progress, get behind me! Yes, stay away from me!

Chuwawa bulges her eyes depicting her seriousness and fearless resolution to defend her family's honor. Out of nowhere, Bimpe the red rooster shows up crowing and disappearing into thin air with the following words.

Bimpe:	Compared to trees, the lifespan of humans and animals alike are so short that life on Earth at the moment is absolutely momentary. As such, I call on all creatures to practice kindness and humility. The lifespan of humans and animals alike are too short, practice kindness and humility. The lifespan of humans and animals alike are too short, be kind to each other. The lifespan of humans and animals alike are so short, live and let live...

2

<u>STAND UP AGAINST THE MACHINATIONS OF BULLIES</u>

Zakondo's Gang On A Robbery Showdown

It is a bright and sunny day. Today is Friday. Robbery is in progress. Zakondo and his gang have just taken over four eighteen-wheeler trucks from a truck rest area. Two of those trucks are carrying Computer products worth about seven million seven hundred and seventy-seven thousand seven hundred and seventy-seven dollars – ($7,777,777.00 United States Dollars - USD). A peculiar thing about the armed robbers is that they are not wearing any form of disguise and it makes you wonder what might have given them the confidence to be self-revealing in a criminal act? Someone bravely but discreetly calls on the police for help. Officer Lansbury is on her radio scanner. She calls in for help while her partner Officer Bengalow is set to shoot. The armed robbers seem to be too smart and well organized for the Officers to handle.

Officer Lansbury: This is officer Lansbury. 10-31, 10-31, 10-31 is in progress. The cross street is Channing in Oxford. Officer requesting backup...

At the time of this writing, 10-31 is a police code for "crime in progress." Pointing to Officer Lansbury's direction, Zakondo, the head of the criminal gang gives the order to disable Officer Lansbury and her crew.

Zakondo: Obispo, blow those police cars into oblivion. Would you?

Obispo: My pleasure.

Obispo aims and fires several grenades in Officer Lansbury's direction. Fortunately, the Officers are able to run for their lives on foot before the grenades hit. The police cars however, are not that fortunate as they are completely blown off. While everyone is running helter-skelter from the flying bullets and grenades, interestingly however, some allow their curiosity to empower them as they pull closer to where the robbery is taking place just to get the first glance of the crime. By this time, police squads are everywhere. You would think that the armed robbers are cornered and about to be brought to justice. As it is, Zakondo and his gang made away with the four eighteen-wheeler trucks via the incapacitated Officer Lansbury's direction.

Doubtlessly, as the gang bombs its way out of the crime scene, the relentless police squads are in pursuit. It became obvious to the police squads that the armed robbers were organized and more than meet the eyes when out of nowhere heavily armed group of men start shooting at the police squads, barricading them from Zakondo and his gang. Before you know it, Zakondo and his gang are long gone. The police were left perplexed wondering about what went wrong and where four eighteen-wheeler trucks disappeared into thin air in a broad daylight and in front of them, all eyes open.

Drones and Helicopters are sent out to find Zakondo and his gang. For several hours in the air looking for the gang or at least any trace of it, both the drones and helicopters come up short. Zakondo and his gang are nowhere to be found neither are they traceable. The search continues.

The Vultures' Fury On Bullies

Lights on Sassy, Mama Fox and Akala, Mama Vulture as they fight for survival and territorial integrity in the jungle.

Simultaneously, their male counterpart Kolokolo, Papa Fox and Igun, Papa Vulture are engaging in the same endeavor.

Igun: This is my space. You are encroaching on my territory.

Kolokolo: Do you know who I am? Aren't you supposed to be afraid of me?

Igun: In what universe would that ever happen? I know that you are confusing me with your helpless victims. You better get out of my presence and go get your facts straight. Get lost!

Kolokolo: What! Do you realize who you are talking to? Look at my sharp teeth that can cut through you like a piece of leaf. Check out my claws. I know that you don't want to mess with me.

Igun: I surely don't! But aren't we rather pompous? While you may have all those qualities that make you a formidable opponent, you are forgetting one important piece of information.

Kolokolo: What is it?

Igun: I have a sharp beak, sharp claws, and I can fly. Can you fly?

Kolokolo: What? Do you have any idea who you are talking to? I am Kolokolo, the master hunter. What is this world coming to where vultures are no longer afraid of Foxes?

Igun: Not even in your dream would it ever happen where vultures would be afraid of Foxes. Yes, we may respect you and your existence, but we have never been afraid of you nor would we ever be afraid of you! You must have not heard the sayings...

Kolokolo: What sayings?

Igun: The saying that the butcher that will kill and devour a vulture is yet to be seen. Yes, there is no butcher that will kill and devour a Vulture. Even the hyenas are afraid to mess with us because of our formidable claws and beaks. Now, if mankind and hyenas dare not to bother us, what makes you think that you have a chance? What is more? We can fly. Kolokolo, you better learn before I school you.

Kolokolo: [In disbelieve of his hearings] Why are you talking to me like that? Do you really know who I am?

Igun: You must be one of the slow ones because you've been asking me the same question over and over again perhaps expecting a different answer. One of the learned mankind by the name Albert Einstein once said and I will paraphrase to make it easy for you to comprehend: "it is insane to do the same thing over and over again expecting a different result."

Kolokolo: What! He really said that?

Igun: One thing that I am going to give to you is that in the universe of mankind, your style of questioning is in use by detectives.

Kolokolo: What is your angle?

Igun: A detective would ask a suspect the same question multiple times or over, and over again so as to have the suspect give multiple answers to the same question and thus, throw him into confusion and abject frustration. Then, the detective would claim that she has caught the suspect in a lie and hence, she got the suspect! I can assure you right now Pappy Fox, that is not going to work with me.

	So, cut it out!
Kolokolo:	No kidding! Are you calling me slow and crazy now?
Igun:	Well, if the hat fits, wear it!
Kolokolo:	This is unbelievable. Oh, it's on now!
Igun:	Having no quarrel or fight with you a priori, you choose to become enviously upset with us. While we do not wish evil deeds on anyone, make no mistake Kolokolo, we will defend ourselves with everything we have!
Kolokolo:	We will see about that, won't we?
Sassy:	Kolokolo, make sure that you tear Igun into pieces! I will take care of the speechless Akala!
Kolokolo:	Count on it! I'm tired of this nonsense.

As Igun and Kolokolo continue their row[30], Sassy is tAunting the quiet and gentle Akala who refuses to give a reply to Sassy.

Sassy:	Akala, you know that my man will tear your man apart like a sharp sword tears a leaf. I know that you know what I do to speechless and powerless ones like you. I will tear you apart and devour you like crazy!
Akala:	[chooses to be nonresponsive – quiet but attentive]
Sassy:	I am talking to you Akala, you better act like you hear me talking to you!
Akala:	[chooses to be nonresponsive – quiet but attentive]
Sassy:	I will not be ignored! I know that you are not going

to ignore me forever! If you do, that's all right with me because it will give me more time to tear you into pieces. Now get ready for this!

Sassy is about to jump on Akala when Igun said the following in a calm voice that shows that Akala is in control of her behavior.

Igun: Sassy, be careful what you wish for. A dove is nagging and uttering some slangs[10] as if the pigeon is deaf and cannot comprehend. The Pigeon comprehends, but ignores the utterances. Yes, the pigeon exercises one of its enduring virtues - patience.

Sassy: O really? Then let's see how your girlfriend here, endures this!

This time, Sassy jumps on Akala and while Sassy is in the air, Akala flies and with her sharp claws she grabs Sassy by her right ear and eye in the air. Then Akala hit Sassy's head on the ground and hold her down right there with her claws still on Sassy's right eye and ear. It does not take any time for Sassy to know that it is about that time to cry for help and suffer defeat. Repeatedly, Sassy tries to break free from Akala's deadly hold, but to no avail.

Before you know it, the fight begins. Igun against Kolokolo, while Sassy pick on Akala. Akala is the quiet one, but her quietness is mostly mistaken for laziness and the lack of ability thereof to defend herself. Sassy is about to find that dogma to be false. With its beak, Igun grabs Kolokolo by its private part between the legs and hold him down right there. At the same time, Akala holds down Sassy to the ground with her claws directly on Sassy's right eye and ear. The excruciating pain that both Kolokolo and Sassy surfer from the claws of Igun and Akala are perceived miles away by mankind via Foxes' horrific outcries.

Igun: Yes, this will tell you not to mess with us again. Don't mess with vultures! Are you enjoying the pain? O, you can't talk now, can you?

Kolokolo: [crying] Please let me go. I won't bother you again, I promise.

Igun: O, I know you won't bother us again and if you do, that may be your last endeavor on this glorious Earth. Remember, the green weed water lettuce that covers the surface of water is always above waters and the pond weed water Lily that covers the surface of the river is always above the river.

Kolokolo: What does that mean?

Igun: It means anytime anywhere you lock horns with me or any of my kin, you will always go down! No questions asked! This is to teach you a lesson. Don't mess with vultures!

Kolokolo: Believe me, lesson learned. I won't mess with you again.

Igun: I know you won't! You just enjoy the pain and never forget it! For a destructive sword has made its way to the intensified bullies, behold the end of bullying and oppression. The remaining bullies and backbiters left behind will have their ears full to where they will become useless even to themselves should they remain obstinate.

Mankind is not the only one who is alarm by the Foxes' outcry. Other curious animals like "Lions, Apes, Hyenas, Eagles, Great- Egrets, Cattle-Egrets, Partridges, Zebras"[28] and more are at the scene. They are all having fun looking at the unthinkable. It seems that the hyenas are having more fun characterize by their laughter.

One of the hyenas going by the name Lethality scornfully discusses the fight with his female partner Felicity in the following way.

Lethality: Hey Felicity, can you see the reason why we do not mess with the likes of Igun and Akala?

Felicity: O yes, my dear I certainly can. I don't think that Kolokolo would be able to use his private part anymore because it seems that Igun is mutilating it.

Felicity is referring to the object that is between Kolokolo' s thighs.

Lethality: Ouch! Kolokolo might be able to use the bathroom but it is going to hurt him like crazy. What about Sassy? Look at her right eye. It seems it's about to pop out of its socket.

Felicity: If nobody helps them out as soon as possible, they might find it difficult to continue living since the beating will leave them disable to hunt for food. Furthermore, they will become easy prey to guys like us.

Lethality: O, that would be great! More food for us.

Felicity: But it would take the fun out of hunting. Chasing our prey is part of the fun in hunting for animals like kolokolo since their blood will be warm and we'll have us a rear meat with fresh taste. O, that is one of the things I enjoy about fresh catch.

Kolokolo finally breaks free from Igun's tight lock. You would expect Kolokolo to take to his heels. But no, not when too many eyes are watching. Kolokolo's concern for his pride and those he represents gives him the dignity, or I should say the stupidity to continue the fight that he has obviously lost. As Kolokolo jumps at Igun, Kolokolo does not have it easy as he may have calculated because Igun flies to meet Kolokolo in the air and with his right claws he grabs Kolokolo's right eye, pins Kolokolo down to the ground and holds him down there.

Igun's claws are long and strong covering Kolokolo's right ear and eye simultaneously. The excruciating pain that Kolokolo suffers now is more than the one he suffered the first time around. So is the cry.

Kolokolo's new cry resembles an elongated violin note, which he does continuously. Sassy is not out of the loop yet. She too has twice break free from Akala's tight lock and each time, Akala renews her catch making the lock tighter than ever before. The view continues. You may wonder why the rest of the wild beasts are not fighting and devouring one another as it is customary in a predator- prey relationship. One of the lions had earlier recommended a truce among the beasts at least for the sake of the fight which is entertaining to all and sundry. You can see a group of Apes harmonizing the following songs antiphonally:

Lead Vocal (LV): Can a fault finder contend with the Almighty?

> A warrior that insolently watches
> the owner of the whole universe
> On thistle thorns he will die
> A hunter that insolently watches
> the sovereign ruler of the whole universe
> On thistle thorns he will rot
> The fight of envy has no gain
> That we are greater than they are
> is not a matter of judicial precedence
> Can a fault finder contend with the Almighty?
> A warrior that insolently watches
> the owner of the whole universe
> On thistle thorns he will die
> A hunter that insolently watches
> the sovereign ruler of the whole universe
> On thistle thorns he will rot
> whosoever acts insolently to the king

Chorus:	will suffer fatal loss and crumbled
LV:	Whosoever underestimates the king
Chorus:	will suffer fatal loss and crumbled
LV:	A wild animal that underestimates the hunter
Chorus:	will suffer fatal loss and crumbled
LV:	Kolokolo underestimates Igun
Chorus:	will suffer fatal loss and crumbled
LV:	Sassy underestimates Akala
Chorus:	will suffer fatal loss and crumbled
LV:	they will suffer fatal loss and crumbled
Chorus:	They will suffer fatal loss and crumbled
LV:	they will suffer fatal loss and crumbled
Chorus:	They will suffer fatal loss and crumbled
LV:	whosoever act insolently to the king
Chorus:	will suffer fatal loss and crumbled
LV:	A wild animal that underestimates the hunter
Chorus:	will suffer fatal loss and crumbled
LV:	Kolokolo underestimates Igun
Chorus:	will suffer fatal loss and crumbled
LV:	Sassy underestimates Akala
Chorus:	will suffer fatal loss and crumbled
LV:	they will suffer fatal loss and crumbled
Chorus:	They will suffer fatal loss and crumbled

LV:	The bullies and the backbiters
Chorus:	will suffer fatal loss and crumble.
LV:	Kolokolo underestimates Igun
Chorus:	will suffer fatal loss and crumbled
LV:	Sassy underestimates Akala
Chorus:	will suffer fatal loss and crumbled
LV:	they will suffer fatal loss and crumbled
Chorus:	They will suffer fatal loss and crumbled

Things That Do Not Work Together Are Illogical

A large group of Mankind come in to rescue the situation and marvel at what they as human beings are looking at. As far as these people are concerned, never have they seen a situation like this before where a bird overpowers a vicious animal like a Fox. They may not have seen an Eagle bold and powerful enough to kill an extraordinarily large wild goat or a mountain goat. So, making it known to these people that an eagle can actually kill and devour a huge mountain goat would be illogical since they have not seen it done before.

Doubtlessly, a Tiger will not be a barber to where a dog dare shows up for a haircut. In general, things that cannot work together do not make sense alike. For example, before mankind was able to travel out of space, the concept that the circular planet Earth hangs upon nothing[34] was highly illogical. At that time, majority of mankind's understanding was based on the fabricated story that the Earth is flat and sits upon giant Elephants, the giant Elephants in turn, stand upon a huge Tortoise or turtle, the huge tortoise swims trough space and the food that both the Elephants and Tortoise eat to keep them nourished and strong for their endless tasks of upholding the Earth is mysterious even to the story tellers and their uninformed audience alike.

There is no wonder that the story was titled "The Great Turtle myth[12]" which was first brought to the public's attention in the 17th century. The curious minds however, found that story to be highly illogical, hence, a myth. Mankind should be grateful in part to science for shedding light on the many things that may not seem logical as a unit, but do work together. For instance, without the scientific on-sight proof, it would have been impossible to fathom let alone believe that like a living thing the planet Earth moves along or rotates on its axis as it revolves around the sun and never deviates from that course.

That the Earth hangs upon nothing would have been illogical if man had not traveled out of space, landed on the moon to experience the workings of the gravitational force and its lack thereof.

There must be a logical explanation for things that work together. The understanding of such logical explanation might be beyond human grasp especially if they are of divine nature. The bottom line is that there is a logical explanation or reason why things work together and why they don't. Things that are illogical do not make sense and things that do not make sense alike just don't work together. However, if illogical things that do not make sense alike do work together, then there must be a logical explanation for them to be working together. Such logical explanation may be beyond human comprehension at the moment, but it exists.

An axiom of the acquisition of knowledge is such that the more you know, the more there is to know. It simply means that the acquisition of knowledge is infinite. This is so, because after spending a considerable amount of time obtaining a set of knowledge leading to a bachelor's degree in Psychology for instance, you will realize that what you have just acquired is a tool to understanding and a key to opening the door into the universe of Psychology where the acquisition of knowledge in the study of Psychology becomes limitless or infinite.

My intention as a Computer Scientist is not to turn this book into a book in the study of Psychology, but the little digression is necessary to explain the fact that while things that cannot work together do not make sense alike and in effect illogical, there are things that do work together that may momentarily seem illogical until the prerequisite knowledge to comprehending the underlying logics is acquired. Now, let's get back to the story, shall we?

The Essence Of Work And The Dignity That Work Provides

As mankind spend few moments digesting the fights between the two Foxes against the two vultures, they come to a realization that vultures do live up to their nick names as scavengers. They'll devour anything resembling food, whether alive or dead as long as such animal can be overpowered. When mankind finally heard enough of the Foxes excruciating cry for help, they scare off the vultures.

Obviously, Kolokolo and sassy are thinking too highly of themselves and too little of others. This is a case where a sculptor is summoned, and the woodpecker shows up. This means that because you are not the only one who can handle a specific job as there can be more than one way to successfully handle the said job, do not think too highly of yourself. Respect others as you may well want them to respect you. Respect is reciprocal. Still in severe pain, the Foxes run into hiding to nurse their wounds with a view to rid their excruciating pain.

As Kolokolo and Sassy are nursing their wounds, they see Chuwawa and her chicks having fun minding their business. Before you know it, the Foxes' hunting skills kick in. As the two wounded Foxes put on their hunting game, Chuwawa starts rapping.

Chuwawa: I know that you two losers are not about to start with me. O yes, I was there, and I saw the vultures Igun and Akala kick your buttocks and you cannot even defend yourselves. You might as well get out of my sight because if I didn't tell you then another Mamma would. Perm on your hair with them slick looking scary curl, reaping where you do not sow, eating where you do not work.

Sassy:	What are you talking about? Eating where you do not work, are you saying we need to work apart from eating you up?
Chuwawa:	Eating me up is not your work. If you have a job and are doing your work, you would not have the time to think about coming to eat me up!
Sassy:	O yeah? Why would I want to work when you are there for me to eat up? That will be dumb. Don't you think so?
Chuwawa:	No! I don't think so! Sassy, you need to take pride in working and providing for your family. You need to know that the essence of work and the dignity that work provides make the birds fly high in the midheavens. The essence of work and the dignity that work provides establish the presence of vultures in the thick forest. The essence of work and the dignity that work provides makes a fish swim in the deepest part of the ocean, the Challenger Deep[11]. The essence of work and the dignity that work provides establish the presence of mice in the thick forest. Yes, the essence of work and the dignity that work provides will make you a better animal to reckon with.
Sassy:	I just want to eat you up right now, right here!
Chuwawa:	Well, that's not going to happen, not even in your dreams. Before the collapse of the bridge, I have gone up to the seashore. A huge log of wood spills out of a huge flame of fire, I made an escape and passed on to victory. So, I am too much for you to handle! Sassy, you are not going to get me! You are not going to eat me.

Kolokolo: Chuwawa, you will not be saying that when we are through with you.

Chuwawa: Whosoever picks up a healthy chicken, will pick up insolent complaints. Whosoever plucks a leaf and deep it in his mouth in the presence of a mute, is seeking to be an adversary to the mute. I am sure that you will be eternally grateful to mankind who came to your aide and saved you from the deadly claws and beaks of the vultures. Now you are here bullying us.

Sassy: We want to eat you!

Chuwawa: O yeah?

Kolokolo: You better believe that!

Chuwawa: Believe this: we are not gullible, but patience. O, no, missy! What I believe is that you can only kiss and mess with the one you are able to grab. If you can't grab me, you surely cannot kiss and mess with me! Remember, the rain will not come down to make enmity with anyone, downpour falls only upon those who avail themselves. Yes, you can only mess with someone if and only if, such one is up for the grabbing, and you have the power to grab her!

Sassy: Really?

Chuwawa: Yes, really. Take for instance, had Igun and Akala the vultures let you grab them; you would have devoured them like crazy. As it were, they proved to be formidable yes, too much for you to handle. Now, you are scared of them. I am sure that you will not mess with them anymore. Would you? They are free from your daunting claws and jaws.

Kolokolo: The vultures may be free from our claws and jaws but you are not!

Chuwawa: O yes, we are! A lepidopteran moth attempting to quench an open flame from a burning candle with its wings, will end up destroying itself. Don't mess with fire. When you mess with fire, you'll get burnt. I am fire and you mess with me, you'll get burnt! Don't mess with me and my family if you don't want to suffer another terrible defeat. Yes, get behind me sore losers.

Sassy: Like my main man, Kolokolo said earlier, the vultures may be free from our claws and jaws but you are not. We will get you now.

Chuwawa: O Really? Watch this.

Chuwawa and her chicks cry out to mankind for help with distinctive emergency outcry. Mankind come running to help Chuwawa and her chicks. When Kolokolo and Sassy behold mankind coming with long tree branches, sticks and machetes, they take to their heels. As they fade into the forest, Kolokolo and Sassy make the following utterances:

Sassy: Save by mankind. We'll catch you later!

Kolokolo: You better believe that!

Chuwawa: You show up next time, you will have your ears slap with words. There is no doubt that a truthful speech pierces like thorns; and it is bitter like bitter leaves. You won't be happy next time you set your weird eyes on me. You better believe that!

Sassy: Yeah! Yeah! Yeah! Like I said, you are save by mankind. Enjoy it while you can. We'll catch you later!

Kolokolo: You better believe that!

Kolokolo and Sassy run away. Ah! Chuwawa and her chicks are safe again. As mankind disperse to their various places of residence the distraught Chuwawa begins her soliloquy right after expressing her gratitude to mankind.

Chuwawa: Thank you Mankind. Thank you for your help. On behalf of my chicks, I express our gratitude for your kind help because any recipient of kindness who chose to be unthankful is like an armed robber who had just made away with someone's belongings at gunpoint.

Mankind: Chuwawa, you are welcome.

Chuwawa: Thank you and enjoy the rest of the day.

Mankind: You too, Chuwawa.

Chuwawa's soliloquy:

Chuwawa: Obviously, everybody except mankind wants to eat up my family and I. May we never see corruption in this life. May we never see pangs of distress in this life. In this life, may we never wear corruption nor pangs of distress as clothing. Just as the fishes that swim in the Challenger Deep[11] do not catch cold nor suffer from hyperthermia, the birds that fly in the midheavens do not suffer from the fear of heights, the water pitchers do not get sick from water nor do they suffer from waterborne illnesses, a spadix does not take ill inside its spathe on a living date palm tree, may we never see corruption in our lives. Yes, may we never wear corruption nor pangs of distress as clothing. Rather, may the joy, yes, the inner peace and happiness that transcend all thoughts pursue us all the days of our lives.

Zakondo's Gang On The Move

Lights on Zakondo and his gang making away with six eighteen-wheeler trucks in Lathrop truck rest area. Who would have thought that possessing guns come with an eighteen-wheeler truck driver's job description? When the gun battle between the truck drivers and Zakondo's gang are over, Zakondo and his gang are seen driving away with four trucks while the truckers are on the ground with severe injuries some of which are fatal. The police department arrives after the gun battle is over. The department's effort to find someone who can tell them in their own words what had transpired ends up being futile.

Officer Mahalo: Did anybody see what happen, can anybody, I mean anybody tell me what happen here? Hey mister, can you tell me what happen?

Azariah: I don't know nothing, I don't see nothing, I don't hear nothing.

Officer Mahalo: Hey! What about you?

Jake: Yes, what about me?

Officer Mahalo: Did you see anything?

Jake: I don't see Jack! Even if I did, I won't tell a soul!

Officer Mahalo: Remember, self-conceit deprives the wasp of honey. How can we help you if you won't tell us what you saw? Don't blame us for not showing up on time. Sometimes they give us guns without bullets; and most of the time it seems that the bad guys have more ammunition than we do. Come on. You have to understand. Come on, tell us something. Tell us something we can use. Anything.

Azariah: Well, it is not like you can do anything now. Zakondo and his gang are long gone.

Officer Mahalo: Well, I guess our hands are tied.

Azariah: Your hands are tied by who?

Officer Mahalo: By you for not wanting to help us help you.

Azariah: Let me ask you this officer. What do you pray for when you feel like praying?

Officer Mahalo: I don't understand what you are asking.

Azariah: I bet you pray for crimes like this to be rampart just so you can feel needed and have a secured job.

Officer Mahalo: Well, one thing we don't pray for is to get shot.

Azariah: Man, I don't have time for this.

Azariah allows the fire fighters and ambulance to help him to the emergency room where the rest of the survivors are equally receiving treatment.

3

<u>SASSY'S FURY OVER CHUWAWA'S INSOLENCE</u>

Lights on Zach and Sean on their way to Cassandra's den to deliver to her the same message that is obviously unpopular to Chuwawa.

Sean:	Hey Zach? Chuwawa was not nice to us.
Zach:	No Sean, she certainly was not.
Sean:	Did you heard Chuwawa call my hair scary curl?
Zach:	Yes, I did. I surely did hear her call our hair scary curl.
Sean:	My hair is not scary, is it, Zach?
Zach:	Well, can I take the Fifth Amendment[13] on that subject? I certainly do not want to comment on that issue at this point because I'm so distraught at Chuwawa's onslaught. Sean, I do not have a stomach for that right now.
Sean:	Ouch! That hurt. You are supposed to be my brother and on my side. My hair is not scary. I am a natural beauty.
Zach:	Sean, oh yes, you are. Oh yes, you are. And don't you let anyone tell you otherwise. You keep your head up!
Sean:	Zach, speaking of heads up, look at those two guys running. I wonder why they are running and where they are running to.

Zach: Sean, not even those two guys know why they are running and where they are running to. Do you know why?

Sean: Of course not! I surely do not know.

Zach: Well, if I tell you that one of those runners is mentally challenged, can you point him out?

Sean: Oh dear. I can surely try. Well, I think it's the one on the left.

Zach: Sean, look again. This time, a little closer.

Sean: Zach, it really does not matter how close I get and how hard I look, I may end up picking the wrong one because the similarities are overwhelming.

Zach: Alright. Can you just try again?

Sean: [with stern look at the runners] Well, I still pick the one on the left.

Zach: Well, you are wrong, Sean! Even after the clue I gave you. When I asked that you try again, that ought to tell you that your first try is wrong. There is no doubt the similarities between the runners are overwhelming, however, a closer look will show the runner on the right to be the one with mental issues.

Sean: How can you tell by sight?

Zach: Can't you see the one on the right picking the hair on his head and scratching his head as if his hair is infested with lice?

Sean: I don't believe I saw that.

Zach: That is why I asked that you look closer. Because if you do, you'll see that he is talking to himself.

Sean:	Ah! That's no reason to think he is crazy. He could be talking to the runner on the left. Or talking to someone on his cellular phone. This days, the use of cellular phones with cordless ear piece make a person look like an insane person who talks to himself like that man.
Zach:	Yeah, yeah, yeah. [Zach's scornful way of saying yes] I'm telling you that the runner on The right is mentally challenged. Everyone knows that except you Sean.
Sean:	I'm just saying.

Zach and Sean at Cassandra's den

Zach:	We are here to deliver a message to you from our mother.
Cassandra:	Really?
Zach:	Yes, really. Cassandra.
Cassandra:	Hold on a second let me finish watching the news on the television about an armed robbery that happened few hours ago at Cedar Point, Ohio.
Zach:	Ok. We'll wait.
Cassandra:	Come in and watch the news with us. It won't be long; it is almost over.
Sean:	Certainly, we can wait.
Stella Gam:	Good Evening. I am Stella Gam. Mekwus Network News MNN Channel 5. We interrupt this program for the breaking news that has been going on for the past few hours in Cedar Point, Ohio. A gang of armed robbers made away with four eighteen-

wheeler trucks with goods costing millions of dollars to their owners. For several hours the police department has been canvasing the air on helicopters and with drones in search of the gang, but to no avail. The leader of the gang going by the name Zakondo vows that his gang will never be caught and they are declaring war against the Police Department and any big company that monopolizes the commercial world.

Zach: Wow! That is deep.

Cassandra: Now, what message does your Mamma have for me?

Zach: My Mamma said come five o'clock this evening you are going to be our dinner.

Cassandra: Really? She said that?

Zach: Yes, Cassandra, she surely did.

Cassandra: Do you mean that my entire family will be your dinner?

Sean: Yes, that is what our Mamma said

Cassandra: I see.

While Cassandra is understandably upset at this point, unlike Chuwawa she does not resort into badmouthing the little Foxes. Unlike Chuwawa, Cassandra becomes unresponsive and quiet. She walks back and forth as if deeply upset, she incoherently quacks and so, are her little Ducklings.

Cassandra: Quack, quack, quack, quack...

Kazzy: Quack, quack, quack...

Mooney: Quack, quack, quack...

Zaffy: Quack, quack, quack…

Akuna: Quack, quack, quack…

Sean: Hey Zach? Can you make out what Cassandra and her little ones are saying?

Zach: No. Oh no Sean. Not a word.

Sean: So, what do we tell Mamma?

Zach: Sean, we are going to tell Mamma that Cassandra did not utter a word in reply. That's it.

Sean: I agree with you and I will stand by you Zach.

Zach: Sean, thanks for the vote of confidence.

Sean: Zach, you are welcome.

Zach and Sean en route to Mamma Fox's Den

Sean: Hey Zach? Can you imagine Chuwawa calling me a knuckle head with scary curl? Does my hair look scary?

Zach takes a Moment to look at Sean's hair style and was bombarded with so many conflicting thoughts. He wants to be as truthful as possible to his brother without hurting his feelings. One of Zach's conflicting thoughts is that Sean had earlier suffered embarrassment when Chuwawa called him names like knuckle head with scary curl. Therefore, telling Sean the truth about his funny looking hair style at least from Chuwawa's point of view may be too much for the little lad to handle being a touchy little fellow in a fidgeting state of mind. So, with sly sarcasm, Zach scornfully and calmly answers Sean as follow:

Zach: No. Oh no Sean. Not at all. The way you wear your hair is perfect.

Sean:	It's not funny Zach. If my hair is funny, you better believe it, yours is too.
Zach:	[busted out laughing and said] That's Ok Sean. I don't mean to laugh like that. Chuwawa will certainly pay for her mockery in just a little while. So. Do not worry my brother.
Sean:	Ok Zach.
Zach:	Come on, let's go tell Mamma the whole story.
Sean:	Alright Zach, let's go.

Now at Mamma Fox's den

Sassy:	Come on in my little princes. How has your day been?
Zach:	Our day is quite interesting and upsetting.
Sean:	Yes. Tell her Zach. Tell her how that Chuwawa called me knuckle head with scary curl.
Sassy:	What? Somebody call my prince Sean knuckle head with scary curl?
Sean:	Yes, Mom, Chuwawa called me that and she said you have a perm on your hair with them slick looking scary curl. Yes, she did.
Sassy:	Seriously?
Zach:	Yes, Mom, seriously.
Sassy:	Really? Are you sure?
Zach & Sean:	Yes, really, we are sure Mom. [They both answer simultaneously]
Sassy:	Now, in your own words I want you to tell me

exactly what happened?

Zach:	Sean, you tell Mom how it went because you are very good at telling stories narratively.
Sean:	I don't think so. After all, you are the older one. So, why don't you act like it and tell Mom our ordeal?
Zach:	Come on Sean, do it for me and I will let you play with my ball.
Sean:	I don't think so.

While Zach and Sean are going back and forth regarding which one of them would tell their ordeal to Mamma Fox, Sassy becomes indignantly impatient and yells out the following.

Sassy:	Boys, somebody better start talking and I don't care who!
Zach:	Sean, would you please tell Mom what happen?
Sean:	No! I won't! You tell her. After all, you are the senior, are you not?
Zach:	Ok. I guess I will have to do the telling. You can kiss playing with my ball goodbye!
Sassy:	Are we going to do this or what?
Zach:	Yes, Mom, I will tell you everything.
Sassy:	And you make sure you don't spare anything.
Zach:	Yes, Mom.
Sassy:	Ok then, let's hear it.
Zach:	Well, we paid a visit to Chuwawa letting her know that you had sent us to her with a message. She asked what the message was and we told her that the message was that come five o'clock PM we are

going to make dinner out of Chuwawa and her family. She did not take the message kindly as she starts rapping and rumbling words that I'm afraid to repeat or relay to you Mom.

Sassy: Boy, didn't I tell you spear nothing?

Zach: Yes, you certainly did Mom. But the words Chuwawa used are too graphic to have them come out of my mouth. You will be upset at me. Except if you promise not to get upset at me Mom.

Sassy: Boy, if you don't start talking at this minute you will regret testing my patience.

Zach: Ok Mom, she said it like this: Well, you go tell your sniffling no good for nothing Mamma that I will be right here waiting for her and her little army.

Sassy: What! She said what? Me and my little army?

Zach: Yes, she said so Mom.

Sassy: What else did she say?

Zach: Chuwawa said tell your Mamma that I will be here waiting for her ragged teeth and smelling little nose.

Sassy: [She's furious] What! Ragged teeth and smelling nose? I'll teach her a lesson with these ragged teeth and smelling nose. Son, go on.

Zach: Calm down Mom, Calm down.

Sassy: Ok son, I'll be calm.

Zach: A cat that sleeps like the lazy one is only looking for something eat. Stay calm, Mom, be cool.

Sassy: All right, I'll be cool. See, I'm calm. So, what else did that town crier said.

Zach: Then Chuwawa starts rapping.

You should see Zach rap out this part.

Zach: because if I didn't tell your Mamma
then another Mamma would
Perm on her hair with them slick looking scary curl
reaping what you do not sow
eating where you do not work
Sticking your nose where it does not belong
Hence, your nose is so short
because it's been chopped
so many times, being where it should not be
Cut your coat according to your size
You've been sharking all them sweet a-pop-a
licking all them sweet a-pop-a
sweet-a, sweet-a, sweet a-pop-a
pop-a sweet-a, sweet a-pop-a
No matter how large the size of a goat may be
yes, it may even be larger than the size of an elephant
but when it faces the wolf, it must perish.

Sassy: Chuwawa called me a goat?

Sean: Mom, she said more than that.

Sassy: Really? What else did she say?

Zach: She says hey boys, what do you call that hair dude on your knuckled heads, Jerry curl? That's not jerry curl, that's scary curl! Now, you get out of my little castle and go give my message to your Mamma! So, we went out of her presence and on our way to Cassandra.

Sassy: No kidding! Those tiny little flies may have forgotten that a Leopard could not be the barber where a dog shows up for a haircut. It must have escaped their tiny little memories that even if some mean dogs put on fiery attires and some mountain goats put on bloody attires, behold the Mountain Lion, yes, the Cougar wrapped inside of a dirty old, ragged attire; the sum total of all those dogs and goats put together will be a hearty meal for the Cougar. When we are through with Chuwawa and her little chicks, they will remember!

Regardless of how things may turn out for the Foxes, we should congratulate Zach for such an astonishing memory and an outstanding performance in rapping out Chuwawa's sayings. Hysterical at this point and full of rage over Chuwawa's challenge, Sassy asks gently.

Sassy: What did Cassandra say in reply to my message?

Sean: Cassandra didn't say a word. She was just quacking, quacking and quacking. So, we left her alone and come back home.

Sassy: Very well then. We are going to leave Cassandra and her family alone for not saying a word. Since she didn't utter a word we don't know her thoughts and how she may have planned to defend herself and her family. They said becareful of the quiet ones, they are the most dangerous ones.

Here Sassy remembers her last encounter with Akala the Vulture where she got away with the skin of her teeth.

Sassy: But as for Chuwawa and her family, we will go and devour all of them this very evening! I am tired of these beasts threatening me, making me feel like I have lost my touch. Get ready princes. Let's go show Chuwawa what these "sniffling good for nothing Mamma and her knuckled head with scary curly hair dude" boys can do. Yes, Chuwawa is right about one thing – "no matter how large the size of a goat may be, yes, it may even be larger than the size of an elephant, but when it faces the wolf, it must perish." Well, she's about to find out who the goat here refers to. Boys, let's go get Chuwawa. Let's go! Let's go! Let's go!

Here, Sassy sarcastically referred to herself and her little Foxes using Chuwawa's insulting words. In essence, Sassy is about to demonstrate her prowess to Chuwawa and thus nullify Chuwawa's boast that the Fox Family consist of good for nothing beasts.

Zach & Sean: All right Mom, we are going, we are going.

Sassy, Zach And Sean En Route To Chuwawa's Den

Exit Mamma Fox's or Sassy's den. Lights on Sassy, Zach, and Sean on their way to Chuwawa's den to devour her family. Let's listen.

Sassy: How dare Chuwawa calls my boys knuckle heads with scary curl and have the audacity to call me a sniffling no good Mamma! We are going to show her what this "sniffling no good Mamma" can do when provoked. And I am definitely provoked beyond compare. Chuwawa is about to find out exactly what that means.

Sean: Yes, Mom. Let's go show Chuwawa that we are certainly not a family to be messed with. Calling me a knuckle head with scary curl like she didn't know what she's talking about. I look good and my hair looks great! I won't let a soul tell me otherwise. I'm handsome.

Zach: I feel the same way brother. Let's go show them we are not a family to be messed with. Yeah!

Sean: Yeah! Let's go!

Sassy: OK boys. Let's go!

On their way to Chuwawa's den they saw a residential building burning and the fire fighters providing escape routes to victims. One last escape attempt by the fire fighters that caught the eyes of the hysteric viewers were one that involved using a helicopter to save a two-month-old baby from the burning building. The most intriguing part of the delivery was when the baby's external demeanor changed from incessant crying to a Moment of silence as she was pulled closer to her rescuer. The baby's Moment of silence was characterized by a display of facial expression of disbelief like "this person is not my mother, is she?" Then the outcry intensified which seemingly proved that the baby did not recognize her rescuer to be her mother. The fire fighters quickly locate the baby's mother to unite her with the crying baby. Thereafter, the baby stopped crying. The fire was finally, quenched[3] leaving behind an uninhabitable building.

Sean: Hey Mom! Mom! Mom! Look! Look! That house is on fire!

Sassy: Yes, it is. I wonder if everyone got out on time.

Look, there is debris[4] everywhere with thick smoke. Hey kids, cover up your nose and eyes with these wet pieces of cloth. [Sassy handed her kids with some damp pieces of clothing that may prevent them from suffocating[5] due to the thick smoke coming out of the burning building.]

Zach: Thanks Mom.

Sean: Thanks Mon. Hey look at that helicopter pulling out something from the fire.

Sassy: Hey, what do you know? The fire fighter is pulling out a baby from the burning building. Isn't that something? That is so cool. [Sassy marvels]

Sean: Can they really do that?

Sassy: Yes, Sean. They are doing it as your eyes are beholding.

Zach: That is amazing Mom?

Sassy: Yes, Zach, it is amazing.

Sean: But the baby will not stop crying.

Sassy: Sean?

Sean: Yes, Mom?

Sassy: If you are being pulled from a burning building, no food, no water and your parents are not around to comfort you, like that baby you too would not stop crying.

Zach: Hey Mom? See, the baby stopped crying after all.

Sassy: Yes, it certainly did. It is as if the baby is glazing at its rescuer and thinking, hey, you are not my Mom, are you? Where is my Mom? What a brilliant kid!

Sean: Yes, Mom, the baby is smart.

Zach: Hey Mom? The baby is crying again.

Sassy: Yes, it is. Now, it is obvious that the baby needs its Mom.

Sean: Hey Mom? The fire fighter is asking for the baby's parents. [At this minute one of the fire fighters is yelling out "whose baby is this?"]

Sassy: Ha look at that. The poor but elated mother, so joyful to have her baby in her arms safe and sound.

[The baby's mother reunites with her baby.]

Zach: But Mom. Why did she run out of the building without taking her baby with her?

Sassy: She must have been so scared that she lost her senses. She was not thinking at the time, maybe because she was in a state of shock that the building was on fire and she wanted to get out before the building collapsed on her. Or, she just did not want to die. You know what they say about death "anticipation of death is worse than death itself." So, she is afraid and in shock.

Zach: But Mom, how can a mother left her baby behind and ran out to save herself from a burning fire?

Sassy: Zach?

Zach: Yes, Mom?

Sassy: Let us assume that you are feeding a baby the same time that you are having your lunch. Your lunch consists of hot spicy soup and as you carefully sip your soup you continue to feed your little baby. Suddenly, an accident occurred and the hot spicy soup splashed into your eyes and those of the baby. Now, as the baby cries profusely for help, you too need help with your burning eyes, which render you temporarily blind. What would you do? Would you help or solve the baby's problem first before you solve your own? Or would you first wash off the hot spicy soup from your eyes so you can see and then help your baby?

Sean: I will first wash off the hot spicy soup from my eyes so that I can see and then help my baby.

Zach: No, that is not fair. The baby ought to be taken

care of first before anything else.

Sassy: There are those who would probably agree with you. But let me ask you this question, Sean. How can you see in order to help the baby in the first place? Remember, you cannot see and you are having an excruciating pain.

Zach: I am confused. What should I do, Mom?

Sassy: Sean is right when he said he would first wash off the hot spicy soup from his eyes so that he can painlessly see and then help the baby. Consider this. How can you help your baby when you cannot see in the first place? What if other dangerous objects that could further hurt you and the baby are lying around?

Zach: Mom? I see what you are saying. If I cannot see, and there are dangerous objects lying around, the baby and I may trample[6] upon those dangerous objects and more harm will be incurred[7]. That would be doing more harm than good. It is better for me to see clearly first before I could help my baby. In that way, I would prevent further injury from occurring.

Sassy: Yes, Zach, you got the point! You see, the baby's mother was not being selfish; she was trying to be in a position where she can safely save her baby. In this case, she needed external help to rescue her baby from the burning building. Hence, the call for the fire fighters.

Zach: I see. I get it Mom. Thanks Mom.

4

<u>TRICKERY, A DIFFERENT FORM OF BULLY</u>

The Fight for Animal rights to Co-exist

Inside the San Francisco Airport, Chuwawa and her chicks are playing and having good times together. Then they see a three-legged puddle dog playing on a bag carousel. The chicks are enticed to join the three-legged puddle on the bag carousel only to find out that the dog is not so friendly after all. The three-legged puddle dog named Smooth has a hash temperament.

Chuwawa:	Do you folks enjoyed the flight from San Diego?
Ikem:	Yes, Mom. We certainly did. How about you Mom, did you?
Chuwawa:	Yes, kids I surely did. I am so glad that you all have a pleasant time.
Ikem:	Hey Mom, can we do it again?
Chuwawa:	Yes, kids, in time, Yes, in time we will do it again.
Ikem:	Hey Mom! Look! That dog only has three legs and its playing comfortably on that bag carousel. Can we join? I want to play on that carousel too. Can we go? Mom please, please, please, can I go?
Chuwawa:	Ok! Ok! Ok! You can go, but please be very careful, OK?
Ikem:	Ok Mom. we will be very careful. Thanks Mom. Come on, Osan let's go!

Chuwawa: You are welcome, my little ones. Be careful.

As Ikem and Osan approach the bag carousel with a view to playing with the three-legged puddle, the chicks are not so happy anymore because the three-legged puddle starts growling and barking with an angry face and signaling its displeasure to want to share the bag carousel with or in the slightest degree to play with the Chicks.

Ikem: Hey doggie, I just want to play with you. Can I? Please?

Smooth: First of, my name is not "hey Doggie" and don't want to play with you.

Ikem: Please let me play with you and I am so sorry for calling you doggie. I'll play nice with you. Please, please, please?

Smooth: I said I don't want to play with you! Can't you get it? The only thing I want to do with you is to chop you up into pieces. If you don't get out of my sight, that's what you going to get!

Ikem: Ok, if you don't want to play with me, can you At least share the bag carousel with me?

Smooth: You must have mistaken me for a Philanthropist. The only thing I want to do with you is to tear out your guts with my teeth and claws. Growl, growl, growl and bark.

Ikem: Ok, Ok, Ok. I am leaving. But you don't have to be so mean and cruel.

Smooth: Come closer and I'll show you mean and cruel. will suffer fatal loss and crumbled

Ikem leaves Smooth alone and return to his Mom, Chuwawa, with his breath zapped out of him. In a trembling state, he says these words to his Mom.

Ikem: Mom, the three-legged puddle is very mean to me. He doesn't want to play with me. He does not even want to share the bag carousel with me. He is a mean and cruel doggie.

Chuwawa: I am so sorry my little one. You see, while some dogs are nice and sweet, others are mean and cruel. That one is mean and cruel. While he has the right not to play with you if he so chooses, he does not have the right to prevent you from playing on the bag carousel. Having said that, I want you to calm down and relax because we are going to go and make him share the bag carousel with you. So, let's go!

Ikem: Thanks Mom.

Chuwawa and Ikem are back at the empty bag carousel with Smooth the three-legged puddle playing on it with its toy.

Chuwawa: Hey doggie! My son told me that you do not want to share the bag carousel with him. Say it is not so.

Smooth: Yes, he is right. I do not want to share this bag carousel with him. He should go get his own. Or else!

Chuwawa: Or else what? This is a free country body, you may have the right not to want to play with my son, you certainly do not have the right to prevent my son from playing on that bag carousel if he wants to so long as it's not yours. My son wants to play on that bag carousel, and I don't see your name on it!

Smooth: Woman? Believe me when I say this to you; you don't want to provoke me. Don't start nothing, there would be nothing!

Smooth is here saying that Chuwawa does not want to start making any trouble with him. Doing so, may be detrimental to Chuwawa from smooth's standpoint. Chuwawa takes the warning for a threat. Chuwawa does not like to be threatened. She meets anything that in the slightest degree bears the resemblance of a threat with everything she has.

Chuwawa: Are you threatening me?

Smooth: If it looks like a rat, smells like a rat, walks like a rat, talks like a rat, hundred and ten percent, it is a rat! Growls. [Smooth growls]

Chuwawa: Do you have any idea who in the world you are talking to? Do you have any glorious idea who on Earth you are talking to?

Smooth: I know you are about to tell me who on Earth it is that I am talking to.

Chuwawa: [Boiling with anger, she starts rapping] You better believe that, doggie. I am Chuwawa the boom, boom destroyer! You better ask somebody if you don't know who I am. Check yourself before you wreck yourself doggie! Don't wreck yourself before you check yourself. I have to tell it to you like it is, because if I didn't tell you, then another Mamma would. Yes, you better cut your coat according to your size before I take you to the bridge and drop you like it is hot!

At this point, many spectators have gathered to get to the bottom of the boiling pot. As they are being amused by Chuwawa's theatrical display of chicken prowess, they encourage Smooth to share the bag carousel with the chickens since they too have animal rights. The encouragement is still in progress when Smooth's owner, Acacia calls for him to leave the scene.

Spectators: [Cheering] Go Chuwawa. Go Chuwawa. Go

Chuwawa. Go! Go! Go!

Suzan: Chuwawa is right. Smooth has to share the bag carousel with others. It is a free country, is it not?

Amanda: It surely is. The chickens are free to play on the carousel as much as dogs are.

Townsend: [Airport security officer] The truth of the matter is that no animal is allowed to play on the bag carousel without proper supervision by his or her owners. In fact, we prefer the bag carousel to be free of animals when it is in motion. We do not want to be responsible for any kind of injury.

Acacia: Smooth! Come on get off the bag carousel and let's go!

As Smooth gets off the bag carousel heeding the call of its owner,

Chuwawa: Yeah! You better recognize! Don't mess with Chuwawa because she'll chew you up!

Smooth: Yeah! You keep dreaming. Save by the bell.

Chuwawa: Yeah! Don't mess with Chuwawa and like a loyal doggie you better keep stepping! There is no fire hot enough to iron or steam press the attires of a dragon parade masquerade. As such, a mountain lion could not be the barber where a dog dare shows up for a haircut!

Smooth: You can have the bad carousel, you little slick! One of these days someone would shut that mouth of yours up and turn you into spicy dinner! What do you know? I may be there to enjoy that dinner. Smooth is out!

Chuwawa: Yeah! I live for that day to come. I'll be there. Just step off! Wow! Ikem, that was close.

Ikem: Mom, what do you mean that was close?
                         Chuwawa: It's so good to have people who cares
                         with us.

Had it not been for them, we would have been done for. These
people made it where that mentally unbalanced doggie Smooth was
unable to harm us.

Fuzza: Mom, do we know any of these people?

Chuwawa: Not a soul. Fuzza, that is the beauty of the essence
                         of mankind. They don't have to know you to help
                         you. Some of them can even put themselves in
                         danger to give you the help you need at no cost to
                         you.

Chuwawa turns to Mankind and say

Chuwawa: Thank you Mankind. Thank you for your help. On
                         behalf of my chicks, I must express our gratitude
                         for your kind help because any recipient of
                         kindness who choose to be unthankful is like an
                         armed robber who had just made away with
                         someone's belongings.

Mankind: Chuwawa, you are welcome.

Chuwawa: Thank you.

Ikem: That is so cool, Mom.

Chuwawa: Indeed, it is cool. Chicks, I've come to a cross road
                         in my life and realize that no matter how poor
                         someone may be, they may even be as poor as a
                         rat that lives in a religious building that people
                         generally refer to as a "church rat," when a
                         stranger offer to come to their aide during crisis,
                         the matter is settle. Now I know and finally accept
                         that mankind is my clothing.

Fuzza:	Mom, that is deep. But why the term "church rat?"
Chuwawa:	People use "church rat" to describe the gravity and the degree of poverty someone may be suffering from. For example, if they want to describe that your standard of living is under poverty, that is, you are poorer than poor. They will say that you are as poor as a church rat.
Fuzza:	Really?
Chuwawa:	Yes, really my son.
Fuzza:	But why?
Chuwawa:	Fuzza, do they store food in the hall of religious buildings?
Fuzza:	No, Mom they surely don't.
Chuwawa:	Correct. Even if they keep food in those halls, they would be locked up tight such that rats will not be able to penetrate. So, if there are rats living in those halls what do you think would happen to them?
Fuzza:	In time, they may die of starvation and the ones that are alive would suffer from malnutrition.
Chuwawa:	Yes, son you have answered correctly.
Fuzza:	So, that is the reason why they refer to people whose standard of living is poor or under poverty as having condition that is similar to a church rat. I see. Thanks Mom.
Chuwawa:	Son, you are welcome.

Acacia walks away with Smooth and the spectators' hearts go out for Smooth because he is missing a limb. You could have heard a pin drop when the spectators watch Acacia leave with her three- legged puddle dog. While Smooth may have temperament that may not be hash to Acacia his owner, make no mistake about the fact that Smooth's external demeanor will be hash to anyone that is not Acacia, or anyone that Acacia and smooth do not consider as a friend.

Zakondo And His Gang – A Public Menace

It is 10:00 PM. On a Monday night The news is on and the Fela's Family is seen watching the news on television. The news is about the 18-wheeler gang of rubbers who is becoming so infamously elusive to the Police Department and increasingly dangerous to the public such that the military force is deployed to arrest the situation and bring the works of the evil armed robbers constituting a public menace to a halt.

Fela: Listen! Listen! listen! The news is on.

Fela calls his family to order just so they can pay attention to the current news on the television. The family of seven is all settle down to pay attention to the news. The news caster is on.

Stella Gam: Good Evening. I am Stella Gam bringing you the news from Mekwus Networks Channel 5. Our top story is on Zakondo, the eighteen-wheeler armed robber who had made away with countless number of eighteen-wheeler trucks with goods costing millions of dollars to their owners. Up until now, Zakondo has not been apprehended and has successfully eluded the Police Department for the past six months. Zakondo's robbery has claimed many lives since its inception.

Sade: Fela sweetie, did you hear that? They have not caught Zakondo for the past six months and he has killed many people. Honey, we are going to have to protect our kids with all we got.

Fela: Sunshine my love; you better believe that! Yes, our little ones are not going to leave our sight. We are going to fix our eyes on them like barnacles on a boat. Let's keep watching, shall we?

Sade: Yes, Pappy.

Sade (pronounced Shadey) kisses her husband affectionately.

Stella Gam: The government is now considering the deployment of the military service men to help capture and put to rest this menace that has tormented the populace for quite a while. Our source tells us that the military deployment will take effect as soon as tomorrow morning.

Fela: Yes! It is time to put an end to this nonsense.

Sade: [second that honey. People are living in fear on a daily basis and that is certainly not acceptable. This is a free country; we must live freely or die trying.

Fela: Sunshine my love; I could not say that any clearer. Let us take out the kids and have a great time out there in the field.

Sade: Big daddy, that would be great. Let us go.

Fela and Sade kiss and hug and they take the kids out to play. When they get on the street, they see the notorious Jackson putting on his game.

Jacky The Wonder – A Bully In His Own Rights

Jackson is an ex-convict who had just got through serving a fifteen-year prison term for armed robbery. He searches up and down, high and low for a gainful employment or even a day laborer job, but to no avail. Then he remembers that when he was in prison, he had a way with illusion. So, he decides to set up a table for the card trick. He is making some money with the card business but not enough to get by. He figures that there are those who would pay money to tickle their hearings with exciting stories that do not necessary have to be true. Now he decides to be a Native doctor going by the name *Jacky the Wonder*.

LeBron street in New Orleans, Louisiana. Jacky the Wonder is seen at the corner of the street preparing herbs to cure a particular disease that is best known to him and at the same time he is telling people who care to stop by that they can pass their unfortunate happenings to other people in exchange of the said people's good fortune by dropping a coin next to the person with which the exchange of fortune is to be made. After dropping the coin, Jacky the Wonder will make an incantation so as to set in motion the exchange of fortune between the two parties. Before that, Jacky the Wonder would request payment from the person asking for service. There are those who may have a prior knowledge of Jacky the Wonder's prison sentence, still, little does anyone know that Jacky the Wonder is not only phony but also an ex-convict pouncing on the miseries of misinformed people. Before going further, it is safe to say that there is a man going by the name Pascal laying down and pretending to be sleeping a few inches away from Jacky the Wonder.

If you live on LeBron street or its neighboring streets, you should know Pascal – a well-educated man with a bachelor's degree in Psychology from Harvard University and usually well dressed. There are those who may share Pascal's view that paying tax for any reason equals slavery. As a free man, Pascal decides not to own any property that will require tax payment. Since almost everything you do in this country requires the payment of some sort of taxes, Pascal decides to be homeless! Pascal is quick at letting people know that he is in no way suffering from any kind of mental defect – he is simply standing up for his rights as a model citizen. Pascal wants people to leave him alone so that he can enjoy his freedom.

One of the gifts that Jacky the Wonder possesses is the ability to talk fast for a long time without getting tired. Some people find that catchy and within a short period of time, Jacky the Wonder receives his first customer going by the name Frederick. Jacky the Wonder explains how his business works including his charge for each service he renders to Frederick. As he points to Pascal, Frederick asks Jacky the Wonder if there is anything preventing him from using the sleeping man for his purpose. Jacky the Wonder answers no, there isn't anything that could prevent Frederick from using the sleeping man Pascal for his purpose, but that Frederick must make his payment first. So, Frederick pays Jacky the Wonder the sum of forty dollars for the service. Jacky the Wonder asks Frederick to cast a coin next to Pascal, and so he does. Thereafter, Jacky the Wonder begins his incantation. Before you know it, the incantation is over. Jacky the Wonder asks Frederick to be on his way and expect good fortunes to come his way.

Frederick goes on his way singing. He only walks a few yards before Pascal wakes up from his pretend sleep, pick up the coin, chases Frederick, catches up with him and pelts the coin at him. Frederick walks back to Jacky the Wonder in haste to ask what will happen now since Pascal casts the coin back at him. Jacky the Wonder explains to him that the request for the exchange of fortune between him and Pascal is null and void. In short, the man's request is not accepted. So, Frederick asks Jacky the Wonder to return the money he had paid for the service.

Jacky the Wonder's refusal results into physical fight between him and Frederick. Spectators and Pascal were laughing profusely at what they are looking at. In the end, two Police Officers arrive explaining to Frederick that Jacky the Wonder is in the right to keep the money since the service he requested was performed regardless of the end result. The Police Officers do not make any arrest because the entire thing is ridiculous. Furthermore, the Police Officers knew Jacky the Wonder to be an ex-convict and a phony. How a nice looking man like Frederick could fall prey to Jacky the Wonder's trickery and deceptions is beyond the Officers' thinking. As it is, a verbal contract between two consenting adults is binding. It is not the job of the court or the officers of the court to argue fairness based on the outcome of the contract. The officers' job is to interpret the verbal contract between Jacky the Wonder and Frederick in the most basic way. Since Police Officers are not actuaries, any complication in such verbal contract can be sort out in court.

The verbal contract favors Jacky the Wonder from the Officers' point of view regardless of his prior convictions. One of the two Police Officers advice Frederick to sue Jacky the Wonder if he is not satisfied with their admonition, but he cannot engage in a street fight with Jacky the Wonder. Therefore, Frederick leaves the scene in a rather shameful manner because he feels that he has been had by an ex-convict notorious to everyone except him.

Fela:	Sade?

Sade:	Yes, Fela.

Fela:	What is this world turning to?

Sade:	Pappy, a funny little place.

Fela:	Sunshine my love; you can say that again. We certainly cannot get tired having fun, can we?

Sade:	No, my dear. We cannot get tired of fun.

Fela:	Sade, did you see that?

Text Not When You Shall Drive, Drive Not When You Shall Text

Fela is pointing to an ongoing accident where a driver of a sedan vehicle isn't paying attention to the road as she is busy texting while driving on a local road in a residential area. Interestingly, the young man that she runs over isn't paying attention to traffic because he is on his mobile smart phone texting.

Sade:	The driver of that car did not even stop to help the young man he ran over. What is this world coming to where it seems that the good guys are disappearing?

Fela: Let's go give him a helping hand. Shall we, Sunshine my love?

Sade: Sure, sweet Pappy.

Fela and Sade walk over to the scene of accident where the young man is hurting but alive. They help him up.

Fela and Sade: Young man, are you all right? What's your name?

Young Man: My name is Obi and I need a doctor.

Fela: Yes, we'll call the ambulance for you, just don't move a muscle, all right Obi?

Obi: OK, I'll try not to. I know it's my fault because I wasn't paying attention to the road before crossing. I didn't even know that I'm about to cross over.

Sade: Why didn't you know that you are crossing over?

Obi: I am so ashamed because my parents told me not to text while walking across the road and especially not to wear loud music on my ears to where I'm not able to perceive the happenings in my environment. Oh, this is so shameful. My parents are going to kill me when the find out. Please, can you promise not to tell them, please, please, please, please, please?

Sade: First thing first. How old are you? What is your age, young man?

Obi: I'm thirteen years old.

Sade: We are glad that you will be all right after seeing the doctor and these men from the Emergency

Response Team will help you further. About your parent, don't worry too much because they will be happy to find out that you will be all right and not dead.

Fela:	Young man, are you going to listen to your parents' advice and obey them from now on?

Fela: Young man, are you going to listen to your parents' advice and obey them from now on?

Obi: Yes, sir. I surely will. I think that I have learnt my lesson.

Sade: Good.

Fela: Nowadays, children think that their parents don't understand or would not understand what they are going through. I wonder if those children ever think of or remember that their parents were once their age and have gone through what they are currently going through; and so, perfectly understand their situation. Thus, based on experience, their parents are in a better position to admonish them appropriately to where they are rescue from their stupor.

Sade: Sweetie, that is so right. I know Obi learnt his lessons now. But I don't know why the lady driving the sedan vehicle did not stop to help the boy.

Fela: She probably was too scared of going to jail.

Sade: But it wasn't her fault that the boy wasn't paying attention to his environment, was it?

Fela: She probably didn't know that it wasn't her fault. She was just too scared because she too was on her smart phone texting and being distracted from driving.

Sade: The Police department will be going after her for fleeing the scene of accident. I just hope that mankind would obey the traffic laws that Congress has put in place regarding texting while driving. If you must text, don't drive! If you must drive, don't text! Is there anything difficult to understand in that instruction?

Fela: I don't think so. In fact, the principle behind that law is that of saving lives — both young and old including those of animals crossing the road. You see my love, life is life. Whether it be those of animals or of mankind, life itself is sacred and has to be respected regardless of personal views.

Sade: Yes, regardless of whose life we are talking about. The bottom line is, such ones are being missed by their respective family who may depend on them for more than anything, support.

Fela: Can you imagine how Obi's parent must have felt if he was killed in that automobile accident?

Sade: They would have been devastated. I cannot imagine losing any of our children and especially you in death. That will be devastating such that I would just die. I don't think that I have the strength to go on without you guys.

Fela: Girl, don't go on thinking crazy like that. If something should happen to me, I want you to summon the courage, the power, the glory and the faith to continue living. One of us at least, has to be there for our children.

Sade: I'll certainly try. I'm just saying that it is difficult for a family to lose a member for any reason and so, mankind must place themselves in the shoes of others when buzzed, drunk, sleepy, texting or doing anything that would hinder their ability to drive responsibly.

Fela: Sunshine, my love; I agree with you totally. If mankind finds itself incapable of driving there is nothing wrong in asking for help like calling a friend, a relative, or a taxi cab. Doing so would be saving lives among other things like prevention of endless guilty conscience and incarceration.

Sade: That is so right, my love.

As There Ever Been the Right Time To Speak Up?

As the couple, Fela and Sade pass through a friendly neighborhood, they catch sight on a handsome young man in his early twenties stirring down his eyes all over a young lady in the same age group, about nineteen. The young man is dying to approach the lady with a view to start a friendly conversation with her but could not summon the courage to do so. As the symptoms of his cold feet become clear to Fela and Sade, after reminiscing on the closeness to home that cold feet behavior had been to Fela on the very first time that he laid his eyes on Sade, Fela and Sade decide that Sade should go and offer the young man some tips that could help him overcome his cold feet.

Sade tell the young man that the young lady that he's obviously having a crush on would not know about it until somebody bring it to her attention. And do you know who should do that? Sade asks the young man. I don't know but I'm guessing maybe I should do that. Says the young man. Sade says yes, you should do it. Sade continues by saying that the worse that could happen would be she turning down

your offer which would allow you to move on to something better or figure out your next move. Sade adds, you are not going to know whether or not she likes you until you try; she may feel like you do, you'll never know until you talk to her. The young man going by the name Holland, is appreciative of Sade's care and advise. However, Holland is not able to bring himself up to approach the young lady.

What Holland sees next is not something that he thinks would happen in a million years. As Holland continues to stir at the young lady, another young man going by the name Hayes, approaches the young lady going by the name Merlot, introduces himself and asks her out for a cup of coffee. Holland is hoping to ridicule Merlot's turning down Hayes' offer, but to his dismay, Merlot accepts Hayes' offer. Holland blames himself for not taking action when he had the chance and vows to put into practice the advice that he had received from Sade the next time around.

The second day is here. Holland is shopping for his Mother and two sisters at a beauty supply store. As he places items into his basket, guess who is walking towards him? Yes, Merlot is. Merlot notices Holland couple of aisles away and decides to go and let him in on a secret. "Hey there, aren't you the guy I saw at the neighborhood stand yesterday?" Merlot asks. "I am ashamed to say yes, I am that guy. But the truth is, I am that guy. What is more, I was literally stirring at you hoping for a miracle to happen where you come to ask me out on a date since I could not bring myself to approach you and ask you out on a date for fear of rejection." Holland replies. "By the way, I am Merlot. May I have your name please?" Merlot asks. "I am Holland and it is nice to finally meet you Merlot." Holland replies. "Yes, it is nice to meet you and it would have been nicer if we had officially met yesterday," says Merlot. "Really?" Asks Holland. "Yes, really, Holland. In fact, I was hoping for you to ask me out because you are a fine young man and I would have said yes." Merlot replies. "Seriously?" Holland asks. "Yes, seriously." Merlot replies.

"You probably noticed that I waited for quite a while hoping to hear from you before Hayes came on to ask me out." Merlot says. "Oh man.

I am so dumb, dumb, dumb." Holland rebukes himself. "Oh, no, no, no, no, no, no, no. You are not dumb at all. As a matter of fact, you are a sensitive and thoughtful young man." Merlot replies. "Yeah, see what it got me, no date. So, much for sensitivity and thoughtfulness" Holland depressingly says. "I tell you this Holland, if things do not work out with Hayes and I, you will be next. I am giving you this promise today that I will personally come and look for you. Do you believe me?" Merlot promises. "Yes, I believe you, Merlot." Replies Holland. Then Holland expresses his appreciation for the newly found knowledge. Merlot stretches out her right hand to Holland for a handshake. They both shake hands and bid each other well and goodbye.

Obviously, Holland is not happy at what had transpired. As he continues shopping, he could not help his soliloquy which he does in despair. Holland speaks out his thoughts when he thinks no one is around and comes to an abrupt stop when he perceives the presence of another being. One of Holland's thoughts goes this way: "She wants me to wait for her as a backup so that when she finishes with that crazy man called Hayes, I'll be next in line. I don't think so, woman! Holland does not wait for ladies; ladies wait for Holland. Yeah, I should wait for you while you are in another man's hand being romanced and loved. And when that go sour, what do you know, Holland will be waiting for you. Oh, really? I don't think so woman! Just as you like kissy, kissy, Holland like kissy, kissy too. In no way will Holland be your rebound, woman! I'm going to go get me my own lady! You better hold on tight to Hayes because Holland is not going to wait for you!"

Well, we feel for Holland and understand why he does not want to be someone else's second hand or rebound. No one should be someone else's second hand or rebound. Aren't we all looking for someone special, that person specially made for us by the creator, that person who always seeks to bring out the best in us through thin and thick, and yes, that person with whom an everlastingly blissful union can be formed? Holland, we feel for you as much as we hope that you have learnt your lesson on not being afraid of who you are and expressing yourself the proper way at the right time.

5

<u>TAKE YOUR STAND AGAINST UNWHOLESOME FLATTERY</u>

Shine the light on the aged Mama Goose named Lefty, due to her deformed left leg from birth. She is ninety-seven years old in Goose-years[9]. Her husband, Papa Goose named Sparky ninety-eight years old in Goose years. They been together as faithful couple for sixty-nine years and have six children together. Since the inception of their union, no formidable force is strong enough to break their bond of union. Sharing a quality time together, the Geese Family enjoys the radiance of the sun as Lefty the Mama Goose educates her family on morality and family values with a story. All members of the Geese Family are present, and Lefty speaks.

Lefty: Hey my beautiful family, gather around me as I am about to tell you a story about a beautiful woman named Vanessa. Vanessa and her husband have been married for a little over ten human years with six beautiful children. Having these six children did not diminish Vanessa's beauty for a bit.

Sparky: Really? Mine, not even for a tiny little bit?

Everyone laughs. "Mine" is an endearing name that Sparky gave to Lefty his wife.

Lefty: Yes, Darlene, not even for a tiny little bit. In fact, if you see Vanessa for the first time, you will think she has no children.

Corvallis: Seriously?

Lefty: Yes, my eldest child. I am dead serious. Yes, as serious as you being my eldest male child

Corvallis: That is so deep, Mom.

Lefty: Thanks son. Now pay attention children, this is how the story goes.

Let the light shine on Vanessa as she walks toward the female restroom to empty her bowel movement in a fancy top-notch restaurant. The restaurant is one that still observes the luxury of the eighteenth or nineteenth century style of restroom, in which a male or a female attendant stands in front of the restroom to direct you to a vacant restroom and another attendant inside the restroom to serve you with a clean towel to dry out your hands right after your hands are washed. These attendants appreciate your generous gifts or tips for the services they render to you. There are so many ways one can describe Vanessa. She is 5 feet ten and one-half inches; married to the same man for ten years with six children. She carries herself in a dignified manner. She is well educated with a master's degree in Computer Science from the University of California Berkeley, California. She is a beauty even to those who meet her for the first time.

Describing Vanessa in terms of breath, she is a fresh breath of life. Describing her in terms of curve, she is perfectly curved with all the curves in the right places. Describing her in terms of substance, she is a flawless diamond whose atomic structures are arranged in tetrahedron. Her flawless skin glows to where you would think that you are in paradise devoid of imperfections. Describing her in terms of a horse, she is an untamed bronco – morally unbroken. To the laymen however, she is a Fox, because it appears to those laymen that the world is full of women who are that physically beautiful but will take you for everything you have and drop you like a hot pot. Hence it is difficult for such laymen to see that beyond the woes of deceptions and beyond the woes of terrible relationships there are women who are physically and morally beautiful. Yes, ladies who strongly believe that having a higher moral standard elevate them over ordinary lives and especially over animals. Describing her in terms of a book, she is a Bible.

Yes, Vanessa is a Bible because she has deep respect for the sanctity of marriage and the institution of marriage. What is more, Vanessa's high morale is due to her firm and immutable believe in the Bible's view of morality in general and the Bible's view of morality respecting married people in particular. Her morality is simply not for sale. There is little or no wonder that of all her many gifts, her appreciation for the institution and the sanctity of marriage stands conspicuous. There is no wonder that her proud husband finds it easy to love her dearly, more than anything in the world. Describing her in terms of moral, her husband will agree with the laymen, she is a Fox. From her husband's point of view Vanessa is a Fox because she is more cunning or sly than the sum total of all those depraved people who in their quest of bringing Vanessa down to their debauched standards, they usually fail woefully. Let us see if Vanessa will hold up to her guard of morality as usual.

This time, a male attendant going by the name Stanley is standing by the restroom door of the restaurant as Vanessa approaches.

Stanley: Hun! Hun! Hun! Hun! Girl, you are fine!

Stanley is a Caucasian American man who actually sing out the above with an attitude coupled with finesse like "G ..I ..r ..I you are fa-a-a-a-aine!" You can imagine that the two words "girl" and "fine" are projected for the longest time in a psychedelic manner. Does Vanessa who had got to go use the restroom really bad appreciates Stanley's sentiment? Let's find out.

Vanessa: Oh, thank you! You are such a gentleman, and you
                   are not bad yourself. What is your name?

Stanley answers with finesse and psychedelic attitude like this:

Stanley:	I am Stanley, but you can call me big daddy.
Vanessa:	You know what? I'll call you Stanley. You see Stanley, I need to use restroom really bad. Can you complete this sentence for me?
Stanley:	Sure! I'll do anything for you, girl.
Vanessa:	If you got to go?
Stanley:	You got to go!
Vanessa:	Yes! Stanley, I have to go really bad.
Stanley:	Girl, I don't think so!
Vanessa:	Why not?
Stanley:	Girl, you are just too pretty! Yes! You are just too beautiful to use the restroom! I cannot let you use the restroom because nothing imperfect can come out of that perfect body of yours. So, I'll take whatever you want to pump out of that perfectly designed and well taken care of body of yours. I cannot let you use the restroom. I just cannot let you. You are way too fine for the restroom.
Vanessa:	Are you crazy?
Stanley:	Girl, you better believe it! I am crazy for your Love girl. As a matter of fact, I'll kill for your love. Girl, don't you ever, ever, ever, ever, ever, ever, forget that I am crazy for your love, and I'll kill for you. Let me prove it to you. Who do you want me to kill? Tell me who? Tell me.
Vanessa:	Man? You are completely out of your mind. You better get out of my way before I run over you!
Stanley:	Girl, you can run over me any time anywhere and it will be my pleasure!

Lefty: Vanessa is furiously agitated because she had to go really bad, and Stanley is not helping. So, she threatens to call the management on Stanley, which can get him fired.

Vanessa: Get out of my way before I call the manager on your crazy self! Don't you get it? If a woman got to go, she got to go! So, you let her go! Get out of my way!

Stanley: Girl, I'll let you go, since you put it that way.

Vanessa: It is about time! Get out of my way! Psycho!

Lefty: Vanessa is understandably becoming more and more impatient and irate partly because she could no longer control or hold her bowel movement and she has been losing her turns for quite a while. Therefore, she forces herself into the women's restroom. Marvel at Vanessa's soliloquy as she enters the lady's room – the female restroom.

Vanessa: I cannot believe what had just happened in a restaurant that supposed to be top of the line. I guess you never know what you can come across when you leave the comfort of your home. That crazy man talking about how I'm way too pretty and beautiful to use the restroom and so he would not let me use it? He must be stoned and gone completely crazy. Who knows? It could be the case that where he comes from pretty women are scarce, if any. You can't blame the man too much for trying harder; can you? I got to hand it to him – he is bold! But Stanley, not today, and certainly not with me!

Lefty: Vanessa is just about done washing her hands when a female attendant named Gail serves her with a clean towel to dry out her wet hands. Listen.

Gail: Madam, can I be of service to you by offering this clean towel to dry your hands?

Vanessa: Sure. Thanks.

Gail: By the way Ma'am, my name is Gail, and I could not help but heard your soliloquy about your encounter with Stanley, one of our attendants out there. I really want to apologize to you on behalf of this restaurant for Stanley's behavior. We've never seen him behave like that before. We are so sorry, and we certainly will appreciate your accepting our apologies.

Vanessa: No problem, Gail, apology is accepted. I am just glad that I did not go on myself. That will have been an embarrassment that I'll be forced to live with for quite a long time. So, since that did not happen, your apologies for Stanley's surprised happenstance is well accepted. Can you make sure that he will not do it to someone else?

Gail: Believe it Ma'am, it will not happen again.

Vanessa: Gail?

Gail: Yes, Ma'am?

Vanessa: You are a good employee and thanks again.

Gail: Ma'am, you are welcome any time. Please have a great day out there.

Vanessa: You too. Bye.

Gail: Thanks for your business and bye.

Lefty:	Vanessa steps out of the restroom into the hallway where Stanley is ushering guests in to use the restrooms. Suddenly, Stanley catches sight with Vanessa who has been trying her best possible to avoid him.
Corvallis:	Really? Mom?
Sparky:	Son, you better believe that. You want to hide from those who cannot take no for an answer. Mine, please continue.
Lefty:	Thanks honey. Can you imagine Stanley yelling in a place that supposed to be one of the best restaurants in town?
Sparky:	This is unbelievable!
Lefty:	Well, let us see.
Stanley:	Ma'am, Ma'am, excuse me Ma'am I just want to apologize for my behavior. It will make me a very happy man if you could let me apologize to you from the bottom of my humble but radiant heart with a candlelight dinner.
Vanessa:	Stanley, while your offer is tempting, I will decline on it. I accept your apology though which is why I will not be filing a formal complaint against you.
Stanley:	My gratitude for not filing a complaint against me. The dinner offers still stand if you change your mind. You know where to find me and I'll wait for you, perfect one.

Vanessa said the following as she walks away.

Vanessa:	Don't hold your breath. You are ten years dead Late!

Stanley: [Yells] I may have to hold my breath because if I cannot have you, Angel, life will not worth much to me. Yes, girl, I'll have nothing to live for without you! So, I will hold my breath for you girl! If I die while holding my breath, you should know that you kill me baby girl.

Lefty: As Vanessa disappears into thin air, Stanley finds himself in a soliloquy. Listen.

Stanley: That girl is fine! She is perfectly built for me. Stanley, that's your girl right there! The girl you can finally take home to Mamma and say Mamma, your son has finally found him the love of his heart!

Lefty: Gail was passing by when she heard Stanley's soliloquy, she says

Gail: And she is going to get you fired if you don't drop it!

Stanley: Oops! She heard me. I did not know that someone is listening to my deep thoughts. I better take a break. I think I have done enough for now. I am going to have to get busy right now.

Lefty: Stanley walks away from the scene and that ends the story. Now, what is the moral of the story?

Courtney: Stay young and pretty?

Corvallis: No Courtney. I am sure that Mom will tell us.

Sparky: Yes, tell us. Mine. I am sure that we are all interested. Do not keep us waiting and guessing.

Lefty: All right then. I will tell you. Listen. In fact, I share the views expressed in the book "Is Silence R e a l l y Golden?" written by Elijah Mekwunye. I will go ahead and read it to you.

Lefty pick up the book, turns to the page she wants to read from, and reads.

I urge you to join me in applauding Vanessa's decisive and eloquent response to a rather tempting situation. As a proud wife and mother of six, she stands resolute to be faithful to the institutor of marriage, her husband, her marriage, and her children, come what may! How would you have reacted if you were in Vanessa's shoes, married and being presented with an opportunity to get it on with someone endowed with attractive physique but whose hands have not been pledged or given to you in marriage?

Remember, Stanley is a very handsome man with strong athletic built. Would your mind be bombard with false reasoning such as, what my spouse does not know would not hurt him? Or would you ask yourself a fundamental question such as, what reaction or response would you expect from your spouse if placed in the same situation of romantic flattery? Think about it. Whatever honest answers you may come up with to the above questions, it pays to always remember that your spouse may someday be presented with the same opportunity where his or her faith and love for your marital relationship may be tested to a high degree. If that happens, how well would you expect your spouse to measure? With your answer in mind, how do you think you should respond to extra marital flattery, which may lead to extra marital affair?

I urge you to remember the golden rule: "Do unto them how you want them to do unto you,"[14] In the same line of thought, "one good turn deserves another." These statements apply especially to the relationship of you and your spouse in particular, and then to your relationship with the rest of the world in general.

Do you notice that Vanessa did not use marriage as an excuse for her chastity in the first place? It was on her way out that she mentioned to Stanley that he was ten years dead late! Which simply means that she has been spoken for some ten years ago and remains spoken for regardless of Stanley's formidable lure. Vanessa stood firm on her ground because of her personal convictions that if you are in a divinely bonded relationship that marriage is, be true to your commission.

Sparky: Let us face it, shall we? It could be the case that Vanessa's spouse may not have most of the attractive physical qualities that Stanley throws on her face. However, one question remains clear in her mind. Can you guess the question? Yes, you are correct. The question is, where was Stanley when Vanessa was dating, courting, and planning her future with her spouse over ten years ago? Another question is, where was Stanley when Vanessa and her spouse were mending their idiosyncrasies over ten years in the making? All humans regardless of who they are, their status in life, and their attractive physique, do have idiosyncrasies or weaknesses. Believe it! While some idiosyncrasies may seem manageable and easy to live with, yet some other idiosyncrasies may be incorrigibly unmanageable and hence, difficult to live with. Vanessa and her spouse have learnt to comfortably live with each other's idiosyncrasies and so Vanessa is not about to let anything, yes, especially those things that are enticing to her eyes to come between her love for her spouse and the sanctity of their marriage.

Lefty: What is more, Vanessa expects the highest degree of chastity from her spouse when her spouse is presented with similar unwholesome opportunity. You probably would agree with me that commending Vanessa for putting into practice what she expects her spouse to do when in similar unwholesome condition is in order. I can tell you that it is not always easy to keep that positive frame of mind partly due to our selfish inclinations. However, when such unwholesome opportunities present themselves to me, I always ask myself this question, what would I expect my spouse to do when in similar condition? Give in, enjoy the ride, and later find a way usually with false reasoning to make it where he is able to live with himself? Or would I expect him to simply flee from that unwholesome condition? Since I will expect my spouse to choose the latter, that is, to flee from that unwholesome situation, which is not always easy but the right thing to do, I expect that of me too. That is how I stayed out of that kind of trouble.

Corvallis: Mom, that is so cool.

Lefty: Yes, I am very happy and proud of doing so. You too can be very happy if you put the interest of your spouse ahead of yours. No one said it is easy not to be selfish. You just have to do it spontaneously when it comes to your spouse and family because it is the right thing to do.

Sparky: Yes, there is no such thing as "love at first sight." But there is infatuation at sight. I mean, how can you be in love with someone you do not know? How can you be in love with someone on the very first time you meet? No, there is a thing called lust. When two strangers meet the first time and hit it off, it is not love but lust. it is a classic definition of infatuation.

Corvallis: Really? Infatuation?

Sparky:	Yes, infatuation. When you marry, the infatuation tends to run out leaving a sense of belonging and that of ownership which may lead to irreconcilable disagreements. And because of imperfections and selfish inclinations, these senses of belonging and ownership are usually abused, or in the barest minimum, taken for granted. When the infatuation is over, what is left?
Lefty:	REALITY!
Sparky:	Then the questions are, can you handle the reality in front of you? Can you handle the reality you are surrounded with? And if the reality is not in your favor, do you have the gut, the endurance, the mindpower, and the selfless heart to make that reality work in your favor? Statistics show that today, at least fifty percent of marriages fail partly because couples are waking up to unexpected reality that is infeasible to work with.
Lefty:	Be nice to your spouse. Be practical in demonstrating your unselfish love to your spouse. Yes, before the opportunity to prove fidelity to your marital relationship presents itself, be resolute in your mind and heart to be faithful to your marriage, come what may! By doing so, it will become easy for you to accomplish that which by nature seems to be difficult.
Corvallis:	Mom, the way you teach us in a practical and fun way is one of the many qualities I appreciate about you. Thanks Mom.
Lefty:	Son, I have to thank you for that observation and appreciation. You see son, many parents do the best they can to teach their children to be good

model citizens on one hand. On the other hand, however, the world around those children teaches them to be bad citizens. Whichever of the two teachings seems to be more fun is usually the one that those children will go for. Your father and I do not want to lose our children to the world around them. Hence, we make it a point of duty to make our teachings more fun and practical. Therefore, when teaching your children, make it more fun and practical for them to follow. By doing so, you will always gain your children instead of losing them to the world around them.

Courtney: Mom, that is deep. You are so cool.

Corvallis: Mom, you rock! You are the bomb!

The term "bomb" used in this context simply means the best in the game at least from a layman's point of view. Corvallis is here praising his mother as the best mother ever! Yes, the best mother on Earth. Of course, Corvallis' mother is happy to be given such a wonderful compliment; especially one that comes from the bottom of one of her sons' hearts.

Sparky: Yes, your Mom is a great storyteller. That is just one of her many wonderful qualities that I cherish from the bottom of my heart.

Rolling her pretty eyes in a sensual way to Sparky, lefty says:

Lefty: You go Pappy. You better recognize. I got skills.

Sparky: You better believe it girl, I do recognize. You are my heart, my blood, and the wind beneath my wings. Yes, you are wind that blows me into your heart and there I will reside forever.

Purdue: Mom, Dad, when I grow up, I want to have what you got. You both have real love.

Courtney: Yes, your love has stood the test of time.

Purdue: They deserve applaud. Wouldn't you say?

Corvallis: Yes, let us all applaud to our great parents.

Everyone applauds.

Purdue: Mom, I want to go and play with Chuwawa's kids, can I go?

Lefty: Purdue, how many times have I told you not to associate with those Chuwawa's kids because they are bad rap? Yes, those kids are bad influence on you. Before you know it, you will start behaving in the same manner as they do.

Purdue: But Mom?

Lefty: Purdue, do not but Mom me! The words that come out of Chuwawa's mouth is bad enough to turn her posterity into a bunch of criminals. Purdue, that is the reason why I do not want you to associate with them. Get it?

Purdue: Mom, I know they are bad rap, but they cannot influence me. As a matter of fact, I am influencing them. I mean, how else can I teach them that which they do not know if I do not know what they do know?

Sparky: Son, that is a good question. Let me ask you another question that is design for reasoning. What if a long-mouthed rat named Asin decides to pay a visit to a Skunk named Yasoyaso, with a view to helping Yasoyaso the Skunk smell better. Would

Asin the gnawer be successful in making Yasoyaso smell better?

Purdue: No Dad, I do not think so.

Sparky: Why don't you think so, son?

Purdue: Dad, I do not think so because when Yasoyaso passes gas, the air in its surroundings will be polluted with pungent smell of the gas a mile away.

Sparky: Exactly! So, what does that tell you about associating with Chuwawa's kids especially when your Mom had asked you not to?

Purdue: It tells me that I should stay away from them. It is not going to be easy, but I will try my best to stay away from them.

Sparky: Son, you see, your Mom has your best interest in mind. She knows from years of practical experience that when you rob your clean hands in dirt, that dirt does not become clean as a result of robbing your clean hands all over it, does it?

Purdue: No, it does not.

Sparky: What about your clean hands, would they remain clean?

Purdue: No Dad. They will be dirty.

Sparky: Yes, son, your hands will be dirty! In the same line of thought, associating with Chuwawa's kids will soon desensitize you to where you will start to think and behave like they do. If that happens, would your Mom and I appreciate it?

Purdue: I certainly do not think so, Dad. I will stay away from Chuwawa's kids. Thanks Dad.

Sparky: Son, you are welcome. I am so glad that your old man can still be of help.

Purdue: Dad, you are not old. I think you are going to be Young forever.

Sparky: Thanks son.

Sparky hugs Purdue.

6

<u>PARENTAL DISRESPECT USUALLY DONE BY A BULLY</u>

Zakondo And His Gang Are Still At Large

It is 10:00 PM. On a Monday night. The news is on and the Lion Family is seen watching the news on television. The news is about the 18-wheeler rubber who is still at large. The military forces are closing in on him.

Zuka: The news is on. Let us listen.

This time, Papa Lion calls his family to order just so they can pay attention to the current news on the television. The family of four is all settle down to pay attention to the news. The news caster is on.

Stella Gam: Good Evening. I am Stella Gam bringing the news to you from Mekwus Network News - MNN, Channel 5. Our top story is on Zakondo, the 18-wheeler armed robbers who have made away with countless number of 18-wheeler trucks with goods costing the owners millions of dollars. Up until now, Zakondo has not been apprehended but the military forces are closing in on him and his gang. Zakondo's robbery has claimed many lives since its inception, coming to a total of sixty including fourteen police officers.

Shelly: Zuka dear, why is it taking this long to capture that thief Zakondo even with the military involvement?

Zuka:	Shelly, the man and his gang are obviously elusive. But worry not, my sweet one, the days of Zakondo and his gang are numbered. It is only a matter of time for the military force to get him dead or alive.
Shelly:	I really want the military to catch him and his gang alive so they can feel the pain that everyone else is feeling thus far.
Stella Gam:	Our source tells us that the military Force is closing in on Zakondo and his gang whose movements are now confined to the State of California. The chase is on. Our correspondence Audrey Somers is covering the chase live in San Francisco, California. Audrey?
Audrey Somers:	Thank you very much Stella. Yes, you can see that the chase is on. Zakondo and four of his gang members are inside the luxurious purple-black Escalade Premium ESP SUV. That is, the longer version of the Sport Utility Vehicle – SUV. Another four of Zakondo's gang members are inside the luxurious black Mercedes-Benz ML450 hybrid. The interesting part of these two chases is that they are going on at the same time. Zakondo's vehicle is on California highway 1 heading to San Francisco. The second vehicle, the ML450, is on California Highway 5 heading to San Francisco. It is obvious that both vehicles are heading to San Francisco. There must be a safe haven for the gang in San Francisco, it seems. We have two helicopters covering the pursuits. I've been talking to Captain Zimmerman the leader of this military hunt and here is his assurance.

Zimmerman: Yes, since we now know that Zakondo and his gang are heading to San Francisco, we are going to get them cornered there in San Francisco.

Audrey Somers: You have them in your sight, can't you take them out from the sky?

Zimmerman: Yes, we can. But we are doing the best we can to mitigate the loss of innocent lives, which will happen if we choose to take them out from the air. Don't worry, we will get them. We will get them sooner than you think.

Audrey Somers: You heard the man. This is Audrey Somers in San Francisco, California reporting live for Mekwus News, Channel 5. Back to you, Stella.

Zuka: That is crazy. The army is about to corner those Hooligans. They may not have a safe haven after all.

Shelly: I really do not think that Zakondo and his gang will surrender that easily without a fight. After all, they have already claimed many lives. It will be a miracle for them to surrender without a fight.

Zuka: Well, let us wait and see.

We now shine the light on the Ape Family of three. That is, Papa Ape, Mama Ape and their son Rawlings. Mama Ape going by the name Fiorina picks up her favorite book "Is Silence Really Golden?" written by Elijah N. Mekwunye, opens it up, and starts to read it to her family.

Fiorina: This story I am about to read to you my lovely family, is about a mother named Florence with her husband named Chiyem and her two daughters, Pamela and Lizzy.

Francesco: I always enjoy your stories sweetie and I am sure this story will be no exception. So, fire away girl.

Fiorina: Thanks pappy. I know that you and Rawlings will enjoy this story.

Rawlings: Mom, I am sure we will. Your stories are exciting to me. I always look forward to your story night Mom.

Fiorina: Rawlings, thanks for your vote of confidence. I'll certainly try my best to keep it up. Let me start reading this to you.

Fiorina reads.

Which of These Two Children Can You Relate To?

Florence asks her two daughters to do chores for her. Pamela the first daughter says yes, Mom I'll do it and leaves, while the second daughter Lizzy stays to argue against doing the chore partly because she has no knowledge of the principle behind her Mom asking her to do the chore order than that of an exercise for physical wellbeing, which she considers as punishment.

Lizzy is a procrastinator who loves gadgets and computer games in the universe of technology; yes, the technology age of distraction. Asking Lizzy to handle a chore at any given time and especially when she is having fun playing with her games and gadgets is like forcing oneself to ride an untamed mustang or bronco. On the other hand, her big sister Pamela is the easygoing kind of a girl. She never argues when asked to handle a chore. She is the dream daughter of every mother. Or is she?

Be Nice To Your Spouse

Before we continue, let me take you on a romantic ride or at least I consider it romantic; you can however decide whether or not it is romantic. It is a fairly sunny day with cool breeze compensating for the environmental heat. Florence is having a very busy day at work where it seems she's carrying the whole world on her shoulder; at least, that is how she feels at the moment. While she is carrying on with her duties in her office as a Senior Director of Finance for a large publicly traded company, she receives a call from her receptionist asking her to come down and accept her package delivery. What is the package and who sent it? You are correct to imagine the question to be one of the many questions throbbing Florence's mind since she is not in expectation of any package delivery. Well, she summons the courage, leaves her office, and go down the stairs to the receptionist's office.

The receptionist's office is not big enough to accommodate these many people who happen to be Florence's colleagues and those she reports to. What are these people doing? They are admiring the beautiful package that has Florence's name on it. In a moment, the crowd behold Florence and hail:

Go Florence! Go Florence! Go Florence! Go! Go! Go!

Go Florence! Go Florence! Go Florence! Go! Go! Go!

Florence wonders why these many people and what are they doing in the receptionist's office. Someone in the crowd says Florence, you have to open the envelop and tell us who sent you this beautiful gift and for what special occasion? Florence asks what envelop and what gift? Like the pathing of the red sea, the crowd paves the way revealing the package. The package blows Florence's mind away from a distance.

As she glazes at the package that renders her speechless, she slowly draws close to the package and could not stop wondering what the sender may have been thinking to have carefully come up with this mind blowing package that turns her busy day into a most cheering one. The package is a freshly cut beautiful flower bouquet. The retail price of the flower bouquet at the time of writing is six hundred and fifty United States Dollars. The flower bouquet consists of one hundred luxurious red roses mixed with one hundred purple Peruvian lilies, one hundred luxurious Magnolia flowers, and one hundred white roses. It has ten balloons each having the inscription "I love you dearly." The vase containing the flowers is colorfully decorated and it is the vase you'll want to keep indefinitely. The flower bouquet is humongous and beautiful floral arrangement.

Florence walks majestically on the cleared pathway toward the flower bouquet, picks up the envelop and open it up. As she takes in a deep breath and a smile, the curious crowd is ready to take in the information inside the envelope. You could have heard a strand of hair drop when Florence begin to read out the words. Someone from the crowd yells out who is it from? Florence answers it's from my husband Chiyem. The crowd simultaneously asks, really? Florence answers yes, really my husband sent the flowers. You could hear the following comments from the crowd: "That is so sweet. That is so cool. That is so wonderful. That is so lovely. That is so nice of him to do that for his love." I will leave the rest comments to your candid imaginations. In the mist of these comments, one person yells out, what is the special occasion? Florence says that according to the information on the card there is no special occasion, my husband sends the flowers to tell me that he loves me for being who I am – his love. Yes, his proud wife.

A gentle voice appears from the thin air saying read the card. Yes, read the card in its entirety and don't leave out a word; would you? Florence says all right and she reads: "Florence my love, these flowers represent my gratitude for being you. The sentimental expression of my love for you as my beloved wife will not complete without saying that you are my blood. You are my heart. You are my love. Yes, you are my life. I love you my dearest baby girl..." Before Florence could finish reading the contents on the card, some in the audience have begun expressing their heartfelt appreciation through uncontrollable tears of joy for what they have heard thus far. Florence receives hugs and congratulating expressions for having such a loving and romantically thoughtful husband. One of Florence's colleagues asks her if she has a brother in-law that is single, available, and as thoughtful as her husband is. During their outburst laughter, Florence nicely says that all of her brother in-laws are married. Girl, I am not surprise, says her colleague. The good ones are hard to come by, she concludes. Four men help to carry the flower bouquet up to Florence's office. Florence no longer feels like she's carrying the world on her shoulder. Now she feels like she is on top of the world.

Florence could not wait to get home to her love. She picks up the telephone and call up her husband. Let us eavesdrop on their telephone conversation.

Chiyem:	Hello, this is Chiyem.

Florence:	Hey you, it's me. How is your day going so far?

Chiyem:	My day is going quite well my sweet baby "Floral." It's so good that you call, my baby girl. How are you doing today?

Yes, your guess is correct. As far as Chiyem is concerned Floral is a shorten word for Florence.

Florence:	My day was so busy, and I felt like the whole world was on top of my shoulders. But when I saw the beautiful gift you sent to me; I remember why I am the most fortunate wife in the entire world. The gloomy day that I was having earlier suddenly turns bright and lovely again.

Chiyem:	So, you like the flowers.

Florence:	I love the flowers. The flower bouquet is so beautiful! Yes, the flower bouquet is so beautiful that I want to lay on it. The vase, O man, that is a knockout! I love you, I love you, I love you! You just know how to push my buttons, don't you?

Chiyem:	I won't take all the credits because you lovingly taught me how to love you. I am just putting into practice that which I learnt from the most beautiful angel my eyes are fortunate enough to see.

Florence: Really? Or are just pulling my legs, Chiyem?

Chiyem: No, my angel, I am expressing my feelings to you. My sweet Floral, you are the most beautiful angel that my hands are fortunate to hold and love so dearly. Yes, my sweet baby Flow, you are the most beautiful angel that I am fortunate to call my own.

Florence: Do you really feel that way, Chiyem?

Chiyem: Yes, I do feel that way, my sweet Floral. You are the ocean in which my fish lives. You are the heaven into which my bird loves to fly. Even if the heavens and the earth do pass away, my love for you will abide forever. The Super-Jupiter cannot contain my love for you. My sweet baby Floral, you are my pride – the breath of my life.

Florence: You see, that is what I'm saying. You are such a romantic man. I'm leaving my office right now. Meet me at home right away.

Chiyem: O dear! Baby girl, you mean it's going to be on?

Florence: O my sweet Chiyem, it's on now! You better believe that! I want to see you at home right away.

Chiyem: Ayayayai! O mama mia! I better go home now.

Florence beats Chiyem to the house. Chiyem barely makes it through the door when like a ravishing lioness Florence pounces on him, kissing, caressing, tearing off the clothes that Chiyem had on, and I will let your imaginations decide what happens next. This is not in a long shot to say that you cannot accomplish the same goal of pleasuring your wife or spouse of many years with flower bouquet that cost less than a hundred or even fifty United States dollars. After all, to a loving spouse, it is not so much about the size and the cost of the flower bouquet that count the most; it is the thought of you caring so much for her and demonstrating that care with actions that count.

Only A Bully Fools The Parents

It is a new day on a Saturday. Florence is home with the girls and Chiyem a structural Engineer is out to see his client.

Florence:	Girls, I need you to do something for me before I get back from the market. Pamela?
Pamela:	Yes, Mom.
Florence:	I need you to handle the laundry. Please make sure that the clothes and linens are clean, fold and put away in the closet.
Pamela:	Yes, Mom. Consider it done.
Florence:	Great! Lizzy?

Florence calls to her younger daughter Lizzy who is busy at the moment playing with one of her gadgets, which she calls her game-fascinator. She has earplug on both of her ears with increased volume of sound, which make it difficult for her to hear any sound from her environment. Therefore, Florence must increase the volume of her voice a second time in order to get Lizzy's attention.

Florence:	Lizzy?
Lizzy:	What Mom? Do you have to yell?
Florence:	Don't you hear me calling you all along?
Lizzy:	I just did Mom. I am busy! I am doing something! What is it Mom?

Florence:	I need you to wash the dirty pots and plates clean before I get back from the market, so that I can have dinner ready.
Lizzy:	Are you kidding me Mom? Why do I have to be the only one handling dirty dishes every time and every day? Uh? What about Pamela?
Florence:	Yes, what about Pamela?
Lizzy:	Why can't she handle the dirty dishes?
Florence:	Don't worry about Pamela. I have given her chores to do too. Or would you like to do the laundry while she handles the dirty dishes?
Lizzy:	No, I don't want to do the laundry either. Why can't I be left alone and not be bordered? Is that too much to ask?
Florence:	Only if you don't want dinner. Even so, you will have to pull your own weight around here with the family. You cannot just eat and play all day in solitary while I watch you play away your life. Get it?
Lizzy:	I get it Mom. But why do I have to wash the dishes every time? Why can't I do something that don't take anytime.

Whenever Florence gets upset, she calls her child by her full name, that is, first, middle, and last names. That child gets the point, pays attention, and does what Florence wants done.

Florence:	Elizabeth Ifeayinchukwu Chizom! I need you to wash the dishes just so I can have dinner ready when I get back from the market! Your sister will do the laundry which takes more time and effort. You know that is the reason why you don't want to do the laundry.

Lizzy:	All right Mom. I will have the dirty pots and plates clean and dry before you get back from the market. I promise.
Florence:	That's my girl! Come here you.

Florence hugs and kisses her daughters before leaving for the market. After Florence left for the market, Lizzy get to work immediately while her sister Pamela dawdles with her chore. Pamela leaves home without laying a finger on her chore. She tells Lizzy that she will do her chore when she gets back from playing with her friends. Pamela is out playing with her friends for hours.

Florence is back home from the market and ready to prepare dinner for the family. Interestingly, she observes that while Pamela's chore is not touched let alone done, Lizzy did her chore as instructed. What is more, Pamela is not home to help prepare dinner. What happen next?

Florence:	Lizzy, thank you very much for doing your chore. You are such a Darlene. I wonder why your sister is not home and she did not even do her chore. Look at the laundry is everywhere. I have to tidy up this place before your father gets back for dinner.
Lizzy:	Mom, I will help tidy up and prepare dinner before my Dad gets back. I can do the laundry too if you want me to.
Florence:	Would you please?
Lizzy:	Of course, Mom, I will. You've been out there in the marketplaces fending for us. It is only fair that we help you with the chores around the house as best as we can.
Florence:	I am so glad to hear that statement from you and am glad you feel that way my Darlene girl. I

wonder what happen to your sister. Even more so, I wonder why she fails to do her chore. I was counting on her.

Lizzy:	Mom, look who is back home.
Florence:	Pamela, where have you been all day? I asked you to do the laundry before I get back from market and you promised you'll have it done. Hello, does it like it is done?
Pamela:	I am so sorry Mom. I thought I'll be back on time to do the chore before you get back from the market, but I lost track of the time. Mom, I am so sorry.
Florence:	Well, you need to apologize to your sister too and be grateful to her for doing your chore.
Pamela:	Lizzy, please accept my apology and gratitude for helping me with my chore. Thank you very much my sister. How can I make it up to you?
Lizzy:	You are welcome. Concerning how you could make it up to me, I will think of something later. Suffice is to say Pamela, you owe me.
Pamela:	Yes, I do, and I intend to pay, Lizzy, my fair lady.
Florence:	All right children, your father is home and dinner is ready. Let's eat.
Pamela:	Hi Dad.
Lizzy:	Hi Dad.
Chiyem:	Hello girls, how was your day?
Pamela:	Not bad at all Dad.

Lizzy: Dad, I did most of the chores today but that is all right. We hope your day wasn't bad at all. Dad?

Chiyem: No, my sunshine, my day wasn't bad at all, but I am famished. Right now, I can eat a house.

Florence: Pappy, you are home now. You can relax and enjoy dinner with your family.

Chiyem: Thanks, my sweethearts. Let's eat. While we eat, let me tell you about an incident that happened on my way home.

Lizzy: Yes, Dad we want to hear it.

Chiyem: Good. I was on my way home when I saw two people arguing. Out of curiosity, I draw closer and heard the black man asks the white man a question.

Pamela: Dad, what was the question?

Florence: Now, before your Dad tells us the question, I must reaffirm my rule about not coming to my kitchen once the kitchen is closed. If after the kitchen is closed you are still hungry and want to eat in bed, then eat those foods whose crumbs will not invite bugs to the bed because I am tired of cleaning bugs out of your rooms and I am sure that you too must be tired of seeing bug bites on your body when you wake up. Is that clear?

Lizzy: Mom, do you mean food like nuts and fruits? Florence: Yes, my girl that is what I mean.

Lizzy: All right Mom.

Florence: Great! Honey, what was the question?

Chiyem: The black man asks the white man, do you mean that I, a black man should give you, a white man a dollar? The white man replies by saying yes, that is what I mean. The black man then says well, it is about time that you people experience what my people have been experiencing for over four hundred years now!

Lizzy: That is not cool.

Chiyem: Do you folks think there would ever be a time where the Caucasians would be the minority?

Florence: When you come to think about it, you'll realize that humans are the only ones that are grouping themselves into categories. Why can't we just have the human race and not group people into categories and classes?

Chiyem: I believe that would be nice and it may solve a whole lot of global problems facing mankind today.

Zakondo And His Gang Are Cornered

Florence: Let's turn on the television for the news.

Chiyem: Sure thing, sweetheart.

Now, the television is on and so is the ten o'clock news. The news caster, Stellar Gam is on.

Stella Gam: Good Evening. I am Stella Gam bringing the news to you from Mekwus News, Channel 5. Our top story is on Zakondo, the 18-wheeler armed robber. Our source tells us that the military Force is closing in on Zakondo. Our correspondence Audrey Somers is live in San Francisco, California. Audrey?

Audrey Somers: Thank you very much Stella. I've been talking to Captain Zimmerman the leader of this military hunt and here is his assurance. Captain?

Zimmerman: Yes, we got him, and his gang surrounded with few hostages after a long chase from New York city in the State of New York. It seems that everyone saw the chase on the television. We are trying the best we can to mitigate the loss of life. It will be nice for Zakondo and his gang to surrender without turning the whole thing into a blood bath. But at this time, there are no guarantees.

Audrey Somers: As the Captain says, there are no guarantees that this chase will be settle without further bloodshed. Considering the fact that Zakondo and his gang have taken seventy lives already, we can only be hopeful for a subtler surrender. This is Audrey Somers in San Francisco, California. Reporting live for Mekwus News, Channel 5.

Chiyem: What a rush! They've been chasing those guys forever! It's about time that they get caught. People will finally see some respite from fear.

Florence: Yes, Pappy, that's right. No more fear when those hooligans are caught.

Parental fight Against The Machinations Of A Bully

You probably expect that Pamela at this point would have completed her chore since she did not argue with her Mom when asked to do the chore. In fact, she promises to do the chore before her Mom gets back from the market. Does she fulfill her promise? On the contrary. At the end of the day, her chore is not done. What about Lizzy, the second daughter who seems to argue her way out of doing the chore? Does she get her chore done? I will answer that question with a resounding yes. Lizzy gets her chore done partly because her

Mom takes out the time and love to explain to her about the underlying principle behind asking her to do the chore in the first place. Lizzy's understanding of the underlying principle is the motivating force behind her getting the chore done.

On several occasion, the above demeanor of the two sisters and Florence their mother is recursive. Yes, recursive in the sense that almost every time Florence asks Pamela and Lizzy to do chores, Pamela will promise to do the chore with a view to put Florence's mind at rest for the time being. At the end of the day, Pamela ends up not doing the chore. On the other hand, Lizzy will automatically attempt to vigorously argue her way out of doing the chore. But later, after Florence's loving explanation of the underlying principle behind asking her to do the chore, Lizzy gets it done.

Does this recursive behavior continue forever? Or did someone let out the cat that changes things forever? Let us find out.

Pamela:	Lizzy, let me ask you this question. Why do you always argue with Mom each time she asks you to do a Chore?
Lizzy:	It's not fair that I get to do all the chores and have little or no time to play with my toys.
Pamela:	Don't you know that the more you argue with Mom the more you will get into trouble?
Lizzy:	Seriously?
Pamela:	Yes. Seriously. Haven't you heard the saying "Silence is golden?" A lay man said it at best, "silence is the best answer for a fool." Now, I am not implying that Mon is a fool, I'm just trying to help you to understand that you don't need to give an answer to every question that comes your way. Get it?

Lizzy:	Yes, I get it.
Pamela:	Take me for example. Have you ever seen me argue with Mom when she asks me to do a chore?
Lizzy:	Come to think of it, you never did argue with Mom. You just promise to get the chore done.
Pamela:	That is correct. Now, does my promise to do the chore makes Mom happy or sad?
Lizzy:	It makes her happy.
Pamela:	Exactly! You will get a kick out of the next question that I'm about to ask you. Did I do the chore at the end of the day?
Lizzy:	No! Come to think of it, I end up doing the chore that was assigned to you. The chores you promised Mom you were going to do. Hey! I actually did the chores you were supposed to do. Hey! That is so not fair. And certainly not cool! Pamela?
Pamela:	Lizzy, let's not get carried away. I am just trying to teach you something here. If you pay attention, you may learn a thing or two. All right?
Lizzy:	I cannot believe this is happening.
Pamela:	You don't have to believe it. Just watch me do it again. Learn from the master. For this to work well, you have to promise not to tell Mom about this secrete. Do you promise?
Lizzy:	Yes, I do. OK?
Pamela:	You better. Anyway, I'll see you later. I've got to go check on my friends out there. Bye my little sister.
Lizzy:	Bye Pam.

Pamela leaves and the flabbergasted Lizzy finds herself in a little bit of a quandary and expresses such a state in a monologue.

Lizzy: What just happened? Can somebody tell me? What just happen here? My own sister has been playing us all along and we've been falling for her deceptions without knowing it. Well, not any more. The fun days of my evil sister are over. I must let in my parent on Pamela's deceptions. I am not going to keep her despicable secrete. I am so distraught. Yes, I am hurt. I am upset. Uh, I feel dirty. Uh, I feel cheated. I'll have to exercise patience at this point. After all, to laugh the last laugh, I must be patient. What is more? I want Mom to catch her in the act.

Enter Florence the mother, who is surprise to see her daughter in an uncomfortable situation.

Florence: Lizzy my love, why are you so disturbed?

Lizzy: Oh Mom, we've been had.

Florence: What? What are you talking about? We've been had? By whom?

In a rather succulent manner yet fill with a sense of betrayal and disgust, Lizzy replies:

Lizzy: Pamela, my sister.

Florence: Pamela, your sister?

Lizzy: Yes, Mom, my sister Pamela.

Florence: What? Are you on drugs?

Lizzy: No Mom, I'm not on drugs. I could not believe it myself when she told me about it and made me promise not to tell you.

Florence: What did she tell you?

Lizzy: Remember each time you ask Pamela to do a chore, she promises to do the chore, but at the end of the day she never gets to do it and I end up doing the chores?

Florence: Yes, I remember. She always looses track of time and have compelling reasons for not getting her chores done.

Lizzy: Mom, Pamela says that is part of her plan to get her off from doing the chores.

Florence: Really?

Lizzy: Yes, really. She also said that she had observed that you don't appreciate us arguing against doing the chores that you asked us to do however unfair such task may be. Hence, she never argues with you but tells you "Yes, Mom" even though in her mind she knows she isn't going to do the chore.

Florence: Oh dear! You had got to be kidding me!

Lizzy: No Mom, I'm not kidding you. In fact, she said silence is golden; and to an ordinary man on the street, silence is the best answer for a fool.

Florence: What? Pamela calls me a fool?

Lizzy: No, no, no, no, Mom. Pamela actually said that she wasn't inferring that you are a fool, nor was she calling you one. She was just trying to explain to me that I do not have to give a reply to every statement or question that comes my way. She concluded by saying that most of the time, I should pretend as if I'm in agreement to what is being said. Doing so according to Pamela, will make life a lot better for me.

Florence:	I'll show that young lady the kind of life that disrespectful children deserve.
Lizzy:	Please Mom. Do not do anything irrational. Pamela made me promise not to tell you about this.
Florence:	She did?
Lizzy:	Yes, Mom. She did. So, can you at least pretend like I did not tell you a thing about this and watch her with a view to catching her in the act? I promise you Mom, if you ask her about this now, she will deny it and it will be my words against hers. So, let her show you by action, then you can reprimand her. Please, Mom?
Florence:	OK sweetie, I agree with you and I will do that for you.
Lizzy:	Thanks Mom.
Florence:	You are welcome my dear.

7

WHEN HUMAN RIGHT CONFLICTS WITH ANIMAL RIGHT - HUMAN RIGHT WILL PREVAIL

Pamela is seen having a good time with her friends on the street when they glance at a patrol officer having her lunch at a roadside restaurant. Police Officers seen eating in public places can be surprising to some people who have never seen any Police Officer eat before, nor could they conceptualize a Police Officer eating, partly because the Police Officers are in a position of authority to enforce the law and therefore, should be ready to go at all times. Since Pamela and her friends have never seen a Police Officer in uniform consumes food a priori, they have the impression that Police Officers do not eat! The degree of surprise that awaits Pamela and her friends when they finally see a Police Officer consumes her lunch is boundless. Not even your imagination can do the trick.

It is a bright sunny day with cool breezy wind blowing across the streets of Fremont city complimenting the hot sunny atmosphere with a tropical Hawaiian feel. People of all ages are out minding their businesses and other peoples' businesses. Even the little ones are out playing, for it is a beautiful day. Pamela and her friends are reminiscing and chanting their way to the mall for girls shopping. Along the way, Pamela and her friends come across a roadside restaurant where people are sitting outside eating. Nothing seems spectacular until the girls catch sight of a Police Officer who is quietly having her lunch.

Pointing to the Police Officer's direction as she gazes at the officer in awe, Pamela says to her friends.

Pamela:	Hey, do you folks see what I am looking at? Do you see that?
Adamma:	Amazing. That is so awesome.
Pamela:	I have never seen a Police officer eat before.
Uchenna:	I ditto that girl. Dove's tail to Pam's statement, up until now my thought is that Police Officers do not eat because they appeared to be authoritative especially when seen in their immaculate uniform. You mean all these years I've been wrong about them? They really do eat?
Adamma:	I know that they had to eat something just not what we eat. I mean just not like us human. You know what I mean Pam, Uchenna?
Pamela:	Yes, we know what you mean. But Police Officers are humans like us too you know?
Adamma:	Yes, I know Pam, but I didn't expect them to eat like we do. That is just strange. Yeah, it is so strange to see the Police Officers eat like us.
Uchenna:	Well, I guess that amazing things never stop Happening.
Pamela:	They surely don't.

Looking at the girls stirring at her with open jaws, Officer Bello intervenes in a rather subtle manner.

Officer Bello:	Are you girls, all right? It seems you have just witnessed the resurrection of one of your long-lost friends. I am only having my lunch girls. That is not against the law, is it?

Pamela: No, officer. That is not against the law. It is just that we have never seen a Police Officer eat like us before.

Officer Bello: You girls must not have been going out much, do you? Because if you do, you will know that not only do we eat good, we also use the restrooms.

Adamma: What? You use the restrooms too?

Officer Bello: Of course, we do. Who do you girls think we are? Robots?

Uchenna: No, we do not think you are robots. We thought that because you control people, you are not people and certainly are not expected to act like one. That is, to eat like we do.

Officer Bello: I got news for you pal, as you can see, we do eat, we use restrooms, we have boyfriends, have girlfriends, have husbands, have wives, have children, and in a nutshell, we do everything that you do except break the law.

Pamela: Wow! This is news to us. We do not know that you do all that.

Police Officer: Sure, we do. Think of it this way, we are humans too. Let your imaginations do the rest.

Pamela: Officer? On behalf of my friends, thank you very much for taking out time to enlighten us. Please accept our gratitude for your kindness; our sincere apologies for stirring at you.

Officer Bello: You are welcome, and your apologies are Accepted. Now get going and stay out of trouble. Would you?

Pamela: You got it! Officer, we will certainly stay out of trouble. Now, you have a wonderful day as you keep our streets free of crime. Bye officer.

Officer Bello: Bye girls.

The Girls: Bye officer.

Pamela and her friends leave. As the girls trek along, they behold a man running vigorously from an angry squirrel who had bitten him earlier for a reason best known to the squirrel. The way the man is running away from the squirrel makes it apparent that the squirrel may have had it from the man and it's not going to take it anymore. The girls help by making all forms of gestures to scare away the squirrel. At first, the scary faces and gestures the girls are making do not seem to be working until Adamma takes out one of her shoes and pretends to want to strike the squirrel with it. The girls are watching as the squirrel runs in the opposite direction with a speed that is equal to the one she uses to chase the man.

The girls, Pamela and her friends finally catch up with the man running from the angry squirrel and ask for an explanation respecting what had just happened. After catching his breath from running, the man going by the name Richard starts by expressing his gratitude to the girls for saving him from the angry squirrel. Richard continues by saying that him and his wife Rachael have been feeding that angry squirrel ever since he was little.

Richard: We decided to stop feeding the angry squirrel because not only was he becoming too expensive to feed, he started to bring several guests along. I mean we are talking about three or sometimes five guests. When we refuse to feed them, they come into our garage and turn it into a disgusting shrine.

Adamma: Seriously?

Richard: Frankly, I cannot take that mess anymore. So, today I decide to chase them away from my property and as they were running away that exceptionally angry one decides to fight back. At first, I did not understand what was going on when the angry squirrel ran toward me. But when he took several bites out of me, it became apparent that the angry squirrel has declared war on me. So, I decide to run. I was doing the running and the angry squirrel was doing the chasing. Now, you girls are here rescuing me. Thank you very much girls.

Pamela: We are happy to be helpful to you.

Uchenna: It is so nice to see someone who cares about the animals I might add.

Adamma: It surely is.

Richard: I think it is all right for the animals not to be afraid of humans, but do they have to attack us too?

Pamela: No. They do not need to attack us. If they start attacking us humans, then we'll have to make them to be afraid of us again. I mean, some of these animals carry with them some diseases that can be deadly to the human race. Therefore, while we advocate animal rights, we must not forget the human rights, which is more superior to animal rights.

Uchenna: In a nutshell, Pam is saying that you sir, do have the right to protect your house from intruders, which includes the angry squirrel.

Richard: It includes the angry squirrel?

Pamela: Yes, especially the angry squirrel.

Richard: Really?

Adamma: Yes, really. You see, animal rights are about not intentionally hurting or mistreating animals both domestic and wild. It does not alleviate self-protection or the protection of one's family from the tyranny of wild and untamed animals like the wild angry squirrel that chased you out from your own home. You certainly do have the right to protect both you and your family from such a degrading abuse.

Richard: What an eye-opening statement!

Pamela: Indeed. My girls are wise. Adding to Adamma's sayings, it would be nice to have a cat or a dog that you can control. What I don't appreciate is people having dogs, cats and other mean animals that they claimed to have tamed and hence, harmless to you. However, when these animals are let loose to the public, they become a menace. Yet, their owners would claim that those animals are the sweetest thing they ever have and that their animals cannot hurt a fly. What a load of nonsense!

Richard: Yes, I agree with you. If you cannot control your pets, don't have them. It certainly does not make sense nor is it fair to place the public in fear in pursuit of selfish pleasure.

Pamela: No, it doesn't make sense. In fact, there is a case in court as we speak in which a Pitbull dog's owner claims that he's unaware of how his dog got out of the house to take a chunk of bite on the plaintiff. He claims his dog is so sweet it could not hurt a fly. The court's attendants have no choice but to laugh at his ridiculous statement. Can you guess what the Judge asks the man after making that ridiculous statement?

Richard: The Judge probably ask the man why is he being sued if his dog is so sweet that it could not hurt a fly?

Pamela: Exactly! In reply, the Pitbull dog's owner says that the plaintiff wants to carve out some money out of him, hence the lawsuit. It turns out that the Judge does not agree with his logic. As a matter of fact, the dog owner's actions flabbergast the Judge solely because of his lack of remorse for causing intentional tort to the plaintiff. Therefore, the dog owner receives the harsh side of the Judge's gavel. Yes, He's on the losing end of the Judge's gavel.

Richard: Wow. Surely, he ought to be found guilty at the bar of common sense too.

Uchenna: Well, it is quite about time for mean dog owners to be held accountable to a higher standard of responsibility regarding the control of their pets. If they cannot control their pets, then they should give them away to those who can.

Adamma: Girl, I agree with you. Yes, while we appreciate the work done by the animal rights activists propagating animal rights to protect animals from mistreat and extinction, humans must be protected from the fear of walking up and down the streets without being attacked by wild and mean animals like that angry squirrel or even Rottweiler. Yes, while they are both important, human rights are superior to animal rights. In order words, human rights supersede animal rights.

Uchenna:	Didn't you folks hear about the Hudson's family? Pamela: Yes, that is so sad.
Richard:	What happened to the Hudson's family?
Uchenna:	They were two little children. The older boy is four years old and have his own bedroom, but their younger son was eight months old when their vicious Pitbull dog mugged him to death in bed just because the baby's mother coughed.
Adamma:	But how did it happen, didn't the parents saw the dog growling at the baby?
Uchenna:	No, the father was downstairs in the living room while the mother, the baby and the vicious dog were sleeping together in the master bedroom upstairs.
Richard:	Do you mean that the mother, the baby, and the dog were in the same bed?
Uchenna:	Yes, Richard that is exactly what I meant. The baby woke up in the middle of the night while his Mom and dog are still sleeping on the bed. The lad was able to crawl off the bed on hearing his father's voice downstairs who at the time was watching a football game on the television. For some unknown reason, his Mom coughed. That cough woke up the dog who then saw something crawling on the floor and probably the dog's instincts mistook the woman's cough for an attack signal.
Pamela:	O, no. Do not say what I think you are about to say.
Uchenna:	Yes, Pamela. The vicious dog mugged the little lad to death.

Richard: That is an unbelievable happening! What about the father, didn't he hear his little lad crying for help?

Uchenna: Don't forget that he was downstairs watching a football game. Besides, he thought his family were asleep.

Adamma: Amazing! But how did they find out what had happened?

Uchenna: The vicious dog proudly woke up the lad's Mom with a view to present to her his catch of the day, except that it's the wrong catch. When the mother saw her little baby being dragged across the bedroom floor, the gates of sorrow and anguish broke loose.

Pamela: Please tell me that they called the police immediately.

Uchenna: Yes, they did. Even in their sorrowful state of mind they knew that calling the court official is the right thing to do.

Adamma: What happened to the dog? Did the animal rights organizations come to rescue the vicious dog?

Uchenna: They tried! One of their arguments was that euthanizing the dog will not bring back the dead boy to life. What is more, as far as the organizations are concerned, euthanizing the dog will mean that the Hudson's family will have two lives to mourn. Nevertheless, both parents of the lad persuade the officers to euthanize the vicious dog that took the life of their precious son.

Richard: What did the officers end up doing?

Uchenna: The vicious dog was euthanized!

Richard: I am so sorry that the Hudson's family had to go through that unfortunate incident.

Pamela: This is a perfect example of what I've been saying all along. If you cannot control a vicious dog, do not have the dog! In fact, there ought to be an enactment or a legislature against having a vicious dog or any vicious animal while raising an infant or a toddler.

Richard: What get to me is listening to these selfish dog owners claiming that they have not seen a well raised vicious dog goes wild on the owner's family. Just because you have not experience something awful or blissful does not mean others have not, neither does it nullifies its truthfulness.

Pamela: We hear you, Richard. I really wish that I could get someone in the congress to listen to me because we must protect our infants and toddlers from vicious animals. In order to alleviate any technicalities in the legislature against having a vicious dog or any vicious animal while raising an infant or a toddler, we'll define a toddler as anyone having the mindset of a toddler. A forty-year old person who has the mindset of a toddler for example, will fall into the category of a toddler.

Richard: That is deep. Pamela, I hope someday, your wish will come true.

Pamela: I hope so too.

Richard: Thank you very much girls and please enjoy the rest of the day.

Pamela: We surely will. You do the same too. Bye Richard. The Girls: Bye Richard.

Richard: Goodbye girls.

Substance Abuse and Addiction Are Bullies

To effectively explain my belief system as to why some people become addicted to alcohol and drugs with respect to what Chemical dependency counseling is, the definition of substance abuse must be established and then differentiate substance abuse from addiction. **Substance abuse** occurs when and only when, the user's functioning is negatively affected due to use of a drug that alters or modifies the mood or behavior of the user, that is, a problem is related to substance abuse if a client's use of alcohol or other mood-altering drugs has undesired effects on his or her life or on the lives of others. The negative effects of the substance may involve impairment of physiological, psychological, social, or occupational functioning (Lewis et al 2018)[58]. For example, if Joe gets drunk from the consumption of alcohol (hard liquor) that modified his mood or behavior but stayed home without disturbing his neighbors, cause harm to himself or to others, nor get into his car and drive off thus causing accident, Joe's behavior will not be considered as substance abuse. Joe's behavior will be considered as substance abuse if and only if, his altered behavior or functioning due to the consumption of alcohol is detrimental to self or to others such as driving under the influence (DUI) of alcohol and causing ghastly accident that may take his life or the life of others, or both his life and the life of others. Lewis et al, (2018 pp 4)[58] defines Joe's problem as addiction only when physical symptoms of withdrawal or tolerance to the psychoactive substance associated with abuse or addiction (such as alcohol, sedative hypnotics, opioids, amphetamines, cannabis, cocaine, and tobacco) are present. When Joe develops a tolerance of the substance (alcohol, in this case) where four shuts are no longer enough to get him high, Joe becomes addicted to the substance, alcohol. The more alcohol Joe consumes the less effective it becomes. At this point, Joe is addicted to alcohol.

Joe did not become addicted to psychoactive substance overnight, he must have become addicted through genetic predisposition – inherited the disease from his parents' genes which may lay dormant like a timebomb ready to explode when triggered, or acquired the diseases through environmental or social entanglement which started off by experimenting the intake of the psychoactive substance probably due to peer pressure, continues the use in social engagements, continue the use at home and other places and it becomes habitual. Habits become abuse when there are negative consequences as discussed above. If Joe continues the substance abuse despite his negative functioning, it becomes an addiction. A terrible thing about this is that if Joe decides to stop using the psychoactive substance, the disease (addiction) continues, resulting to death. There is no wonder that while insurance does not cover substance abuse (not life threatening), it covers addiction (life threatening). This is so because addiction is permanent and progressive. If left untreated as the addiction progresses, it becomes irreversible and at this point treatment may be too late and death becomes inevitable. A professor of Psychology, Dr. Jimmy R. Turner (2018) revealed that the goal of a disease (like the two addictions that require medical support: addiction to alcohol and benzodiazepine - any of a class of heterocyclic organic compounds used as tranquilizers, such as Librium and Valium) is to kill you if left untreated. Therefore, it will behue Joe to seek professional help for his chemical dependency before it is too late.

Why Some People Become Addicted To Alcohol and Drugs

Gone are those days when people who are addicted to alcohol and drugs were viewed as weak-willed individuals with no moral compass or conscience to decipher between good, evil and have the willpower to practice goodness. Now we know addiction is a chronic and complex brain disease that alters the brain's structure[46] or chemistry in such a way that it fosters compulsive drug seeking and relapsing behaviors, despite common sense and the inbuilt will to live forever without dying. Studies have shown that there are several factors that make some people more vulnerable than others as it relates to addiction (Lewis et al 2018)[58] which constitute my belief system and these factors are not limited to the following:

Disease – As stated above, addiction is a mental disorder due to drug abuse that alter the brain's structure and function, resulting in changes that persist long after drug use has ceased. There is no wonder why alcohol and drug abusers are at risk for relapse even after long periods of abstinence and despite the potentially devastating consequences[58]. Almost half of drug abusers and about a third of alcoholics are also coping with a mental illness, such as depression or anxiety. Likewise, half of those living with a severe mental illness, like bipolar disorder or schizophrenia, have substance abuse issues. The existence of both mental illness and addiction is very common and referred to as dual diagnosis, comorbidity, or co-occurring disorders that is, drug abuse and addiction are both mental disorders which often co-occur with other mental illnesses. Patients who are diagnosed with PTSD for example, may also be diagnosed with Antisocial Personality Disorder (APD) and when these problems co-occur or comorbid, treatment should address both disorders, including the use of medications as appropriate (Lewis et al, 2018[58], APA 2015[41]).

Genetics – Some are genetically predisposed to alcoholism and drug abuse which is passed on to them from their parents. Genes provide information on how our bodies respond at a cellular level - 99% of our genes are the same, while the 1% that are different account for things like hair and eye color, height, and even the potential for heart disease, diabetes or addiction to drugs and alcohol.

Earlier research has shown that the presence of specific genes involved in alcohol metabolism and the transmission of nerve cell signals, increases the risk of becoming dependent on drugs or alcohol or both (Lewis et al 2018[58]). Those specific genes are are bullies to the bearer and you can fight back by refraining from the illicit use of alcohol and drugs.

Social Environment – Peer pressure during social interactions and environmental circumstances fire up the brain's reward pathways. The ability to want to have fun with friends and not be judged can have both positive and negative affects on different individuals. Peer pressure can occur at home with siblings and neighbors, at school, or even at work environments where alcohol and drugs are widely used to make friends and bond or daring each other and betting on who can consume more alcohol and drugs and stay sober. Studies have shown that individuals in such environments are more likely to fall into patterns of substance abuse and addiction. What a bully peer pressure can be!

Coping - To hide Emotional pain or trauma suffered earlier. There is Early Childhood Trauma (ECT) on one hand due to neglect, physical and emotional abandonment, sexual, physical, and psychological abuse. Scientists know that this kind of distress alters the brain structure or chemistry of children and makes them more vulnerable to addiction later in life as even moderate levels of abuse of alcohol and drugs can damage their brains, which are generally not fully matured until the age of 25 (Lewis et al 2018). On the other hand, there is Adult Trauma (AT) which is like childhood trauma except that it occurs later in life. Adult trauma can be due to the loss of a loved one, such as a child, friend or spouse, or develop post-traumatic stress disorder (PTSD) which may be the result of combat experience, a car wreck or sexual assault. People with adult trauma have a propensity to self- medicate using drugs and alcohol as a coping scheme to help deal with the pain which often leads to chemical dependency or addiction. Addiction to alcohol and drugs is a bully!

Cultural Crimes – are crimes committed against a specific culture by destroying the cultural artifacts of that specific culture with a view to gaining superiority over them. The oxford English dictionary defines culture as a set of beliefs, attitudes, values, and behavior that is passed down from generation to generation. Culture is all-encompassing, and is shaped by many factors including race, religion, and ethnicity. Culture also affects perceptions of stress, trauma, abuse, and reactions to all of those environmental mishaps. The native Americans are the first to settle in this country with their culture which was associated with their form of religion. When the Caucasians came from Britain with their guns, they battle with the native Americans, stealing their lands and destroying their cultural artifacts with a view to gaining superiority over the native Americans. The Caucasians won the battle and tried to force Caucasian cultures on the native Americans through a process called naturalization. Whoever refuses to be naturalized by the Caucasians was either killed, starved to death, or given a piece of land that was so difficult to cultivate for food. What is culture to a starving man? Gradually, the native Americans went from glory to despair, from hero to zero. Their cultural heritage was reduced to nothing and they were dump in reservations in the remote part of the country with most harsh weather conditions that may not suitable for farming such as the State of Alaska, the deserts of the States of Arizona, Nevada, New Mexico and the like. Farming that used to be one of the native Americans' pride becomes unattractive due to the harsh weather conditions that are not condusive for agriculture. So, the native Americans turned those harsh lands into casinos. When a culture has been decimated, the surviving members of that culture would resort to the addiction of psychoactive substances such as alcohol and drugs, which were peculiar to the native American society down to this day. Cultural crime is a bully!

Structural crime – are accusation crimes stacked up against someone due to his racial background and color. Usually, structural crime affects African or Black Americans in particular, and people of color in general. The idea calls down judgment against someone from birth that because of the person's race, (black in this case) the baby is born to fail in life and so the destination of such one is the prison. As such, the secure base (a place or someone to run to for security, protection, relief, resources and assurance or hope for a successful future) of such one becomes threatened daily as the police department get away with daily abuse and mistreat of such Black American who may have no choice, at least from the perspective of such one, but to become addicted to alcohol and drugs. Structural crime persists all the way to graduate school for those Black Americans who are fortunate enough to graduate from the institution of higher learning despite the many bullylike challenges they are born to face. Consider the institution of higher learning like the University of California system or the ivy leagues for example, suppose these institutions are accused of racial discrimination against black students and to refute such accusation, the institutions matriculate as faculty members a couple of Black Professors whose sole purpose, from the standpoint of the institution is to bring in black students under their tutelage. It turns out that to maintain their prestige, if any, or to gain prestige among fellow faculty members who are mainly offblacks, these black Professors want offblack students only – also an example of "black on black" crime, a severe case of bully. Either way, black students seem to be at the losing end of the judge's garvel. There is no wonder why some black students are addicted to alcohol and drugs. Structural crime is a bully!

Sexism and **Racism**-The Oxford English dictionary defines sexism as prejudice, stereotyping, or discrimination, typically against women, based on sex. Imagine an African American woman finding it extremely difficult to secure a gainful employment since employers hope to give the jobs to men who do not have any reproductive issues like taking off during childbirth, and so she resorts into prostitution. Studies have shown that prostitution breeds addiction to alcohol and drugs. Like sexism, racism is prejudice based on race. Racism is the belief that all members of each race possess characteristics or abilities specific to that race, especially to distinguish it as inferior or superior to another race or races. Some white supremacy (mostly Caucasians) proclaim superiority over other races. This behavior breeds hatred against other races that are not Caucasians. It is no wonder therefore, that some police departments composed of mainly Caucasians are cruel to especially African American communities whose secure base are constantly under threat. Threats breeds fear, fear breeds pain and to deal with the pain comes the addiction to alcohol and drugs. What a bully sexism and racism are!

Mixed Models- the idea of mixing two or more different psychoactive substances together. The mixture of Cocaine and alcohol use for example, is one of the most common combinations among drug users because of the powerful high that both substances produce. Cocaine is a stimulant that increases your blood pressure, heart rate and alertness. This helps alcohol reach the brain quicker. Mixing cocaine and alcohol causes coca ethylene, which produces intense feelings of pleasure. Other risk factors of combining cocaine and alcohol include heart attack, overdose, or death. Chemical dependency is a bully!

Spiritism - While witchcraft is practiced secretly in Africa, Asia and other third world countries, in United States however, witchcraft is practiced openly as an art due to the freedom of religion the constitution provides. There are some religious groups that are not related to witchcraft and the commonality for both religious practices are the use of psychoactive substances that members consume with a view to conjuring the spirits. Along the line, most of these members become addicted to these drugs like marijuana and alcohol. The use of psychoactive substances is a bully!

Cognitive distortions - are ways in which our mind convinces us of something that is not true or something that is not there. These inaccurate thoughts are usually used to reinforce negative thinking or emotions — telling ourselves things that sound rational and accurate, but only serve to keep us feeling bad about ourselves. These distortions have been shown to relate positively to symptoms of depression, meaning that where cognitive distortions abound, symptoms of depression are likely to occur as well (Burns, Shaw, & Croker, 1987). Interestingly, where symptoms of depression abound, so will the addiction to alcohol and drugs to help cope with the depression. Cognitive distortion is a bully!

Cognitive Dissonance: Myers, D.G. and Twenge, J. M. (2016)[42]

define Cognitive dissonance as the tension that arises when someone is simultaneously aware of having two inconsistent cognitions or thoughts. Cognitive dissonance is the mental discomfort (psychological stress) experienced by a person who holds two or more conflicting beliefs, attitudes, or values, all of which have the same degree of importance. This mental discomfort is triggered by a situation in which one's belief clashes with new evidence perceived by the person. Cognitive dissonance is the motivation to reduce the tension that you feel or to alleviate the discomfort that happens when your attitude and your behavior are at odds with each other or when you are acting in such a way as to be at odds with your attitudes, values, or beliefs. Cognitive dissonance is deeply rooted in classic Social Psychology and Cognitive dissonance theory was proposed by Leon Festinger in 1957, which says that we often bring our attitudes to line with our actions - attitude follow behavior principle.[42] A classic example is the case of a cigarette smoker, who may have two distinct thoughts, one of which is to smoke cigarettes on a regular basis and the other is the knowledge that smoking cigarette is unhealthy. These two conflicting thoughts that the smoker is simultaneously having and thus acknowledging both dichotomous thoughts as **facts** would seem inconsistent with one another. If you know that smoking is bad, then logically, you probably would not be engaging in that activity, and because there is inconsistency in the smoker's thoughts, psychological stress or pain is experienced. The smoker may want to alleviate the pain by engaging in the abuse of alcohol and drugs. Cognitive dissonance is a bully!

The Role Of Counselor In Addiction Treatment

Chemical dependency counseling is a process in which a trained or licensed counselor helps people like Joe to understand and overcome the root causes of drugs and alcohol addiction. It addresses the ways in which drugs and alcohol affect people on personal and physical levels or psychophysiological level (the way in which the mind and body interact)[58] and in their relationships with others. A chemical dependency counselor coordinates his efforts with those of other agencies and counselors to get patients the help they need to break their harmful addictions by working collaboratively with these patients with a view to building bridges to recovery and not burning them. A counselor needs to know where the resources are to recommend them to patients. A counselor is not meant to be the solution but a guide to patients. That is, a counselor is the fulcrum of the will connecting patients to service. There are situations where a counselor is well vast in experience to provide solution to a patient which is all right. However, the counselor should not feel that he must be the solution to the patient. His job is to effect positive change in the patients' behavior. The active ingredients of counseling characteristics of a good counselor depend upon the facilitative qualities such as **empathy** (being able to access the degree of your painful experience relate it to your patient's feeling, stating your perception, legitimizing the feeling and offering support and partnership in managing their situation.), **genuineness** (be real, be yourself and let your external behavior matches your internal feelings. Your patient can tell the difference.), **immediacy** (display of real feelings.), **warmth** (nonverbal display of genuineness), and **respect** (let the patients know that they are capable of surviving in a difficult environment and are bright and free to choose their own alternatives and participate in the therapeutic decision-making process.) that the counselor brings to the process and the strategies that he or she uses to create a positive environment for exploration and change (Lewis et al 2015 pp 104)[58]. An ideal culturally competent treatment models entails that the counselor must demonstrate cultural sensitivity to the patient taking into consideration the patient's cultural background which may explain some of his behaviors as some experience may be part of cultural message with individualized implications.

My ideal counseling is one that effect positive changes in patients' behavior, and it involves six *stages of change*[58] which are:

1. **Precontemplation** – In this stage, patients have no belief that they need to change. They feel that they are mentally healthier than any mentally healthy person you can think of. These patients may have come to that conclusion because of their status in life. You may know some celebrities, successful business leaders, and the likes that refused to get help, some of whom end their life. You are encouraged to do your very best to convince such ones that they need this help that they seek when they come to your presence.

2. **Contemplation** – Patients relapse and recognize that there are problems that are not within determination. In this stage, patients understand that even with their vast wisdom, there are unknown unknowns, which according to the former Defense Secretary Donald Rumsfeld, are the things we do not know that we do not know. So, these patients rely on your expertise to help them figure out the unknowns.

3. **Preparation** – In this stage, there are actions that a patient must take to show that she is ready for the action stage. You can help to prepare her heart for the action stage. Does she have the prerequisite skills to understand the underlying logic behind the action she is about to take? Can we expect a smoker for example, to quit smoking if she does not understand the danger that smoking presents to life? Can we expect her to quit smoking if there are no alternatives to smoking? Can we expect children to get themselves dressed every morning if their dresses are not within reach?

4. **Action** – In this stage as a counselor, you need to know what action looks like, so you can help your client make or take that action. If your patients' goal

is quitting smoking for example, as a counselor, you need to understand that quitting smoking can be daunting and life changing. So, you could encourage your patients to take the action that mitigates her cravings to smoke. Instead of giving in to her cravings for example, you could encourage her to chew gum, wear prescription patch, or do things that will help mitigate her cravings to smoke. These actions must be crystal clear in your mind as a counselor, so you can help your patients to take them.

5. **Maintenance** – In this stage, patients should maintain the action of a good recovery. Self-actualization - fear alone would not keep you from addiction but maintenance would help you reach your goal. Once you have attained the action of a good recovery, like barnacles on a boat, stick to it.

6. **Termination** – stages of motivation to change is about your motivation to want to change, and when such changes have been made, the goal is reached.

As Imperfect people, we live in an imperfect world and sometimes things may not go the way we have planned. Therefore, relapse may occur with our patients. Usually, relapse from the specific addiction we want to change occur from stages 2 to 6.58

Defend Your Communities Against The Spread Of Narcotics

The girls depart from Richard. As they walk on, they come across two men selling something that's not currently visible to the girls. The two men make a pass at the girls and when the girls finally realize what these men are selling, they fearlessly make plans to secretly involve the Police Officer that they had met earlier. What are the two men selling? Yes, you are correct. They are pushing hard drugs into the neighborhood. These two men are equally looking to recruit from the neighborhood. One of the interesting behaviors about these men is that they are residents of a different city that is far away from the city in which the girls reside.

The girls already know what to do. First, Pamela pretend as if she had left her wallet at the restaurant where the Police officer is still staking out. Adamma and Uchenna stay behind to keep the men company until the police arrives. While waiting. Adamma and Uchenna trick the men into thinking that they want to buy as much hard drugs as the men can supply. What do you know? The plan works. Not long, Pamela shows up with four Police officers with guns. The officers arrest the two men, confiscate their hard drugs, and force them to reveal their employer. It ends up being a major burst involving three connecting cities and one town. The success of the drug burst can rightly be attributed to the bravery of the three girls who are determined to keep their city free from hard drugs and their distributors.

The relationship between drug dealers and consumers of these hard drugs is such that, while the drug dealers are getting richer and healthier, the consumers on the other hand, are losing control of self as they dwindle in health and acumen. You would think that at some point in time, these consumers will seek help in order to be free from the control and stigma that the use of narcotics or hard drugs (e.g. cocaine, heroin, opium, methamphetamine, etc.) exert on them. In most cases, that thinking may be farfetched as some have argued that the good feeling derive from the use of these hard drugs is as if the user is under the spell of an external force over which he has no control. When he is under this spell, he barely remembers any of his many problems until the drug wears off. If he is someone who does not want to deal with his problems, like a dog that goes back to its vomit, it will only be a matter of time before he goes back to his vomit. Is this person beyond help? I do not think so. His first step to recovery may be to face up with the fact that without dealing with his problem squarely, these problems will always be there. So, he needs to deal with the problems that led him to use hard drugs in the first place. The problem may be the result of bad associates daring and thus, compelling him to try these hard drugs which he may get hooked on his first try. If that is the case, how wise would it be to keep that association? There are those who would argue that the said association must be forgone effective immediately and thus, replacing that association with a better and caring one. Yes, the association you want to keep should be one that will appreciate, encourage, and strengthen your useful behavior, not the opposite.

Yes, there are those who may think that such step may be too difficult to accomplish. There is no doubt about that except that you need to think about what is most important to you at this point: your sanity or your association especially if you can make new and better friends? I want to agree to disagree with those who are for gradual change of harmful habits. A cigarette smoker for instance, who has been given the medical advice to quit smoking for health reasons may think that he does not have to quit immediately but gradually. That is, if he is currently smoking one packet of cigarette a day, he can reduce it to half a packet a day for the next three months. Thereafter, he can smoke half of one half a packet a day for the following next three months. The reduction in consumption continues until he finally quits smoking. At that rate you will wonder whether he'll ever quit smoking. Information can empower you to make the decision and stick to it. The 2020 Surgeon General's report on Smoking Cessation highlights the latest scientific evidence on the health benefits of quitting smoking, as well as proven treatments and strategies to help people successfully quit smoking. The knowledge that the consumption of cigarette is not good for your health and for the health of those around you should motivate you to stop its consumption on the assumption that you want to be healthy, remain healthy and care about others.

Imitate The Stellar Example of The Former Magic Practicers

I completely understand that it can be very difficult to be well disciplined in making a specific stand without regrets. However, when

I'm faced with the problem of not going back on a prior decision involving harmful habits, I usually draw comfort and strength from the Stellar example given by a number of magic practicers during the Apostle Paul's day in the Bible book of Acts 19:18,19. When these magic practicers became Christians, they confessed and reported their practices openly, brought their expensive books together and burned them up before everybody. That was a remarkable swift but difficult decision made, which these former magic practicers never regretted nor did they gave it a second thought respecting the high cost of the books and the great feelings they usually derive from the practice of magic. They stood resolute to remain clean in mind, soul and spirit come what may! If those men can do it, you and I can certainly do it too.

What if those former magic practicers kept on thinking about their priceless magic books that they have destroyed in fire and the pleasure they used to derive from the magic practices? They probably would have fallen prey to such depraved thoughts and like a dog that has gone back to its vomit, they too would have seen the need to go back to their former magic practices. As it were, those former magic practicers replaced any thought that will call to mind the regret of their brave actions with the joy of their newly founded understanding, which released them from the bondage of magic practices, beliefs that subjected them to slavery of timid fears, superstitions, and corruption.

In the same line of thought, when you have made the progress to regain the control over smoking and the illegal use of narcotics, like the former magic practicers, stand resolute to uphold that brave decision. As an imperfect person that we all are, if you put too much thought into what you think you had forgone by letting go of those harmful habits or vomit, which subjected you to slavery of narcotic influences, like a dog that goes back to its vomit, you too, will go back to your vomit. In order to prevent you from going back to your vomit, you need to detest that former course of action such as smoking and the use of hard drugs that you have vomited out of your system and unlike a dog that went back to its vomit, repudiate your vomit. Should you for any reason relapse in your resolution due to feelings of withdrawals and the perception that you are missing out on the so-called "good old days" when you are under smoking and narcotic influences, do your very best to replace those thoughts with freedom. Yes, freedom - the joy of your newly founded freedom from the brutal control that smoking and hard drugs used to have on you. Enjoy the freedom and make it last.

Secondhand smoke is A Bully

Here at Chizom's home, we see Pamela and her sister Elizabeth reminiscing as some sisters would do. I invite you to listen. Shall we?

Lizzy: Hey Pammy?

Pamela: Yes, Lizzy.

Lizzy: Have you ever wonder why Taylor died of lung cancer? She was only fifteen? I thought lung cancer only happen to heavy smokers. Taylor is young and never smoked a day in her life. Why did she die of lung cancer? Pammy, I am so confused.

Pamela: Lizzy, do not be confused. Taylor may have never smoked a day in her life, remember that her father is a heavy smoker. So, Taylor had been around smokers all her life.

Lizzy: Yes, that is true. But Pammy, what has Taylor being around smokers have to do with her dying from lung cancer? She's not the one smoking. Was she?

Pamela: Lizzy?

Lizzy: Yes, Pammy.

Pamela:	Have you ever heard of the phrase "secondhand smoke" also called passive smoke or environmental tobacco smoke?
Lizzy:	Yes, Pammy. I have heard of it, but I don't think I know what it means. What is secondhand smoke?
Pamela:	Very well. Then I will tell you the meaning of secondhand smoke. According to Merriam-Webster dictionary, the "Medical Definition of secondhand smoke is tobacco smoke that is exhaled by a smoker or is given off by burning tobacco (like a cigarette) and is inhaled by persons nearby" which is also known as "passive smoke" or "Environmental tobacco smoke."
Lizzy:	Really?
Pamela:	Yes, really. I like the way that the Webster English Learners dictionary defines secondhand smoke as "smoke from a cigarette, cigar, pipe, etc., that can be inhaled by people who are near the person who is smoking."
Lizzy:	Wow! Pammy, so, you do not have to be the one smoking. If you are with or around someone who smokes, then it will be like you are the one smoking?
Pamela:	Yes! Lizzy, you got it!
Lizzy:	Hey, but that is not fair!
Pamela:	Tell me about it. Mankind is faced with so many unfair situations. But what can we do about it?
Lizzy:	I have no shredded idea.
Pamela:	Hey Lizzy?

Lizzy: Yes, Pammy.

Pamela: Do you have any idea how many Americans die from smoking without even lighting up a cigarette a day in their lives?

Lizzy: Pammy, no shredded idea!

Pamela: Well, according to a new study carried out by a group of researchers led by Dr. Wendy Max, a professor of health economics at the University of California, San Francisco; over 42,000 people died of secondhand smoke each year, including 900 infants.

Lizzy: Wow! That is so alarming! Are you sure these are people who never smoked a day in their entire lives? Pammy?

Pamela: Yes, Lizzy, that is what the study says. Have you seen an infant that smokes?

Lizzy: No. Pammy, that would be weird.

Pamela: That's right, Lizzy. Furthermore, the study shows that going by the numbers I just gave you, about 600,000 years of potential life was lost in total and that is an average of 14.2 years for each nonsmoker who has died prematurely as a result of someone else's smoking. Lizzy, do you know what that equates in lost productivity?

Lizzy: Pammy, I have no shredded idea.

Pamela: Well, in lost productivity, that equates $6.6 billion according to the study, which amount to $158,000 per death.

Lizzy: Now, Pammy, that is a lot of money for a country to lose.

Pamela: Lizzy, you can say that again! All that happen because of being around people who smoke. That study also shows that despite public health efforts to reduce the use of tobacco, secondhand smoke continues to take a grievous toll on nonsmokers. How tragic!

Lizzy: Yes, Pammy, that is so tragic. I promise this to you Pammy, from now on, I will emphatically let smokers know that in my environment, there is no place for them. I will not let them poison my environment. I will remonstrate with them to the best of my ability to keep my environment clean.

Pamela: Me too, Lizzy. Me too.

Lizzy: Pammy, where did you get that study you shared with me?

Pamela: The study was published on Sept. 20, 2012 in the American Journal of Public Health.

Lizzy: That's way past my brain. Thanks, Pamela.

Pamela: Lizzy, you are welcome!

When people who have never smoked a day in their lives are diagnosed with lung cancer, one of the questions they understandably ask is: "I never smoked a day in my life, why do I have lung cancer?" In being empathetic to such ones, a prevailing question to ask them would be, even if you have never smoked a day in your life, what about your environment? Has your environment been rid of smokers in order to avoid completely, secondhand smoke or passive smoke which may have the same effect as if you were the one smoking - the primary smoker? You should think about it because you may be inhaling the poison that smokers in your environment are exhaling. Who are your friends and companions? Does any of them smoke around you? Give this a thought, would you? Clean up your environment and insist upon its cleanliness.

As a Board-Certified Behavior Analyst (BCBA), Gershom met a seventy-five-year-old woman going by the name Jennifer, a heavy smoker in her own rights. Gershom's goal is to help Jennifer get rid of her harmful habits of smoking. However, Jennifer had earlier informed Gershom that she has been smoking heavily for the past fifty years.

She felt that she had beaten death hands down and proud of smoking. Gershom asks Jennifer what she meant by "beaten death hands down"? Shall we listen to their conversation?

Gershom:	Hey Jennifer, what do you mean by the phrase you had "beaten death hands down"?
Jennifer:	I have beaten death hands down because while my husband, my three daughters and a son were all dead, I am still here. So, death has nothing on me.
Gershom:	Wow! That is so interesting. I am so sorry for your loss.
Jennifer:	Oh, that is all right and thanks for your condolence.
Gershom:	Please, may I ask what your family died of?
Jennifer:	Sure. They all died of some sort of lung cancer.
Gershom:	Were they heavy smokers too?
Jennifer:	None of them, my husband, my three daughters and my son. That is the funny thing about it all. While none of them ever smoked a day in their lives, I do all the smoking. Lo and behold, they are all gone but I am still here. Hence, I said, death has nothing on me. Yes, so I am not afraid to die. So, I am going to keep smoking!
Gershom:	Oh, I am so sorry to hear you say that because one of my goals is to see how I can help you to replace your smoking habit with something better.

Jennifer:	Well, I don't think smoking is a habit to me. Smoking is who I am. Who wants to live forever anyway? That will be so boring.
Gershom:	I will love to live forever under blissful conditions on this Earth as eternity to me can never be boring. There are so many things to do on this Earth and time is always considered as an enemy of progress for a reason.
Jennifer:	Yes, because we usually don't have enough time to accomplish our goals before we kick the bucket.
Gershom:	Is that not the reason why some people make a bucket list of things they would like to do on Earth before they kick the bucket?
Jennifer:	Yes, that is right. In fact, I have my own bucket list too.

Gershom: Amazing! Consider this, Jennifer. One of the reasons why some people think that the idea of spending eternity on this Earth would be boring is because of all the bad conditions that exist on it; like sickness, pain, sorrow, stress, mental health issues or mental disorders, hatred, racism, unrest, war, bad habits like smoking, the abuse of narcotics, and other bad conditions that you can think of. L et's assume that for a change, we can remove all those terrible conditions and replace them with great conditions like great health, feeling great daily, looking great, enjoying life with your loved ones, creating beautiful things and the ability to appreciate and enjoy the beautiful things you have created, no pain, having real love for one another, being your brother's keeper, unity among all mankind, prosperity for all with beautiful homes in beautiful environment, replacing competition with cooperation, replacing hatred with love and the likes. Would eternity be boring under those blissful conditions?

Jennifer: Certainly not since you put it like that. I really do not think so. I don't think I'll be so stressful to resort to smoking or have friends that will dare me to smoke under those beautiful conditions that you have stated. My family would have been alive and healthy. I probably would not have missed out on the opportunity of having my own grandchildren and avoiding the possibility of being lonely.

Gershom: Jennifer, my condolence. Please Jennifer, I need you to understand that humans are endowed with the power to create[46] and time is needed to get it done. As it is, time has been an enemy to humans' ability to create. Take Steve Jobs the co-founder of apple computers and the inventor of iPhone for instance, who knows what more he would have contributed to humans' welfare if he had not lost the battle to pancreatic cancer? If Steve Jobs is alive today and you have the opportunity to ask him this question: "Steve, now that you have accomplished so much and given so much to this world, would you like to die, or isn't it time for you to die happy? What do you think Steve Jobs' answer to you, would have been?

Jennifer: Well, I don't know. He'll probably be mad at me that I'm wishing him dead.

Gershom: Or, he'll probably tell you that he has not even started. He's just warming up. As such, to the prudent, like Steve Jobs, eternity cannot be boring. Yes, eternity is not boring to the wise as we need time to create and enjoy our creations.

Jennifer:	That is so interesting. I never thought of it like that. I mean, if you really think about it, nobody wants to die. So, eternity is boring only to the fools. Hey Gershom, I'm curious, who can bring about those beautiful conditions you've mentioned to this Earth for us to enjoy?
Gershom:	Well, Jennifer, I'm afraid that the answer to your wonderful question is beyond the scope of this discussion. However, suffice is to say that those beautiful conditions that will take place on this Earth are promises that are of divine[56] utterances.
Jennifer	Wow! That is so awesome.
Gershom:	Jennifer, you said earlier that smoking is who you are. If I may ask, were you born a smoker?
Jennifer:	No, Gershom. I was not born a smoker.
Gershom:	Did you smoke when you were a baby?
Jennifer:	No. I started smoking when I was fifteen years old and my friends back then did smoke too. So, it was common for youngsters to smoke when I was a teenager.
Gershom:	Jennifer, would it be safe to say that you learn to smoke when you were a teenager because your friends smoked?
Jennifer:	Yes, that is right.
Gershom:	Therefore, Jennifer, would it be safe to conclude that while you were not born a smoker, the habit of smoking is what you picked up or learned from your associates as you grew older?
Jennifer:	Yes, you can say that.

Gershom: Jennifer, considering what we have discussed so far would you conclude that you are a born smoker?

Jennifer: No, Gershom. I was not born a smoker. It is a habit I craved to blend in with my friends as I grew older and before I knew it, I got hooked on it.

Gershom: While I am not an expert on getting unhooked on smoking, as a matter of fact, nobody claimed to be an expert on quitting smoking. What we can do is to offer suggestions, but the willpower to put those suggestions into action, will come from you.

Jennifer: I understand completely. Gershom, can I ask you a question?

Gershom: Of course, you can.

Jennifer: A while back, you said one of your goals is to replace my smoking habit with something better. What do you mean?

Gershom: Yes, you are right Jennifer. I said that. What I meant was that in my line of work, there are steps I take when helping people to change from their maladaptive behavior to preferred behavior.

Jennifer: What is maladaptive behavior and preferred behavior?

Gershom: In its most basic term, maladaptive behavior are those things or stimuli that get in the way of doing the right thing. The term "maladaptive behavior" is used to describe behavior that adapts, modifies, or adjusts poorly. Maladaptive behavior is a series of behaviors that react and behave inappropriately to internal or external stimuli. Take smoking for example, your cravings to smoke would be your internal stimuli because they are inside of you or they are coming from within you which a Social Psychology Professor, Dr. Jerry M. Burger referred to as "intrapersonal processes."[40]

Jennifer: What? What on earth is intrapersonal processes?

Gershom: In describing the second part to personality in his book,[40] Dr. Jerry M. Burger describes intrapersonal processes as that which involve our emotional, motivational, and cognitive processes that go on inside of us and they influence our feelings and actions – that is, inside of us are emotional, motivational, and cognitive processes that affect how we feel and act.

Jennifer: So, are you saying that my cravings to smoke can be part of my emotional process, motivational process, Cognitive process, and because they are happening inside of me, they are my internal stimuli that subjected me to smoke the way I do?

Gershom: You can say that.

Jennifer: Wow! That is interesting. So, if I have the power over my cravings and stop my cravings to smoke, then I can stop smoking.

Gershom: You can say that.

Jennifer: So, Gershom, would it be safe to say that intrapersonal processes are the same as interpersonal processes?

Gershom: Not quite. You see, Jennifer according to Dr. Jerry Burger, intrapersonal processes totally different from interpersonal processes.

Jennifer: Really?

Gershom:	Yes, really. While intrapersonal processes is about the emotional, motivational and cognitive processes that occur inside or within an individual which affect the way that individual feels and acts, Interpersonal processes on the other hand, take place outside of your body between different individuals in an environment. An example of interpersonal processes is, in each environment, some people are smokers while the nonsmokers are subjected to secondhand smoke.
Jennifer:	I see. So, intrapersonal processes are about internal stimuli while interpersonal processes are about external stimuli that may affect how a person feels and acts.
Gershom:	You can say that.
Jennifer:	You keep on saying "you can say that, you can say that, you can say that." What exactly do you mean by the sentential phrase "You can say that."?
Gershom:	What I mean is that while you may have the information and the willpower to stop smoking, you must develop a hatred to smoke. Without detesting the urge to smoke, all the willpower and the information you have on smoking would amount to nothing.
Jennifer:	Oh, so, are you saying that I need to put into action my current knowledge on smoking and loathe my habit to smoke before it can work for me?
Gershom:	Exactly!!! What importance is having knowledge if you will not apply it to yourself?
Jennifer:	Useless. No importance.

Gershom: That is right, Jennifer. Would doing without your cravings to smoke kill you?

Jennifer: No! it will not.

Gershom: Yes, it may render you uncomfortable, but it certainly, will not kill you. So, to make the sacrifice of not smoking will not only be in your own interest but will also be in the interest of those in your environment.

Jennifer: Tell me about it. It would have been nice to know that I was hurting my family before now. Gershom, you mentioned earlier, preferred behavior and replacing my maladaptive behavior with it. What do you mean?

Gershom: Yes, Jennifer. Preferred behavior is the behavior that we want – one that is conducive to human consumption. Preferred behavior is the opposite of maladaptive behavior. In your case, Jennifer, not smoking anymore is an example of preferred behavior – that is, good habits you can cultivate or do instead of smoking.

Jennifer: I see.

Gershom: So, whenever you have the cravings to smoke, you could replace that with doing those things that will help to mitigate, if not eliminate your cravings to smoke.

Jennifer: Really?

Gershom: Yes, really. Jennifer, please do not forget that you need to detest smoking and you need to want to quit. You also need to figure out what led to your maladaptive behavior as maladaptive behavior can be the result of having a gleam future or not seeing a clear path to your desired future.

Jennifer: Seriously?

Gershom: Yes, seriously. You see Jennifer, if the prospect for your future is gleam or you just cannot see a clear path to your desired future, that may be the result of a major change in your lifestyle, or even chronic illness that may reduce your standard of living due to loss of job.

Jennifer: Wow! Gershom, that is so amazingly true because when I think about it, I started smoking when I was fifteen years old, the same time that my dad lost his job and we were forced to move to a neighborhood of lesser standard of living. I hated it so much that for two days I just could not eat anything. I was so depressed.

Gershom: Oh, I am so sorry about that.

Jennifer: Thank you for that, Gershom. It turns out that the new friends I cultivated in the new neighborhood were able to convince me that the reason for their smoking was to relieve pain from poor standard of living. Now that you said it, I certainly, can relate to that. Wow!

Gershom: You see, as humans, Jennifer, we are endowed with defensive mechanisms to fend off terrible thing that has happened to us or, about to happen. With maladaptive behavior, self-destructive actions are taken to avoid undesired situations.

Jennifer: Gershom, you are not saying that I resorted to smoking to avoid the undesirable situation caused by my Dad's losing his job such that, we have to move to a less desiring standard of living. Are you?

Gershom: You are saying that yourself. Jennifer: I   agree with you totally.

Gershom: Jennifer, you can read up on the "Smoking Cessation" study by the Centers for Disease Control and Prevention (CDC), which offers practical suggestions on quitting smoking.

Jennifer: I certainly will. But what is defense mechanism? Gershom: Well, in order to fully understand defense mechanism, I must take you on a journey back to the past, say 1923 when Sigmund Fraud[39], the founder of psychoanalysis, divided the human brain or personality psyche into three parts:

1. **id**: id only cares about instant gratification of basic physical needs and cravings. This is an impulse to pleasure yourself. It operates entirely unconsciously (outside of conscious thought). Your cravings to smoke which can be aggressive are the strong desires of the id.

2. **Ego**: According to Sigmund Freud, the job of the ego is to balance the aggressive/pleasure- seeking drives of the id with the moral control of the superego.

3. **Superego**. The superego has to do with morals and social rules that are developed from childhood. As those children grow, they learn from their parents and the world around them regarding what they consider to be right and wrong. By doing so, morals and social rules are formed which most people would call their" conscience" or their "moral compass." Your superego will not let you yield to your cravings to smoke.

These three parts of the brain are collectively called the **Structural model** of personality.

Jennifer: Really? That really exist? I have heard people use the words ego and superego; you mean they really exist?

Gershom: Yes, they do exist. Sigmund Freud was able to respectively map the contents of the structural model (the id, the Ego and the Superego) to contents of the **Topographic model** which consist of three parts:

1. **Unconscious** – where unconscious materials are kept, and not available to human awareness.

2. **Preconscious** –unrepressed unconscious thoughts that are available for recall and capable of becoming conscious and

3. **Conscious** - where conscious materials are kept and are available to human awareness.

[Gershom shows the following list to Jennifer]

Structural model	Topographic model
1. Id ⬅———➡	Unconscious – where strictly unconscious materials are kept
2. Ego ⬅———➡	Preconscious – unrepressed unconscious thoughts that are available for

recall and capable of
becoming conscious

3. Superego ←——————→ Conscious - where conscious
materials are kept

List 1.1: *topographic model is the playing field; the structural model are the characters on the playing field[40].*

Gershom: Jenifer, what can you deduce from this list?

Jennifer: Well, the list shows that the id is mapped to the unconscious, which means that the unconscious materials are kept in the id part of our brain.

Gershom: Jennifer, that is correct. What about the next one? Let's do the superego. Shall we?

Jennifer: The list shows that the Superego is mapped to the conscious, which means that the conscious materials are kept in the superego part of our brain.

Gershom: Yes, that is correct. Now, let's do the one for Ego.

Jennifer: The list shows that the Ego is mapped to the preconscious, which means that the unrepressed unconscious thoughts that are available for recall and capable of becoming conscious are in the Ego part of our brain.

Gershom: There is a reason why I want you to do the Ego last.

Jennifer: Really?

Gershom: Yes, really. The reason is that the Ego is the "go-between" the id and the superego. There is constant battle between the id and the superego.

The ego travels between the id and the superego as it resolves the issues that exist between them by repressing harmful thoughts, emotions, childhood and other harmful experiences into the unconscious mind, the id.

Jennifer: Seriously? Gershom, you mean issues can exist between the id and the superego?

Gershom: Yes. Jennifer, they do exist. When the unconscious materials are struggling to force their way from the id (the unconscious) into the superego (the conscious), it is the job of the Ego to prevent that from happening.

Jennifer: Wow! That is so cool. But Gershom, what are conscious materials and unconscious materials?

Gershom: Well, Jennifer, that is a good question. You see, unconscious materials are those intrapersonal processes we mentioned earlier such as emotions, motivations, thoughts, and experiences that are harmful to humans. Sigmund Fraud believed that humans are constantly bombarded with harmful thoughts or unconscious themes such as your Dad losing his job where you have to move out of your comfort zone, incestuous thoughts, memories of traumatic childhood, hatred for one's parents, aggression towards one's spouse, aggression towards schoolmates and the likes such that, when acted upon, the result would be devastating.

Jennifer: Wow! So, the unconscious materials are our bad experiences in life. When we act upon those bad emotions, motivations, thoughts and experiences, the result can be catastrophic.

Gershom: Yes, Jennifer, you got it! Jennifer, an example could be your Dad losing his job thus reducing your standard of living which may be a traumatic experience to you.

Jennifer: Yes, it was traumatic to me. We nearly lost everything when my Dad lost his job.

Gershom: Can you imagine what would have happened if you had acted upon that traumatic experience?

Jennifer: Tell me about it. I probably would have been dead or something.

Gershom: Or, because your standard of living was reduced where you have little or no money at some point, you might have been forced into prostitution, robbery and other illegal acts that may not make you a happy camper.

Jennifer: That is so true. Now we know what unconscious materials are. What about conscious materials. What are they?

Gershom: Well, Jennifer, conscious materials are those experiences that are not harmful to humans. They are also intrapersonal processes such as emotions, motivations, thoughts, and experiences that are not harmful to humans. Yes, these are the good intrapersonal processes that will not drive you crazy and may make you a happy camper.

Jennifer: So, how does the Ego relate to all these? I mean, how does the Ego relate to the id (where the unconscious materials reside) and the superego (where the conscious materials reside)?

Gershom: Jennifer, you ask great questions.

Jennifer: Thanks.

Gershom: One of the jobs the Ego has is to take the harmful emotions, harmful motivations, harmful thoughts, and harmful experiences and repress or confine them into the id, the unconscious mind. By doing so, that person will not have to deal with those traumatic experiences.

Jennifer: Gershom, are you saying that the contents of the unconscious mind or the id are hidden away from the person such that, she is not bothered by those harmful intrapersonal processes?

Gershom: Yes, Jennifer. The unconscious materials inside the id are hidden from that person. Only the conscious materials inside the superego – the conscious mind, that a person is aware of.

Jennifer: So, a person is not aware of the stuff inside the id - the unconscious mind, she is only aware of the stuff that are inside the superego - the conscious mind.

Gershom: Exactly! Now, whose job is it to keep those harmful intrapersonal processes inside the unconscious mind, the id?

Jennifer: I believe that it is the job of the Ego to make sure that the unconscious materials do not escape from the id, the unconscious mind.

Gershom: That is so correct! Is a person aware of what goes on in his unconscious mind, the id?

Jennifer: Capital N, capital O, exclamation point. No! A person is not aware of what goes on in her unconscious mind, the id. She is only aware of what goes on in her conscious state, her superego.

Gershom: Jennifer, you have answered correctly. Now, are all intrapersonal processes harmful?

Jennifer: No. Not all intrapersonal processes are harmful. Some intrapersonal processes like blissful emotions, great motivations, beautiful thoughts, and experiences are good.

Gershom: What happen to those blissful emotions, great motivations, beautiful thoughts, and experiences?

Jennifer: Aha! The Ego stores them in the conscious mind, the superego so, we can be aware of them and possibly use them as often as we want.

Gershom: Great! Now that we have the prerequisite knowledge, we can discuss the term, defense mechanism.

Jennifer: Yes, what is defense mechanism?

Gershom: Dr. Jerry M. Burger defines defense mechanisms[40] as the techniques that the Ego uses to deal with harmful intrapersonal processes such as unwanted thoughts and desires with a view to reducing or avoiding anxieties.

Jennifer: I see.

Gershom: As a defense mechanism, the ego uses a huge amount of energy to repress things that trigger painful experiences and harmful unwanted thoughts and desires into the unconscious and thus, preventing them from getting into consciousness.

Jennifer: So, as a defense mechanism, the ego uses huge amount of energy to repress things that trigger painful experiences and harmful unwanted thoughts and desires into the id, the unconscious mind so as to prevent those harmful thoughts and painful experiences from getting into the superego where consciousness resides.

Gershom: You got it! Jennifer, what do you think would happen if the ego fails, or if the ego is not strong enough to prevent the unconscious impulses from getting into consciousness?

Jennifer: Catastrophe?

Gershom: That is close, Jennifer. Should the ego fail in its plight to prevent those painful experiences and harmful unwanted thoughts and desires that are in the unconscious mind from getting into consciousness, the result would be what Sigmund Freud called neurotic anxiety – a mental disorder marked by anxiety or fear.

Jennifer: Really? That is psychotic.

Gershom: Not really. It is a mental disorder.

Jennifer: Wow! That is unbelievable!

Gershom: Studies show that there are times where a patient may suffer neurotic anxiety without having to do with the anxiety that is sparked by the sensation of the ego's inability to prevent the unconscious materials from bursting through the awareness barrier and materialize themselves into consciousness[41].

Jennifer: So, sometimes a patient may suffer neurotic anxiety that has nothing to do with the anxiety that is caused the ego's inability to prevent the unconscious materials from getting into consciousness – the superego.

Gershom: That is correct.

Jennifer:	Would it be safe to say that an example of such neurotic anxiety could be schizophrenia?
Gershom:	Not quite, Jennifer. The neurotic anxiety Sigmund Freud is talking about is less severe than psychosis because it does not involve detachment from reality. Schizophrenia and hallucination are example of psychosis because they involve detachment from reality.
Jennifer:	If that is the case, what are example of neurotic anxiety, a mental disorder marked by anxiety or fear?
Gershom:	According to the American Psychiatric Association[41], examples of neurotic anxiety are Bipolar Disorder, Autism Spectrum Disorder (ASD), Opositional Defiant Disorder (ODD), Conduct Disorder (CD), and many others which do not involve detachment from reality.
Jennifer:	That makes a whole lot of sense.
Gershom:	You see, Jennifer, since there are so much battle going on between the id and the superego, defense mechanisms are tools that the ego uses to trick the mind with a view to preventing such neurotic anxiety from happening.
Jennifer:	I see. So, Gershom, you said earlier that when you help me to stop smoking, you will give me something that will replace or something that will fill the void that will be created when I stop smoking. What do you mean?
Gershom:	Yes, I'll tell you what I mean. You see, Jennifer, when you stop the habit of smoking, you need to fill that habit with a better one. Otherwise, the

void created by not smoking may compel you to resume smoking. We do not want that, do we?

Jennifer: No! We most certainly do not want that. Earlier, Gershom, you said there are steps you will take to help me stop smoking. What are they?

Gershom: Yes, Jennifer. I mentioned steps and there are five of them on my mind.

Jennifer: What are they, Gershom?

Gershom: Well, Jennifer, you kind of did the first step when you call for my service.

Jennifer: Seriously?

Gershom: Yes, seriously. You see, Jennifer, the first step is to decide to let go of that maladaptive (or smoking) behavior. Your calling on me, let me know that you have decided to let go of smoking. Am I correct with that assumption?

Jennifer: Gershom, you are correct.

Gershom: Thank you Jennifer. The second step is to develop a hatred for that habit of smoking. A way to do that is to pay attention to what scientists including medical doctors are saying about how bad smoking and secondhand smoke are for human consumption.

Jennifer: Oh, there are many studies out there even from the Surgeon General condemning smoking and secondhand smoke. The fact that my family is gone, and I am still here, made a believer out of me that secondhand smoke can be fatal. I wish I had known this before now.

Gershom: Jennifer, it's never too late to use that knowledge to help the living. Do it for those you love.

Jennifer: Yes, most of whom are dead. I wish I have this knowledge before now, my family may have been alive. What a loss!

Gershom: I am so sorry for your loss. Jennifer: Thanks for your condolence.

Gershom: Jennifer, the third step is to replace that maladaptive behavior or in your case, the habit of smoking with a preferred behavior which in your case may be to chew some gums, use prescription patch on your skin, and other endeavors that will help mitigate or eliminate your cravings to smoke. There are valuable suggestions in the "Smoking Cessation" by the CDC.

Jennifer: Oh, that is what you mean by replacing my smoking habit with something better.

Gershom: Yes, that is correct. Now, the fourth step is that of maintenance which has two folds. The first fold being to do a thorough examination of your friends. Are they smokers too? Would they respect and support your decision to quit smoking and never go back to it?

Jennifer: I agree with you. Is kind of like I need a support group and if my friends cannot be my support group or at least respect my decision, then I'll have to find a new set of friends who will support my decision and be my support group.

Gershom: Yes, Jennifer. That is vital because the second fold of the maintenance relates to our imperfections as humans. That is, should your cravings to smoke and the sense of what you feel you had lost for giving up smoking crawl back to mind, then you need to reinforce your developed hatred for the habit of smoking and reinforce your joy for the preferred habit.

Jennifer: I get it. So, my preferred habit would be to chew some gums, administer prescription patch on my skin, and other activities that will help to mitigate or eliminate my cravings to smoke.

Gershom: That is correct. Now, the fifth step is to seek the help of other licensed mental health professionals like me, BCBA, Licensed Psychologists, licensed Psychiatrists, and medical specialists.

Jennifer: You mean in conjunction with you because you are a Board-Certified Behavior Analyst - BCBA?

Gershome: Yes. Jennifer, in conjunction with me because you probably need all the help you would get to reach your goal.

Jennifer: Oh, you better believe it Gershom. I need all the help to quit smoking. Yes, I need all the help that I can get to help quench my urge to smoke so I can have a clean environment.

Gershom: Exactly!!! You got it! [Gershom and Jennifer clap] Now Jennifer, with all that is going on, what would you conclude about the ego as a character?

Jennifer: Well, we know that the id and the superego as characters constantly fight with each other. So, the ego's character would be that of a referee that constantly intercedes between the id and the superego.

Gershom: Good. But what if the ego is less powerful than the id and the superego?

Jennifer: In one word? Catastrophe! Yes, that person will be an insane camper.

Gershom: That is correct, Jennifer. Now, in terms of power, do you think the ego ought to be powerful or powerless based on its responsibility?

Jennifer: I believe that the ego ought to be more powerful than the id and the superego. I mean, that is the only way the ego can successfully do its job of preventing the id from bullying the superego and vice-versa.

Gershom: Exactly!!! I appreciate the way you phrase your answer, it shows insight. What happens if the id succeeds in bullying the superego?

Jennifer: That will mean that the ego has lost the battle to the id, which means that the ego is not strong enough to prevent the unconscious impulses in the id from bursting through the walls of consciousness. In that case, the person would be more prone to be a bully, aggressive without morals and in short, a criminally prone person.

Gershom: Excellent! What happens if the superego succeeds in bullying the id?

Jennifer: You may have heard of the words "over righteous" and "Goodie two shoes." Have you?

Gershom: Yes, I have.

Jennifer: Then a person referred to as being "over righteous" or "goodie two shoes," is the result of that person's id succumbing to the superego's bullying.

Gershom: Once again, Jennifer, you have answered correctly. According to Sigmund Freud the founder of psychoanalytic therapy[40], the difference between a mentally healthy person and a mentally ill person is a weak ego. While mentally ill person has a weak ego, a mentally healthy person has a strong ego.

Jennifer: Really?

Gershom: Yes, really. Jennifer, now you know that it is not a good thing for the id to successfully bully the superego and vice-versa. As such, the ego must be strong to balance the aggression and pleasure-seeking impulses of the id with the moral control of the superego.

Jennifer: Amazing!

Gershom: Do you know what the primal of these defense mechanisms is?

Jennifer: Not a clue.

Gershom: The primal of these defense mechanisms is that they allow us to be our authentic self.

Jennifer: Yes, that makes a whole lot of sense because without defensive mechanisms humans will probably be acting like animals or insane.

Gershom: Something like that and who knows, we may all be criminals or moral geniuses.

Jennifer: None of which would have been to our advantage. Gershom: Jennifer, you can say that again.

Jennifer: You mention willpower earlier, Gershom, is willpower the same as self- control? I guess what I'm trying to ask is, what is willpower and how can I increase my willpower to stop smoking?

Gershom: Jennifer, you ask great questions. While Willpower is not Self-Control, Willpower is one of the three essential factors of Self-control (Standards, Monitoring, Willpower) – Myers and Twenge 2015[42]

Jennifer: Oh, so, although Willpower is not Self-Control, it is part of the three components of Self-Control which are Standards, Monitoring and Willpower.

Gershom: That is correct.

Jennifer: I see. Well, since I know what Standards and Monitoring are, what is willpower?

Gershom: Will-power is the energy needed to accomplish your set of goals after awareness and initial change of thoughts have been accomplished. Without awareness, we will have problem with self-control or willpower (Myers and Twenge – 2015)[42].

Jennifer: Yes, humans are not aware of the unconscious materials repressed inside the id but are aware or conscious to the conscious materials in the superego.

Gershom: Jennifer, that is correct. Humans have a threshold of 50%. That is, anything below 50% are in the realm of unconsciousness, which means humans will not be aware of it. However, things that are from 50% and above are in the realm of consciousness, which means humans are aware of it[40].

Jennifer: I see. So, the knowledge of Sigmund Freud's topographic model and structural model are still in play here.

Gershom: Jennifer, you can understand why I had to cover that aspect first.

Jennifer: I understand now. It is as if the models are the basis of everything regarding awareness or consciousness.

Gershom: That is somewhat right. However, the definition of Willpower will be amiss without a proper understanding of Self-Regulation relating to the achievement of set goals such as quitting smoking.

Jennifer: I see. What is Self-Regulation?

Gershom: Self-Regulation is "the self's capacity to alter or change itself and its states to bring them into line with goals, ideals or rules." – Baumeister and Finkel (2010), also cited by Myers and Twenge (2015) [42].

Jennifer: Gershom, that is deep. Can you explain what that mean?

Gershom: Jennifer, it means that we set our initial goal with self-awareness, and it will take a lot of energy to meet this goal of not smoking in your case, since according to Sigmund Freud, our ego expends huge amount of energy to carry out this process.

Jennifer: Really?

Gershom: Yes, really Jennifer. When the goal we set is unmet, like amoeba bounces back from a terrible object, we want to bounce back from a failed goal and set a new realistic goal with changed thoughts.[41]

Jennifer: That sounds interesting.

Gershom:	As humans, Jennifer, we are almost always self-aware in relation to some standards like our social groups with social rules and effective self-regulation is guided by effective feedback loops as with cybernetic theory, which is TOTE - Test, Operate, Test, Exit.[41]
Jennifer:	So, "Test - Operate - Test - Exit", is an iterative problem- solving strategy based on feedback loops.
Gershom:	Correct. After awareness and initial change of thoughts have been accomplished, then the energy needed to accomplish that goal is, the willpower.
Jennifer:	Wow! That is amazing.
Gershom:	The folk notion of willpower has some merits that could be reckoned with - when people exert self-control, they use up some of this energy, leaving them in a temporarily depleted state. The American Psychological Association (2015) states "A growing body of research shows that resisting repeated temptations takes a mental toll."
Jennifer:	Really? It makes people tired mentally?
Gershom:	Jennifer, you can certainly say that. Some studies describe willpower as being like a muscle that gets fatigued with heavy use.
Jennifer:	Wow! That's how I feel and even the thought of me quitting smoking makes me so tired. It's a drag.
Gershom:	I can understand that, Jennifer. I hope you can draw comfort from the knowledge that willpower is like muscles that become exhausted by exercise

in the short term, they are strengthened by regular exercise in the long term.

Jennifer: I see. So, by regularly exerting self-control the strength of willpower may improve.

Gershom: Sure. Self-control is a central function of the self and an important key to success in life (Myers and Twenge 2015)[42]. The self or a person utilizes huge amount of energy to exercise self-control for the first time. Following that initial act of self-control, performance on a second unrelated self-control task is often impaired suggesting that energy was expended.

Jennifer: I see. So, because that person had expended a huge amount of energy for the first act of self-control or willpower, the second act of self-control on unrelated matter may not succeed because less energy is available for use. Because the huge amount of energy needed to exercise self-control the second time has been depleted on the first act of self-control, the second act of self-control may be impaired.

Gershom: Yes, Jennifer. That is correct. So, expending or depleting the energy is called "Ego-depletion."[41]

Jennifer: There we go again with the "ego."

Gersom: Yes, Jennifer. In a manner that muscles get tired from exertion, acts of self-control or in this case willpower, cause short-term impairments (ego depletion) in subsequent self-control, even on unrelated tasks.

Jennifer: That is amazing! Now I understand why I'm always tired as if I ran out of energy to do anything.

| Gershom: | The Executive function involves planning, decision- making, information updating and monitoring. Research shows that after people make choices their self-control is impaired as they use the same energy for decision-making and acts of self-control[41]. |

Jennifer: Then how do I increase my willpower?

Gershom: Jennifer, you probably know that after depletion of glucose, people are more likely to make irrational decisions.

Jennifer: Really?

Gershom: Yes, really. As a matter of research, biological or psychological, ego-depletion studies have linked self- control to glucose in the blood that provides fuel for brain processes and after acts of self-control (willpower), blood levels of glucose are diminished (Gailliot & Baumeister, 2007), cited by Myers and Twenge.[42]

Jennifer: You mean after an act of self-control or willpower, blood levels of glucose that provides fuel for brain processes are diminished too?

Gershom: Yes, that is right. The biological explanation of willpower is such that during demanding tasks, blood glucose levels in the frontal lobes drops. In a video titled "Behave, the biology of humans at our best and worst" (2017) Professor of neurology Robert Sapolsky of Stanford University argued that if subjects are given a sugary drink, the frontal lobe functioning, and glucose levels will improve. When people are hungry, they become less charitable and more aggressive. As such, willpower is probably a combination of cognitive capacities and ego- depletion.

Jennifer: So, the consumption of sugary drinks will help improve willpower?

Gershom: Yes, according to the studies, it will. Another way to improve willpower is through motivational incentives which can encourage people to overcome ego- depletion. Thinking at a highly meaningful abstract level that incorporates long-term perspectives can improve self-control even with ego-depletion. Studies have shown that people can improve their willpower by engaging in frequent exercise of willpower. The logic behind that reasoning is such that muscles get stronger from regular exercise, so engaging in some extra self-control activities for couple of weeks produces improvement in willpower, even on tasks that have no relation to the exercise activities.

Jennifer: What are examples of exercise of willpower? Gershom: Professor Roy F. Baumeister, a social psychologist at Florida State University suggested two kinds of exercise to improve willpower – arbitrary and meaningful exercises. An arbitrary exercise could be using your left hand instead of your right hand to open doors and to brush your teeth. A meaningful exercise could be managing your money better and save more.

Jennifer: That's not bad at all. Anybody can do that without a problem.

Gershom: The important thing is to practice overriding habitual ways of doing things and exerting deliberate control over your actions.

Jennifer: So, controlling my cravings to smoke would be an example of overriding habitual ways of doing things and exerting deliberate control over my actions.

Gershom: That is correct. This is the case where "practice makes perfect." Yes, practice, practice, practice, practice. That is, as you practice exerting deliberate control over your cravings to smoke, as time goes on, that practice will improve your willpower[41] over smoking.

Jennifer: That makes sense. We cannot overestimate the power of practice. So, as I practice exerting deliberate control over my cravings to smoke, over time, that practice will improve my willpower[41] over smoking.

Gershom: You got it! Summing up what we've discussed thus far, decades of studies and trials backed with scientific rigor reveal that intelligence and self-control, or willpower are the two main traits that Psychology identified as beneficial to people. While there is not much that one can do to produce lasting increases in intelligence as far as Psychology is concerned, thus, making intelligence an innate gift, on the other hand, self-control can be strengthened[41]. Therefore, do your utmost, yes, your very best to strengthen your willpower to quit smoking.

Jennifer: Gershom, for the sake of humanity and self, I will certainly do my best to heed your candid counsel by strengthening my willpower to quit smoking.

Gershom: We don't want to forget that there are other factors that are responsible for self-control like the prefrontal cortex – an area that is responsible for self-control, which according to the study conducted by Dr. Adrian Raine[46] and his research team shows that the prefrontal cortex is 14% less active in murderers than in normal people (excluding those that had been abuse by their parents) and 15% smaller in antisocial personalities. So, the size of the prefrontal cortex matters to self- control. Getting proper sleep is very important because the study also shows that sleep deprivation reduces activities in the prefrontal cortex.

Jennifer: That is another area I will have to improve because I barely had six hours of sleep without restlessness let alone eight or nine recommended hours of sleep.

Gershom: Jennifer, respecting our discussion thus far, it is important to understand that you need to set a SMART goal. We all know what it means to be smart, but here, I am using it as an acronym in which the letter 'S' stands for **S**pecific goal, 'M' stands for **M**easurable goal, 'A' stands for **A**chievable goal, 'R' stands for **R**ealistic goal, and the letter 'T' stands for Time-bound goal. Therefore, to successfully reach your goal, your goal must be:

Specific: In setting your goal, you want to avoid vagueness. Unlike a Hamster, you do not want to aimlessly direct your blows everywhere and not hitting your target – that is what setting a general goal will do, setting you up for failure. You want to be specific about what you want to accomplish. It may help to set one specific goal at a time and when that goal has been accomplished, then you can set another reachable goal. In a nutshell, within an environment such as home, work, school, or social setting, work on one specific goal or project at a time. So, if I ask you to set a specific goal, what would it be?

Jennifer: Quit smoking.

Gershon: Great! Jennifer, you got the point. Next, your goal should be

Measurable: Your goal should be measurable. Measurement is how we track levels of a behavior, the success of an intervention, and make programming decisions. That is, you need to find a way to measure how well you are doing respecting your set goal. If your set goal is not measurable, then it might be difficult to determine whether that goal is achievable. So, we want to be able to measure our set goal. In my line of work, there are few ways in which our goals can be measured, however, specific to your goal, we could use two measuring procedures such as (1) Frequency - which means tallying the number of occurrences that you are able to control your cravings to smoke or counting the number of occurrences that you yield to your cravings to smoke per day, per month or per year and (2) Accuracy - you are able to measure your success rate. As such, the industry considers 80% and above as a good success rate per several trials.

Jennifer: So, I need to measure my performances.

Gershom: Yes, Jennifer, that is correct. Measuring your performances will allow you to monitor your progress.

Jennifer: I see.

Gershom: Next, your goal should be

Achievable or **Attainable**: If your goal is not achievable, like amoeba you want to abandon that goal and set a new one that you can achieve. You need to have the prerequisite that will afford you the understanding behind the underlying logic of achieving your goal. Yes, you need to have a prerequisite skill that will help to achieve your goal. So, Jennifer, if you want to stop smoking, what prerequisite skill should you have?

Jennifer: Well, in my case, I think figuring out my maladaptive behaviors and replacing them with preferred behavior. Understanding that there are alternatives to smoking and the skillful knowledge of applying the alternatives to myself.

Gershom: Right. Next, your goal should be

Realistic or **Relevant**: Do you realistically have the prerequisite to achieve your goal? And is this goal relevant to you? For example, if it's your goal to be a medical doctor, would it make sense to concentrate on Finance for a major? If your goal is to quit smoking, would it make sense to associate with heavy smokers? You will be taking that step if your goal is not relevant to you and you will thus, render that goal unrealistic since the friends you choose can influence you to either quit smoking or indulge in it. Relevant goals are goals that will make a difference in life and if the goal to quit smoking is relevant to you, you will stay away from smokers. By doing so, you will be demonstrating that your goal is relevant to you, your goal is reachable, and your goal is realistic. Jennifer, what could you do for your goal to be realistic?

Jennifer: I need to rethink the caliber of my friends, making sure that none of them smokes and that they would support my decision to quit smoking.

Gershom: Right. Next, your goal should be

Time-bound: You need to set a time frame in which your goal will be accomplished. You need to set a start time and an end time or deadline for your goal. If the deadline comes and your goal is not accomplished, you will have to rethink whether you have set an achievable goal. If not, like an amoeba that retreat from a dangerous object you want to retreat or step away from that goal and set a new one. Otherwise, you could give your current goal another time frame to complete. Jennifer, if I should ask you to set a time frame for your goal, what would it be?

Jennifer: Well, Gershom, I would say six months starting today. I'll get everything ready after you leave.

Gershom: That sounds good.

Jennifer: Thanks.

Gershom: Jennifer, you are welcome. On a different note. There is something else that you need to do every day as it is the guiding force that would help you to apply the previous steps. Although in the universe of research, especially that of scientific rigor, there are those who have not accepted the importance of this step because of varying beliefs, deceptions, and the hypocrisy of those who ought to be leading by example. But this is something you need to think about as it is something you must do on your own.

Jennifer: Gershom, what is it?

Gershom: It is personal prayers.[47] The proof of the existence of the supreme being that you should pray to, is beyond the scope of this discussion. However, suffice is to say that you are a living proof of his existence. Think about it, with all these many gasses there are in the atmosphere, how do you know how to breathe in only oxygen, exhaling carbon dioxide as waste product which is naturally recycled among plants? How do trees know how to inhale only carbon dioxide and exhale oxygen as a waste product which is naturally recycled among animals? Do all those brilliant designs came by chance, or are they acts of a brilliant supreme designer?

Jennifer: That is amazingly some good food for thought.

Gershom: Whether you believe in the existence of the supreme being, the creator of the whole universe or not, prayer is something you need to do on your own as it is a personal and solemn request for divine help to quit smoking. Since quitting smoking is of divine will, your prayers will be answered so long as you are living according to your prayers.

Jennifer: Gershom, what do you mean by so long as I am living according to my prayers?

Gershom: What I mean by living according to your prayers is, as you ask for divine help to stop smoking, you do not want to intensify your smoking habits with a false reasoning of expecting God to perform a miracle by forcing you to quit smoking. That is not how it works since God does not force you to do anything, he gives you the "free will"[48] so that your good deed may be done not under compulsion, but from your heart. As such, what you do is entirely up to you. So, when you ask for divine help, you are expected to live according to your request by exerting your willpower over your cravings to smoke and thus, stop smoking.

Jennifer   Oh, I see. So, it is like me doing my very best to stop smoking and him guiding me all the way through the process.

Gershom: Yes. Jennifer, just as you are getting physical help from me and other licensed mental health professionals, you need divine help too.

Jennifer: Gershom, I understand completely. You also said it is something that I must do on my own, what do you mean by that?

Gershom: There are those who would go to some acclaimed religious leaders to lay hands on them for prayers. No. You do not need to do that as your God want to hear your request directly from you, certainly not through some medium. Your solemn request must be accompanied by your voice not someone else's. Your request, your voice, your prayer.

Jennifer: Oh, I see. My request, my voice, my actions.

Gershom: Yes, it is completely up to you to get the best help all around that will yield the best result. I am not saying here that you cannot ask others to pray on your behalf because we all need someone to include us in their prayers. I am saying that when it comes to a request like quitting smoking which is difficult for most people to do and can have a huge impact on your life, the request must be personal, private, and solemn.

Jennifer: I got it. Thanks, Gershom.

Gershom: You are welcome, Jennifer.

Gershom is treading carefully not to upset his client, Jennifer, as he reasoned with her, leaving her to draw up her own conclusion that she was not born a smoker. She learned the habit of smoking from her teenage friends. So, smoking is not who she is. While at the moment, it may be difficult to grasp the logic behind Jennifer's smoking for years but still alive and seemingly free from the diseases that are incidental to smokers, whereas her husband and children who have never smoked a day in their lives are dead from lung cancer. Suffice is to say that we are glad to see the growth of our comprehension of secondhand smoke or passive smoke or environmental smoke to be a deadly force against those who have never smoked a day in their lives. As such, do you have to be around those smokers who due to selfish inclinations and desires do not care that much about your wellbeing? May your answer be a resounding NO! You do not have to be around those smokers nor have them around you. Jennifer's husband and children may have chosen not to exercise their rights to insist on a smoke free environment hence, they suffer fatally. You, however, need to insist on your rights to have and maintain a smoke free environment. Yes, you need to have an environment that is free from secondhand smoke. Good health to you.

There is no doubt that replacing harmful habits with preferred habits will pose fearful thoughts to the bearer. However, having courage can help you to overcome that fear. The English Learners dictionary defines courage as a "mental or moral strength to venture, persevere, and withstand danger, fear, or difficulty. " The word "Venture" in the definition for courage means to "proceed especially in the face of danger." Therefore, courage is doing the right thing in the presence of fear or danger. Yes, even with an intractable problem, there is tractability. That is, even with a difficult problem like quitting smoking, quitting illegal use of narcotics; you can still find a way to do the right thing – quit it.

Concerning wisdom, the Bible book of Ecclesiastes 7:12 says "For wisdom is a protection just as money is a protection, but the advantage of knowledge is this: Wisdom preserves its owner." May you never be one of the inexperienced who sees the danger in smoking, the danger in secondhand smoke, the danger in illegal use of narcotics; keep right on going and suffer the consequences. Rather, may you be one of the shrewd ones who sees the danger in smoking, the danger in secondhand smoke, the danger in illegal use of narcotics; and conceals himself.[43] By doing so, you will be building your house on the rock,[44] not on sand, withstanding all naturally occurring disasters.

Wisdom is the application of knowledge. When you acquire the knowledge that smoking cigarettes is not advantageous to your health and so is the illegal use of narcotics, applying that knowledge to yourself is wisdom. Kindly protect yourself from the bullies of illegal use of narcotics, secondhand smoke, and smoking.

8

MOTHER DEALS WITH CHILD'S CRAFTY ACTS

The girls depart from the scene of the hard drugs distributors. As they walk on, they come across two boys Ikem and Sina (pronounced Shinau) who had earlier made a bet on whether or not chickens can be fed satisfactorily at a given time. Ikem's stance is that chickens have stomach and appetite whose depth is equal only to that of the abyss, the bottomless pit. What is more? Ikem contends that because chickens have throats deeper than the bottomless pit, it is impossible for them to be fed satisfactorily at a given time. In a nutshell, Ikem's contention is based on one of his beliefs that chickens have insatiable appetites and therefore, it is impossible to feed them to their satisfaction in a given time. Of course, Sina disagrees with Ikem and the vie leads to a betting game.

Addiction To Gambling Is A Bully

Devoid of the boys' knowledge, the girls decide to have their own betting game. The question is, is it impossible to have fun playing games without sacrificing your valuables?

Pamela and Uchenna take side with Sina. Adamma sides with Ikem. In order to make the game more interesting and finite, the boys hold constant some variables. The first variable they hold constant is that the said chicken must eat out from the big plastic bowl where the boys will put sufficient amount of blended corn, plain corn or seeds and replenish it when necessary. Holding that variable constant ensures that as long as the chicken eats from the plastic bowl at that given time, it is still hungry. The chicken satiates when after eating walks away from the plastic bowl. The second variable that the boys hold constant is that when the chicken walks away from the plastic bowl after eating, it must not peck on the ground for food or anything resembling food until it disappears into oblivion or completely out of the contestants' sight. Ikem wins the bet if the chicken pecks the floor after eating from the plastic bowl. Otherwise, Sina wins.

Mysteriously, the news about the betting game get to other people and before you know it there is a little crowd with curious hearts gather around to see the outcome of the game. More so is to engage in the betting game by taking sides on the issue at stake and of course giving their money to a stakeholder. While some of the contestants bet with nothing at stake order than for the fun of it with regards to whose logic is more credible, others however, bet with something of value at stake, which may be in the form of money or service. The environment for the betting game is set. The contestants are set and ready to go. The chicken is in place. The game is on. The spectators are chanting:

Go Chuwawa Go!

Go Chuwawa Go!

Go Chuwawa Go!

Go Chuwawa Go!

Chuwawa is having a blast as it devours the food. The boys replenish the bowl with more food and Chuwawa continues to massacre the food. Few minutes into the game with more people joining the fold as they are enticed by the chanting of the zealous spectators, Chuwawa gives up. Or does she?

Well, Chuwawa comes out of the plastic bowl and the spectators as well as the contestants think for a Moment that Chuwawa has done eating to her satisfaction and cannot take in any more food. Therefore, Sina and all those contestants who bet against the notion that chickens have insatiable appetites and therefore, it is impossible to feed them to their satisfaction are declared winners. Or are they?

The winners are celebrating and collecting, while the losers are not. All eyes are still on Chuwawa since she must not peck on the ground for anything as she walks out of the spectators' sight. It turns out that as Chuwawa takes a few steps away from the plastic bowl; you could hear a pin drops when she pecks on the ground. Who cares for the reason that Chuwawa may have had for pecking on the ground at this Moment? The bottom line is, that changes things one hundred and eighty degrees from where they are at the moment. Suddenly, on one hand those celebrating stop jumping up and down for joy regarding the jarring sight. On the other hand, the once mourners start celebrating with an indescribable joy as the new winners. The new winners become collectors of the stakes.

Of course, there are arguments as to whether or not Chuwawa satiates her deep appetite when she pecks on the ground. The bottom line, however, is the fact that Chuwawa pecks on the ground after eaten from the plastic bowl, which in the eyes of the majority signifies that Chuwawa is still hungry. Hence, she pecks on the ground for more food.

There is no doubt in someone's mind that all those contestants who bet against the notion that "chickens have insatiable appetites and therefore, it is impossible to feed them to their satisfaction" really do have a point or two. Their logic for example, is based on the fact that chickens are beings with finite bodies and a finite body has a finite or a definite stomach with a perimeter. You can only put so much food in a stomach as little as that of a chicken. Therefore, as far as the opponents of the notion are concerned, it is possible to feed chickens to their satisfaction. The problem is that they are not counting on one of the natural behavior of chickens, which is to peck on the ground for reasons that are best known to them, even after they have been well fed. The only period of time that chickens do not peck on the ground is when they sleep. The winners including Sina capitalize on this knowledge to win the bet. The beat goes on as everybody minds his or her own business.

Several yards away, a young teenage boy named Isaac behold two teenage boys fighting over the bet as the loser refuses to pay up. One of the fighters named Ezechi is fourteen years old and the second fighter going by the name Mide is about the same age. Isaac runs toward the fighters with a view to separating them and eventually bringing an end to their quarrel. When he gets to the scene, an unfortunate thing happens to him. Mide throws a blow at Ezechi who successfully evades it and the blow lands on Isaac. Oh dear! Isaac is hurt and unhappy to the point of joining the fight by throwing blows at Mide. The fight that involves two people a priori, now takes a toll on three participants. As Mide defends himself against Ezechi and Isaac he explains himself to Isaac that he does not mean to hit him, it is unfortunate that he gets in the way. It does not seem that Isaac is listening as the fight intensifies calling to it spectators in multiple.

Three men are bold enough to separate the fight by pulling off each participant simultaneously. While the spectators understand the logic behind the quarrel between Ezechi and Mide, they don't quite get the logic behind Isaac joining in on the fight. So, they ask Isaac for an explanation. Isaac starts off by saying it is quite simple. Pointing at Ezechi and Mide, Isaac says I saw both of them fighting against each other from a far of, so I ran to stop them from fighting. When I got to the scene, I was greeted with a dirty blow coming from Mide. I tell you people; I have never felt such an excruciating pain in my entire life! It was out of anger that I hit Mide and the rest? I think you know the rest. Stanly, one of the three men who separated the teenagers from the fight says Isaac, we understand, and we sympathize with you. When you see two people fighting with each other next time, get help. Ok? Isaac answers yes, I will. The beat goes on as everybody goes about minding his or her own business.

One thing worth mentioning is that remember the three men who separated the fight above, one of them is a forty-year old moderately heavy built man with beards who has braces on his teeth with a pair of silver earpiece of the frame hanging on his ears. While braces are normal, the pair of silver earpiece of the frame hanging on his ears is cool for his age during the nineteen-seventies or the era when braces are first discovered or invented. Currently however, the silver earpiece of the frame hanging on his ears at his age will certainly draw unnecessary attention couple with ridicule to self. No wonder, the spectators will not stop laughing as they leave the scene of the fight. In fact, they remember the braces more than they do the fight.

The light shines on the Ape Family. Fiorina, the mother continues to read from the book "Is Silence Really Golden?" to her family.

Rawlings: Mom, I wish I was there playing the chicken game with Ikem and Sina. I can see myself winning the bet. It is a no brainer.

Francesco: Son, you really think so?

Rawlings: Yes, Dad, I really think so. I mean, who does not know that chickens always peck on the ground even after they are done eating? That is one of the chickens' hallmark.

Fiorina: Son, that is wonderful. I mean, not everybody knows that and so son, it is a gift that you know it.

Rawlings: Thanks Mom.

Fiorina: Son, you are welcome. Now, let us go back to see how Florence handles Pamela deceptions.

Francesco: Oh yes. I would like to know how that ends. Pamela is not only cunning she is always a bold face deceiver. I want to see how her Mom takes it when she finds out and how she deals with Pamela.

Fiorina: Great! Then let me continue reading the story. Fiorina reads:

A Mother Deals with Unruly Young Adult

We shine the light on Florence and her two daughters, Pamela and Lizzy. Florence is home with her daughter Lizzy. Both are having a good time playing with Lizzy's computer game. Not long, Pamela walks in demanding for her dinner.

Pamela:　　　　　Hi Mom. Hi Lizzy.

Lizzy:　　　　　Hi Pamela.

Florence:　　　　Hi Pamela. How are you and how are your friends been doing?

Pamela:　　　　　I am starving. My friends are doing fine. Thanks for asking, Mom. The only thing is that we've been out all day without food, and I am famishing I could eat a cow.

Florence:　　　　Really?

Pamela:　　　　　Yes, really. You know what's funny? I don't see any sign of dinner made. What's up with that? I mean what on Earth is the idea of you not having dinner ready, Mom?

Florence:　　　　Girl, we are waiting for you to come and help us to prepare the meal.

Pamela:　　　　　Seriously?

Florence:　　　　Yes, seriously. We better get going.

Pamela:　　　　　All right Mom.

On any given day before now, Florence the Mom, always have dinner ready by now and do not require the children to be home to get it ready. This time, things change partly because Lizzy had earlier laid a justifiable complaint against her sister, Pamela. In her quest to get to the bottom of that complaint, Florence now requires her girls to help with the preparation and serving of the meal. What is more?

Florence wants to teach her daughters to be better chefs at least for their own sake. Pamela who at the Moment is in a quandary with the thought of whether or not her sister Lizzy has broken her promise to protect Pamela's secret from Mom. So, Pamela secretly asks Lizzy if she had told her secrete to Mom. Lizzy reassures Pamela that her secrete is safe. Like a load has been lifted off from her shoulders, Pamela expresses her gratitude to her sister for keeping her secrete safe. The all cook and dine together. The night is over and it is the next day.

Days go by and Florence's trap is closing in on Pamela devoid of her knowledge. A new day has begun. As usual Florence gives chores to her daughters and expects them to do it before she gets back. This time Lizzy pretends to argue with her Mom respecting the unfairness of being asked to do her chore. She is so good at acting out her part that she is able to fool Pamela into trusting that her secrete is still safe. With that knowledge in mind and after telling her Mom "Yes, Mom, I'll do it," Pamela leaves the house as usual in quest of her friends. Florence also pretends to do what she does best. That is, pretends to be heading to the market places to get things for dinner. So, things are going as normal as possible and no suspicions.

The day is almost over. Florence is back home from the marketplaces and Lizzy is playing games on her computer. Pamela gets home as usual asking for dinner while her chore patiently waits for her. Florence scornfully and sarcastically says to Pamela

Florence: Pamela, you are asking for your dinner as if you have paid maids that cook for you and do your chores too. Behold and listen very carefully.

Florence points to Pamela's chore with her left hand, with her right hand she pushes her right hear forward from behind and scornfully continues:

Florence: Can you hear your chore crying out to you saying: "Oh Pamela, please do me, please do me. I'll be nice to you. I won't be any of trouble to you. Oh Pamela, please do me, please do me."

Pamela:	Mom, I thought you will ask Lizzy to do the chore for me since I lost track of time and besides, I just can't leave my friends hanging. They need me Mom. Can't you understand that I am their leader and they look up to me?

Lizzy:	Sister, I look up to you too.

Florence:	There you go. Pamela you see, your own sister looks upto you too. What example are you setting for her if you do not fulfill your assignments on a continuous basis? Don't you know that your pride is in your work? Pamela, take pride in your work.

Pamela:	Mom, I didn't do it on purpose. I just lose track of time. Since the day is not over yet and there is time for Lizzy to help, why can't you tell her to help me with the chore?

Florence:	Really? Let's ask her. Hey Lizzy my girl, would you be a Darlene by doing your sister's chore because she lost track of time?

Lizzy:	No Mom, I won't be a Darlene! Lizzy does Lizzy's chores Only. If not doing Pamela's chores means not being a Darlene, then I don't want to be a Darlene. Pamela should learn to take up her responsibilities and leave me alone!

Florence:	Well, that settles it. Pamela, all these times I thought you are my favorite daughter. I didn't know that you've been playing your own mother all along for a fool! I'll make you pay for it by doing all the chores including your sister's. And as you do these chores always remember that you bring it upon yourself; for a teacher who thinks she can outsmart her parent has a fool for a student. You will do the chores in this house for one full month. Do you get it, Pamela?

Pamela: But Mom please don't do me like that?

Florence: Don't do you like what?

Pamela: Mom, I mean don't treat me like I'm some orphans that have no choices, no parents, no siblings and no help. Please Mom.

Florence: Well, you should have thought about that before playing me, your own mother, for a fool. Pamela, you know you ought to apologize to your sister for treating her in such an unkind way. Having her do your chores all these times is not cool.

Pamela: Well, I'm going to be doing her chores now. Who's going to apologize to me for doing her chores?

Lizzy: That's all right, Mom. She doesn't have to apologize. That she cannot fool you anymore, is good enough for me.

Florence: Very well then, we'll leave that alone. Pamela?

Pamela: Yes, Mom.

Florence: One more thing. I need you to think! Think! Think about what you have done! You know how people say "use your mind or your brain to think and your heart to feel?

Pamela: Yes, Mom I think I've heard that before.

Florence: Well, Pamela I am reversing that today. I need you to think with your heart. Yes, don't use your brain, don't use your mind; use your heart to think about what you have done to your sister and I. The heart is the seat of motivation and I need you to feel the thinking about what you have done to your sister and I. Maybe then you'll see the need to apologize to us from the bottom of your heart.

Lizzy: Thanks, Mom.

Zakondo And His Gang In Military Custody

Florence: You are welcome, my Darlene. It's almost 10:00 PM let's turn on the television for the 10 o'clock news. I want to know if Zakondo and his gang have been caught or still at large.

Pamela: You mean they have not caught the man and his gang yet?

Lizzy: No, they have not caught them yet.

Pamela: Seriously?

Florence: Yes, seriously. The news is on now. Let's Watch.

Stella Gam: Good Evening. I am Stella Gam bringing the news to you from Mekwus News, Channel 5. Our top story is on Zakondo, the 18-wheeler armed robber who had made away with countless number of 18-wheeler trucks with goods costing millions of dollars to their owners. Fear no more for Zakondo and his gang are now in the military custody. Our correspondence Audrey Somers is live in San Francisco, California. Audrey?

Audrey Somers: Thank you very much Stella. Yes, we have good news for you, and I want you to hear it from the horse's mouth, Captain Zimmerman the leader of this military hunt. Captain?

Zimmerman: Yes, we got him! Zakondo and his gang gave up when they run out of stake to bargain with. We threaten to view the hostages as collateral damage and smoke him and his gang out of the hole, dead or alive, it really doesn't matter to me. I threatened, soon enough, he surrendered, and the few hostages were release with no harm done to them. It is a glorious day! No bloodshed after all.

Audrey Somers: Yes, indeed! It is a glorious day! Take the news to the jungles, Yes, take it to the city! Take it to the country! Yes, even to the suburban! Tell them, Fear no more! For the notorious Zakondo and his infamous gang have been captured and awaiting their fate in the military tribunal. I am so excited! I am Audrey Somers reporting to you live in San Francisco, California, for Mekwus News Channel5. Back to you, Stella.

Florence: They finally catch them. It's about time.

Pamela: Mom, like the news says, no more fear. My friends and I can go wherever we want to go now without fear of those horrible gang. Isn't that so?

Lizzy: Yes, no more fear!

Florence: But you steal have to be very careful out there.

Lizzy: Yes, Mom I will. May I be excuse for now?

Florence: Yes, you may Lizzy.

Lizzy: Thanks Mom. [Lizzy leaves]

Pamela: Mom, I just don't get it.

Florence: Pamela, what don't you get?

Pamela:	I really don't get how to think with my heart and not the mind. Can thinking process take place in the absence of the mind?
Florence:	The mind is not absent my dear; the mind is there monitoring your thinking process. It's just that with the heart you'll feel your thought process. Doing so may help you see yourself in the shoes of others like your sister and I in this case. Thus, asking yourself a fundamental question: if the table should turn placing you in the receiving end, how would you feel?
Pamela:	Mom, I see what you are saying. So, it's about treating others in the same way that we want to be treated.
Florence:	Girl, you got it!
Pamela:	Thanks Mom. I think that I'm ready to apologize from the bottom of my heart to my baby sister. Mom, I am so sorry to have put you and my baby sister through this experience.
Florence:	My baby girl, I accept your apology from the bottom of my Heart.
Pamela:	Thanks Mom. Now I have to figure a way to talk to my baby sister so she can feel the gravity of my apology and make her trust me again.
Florence:	That shouldn't be hard since your sister is an understanding smart girl.
Pamela:	Indeed, Mom. Lizzy is a smart girl indeed. Let me go and look for her. Mom, may I be excuse?
Florence:	Yes, you may, Pamela.
Pamela:	Thanks Mom, see you later.
Florence:	Sure. [Pamela leaves]

9

<u>POVERTY IS A BULLY</u>

Shine the light back on the Ape Family of three. That is, Papa Ape, Mama Ape and their son Rawlings.

Fiorina: Do you folks enjoy the story?

Francesco: I certainly do enjoy it girl. I am glad that the notorious gang and its leader are caught.

Fiorina: Yes, I am glad about that too. Catching that gang alleviates fear from the people. And that is a good thing.

Rawlings: Yes, Mom. That is a good thing.

Francesco: I have to tell you folks something that happen on my way to work this morning.

Fiorina: Yes, tell us pappy.

Francesco: It was a bright shining day. The sun was just right as it complements the cool blowing breeze. O, it was so nice, and it felt so good. On my way to work this morning, I saw a man talking to someone on a cellular telephone outside Greg's coffee shop. Let us call him Jerome. As Jerome was talking, another man going by the name Raymond was also talking to someone on a cellular telephone too. Raymond walked toward the location where Jerome was standing and when he got there, he stood right in front of Jerome, continued his telephone conversation with an increased volume and looking directly at Jerome.

Fiorina: Really? Raymond was rude. I mean it is one thing to stand in front of someone and talking loud on the telephone, which by itself is rude; it is even ruder to stir at someone while talking as if that person you are stirring at is the subject of your telephone conversation.

Francesco: My Darlene, so it seemed at that moment. Jerome was about to ask Raymond in a nice way to move to a different location if he could not keep his voice down in consideration of other people who are trying to enjoy the day. Besides, of all places there are to stand and talk over the phone, why would Raymond want to stand in front of Jerome in the first place? Jerome reasoned. But as Jerome looked intently at Raymond, he observed that Raymond's cellular phone was invisible.

Rawlings: What? Dad, do you mean that Raymond's cellular phone was invisible all that time?

Francesco: Yes, son. Raymond's cellular phone was Invisible to human sight.

Rawlings: But dad, I don't think they've come up with invisible cellular phones yet, have they?

Francesco: No, son. They have not come up with invisible cellular phones yet. But what does that tell you about Raymond using an invisible cellular phone?

Rawlings pauses for few seconds to think about his Dad's question. Then he says

Rawlings: Dad, the only person that could use an invisible cellular phone that has not been invented is someone with loose nuts in his or her mind.

They all laugh simultaneously.

Francesco: Now you can understand why the people who were present at the scene laughed profusely. In fact, their laughter gave it away to Jerome who finally figure out that Raymond must be having some mental issues. Therefore, instead of asking Raymond to move to a different location if he could not keep his voice down in consideration of other people who are trying to enjoy the day, can you guess what Jerome did?

Fiorina: Jerome moved to a different location without a word.

Francesco: Exactly, my love. While people were still laughing, Jerome moved to a different location leaving Raymond alone. Raymond continued his conversation with his imaginary friend over his imaginary or invisible cellular telephone.

Rawlings: Dad, that is so hilarious.

Fiorina: Yes Indeed, it is hilarious.

Francesco: Thank you very much my people. It is my pleasure to entertain you.

Rawlings: But Dad, was anyone able to make out what Raymond was saying over his imaginary cellular phone?

Francesco: Yes, son. Some of what Raymond said was Comprehensible.

Rawlings: Really?

Francesco: Yes, really. Part of what Raymond said was that the life of his entire family was threatened by drug dealers. He also said that those drug dealers and gangsters killed his wife and children and he was getting ready to go and kill all of them for destroying his family.

Fiorina: What? Pappy, you mean Raymond's family was assassinated by drug dealers and none of the people who heard him could help him by calling the police?

Francesco: Sweetheart, you are forgetting one important information. Raymond is mentally challenged.

Fiorina: You mean Raymond is really crazy?

Francesco: Of course, he is really mentally disabled or at least that is what he wants people to think just so they would give him handouts for being homeless.

Fiorina: Seriously?

Francesco: One thing for sure is that Raymond is a well-dressed homeless person who treks from street to street and city to city in search of his daily bread. Yes, if you live or work in the city of Rosemary or in Manchester city, you should have come across a six feet and seven-inch man with an untrimmed bearded face who usually wears a long khaki or tan colored trench coat come rain or shine.

Rawlings: Dad, did you just describe Raymond?

Francesco: Yes, son. I just did. Remember, I left out the race of the two men because it's not about race. People of all races seem to have the same problems like homelessness, poverty, mental anguish, and ailments. These are all global problems that face the human race today.

Rawlings: Raymond always talk to himself.

Francesco: Actually, he talks to himself only when he comes across people just so they'll think he is crazy and disabled.

Rawlings: But why would he want to do that Dad?

Fiorina: Rawlings, the simple answer to that question is that Raymond wants people to think that he is mentally disabled and hence cannot work. By doing so, people would show him mercy by giving money or as your Dad would call it handouts to him.

Rawlings: Really?

Francesco: Yes, really. It may be the case that Raymond is really mentally challenged. However, when he is alone, he barely talks to himself. But as soon as he draws closer to where people are, he starts talking to himself. Those who have closely observed this behavior from Raymond do not think that he has mental problems. To such ones, Raymond is a bad actor who begs for a living; certainly not mentally Challenged.

Fiorina: As situation gets critical, it becomes difficult to blame people like Raymond who feel that they must put up a show of deception to get a buck or two; yes, to make a living.

Rawlings: Mom, isn't that something?

Fiorina: Certainly, son. It certainly is.

Are My Children My Parents' Children too?

Rawlings: Hey Dad?

Francesco: Yes, son.

Rawlings: Telling great stories is one of those things you can do better than I can. There is one thing that I can do better than you, Dad.

Francesco: What might that be, son?

Rawlings: You know how you have only one child and I have seven children?

Francesco: That is correct, son.

Rawlings: Dad, why don't we throw a party to the villagers and count our children in their presence? Whosoever has the most children will be declared the winner. Dad, what do you think?

Francesco: I think that is a good idea.

They quickly made arrangement to have the villagers present and the party is on. What turns out to be a joke is now reality. Well, Rawlings is given the honor to count his children first, thus granting Francesco's request.

Chairman: Rawlings, you have the floor.

Rawlings: Thank you Mr. Chairman and thanks to everyone for honoring our invitation. I will start by counting Leslie, Samson, Dakota, David, Isabella, Gershom, and Rebel. I counted seven of my children. Dad, I believe it is your turn to count your child.

Here Rawlings is confidence that his father will lose because he only has one child, Rawlings. Rawlings is however, in for a surprise.

Chairman: Rawlings has seven children. Now let us yield the floor to Francesco, Rawlings' father. Francesco.

Francesco:	Mr. Chairman, I want to thank you so very much for Coming. Our guests the villagers, I cannot thank you well enough for coming even at a time that you are all so busy. It shows that you find us worthy of your love and deep respect. We love and deep respect for you too. Respect.
Villagers:	Respect.
Francesco:	We are here to count my children.
Rawlings:	Dad, you are here to count your child. So, let us get on with it just so I can claim my victory.
Francesco:	Patience my son, patience. Patience is beneficial. Now, I will start by counting Rawlings my son, Filomena his wife, Leslie, Samson, Dakota, David, Isabella, Gershom, and Rebel. So, my children are nine in number.
Rawlings:	Whoa! whoa! whoa! whoa! Time out, Time out, Time out, Time out, Time out! What is happening here? Why is my Dad counting my children and wife as his children?
Chairman:	Because they are his children just as you are his child.
Rawlings:	But why? My Dad did not give birth to them or cause their birth like I did, did he?
Chairman:	Well, think about it. Without you would your children Have come into existence?
Rawlings:	No, my children will not have come into existence without me.

Chairman:	Good. Now, would you have come into existence without your Father?
Rawlings:	No. I would not have come into existence without my Dad.
Chairman:	Good. Since your father caused your birth to where you come into existence and you caused the birth of your children to where they come into existence, won't you conclude that your father actually caused the existence of your children, hence their grandfather?
Rawlings:	If you put it like that, yes, my children are my Dad's grandchildren. Congratulations to you, Dad. Francesco: Thanks son. I am glad that you finally got the point. Rawlings: Yes, Dad I did get the point.
Francesco:	Son, don't beat yourself up. You see, "experience is the best teacher" and because I was once your age I can empathize with you and I promise you son, as you watch your children grow to where they get marry, you would acquire most of the experience necessary to make you see things my way.
Rawlings:	Dad, I know it's going to take some time for me to catch up with you and I will continue to do my best to pay attention to your teachings.
Francesco:	Son, can the Partridge bird find out where the Cattle-egret white feathered bird washes itself?
Rawlings:	I don't think that I have any idea or am I equipped well enough to answer that question. However, based on how you phrased the question, Dad, I can only guess that the Partridge bird cannot find out

where the Cattle-egret white feathered bird washes.

Francesco: Son, you guessed right. Where the Cattle-egret white feathered bird washes, the Partridge bird will never know. But does it mean that the Partridge bird is completely out of hope to be as clean as the Cattle-egret white feathered bird?

Rawlings: Only if the Cattle-egret white feathered bird wants to teach the Partridge bird how to be clean would the Partridge bird not be out of hope completely.

Francesco: Son, you have answered correctly. The Partridge bird can learn to be as clean as the Cattle-egret white feathered bird by following the Cattle-egret white feathered bird where ever it goes with a humble heart, attentiveness, and readiness to obey the Cattle-egret white feathered bird.

Rawlings: Wow! Dad, that is deep.

Francesco: The same quality is expected of a student in a teacher-student relationship, of a child in a parent-child relationship, and in any kind of relationship that involves teaching and learning. Therefore, you will be successful more that I could ever be if you pay constant attention to the teachings of parents - yes, your Mom and Dad with deepest respect regardless of your age.

Rawlings: Dad, I cannot thank you well enough and I will always be in your debt. My prayer is that you and my Mom will be there for your grandchildren as you have been there for me.

Francesco: Son, be rest assured that your Mom and I will always be there for you and our grandchildren.

Rawlings: I believe so Dad. Thank you very much Dad. I am proud and fortunate to have you and Mom as my Parents.

Francesco: Son, we are very proud to be your parents too.

Filomena: Hey Rawlings, could you be a Darlene and help that man being chase by his own Rottweiler?

Rawlings: What? You mean that is his dog chasing him?

Filomena: Yes, it is. In fact, it's a long story. The short version is that Tyrese was playing with the dog at one time. During that time, Tyrese fed the dog with a juicy steak in which the owner wasn't too grateful for as he contended that he doesn't like his dog to be fed by strangers or anyone other than him. One thing led to another and the misunderstanding between Tyrese and Mambo was in place. Before you know it, Mambo, the owner of the dog gave a command to his dog to attack Tyrese. When Tyrese observed that the dog had refused the owner's Command, Tyrese gave the dog his own command to attack Mambo. What do you know? There goes the Rottweiler chasing his own master. Please, sweet Rawlie, kindly help the man from his own dog. Would you?

Rawlings: Sure. Give me a minute and I'll be right back.

This time, the dog is all over Mambo and you could hear Mambo asking for help to stop his dog from the attack. Rawlings and Tyrese help to rid Mambo of his vicious dog. Rawlings figures a way to reunite Mambo with his dog one of which is to make sure that Mambo does not exhibit any hint of fear to go close to his dog with a huge reward like juicy steak on his hand. Then Francesco gives his admonitions on being nice to animals.

Francesco: When you think about it for a moment, you'll realize that the dog was nice to Tyrese because Tyrese fed the dog with a nice juicy steak and we cannot say the same for Mambo the owner of the dog who may have not fed the dog for quite a while.

Filomena: I thought dogs are supposed to be faithful to their owners regardless of whether or not they are maltreated.

Rawlings: Obviously not. As you've seen for yourself there has been a transfer of power in the chain of command to a stranger Tyrese, who was nice to the dog and his command was carried out by the dog against his own master.

Francesco: All in all, you should be nice to these animals if you want to get control of them at all times in most cases. Remember, I said in most cases because there are some extenuating circumstances in which my premise may be rendered futile. Remember, animals in general act on instinct not on love like we do, and a Rottweiler is no difference. Furthermore, some dogs have impulse control – the ability of a dog to do things that he generally would not want to do.

Filomena: I kind of agree with you Dad, but I think I need more clarification.

Francesco: Filomena my dear, let me give you an example. Do animals have morals like we do?

Filomena: I will say no, they don't.

Francesco: Think about rape for a moment. If someone tells you that your dog raped her dog, would she be taken seriously?

Filomena: Of course not. That is what animals do. I mean, animals don't give you notice that they want to do something like that, they just do it.

Rawlings: And because that terrible behavior has been accepted for quite a while, it becomes "the norm." That is, the acceptable normal thing to do - the banality of evil.

Francesco: Are you saying that a time is coming when mankind would finally accept rape as "the norm" because it has been practiced for such a long time?

Rawlings: Of course not, Dad. That behavior is barbaric, animalistic, vandalistic, wicked, mean, and every disgusting thing that is against the very fiber and the magnitude of love.

Francesco: Son, it is not my intention to get you started. But it is clear to me that you get the point on the fact that animals do not act on love like humans do. They act on instinct. If we bring the behavior of the animal world into that of mankind, would it not be chaotic?

Filomena: Certainly. It would be chaotic. So, the Rottweiler was acting upon its instinct to be nice to those who are nice to the dog and be mean to those who are not nice to him. That is the reason why the dog was nice to a stranger like Tyrese for his kindness but mean even to his owner. Yes, some dogs can be trained to control their impulses or instincts.

Francesco: Exactly. So, when people say that my dog loves me.

Filomena: They really mean that based on their dogs' trained instinct of being treated nicely and feeding them at the right time, they obey their owners' command. The reverse would be the case if treated harshly.

Rawlings: You got it, girl.

Fiorina: All right boys, let's pay attention to our guests now.

The Francesco family gets back to the guests.

10

<u>A FAMILY BULLY IS A HOUND DOG</u>

It is a bright day and the sun shines on the institution of higher learning in Berkeley, California where students, faculty members and staffs are having their lunch breaks. While some choose to have lunch in their offices, some choose the cafeteria lounges and others prefer the outside open space which allows them to bond with nature as they consume their meal. In the midst of those uncontrollable noises, everyone is able to count the number of times that the bell from the huge clock on the tower rings. Yes, they are all right. The bell rings twelve times signifying that it is twelve noon, which means that it is lunch time.

Kachi Meets Pamela

Kachi is a quiet, shy but an intelligent young man. He is having his lunch alone as usual at one of the restaurants in the college campus that he is attending. As he enjoys his meal with his face on a computer science book that he's glancing through, a young lady by the name Pamela approaches. So far, we know little about Pamela in the past chapters and we are about to find out more. There is an empty chair at Kachi's table and as he enjoys his meal, Pamela asks with a gentle airy voice. Shall we listen in on their conversation? I agree with you. Let's do that.

Pamela: Excuse me, is this seat taken?

Kachi: [his eyes are still buried on the book] No, kindly help yourself to it.

Pamela: Well, thanks. [Pamela takes the sit] By the way, I am Chiyem. Pamela Chiyem, a senior in the Psychiatry Department, UC San Francisco Medical school. What is your name if I may ask?

Kachi: [He finally takes his eyes off the book and look up to see a beautiful lady, a kind he has never seen before. So, he says] Wow, God has sent me a visitor from heaven. Angel, are you from heaven?

Pamela: The name is Pamela. The answer to your question if I'm from heaven, I do not know about that.

Kachi: You are so beautifully made and there are no imperfections in what I'm looking at. But what are you doing sitting in front of me?

Pamela: First, thanks for the compliment. I ask earlier if the chair was taken to which you said I should help myself to it, and I did. I introduced myself to you as Pamela Chiyem and I am hoping that you will do the same anytime now.

Kachi: Well, I am running out of words...

Pamela: Why don't you start by telling me your name?

Kachi: [with a smile on] That is a good idea. My name is Onyekachi Chimebelem. My friends call me Kachi.

Pamela: Then I will call you Kachi since I want you to consider me as a friend. Is that OK with you, Kachi?

Kachi: Sure. No problem at all, Pamela.

Pamela: Oh, I like that. So, what is your major course of study?

Kachi: Computer Science. Yes, I know that there are those who consider it as a boring major, but I find it

	fascinating. The way we use computer to model or simulate real life object can be amazing.
Pamela:	I am not one of those who view Computer Science as boring. In my years of studies, I've observed that any course of studies can be both boring and interesting. It depends on what you are doing at that point in time, how long it takes to do it and whether or not it would yield exciting results.
Kachi:	Yes, that is true. What I find interesting is that when designing a program, enter the code into the computer and when I run it successfully, I share the feeling that God had after creating the universe and found that it was good. I am usually elated about that.
Pamela:	The most important thing is to enjoy what you do, because if you don't, you would be like a piece of paper blown about by the wind and never satisfied with what you have.
Kachi:	I hear you Pamela. I agree with you totally.

Gouging Prescription Price Is Bullying The Affected Ones

Kachi and Pamela's informal date isn't over just yet as we see them walk toward the main street. As they do, they see a gathered group of people listening to a middle-aged bearded Caucasian man arguing with a middle-aged Asian man about how gouging prescription price should be illegal. While the Asian man argues against the gouging of prescription price as an inhumane behavior, the Caucasian man however, vigorously argues that so long as the people are willing to pay the price thus creating the demand for it, the congress must not criminalize the gouging of prescription price. When the Asian man ask the Caucasian man how he would feel if his mother is to be part of the victims of prescription price gouging, the

Caucasian man responds by making the following statement: "I cannot hear you when you are shouting! Why don't you go back to Asia if you don't like how things are run here?" The Asian man makes it clear that he is as much a citizen of this country as anyone else is. So, he is staying to fight the injustices against humanity. The Caucasian man responds by making fists and saying: "bring it on! If it is fight you want, don't keep me waiting. Let's get it on!" The crowd intervene as the two men are about to get down on it.

One may not be able to successfully put up an argument for the gouging of prescription price since the principle behind the gouging must be considered as stealing from the infirm. Yes, the gouging of prescription price is nothing short of bullying the infirm.

Stores That Dupe Their Customers are Bullies

There are two different products of interest. The first product is "Plantain (Fufu) Flour" made from 100% dehydrated Plantain, which you make Plantain Fufu out of by stirring Plantain Flour in a boiling water – people who are concern about their health love this product for its natural vitamins, taste, and its inability to spike the blood level. So, it sells like a hot cake. The second product is "Yam (Elubo/Amala) Flour" made from 100% dehydrated tropical African yam tuba, which you make Amala or yam fufu out of by stirring the Yam Flour in a boiling water – not many people buy this product characterized by fewer patronage - not as much as they buy Plantain (fufu) flour. The interesting thing is that the price of Plantain (fufu) Flour is almost triple the price of Yam (Elubo/Amala) flour. That is, Plantain (fufu) Flour cost $14.99 for a five pounds package while Yam (Elubo/Amala) flour cost $5.99 for a five pounds package.

Can you see if you can relate to the following scenario? You are in an Asian (Chinese) store, shopping. Suddenly you see what you have been looking for quite a while because of its scarcity. Let us call the product "Plantain (Fufu) Flour." On the package is an inscription "100% Plantain" and that is what you want. Each package weighs five pounds or 2.267 Kilograms. You happily buy four packages of the product and take them home. At home, you open three of the four packages and pour them in a nice container for better storage. The next day is here, it is lunch time and guess what you are dying to have for lunch? Yes, the Plantain fufu. So, you bring the water to a boiling point, pour four cups of the Plantain (fufu) flour inside the boiling water and as you stir the content, to your dismay, you observe that the product you had initially thought to be 100% Plantain flour out of which Plantain fufu is made, isn't Plantain flour but, tropical African "Yam (Elubo/Amala) Flour" made from 100% dehydrated African Yam tuba – a product that you do not want. How would you feel about this dilemma? Remember, you have already opened three bags which you cannot return to the store for a refund and since they are not what you want, you going to have to throw them away at loss. You were able to calm yourself from the frustration of the whole experience.

You take the last package that has not been open and the three empty packages with your receipt and head out to see the manager of the Asian (Chinees) store who can barely speak in English language as much as you can barely speak in Chinees language. Since there are no translators, you tried the best you could to explain to the store manager that the product the store had sold to you was the wrong product – it was actually "Yam (Elubo/Amala) Flour" packaged as "Plantain (Fufu) Flour" which ought to be a criminal act in the United States of America. The store manager's argument was that the manufacturer packaged the product as such. So, the store manager refunded $14.99 to you for the unopened package, and the rest three opened packages? Your loss. Is losing $44.99 fair to you, especially when you are not at fault? You let it go because you feel that it does not worth the effort to pursue the matter any further. Then you wonder if Asian (Chinese) stores operate on a different set of rules that allow them to get away with such dishonest business practices that do not exist among the conventional American stores.

Interestingly, you are not the only person this store has been steeling from. For some unknown reason, this store was able to get empty packages from the manufacturer bearing all the inscriptions to advertise a product as Plantain (Fufu) Flour. Then, the Asian (Chinese) store will repackage the unsold Yam (Elubo/Amala) Flour that have been sitting there on the shelf and no one is buying, as Plantain (Fufu) Flour at a higher price. You will think you are buying Plantain (fufu) Flour at a higher price and will not know the truth until you open up the package at home, cook it and realize it isn't Plantain (fufu) Flour. The catch is, once the package is opened, it cannot be returned for a refund. The rule of not returning an opened package for a refund should only apply to packages that are correctly advertised. That is, the package has the correct product that it advertised. Packages that are incorrectly advertised, that is, the package contains the wrong product, should be considered as criminal, which is bullying the customers.

The District Attorney ought to prosecute stores that dupe their customers by falsely advertising a product to fool the customers. This is a case where you will say "fool me once, shame on you. Fool me twice, shame on me." But I'll say "fool me once, shame on you. Fool me twice, shame on you. Fool me many times, shame on you many times." This is so because no store should have the business of fooling its customers for profiteering. Someday, Asian (Chinese) stores and their allies will be brought to justice for duping their customers in the United States of America and wherever they operate. What a bully!

Pamela's Childhood Ordeal

Pamela is dating this young man she met in college. The interesting thing is that in shielding herself from the physical and psychological pain she suffered from the hands of her Uncle and her Uncle's friends since she was a toddler until preteen, Pamela is afraid to get involve with anyone for fear that such involvement may lead to an unwanted relationship. Pamela creates a formidable wall to shield her from people whose view is clearly to have a relationship with her. Unlike a so-called "normal girl," Pamela is not interested in dating even though she has the cravings of a normal girl and very beautiful. If you are thinking that Pamela's parents ought to have helped Pamela through years of therapy when she was a tween (or a preteen), your thought is in order.

An exception to that thought is that Pamela's parents at the time, do not have the knowledge and the technical knowhow to decipher the anguish that Pamela will suffer then, now, and in the future if her condition does not receive the proper treatment on time. Be that as it may, Pamela seems to be doing well at home and at school. In fact, she is an "A-student"[26] and usually the teacher's favorite because of her smart participation in class lectures. There is no wonder why Pamela's relatives and friends who knew about her childhood trauma could not see beyond the wall surrounding our dear Pamela.

Pamela is now nineteen and a senior in a prestigious university – the University of California San Francisco Medical School, department of Psychiatry. Her childhood trauma drove her to choose Psychiatry as a major course of study. Kachi her friend, is also a senior in the Computer Science department at the University of California, Berkeley. Pamela is yet to introduce Kachi to her family and so is Kachi in honor of Pamela's request who want to wait until the dating becomes promising.

Kachi And Pamela On A Dinner Date At A Restaurant

Kachi invites Pamela to a dinner date at a nice restaurant on the ocean in Berkeley, California - the City and State in which the university they are both attending resides. Pamela joyfully accepts the invitation. Prior to the dinner date, Kachi had made contact earlier with the restaurant requesting that the flower bouquet he had ordered for Pamela be brought in about ten minutes after they had sat down and begun feasting. Kachi had the restaurant's management put a diamond fourteen carat gold engagement ring inside a little envelope attached to the flower bouquet. Pamela will see the ring when she opens the envelope.

At the restaurant, the waitress leads Kachi and Pamela to their table next to a window. On the table sit two burning candles with the restaurant's lights already set for a romantic dinner for couples. Looking out through the six feet by six feet window is the beautiful ocean turning its waves into beautiful songs if you listen carefully. Kachi pulls out a chair for Pamela to sit and he plants a kiss on her forehead. Pamela gives Kachi the priceless smile and Kachi reciprocates the smile with a bowing gesture before taking his sit. Let's listen to their conversation. Shall we?

Kachi: Girl, you are ravishing! In fact, you make that dress look awesome! Nothing of this Earth is as beautiful as you, my girl.

Pamela: [Pamela blinks her eyes with an inviting smile] Thank you Kachi. You are not bad looking either. This is a nice restaurant. How did you find it?

Kachi: I have my ways, baby girl.

Pamela: It's very nice. I like it.

Kachi: Thanks. I'm glad you do. Would you like a glass of "Mekwus unadulterated pure red wine?"

Pamela: Sure. I certainly would. Now, you are not trying to get me drunk, are you?

Kachi: On the contrary, I need you to have a hundred percent control of yourself.

Pamela: You know I was kidding right?

Kachi: Oh, are you?

Pamela: Of course, I am. It will take two or three of those glasses to get me drunk. Besides, I love Mekwus unadulterated pure red, red wine. The thing is, I have projects due this week and so I cannot afford to get drunk just yet. Hey Kachi, can you see what I'm looking at?

Kachi: Do you mean that waitress walking towards us with a flower bouquet?

Pamela: Yes. That is one beautiful flower bouquet.

Kachi: Do you really think so, baby girl?

Pamela: Yes. I know so. But she's walking towards me. Are you kidding me? Do you mean the flower bouquet is for me?

Kachi: Yes, Pamela it's for you.

Pamela: Wow! It's so beautiful.

Kachi: Yes, but you are much more beautiful than the flowers do.

Pamela: Wow! Thank you so much. The flower bouquet is so beautiful. I cannot believe it.

Kachi: Do you like it?

Pamela: Are you kidding? I love it! I love it! I love it! Thank you so much Kachi.

Kachi: You are welcome my baby girl. Would you like to open the envelope and read the card?

Pamela: Sure. I love to.

Pamela opens the envelope and pulls out the card and the diamond ring falls on the table. Pamela is elated as Kachi put the ring on her finger and reads the card.

The Proposal That Leads To Pamela's Revelation

Kachi: Pamela, I have known you for quite a while and you have become the girl that my humble yet dignified heart aches for. In my book, Pamela, you are worth more than a million wives and concubines combine. Not even King Solomon in all of his glory would be as fortunate as I am if you will do me the honor to be my love, yes, my best friend forever. Pamela, would you be my love?

Even in her elated state, tears rain down Pamela's eyes as she remembers her childhood trauma.

Kachi: Pamela, why are you crying? A simple no would have suffice. I'm a big boy you know. I can take disappointments.

Pamela: Kachi, you don't understand. I am not saying no because I want to. The thing is, if you know the real me, you won't want me.

Kachi: Pamela, please do not tell me that you are a prostitute. Are you?

Pamela: No! I am not! How are you going to sit there and ask me such a crazy question, Kachi?

Kachi: Hey, don't blame me. You said if I know you, I won't want You. I'm only asking question about the things I won't want in a lady that I want to get close to. OK?

Pamela: You are right and I'm sorry, Kachi.

Kachi: That's all right Pamela. So, did you kill someone?

Pamela: No!

Kachi: Did you murder your parents?

Pamela: No! Are you serious, murder my parents?

Kachi: Then there is nothing you can tell me that will make me not to want you. Everything else can be worked out with love and God's beauty. So, baby girl, what is bothering you? Share your pain with me, would you?

Pamela: [Pamela asks Kachi to come closer, then she whispers to his ear] When I was a preteen, my Uncle and his friends raped me. Down to this day, I don't know how to deal with the trauma neither do I know how to move on with my life. I didn't tell you this before because I value our friendship so dearly and I thought that you will dissolve our friendship when you find out about this dark side of my life. I did not tell my parents or anyone until I was eighteen because I thought it was my fault and I'll be blamed for it.

Kachi's Consolation And Admonition To Pamela

Kachi: Pamela, thank you so much for confiding in me. I know that it is not easy for you to open up your heart and tell that to me. Like I said earlier, there is nothing you can say that will make me not to want you.

Pamela: Thanks for understanding, Kachi.

Kachi: Now that you have open your heart to me, I want you even more than ever before.

Pamela: Are you serious?

Kachi: Baby girl, don't you ever close your precious heart to me especially in the face of hardship. Pamela, we are in this together and if it is any consolation to you, my mother suffered the same ordeal when she was that age.

Pamela: Really?

Kachi: Yes, really. So, you see my fair lady, you are not alone. You cannot be alone. Yes, we will put our heads together to battle that dreadful pain. Baby girl, if you have never believed anything before, believe this: together, we will come up victorious over that dreadful ordeal. Remember, my dear one, a single lion does not stand a chance against a hippopotamus or a rhinoceros. Collectively however, a group of lions working together in unity can defeat the hippopotamus or rhinoceros.

Pamela: Kachi, that is an amazing statement. Thank you for that thought. I did not know that your Mom has gone through so much odds in her life.

Kachi: Yes, she has. It's not something she likes to talk about or even discuss because as far as she's concerned she is not going to let those bad people posing themselves as family members to have a hold on her nor define her future neither would she let them deprive her of her inner joy and happiness. She's just going to concentrate on her God, her husband, and her Children.

Pamela: That is so wonderful. How's that been working out for her?

Kachi: One of the many things that my Dad appreciate about my Mom is that she always looks up to my Dad for affection and accept my Dad's affection with the deepest respect and loving attitude regardless of how sad the day may have gone.

Pamela: Kachi, what do you mean by that?

Kachi:	My Mom is a very beautiful and industrious woman. As a Vice President of a large conglomerate corporation, it is safe for me to say that she makes more money than my Dad does. But she always shows my Dad that she needs him so much especially for spiritual and emotional affection through constant hugging, kissing, and saying beautiful things like "I love you more," "without you my love, my existence would have no meaning," "you are my love, my life, my heart, my blood and the better half that completes me." Of course, my Dad reciprocates that loving gesture in a large way that blows her mind every time.

Pamela:	Wow! That is so loving and nice. It seems the elephant has climbed out of its quandary in your Mom's case. Good for her!

Kachi:	Pamela, my Mom and Dad never give each other any reason for unwholesome jealousy through flirting or doing horrible things that people who have no regard for the institution of marriage do. You know how people get emotional with their coworkers and have countless reasons for doing so, my parents see that behavior as abomination. They give each other the priceless peace of mind that I wish to have when I get married.

Pamela:	Kachi, I am sure you will.

Kachi:	Oh, you think so?

Pamela:	I know so, Kachi. You are a very good man and don't let anyone tell you otherwise. By the way, our parents share the same values and I'm sure that they'll be fond of each other because birds of the same feathers usually flock together.

Kachi: Thank you very much my dear lady.

Pamela: You are welcome, Kachi. Is your Mom implacable or pliable?

Kachi: My Mom is implacable with deep respect; she is pliable only to the highest of the highest, the Most High God. She always asks my Dad to include our God in their decision-making process. My Dad appreciates it like crazy.

Pamela: How is that working out for them?

Kachi: In a surpassingly amazing way. My parents have really been enjoying their marriage for the past fifty years. On several occasions that I peeped into their bedroom during the night, it seemed like they can't get their hands off of each other.

Pamela: Seriously?

Kachi: O yes, seriously. Ever since I know them, their down time has been ten minutes and not more.

Pamela: Down time? What do you mean by the term "down time?"

Kachi: When they are upset at each other, ten minutes later my Mom and Dad become friends again and they'll behave as if nothing had happened a priori. Down time is the period of time that my Mom and Dad chose not to speak to each other because they are upset at each other.

Pamela: That is amazing, and it tells me that your Mom has overcome her childhood ordeal.

Kachi: I think so. Like you said earlier, the elephant has climbed out of its quandary. As a matter fact you can ask her when both of you become friends. I'm

	sure she won't mind. Pamela. My Mom is not going to fit into any of the templates for rape victims that you are learning about at school. You see my dear, my Dad helped my Mom to see the need to rely on God as her personal doctor and therapist.
Pamela:	Really? How is that working out for them?
Kachi:	Considering the way things are ever since I was born, I'll say It has been working out for them really well. In fact, I once ask my Mom why she's so different from most married women that I've seen. I mean, her deep respect and her deep love for my Dad is unique. You know what she said?
Pamela:	No, I don't.
Kachi:	She said that she's not doing anything extraordinary other than gladly obeying the institutor of marriage who is indeed our most high God. She also said that as she enjoys giving my Dad his dues, my Dad enjoys doing the same for her in line with the Holy Scriptures. Then she reminded me of our neighbor who suffered from intra-familial molestation as she did; things are not going well with the woman and her husband because the woman could not separate her husband from her childhood rapists.
Pamela:	Seriously?
Kachi:	Yes, seriously. My Mom said that it is a big problem for a married couple to go through if you cannot separate your spouse from your offender. Think about it, Pamela, your molesters are your offenders.
Pamela:	That is true.

Kachi: Pamela, how would you relate to your spouse if you are not seeing eye-to-eye leading to constant argument and disagreement, won't you see him as an offender?

Pamela: Kachi, I see your point.

Kachi: My Mom explained it to me that when she and my Dad have a heated-up argument, she relates my Dad to her childhood molesters. When, that happens, she'll pray deeply about it. Thereafter, she tells herself that while her molesters' actions are based on hatred, my Dad's love for her is deeper than the abyss. So, she'll immediately hug my Dad, both express their apologies and life goes on amicably.

Pamela: That tells me that married couples, especially those ones that suffered from intra-familial rape or any other kind, should curb the urge of blaming their spouses of any miss happenings. They must come to a realization that their spouses are definitely not their offenders. By so doing, they will not be re-living the past. I know that is a sensitive issue. But like your Mom, it can be done.

Kachi: It certainly can be done. It is sad because there are those that do not see it that way.

Pamela: Really?

Kachi: Yes, Really. Pamela, I know of some who were raped by people they trusted during childhood like their Uncles, nieces, even fathers and mothers.

Pamela: Hew! That is just gross!

Banality Of Evil

Kachi: Because such ones did not get the needed help like intense therapies to wean them out of the thought that there is nothing out there better than the kind of lifestyle they were involuntarily exposed to, and because the ordeal has been going on for such a long time, it becomes normal and acceptable to such ones. Such that having and keeping a relationship with the opposite sex can be daunting, if not impossible.

Pamela: Kachi, that is a plausible thought.

Kachi: There are those who would consider that behavior as normal. Others are coming up with different forms of relationships the end of which are not in sight.

Pamela: So because nobody does anything to help them and since it's been going on for such a long time, the ordeal may become normal to the victims.

Kachi: You can say that. Normal with much sadness. Pamela: That sounds like the "banality of evil"[19]. In fact, much has been written about it by scholars in the fields of Psychology and Philosophy.

Kachi: Seriously?

Pamela: Yes, Kachi seriously. The banality of evil is characterized by a belief that what one is doing is not evil, rather, his action is a behavior that has been made normal by the society of his residence. The horrendous behavior of such evildoers is no longer considered as evil but normal and acceptable to that society.

Kachi: You can imagine that if no one blows a whistle against such demonically induced behavior, the damage will continue to where it affects relationships and the inability to really love someone and let yourself to be loved by someone. Your home that supposed to be your haven warmed up with love becomes so cold and shallow that you want to scream. There are those who would see that cold condition as normal and you said it right – the banality of evil.

Pamela: I cannot imagine not given the proper due to whom it is due.

Kachi: Pamela, what do you mean?

Pamela: I am just thinking about that cold and shallow behavior in some married peoples' home. I mean, how can you love or in the least, give your romantic love to someone who has not been pledge to you in marriage but withhold it from someone who had? I just cannot see the logic in that behavior.

Kachi: Pamela my dear, you cannot see the logic in that behavior because there is none to see. That behavior is just plain evil, hence, cold, and shallow. The banality of evil.

Pamela: Indeed, it is. One of my friends let me know that the reason why her parents broke up was the lack of affection that plagued their marriage and that as they lay in bed every night the gap between her parents got wider and wider each night until they fell out of the bed.

Kachi: That is so sad. Maybe her parents did not see the need to close the gap before it is too late if they truly love each other.

Pamela: My friend also said that they always fight about the fact that her mother had her youth taken away from her when she was a youngster by her Uncle. I asked her if her parents went through therapy, she said no, they did not. Then I asked if her Mom did see a therapist when she was younger. She said when she asked her Mom about that, her Mom said she did not because they did not see it as something that can pose potential problems to future relationships back then when her Mom was younger. Besides, they probably couldn't afford the needed countless number of therapies.

Kachi: Who knows? That may have helped them not to dwell in the past since the ability of not dwelling in the past would have helped them to move forward unitedly.

Pamela: Kachi, how does your Dad feel about your Mom's expression of emotional affection to him?

Kachi: Although he never wins a sweepstakes before, on a daily basis however, my Dad feels like a sweepstakes winner. I believe that if anything should happen to my Mom, my Dad may end his own life. I just cannot see him living without my Mom.

Pamela: Wow! Isn't that real and strong, Kachi?

Kachi: It is stronger than you can imagine, my dear one.

Pamela: I can tell that your Mom is going to be my best friend.

Kachi: Not that I am jealous, but I would like to be the one. I mean, I want to be your best friend, you know?

Pamela: Kachi, you are my best friend already!

Kachi: Oh, OK.

Pamela: Kachi, I am so crushed by what my Uncle and his friends did to me. They hurt me so badly that I had to shield myself from the outside world.

Kachi: I am so sorry that you had to go through that horrible treatment from someone you trusted. Hurtful feeling is a terrible thing to bear alone. Pamela, hurtful feeling can be likening to a viral infection (endemic or pandemic influenza) whose cycle may be up to two weeks or even more. If your doctor does not see the need to prescribe an antibiotic medication for your consumption, maybe because he thought prescribing such medication at this point in time may not be wise, he may however, make recommendations for over- the-counter medications for your consumption to make you feel comfortable during the viral cycle. In the same line of thought, when experienced and mature men and women who have your best interest at heart do come to your aide with practical admonitions devoid of self-promoting views that lack divine wisdom, your hurtful feelings may tend to dissipate, if not completely eradicate.

Pamela: That is so true.

Kachi: Alas! Your hurtful feelings are being replaced with a sense of elation and gratitude to have such selfless mature men and women as friends. Then you'll realize the true meaning to the phrase "no man is an island" and your fellow human can indeed, be your clothing.

Pamela: I believe you, Kachi. I am just afraid that in pleasing you, I may fall short because my heart has been torn apart by someone I trusted. I feel like I have nothing to give you, Kachi.

Kachi: Pamela my dear girl, you have a lot to give me. You just don't know it. I want to stand in place of those experienced and mature men and women that you have not been fortunate enough to have all those years. I need you, Pamela.

Pamela: Really? Do you, Kachi?

Kachi: Yes, of course I do. Pamela, the simplest way to explain the fact that with all our many challenges in life, we have some goodness in us that others can benefit from if we let them is through an illustration.

Pamela: Seriously? Please explain it to me. Kachi, would you?

Kachi: Consider the termites' colony. The Soldiers termites have large jaws or mandibles and poisonous glands to protect the colony, but they cannot care for themselves. Therefore, they must be fed and groomed by the worker termites. The Worker termites do all the work in the colony including the construction of new tunnels, caring for the young, and grooming the soldier termites but they do not have wings to fly nor do they have jaws to fight. The Queen and King termites are the reproductive of the colony. They are founders of new colonies by using their swarmers who have developed wings to fly out and form new colonies. But they cannot build nor protect the colony. What does that tell you?

Pamela: Well, that tells me that the soldiers, the workers, the king and queen termites cannot survive individually. They all need each other to survive. They can only survive collectively.

Kachi: Exactly! There you go. No man is an island. We need someone to lean on as much as someone needs us to lean on regardless of how terrible we may think we are; we don't want to be an island. We are a community of talented people. Like termites, we need each other.

Pamela: I totally agree with you Kachi. Especially when you put it like that, you cannot get an argument from me. I agree with you.

Kachi: Pamela, it is quite understandable why some relationship should be scary since they can be likened to risk-taking, which can sometimes be a failing adventure. However, before we see a blue feathered woodcock bird like the blue feathered Cardinals[28], Great Blue Turaco or the Blue Grosbeak[28], our eyes will hit the blue dye of its plumage. Before we see a red feathered species of woodcock bird like the red feathered Cardinals[28], Scarlet Ibis or the Ruddy Kingfisher or even the Rose finch birds, our eyes will hit the red dye of its plumage. Without the existence of the Cattle-egret, a white feathered bird, no one would have appreciated the importance and the value of pure white especially, in clothing.

Pamela: What? What are you saying?

Kachi: Well, that simply means that without bitter taste, no one would have appreciated a sweet taste and without failure, success would have been taken for granted. The rareness of gold gives it its enduring value. What is more, the size of an object does not equate the degree of the appreciation for its value. It takes an effort to catch sight with the Blue Grosbeak for instance. When we do, our appreciation for beauty increases enormously. Pamela, we all need someone. Yes, we need each other.

Pamela: Kachi, you are an amazing young man. Your sense of reasoning is unmatched.

Kachi: Pamela, usually some people are so focused on preventing the mate whom they are trying to form a lasting relationship with from knowing their terrible past. Thus, blocking this mate from getting to know their true essence. Yes, who they are and who they have the potential of becoming in the future.

Pamela: Oh, yes, Kachi that is so important.

Kachi: One question that my Mom always ask us the children, which has been part of my driving force is: "Should it really be about someone not finding out your terrible past that should matter? Shouldn't it be about your behavior going forward that should matter regardless of your terrible past?"

Pamela Accepts Kachi's Proposal

Pamela: That is deep and so true that one's behavior or character going forward should matter more than the past. Kachi, could you please ask me your question again?

Kachi: Sure. Pamela, would you be my love and friend forever?

Pamela: Yes, I will. Kachi, with you by my side, I have nothing to fear. Not even fear itself. I will make a very happy man out of you, Kachi.

Kachi: Pamela my Darlene, you have already made a very happy man out of me, such that King Solomon of ancient Israel has nothing on me. Yes, he has no hold on me! Baby girl, you better believe it!

Pamela: Oh, I believe it, tiger!

Kachi: I know you'll recognize.

Pamela: Oh, I do recognize. Kachi, I do.

Kachi and Pamela are both laughing and enjoying the rest of the gourmet meal. While Kachi is having Prime rib serve with peppercorn, horseradish, matched potatoes, and the restaurant's proprietary special sauce in which he dips the beef before masticating it; Pamela is enjoying her vegetables, garlic noodles with roasted Dungeness crab that she dips in a sauce made with butter, balsamic vinegar, and roasted garlic.

Pamela: Kachi, you have to taste this noodles and roasted Dungeness crab. It is so good and if I don't know any better, I'll say it's from heaven. [she rolls up the noodles on her fork, pins the roasted crab with the garlic sauce and slowly dips it into Kachi's mouth.]

Kachi: Umm, it tastes delicious. But not as good as mine.

Pamela: Seriously?

Kachi: Yes, seriously.

Pamela: Then give me some.

Kachi: Here, take it.

Pamela: No, tiger. Give it to me like I gave mine to you.

Kachi: You mean I should cut a piece and put it in your mouth?

Pamela: Yes! Hello? That is exactly what I mean, Kachi. Cut a piece and slowly put it in my mouth like you are feeding me. [She passionately blinks her gorgeous eyes at Kachi.]

Kachi: I got you baby girl. Here we go. [Kachi seems shy but cut out a piece of his prime rib, dips it in the special sauce and slowly serves it directly into Pamela's mouth as he was taught. As Pamela chews, Kachi enjoys the view.]

Pamela: Ummm. Kachi, you are right! The prime rib tastes delicious. I love it! Give me another piece like you did before and I will do the same. This time let's do it slower than before and simultaneously to where our hands slowly cross paths.

Kachi: OK. Let's do it.

Pamela: O, I like that.

Unknown to Kachi and Pamela, some restaurant guests are watching and paying attention to what the two love birds are doing. As Kachi and Pamela are feeding each other according to the above plan, a couple said to them, that is so romantic and we going to have to try that too. Before you know it, all couples in the restaurant are doing the same thing. Suddenly, they all burst out laughing. You should have been there; it would have been a sight for your enjoyment. The evening at the restaurant continues.

Pamela: Thank you very much, Kachi.

Kachi: Pamela, you are welcome!

Pamela: No, I mean thank you so very much.

Kachi: I thought when someone say thank you to me, I am supposed to say you are welcome.

Pamela: Yes, you are supposed to, but you don't understand why I am thanking you.

Kachi: Seriously?

Pamela: Yes, seriously. My gratitude is for your willingness and ability to break the wall that I've built to shield me from the rest of the world just so they will hurt me no more.

Kachi: Really?

Pamela: Kachi, I never thought that there was anyone out there who could break this wall, let alone try for that matter. Here you are however, making your way right into my heart. Assuring me that with you by my side, I will be all right. That someone like you could love someone like me, with all my baggage, that makes me feel special.

Kachi: [Kachi stretches out his hands, gently take Pamela's Hands, and with an airy baritone voice he tenderly pours out his heart with the following words.] Pamela my dear baby girl, you are very special! Let no one tell you otherwise. I love you so dearly, my baby girl. You are so beautiful.

Pamela:	[Pamela expresses her deep emotions as tears roll down her cheeks with the following words.] I can honestly from the bottom of my heart say to you Kachi, I love you even more. Thanks to you Kachi for making me believe that I am good enough to love and be love by someone with a big heart like you.
Kachi:	Pamela my baby girl, you are worth more than a million best ladies put together. Don't you ever forget that I love you and you are the best thing yet that happen to me.
Pamela:	I feel the same way too. I love you, Kachi.

After expressing their feelings through tender kisses, they make plans to continue the evening on the shore of the ocean upon which the restaurant they just left is situated. Before that, on their way out of the restaurant, Kachi and Pamela received a standing ovation, applaud and best wishes from the guest and the management who had earlier discounted Kachi's bill for giving them an evening to remember. On the shore of the ocean, Kachi and Pamela are seen having heart to heart discussion. Let us eavesdrop on their conversation.

Empower The Inner You -
Do Not Make You A Victim Of Your Offenders

Pamela:	Kachi, can you explain to me what your Mom meant by the question "shouldn't it be about your behavior going forward that should matter regardless of your terrible past?"
Kachi:	Oh, you remember.
Pamela:	Oh yes, Kachi. Of course, I do remember.

Kachi: Pamela my girl, your memory is as remarkable as your looks. My Mom meant that if you have pains inflicted on you, would you want to live with the pain forever with self-pity and thus, making you a lasting victim of your offenders? Or would you rather seek help to have the pains treated and rid you of slavery to your offenders?

Pamela: I would rather seek help to cure the pains.

Kachi: If the kind of pain that the victim suffers are emotional, psychological, and physical, then the victim would need more than just the conventional medication to get better.

Pamela: Really?

Kachi: Yes, really my dear girl. While the medication may help with the physical aspect of the pain, you need someone to help repair the emotional and psychological damages. Someone that can reach your heart and implant the fact that the ordeal you had suffered is not your fault and will never be your fault.

Pamela: [Mystifies and expresses her emotions as tears run down her cheeks. Kachi hugs Pamela tenderly as he nurses her tears away.]

Kachi: Pamela, you need someone who can remind you that there are bad people in this world that just want to hurt good people like you, not because you are bad but because that is who they are —bad people. If you let them into your mind and heart, you will be empowering them. Therefore, do not let them in. You need to live your life out of the box by blocking them out of your mind.

Pamela: But how can I block them out of my mind since my Uncle is one of them and he is my family?

Kachi: Yes, baby girl. I know that can be daunting. However, one way to accomplish that is to forgive him and protect yourself by making sure that you are never alone with him.

Pamela: Forgive him? How can I forgive someone that hurt me so badly?

Kachi: I understand that can be very difficult. But when you forgive him, he'll become less and less significant. Yes, he'll become insignificant, and you will no longer be afraid of him. On the other hand, if you do not forgive him, he will always be on your mind hurting you over, and over again. Moreover, when he comes around, his presence would influence your mood and you do not want that, baby girl.

Pamela: No, I certainly don't.

Kachi: Pamela, forgiveness is letting go of all resentments that the ordeal may have caused. You must also forgive yourself which happens to be the most difficult thing to do.

Pamela: Forgive myself? Why, you said it yourself, it wasn't my fault?

Kachi: Sure. It's not your fault but has that stopped you from blaming yourself for the ordeal?

Pamela: No. I still do.

Kachi: Don't blame yourself and always know that it wasn't your Fault. Another thing you need to do is to immediately tell your ordeal to the parent that is not biologically related to your Uncle. If your Dad is biologically related to your Uncle for example, then you want to tell your Mom about it. On the other hand, if your Mom is biologically related to your Uncle, then you want to tell your Dad about it. He or she will understand your situation, believes you without reservation and take swift action to protect you immediately.

Pamela: That makes sense, Kachi. But what if the parent that is biologically related to my Uncle is the one I see first?

Kachi: Now, I'm not saying you should not tell it to that parent, I'm saying that it is possible for that parent to be in denial of your situation and thus, question your truthfulness as to whether or not your ordeal did happen at all. Or better yet, he or she may feel that you are just a spoilt little brat.

Pamela: That makes a lot of sense. In fact, that is the reason why I was not able to tell any of my parents because I thought they will blame me for it and claim that I want to tear our family apart. At least, that was what my Uncle threatened would happen if I dare tell my parents about his pedophilia or child molestation against me.

Kachi: Exactly! I have to let you know that you did the right thing, Pamela.

Pamela: I did the right thing not telling my parents about my ordeal when it happened in my preteen age years?

Kachi: Yes, you did great as a child. Remember, you said your Uncle threatened you not to tell anyone, your parents especially.

Pamela: Yes, that is correct, Kachi.

Kachi: Can your parents protect or be with you for twenty-four hours a day, seven days a week, and three hundred and sixty-five days a year?

Pamela: No, they cannot.

Kachi: And since he is your Uncle, he practically knows when your parents will not be around to protect you.

Pamela: That is so true.

Kachi: If you had disobeyed your Uncle by telling your parents about the ordeal you had suffered from him and your parents refused to believe you maybe because they do not have a clue about how to help you and so, it is easier to deny it ever happened. It will be very bad when your Uncle finds out that you had told your parents on him, and your parents did not believe you. He will increase your ordeal in multiple.

Pamela: That would be horrible.

Kachi: Of course, it would have been more horrible than it is. So, you have done great as a preteen.

Pamela: But earlier, you said that I should tell my parent, the one that is non-biological to my Uncle.

Kachi: Yes, I did say that. But you didn't do that did you?
Pamela: No, I did not do that.

Kachi: The point that I'm trying to make here is that the consequences of the choices you made as a child should not be held up against you because you do not have the reasoning tools and the manpower to make the right decision.

Pamela: Really?

Kachi: Yes, really. Pamela, you are never at fault for whatever you may have done wrong as a child. You kept safe by not telling your parents about your ordeal in response to your Uncle's threats. That is great! On the other hand, if there was a telephone around and you've been taught how to dial for emergency, I am sure that you would have picked up the telephone and call for help. Then the Police Officers would have showed up to protect you from your abusive Uncle.

Pamela: That seems plausible.

Kachi: The Police Officers may also have had the opportunity to educate your parents of the need to have you treated psychologically and psychiatrically at that early age. That would have been a wonderful help, don't you think?

Pamela: Yes, Kachi. I really think so.

Kachi: Now, since the needed help was not given to you at that right time, does it mean that all hope is lost?

Pamela: No. I do not think that all hope is lost.

Kachi: Exactly! You've done quite well for yourself in spite of that ordeal. However, going forward you are not going to let those losers control your life. You will do your best to let go the pain by letting go of the resentments you may have for those evildoers.

Letting Go of Your Pain Is About Remembering Your Blissful Future Upon Which Your Perpetrator Has No Hold.

Pamela: Kachi, I try not to think much about the past because when I do, I usually fall into deep depression and pain. So, I try my best not to think much about the past.

Kachi: Pamela my dream girl, letting go the pain is not about forgetting the past because the past is part of your history which has made you a better person. No! Pamela my dear, letting go the pain is about remembering the future.

Pamela: The future? Kachi, what future?

Kachi: The blissful future that you and I will have together. You will no longer go through your pain alone since I am here for you. Yes, Pamela, I will be there for you all the way my Darlene.

Pamela: Will you?

Kachi: Yes, I will. Pamela, we deal with adversity by moving onward and not looking backward. Do not lose your focus of not being his victim as you look beyond the woes of your persecutions.

Pamela: I'll do my best.

Kachi: Do not be a helpless victim of your past. Pamela, you are not a helpless victim of your past. Set your goals and do your utmost best to achieve them. That is the meaning to my Mom's question of it not being your past but your behavior and the character of whom you choose to be now and in the future that should matter.

Pamela: Thank you so much Kachi for making yourself available for this poor little girl with so many damaged goods to lean on.

Kachi: You are welcome, Pamela my baby girl. Pamela, we all come with different damaged goods because we are all imperfect. The chirping of a small bird like Canary differs from that of a Partridge bird. The chirping of a Partridge bird differs from that of an Eagle and the chirping of an Eagle differs from that of any other bird you can think of. However, when an Eaglet chirps, she does so with the voice of a bird and when an Eagle chirps, she does so with the voice of a bird. When an Eyas chirps, she has the voice of a bird and when a Falcon or a hawk chirps, she has the voice of a bird. Compare not the venom of a black mamba snake to that of a wasp. Compare not the venom of a viper to that of a schemer. Compare not the head of an Ostrich[28] to that of an Emu[28] for Ostrich is the largest of all birds, yes, the prince of birds. In a nutshell, my dear Pamela, we can learn from our many damaged goods and use the knowledge to help each other to thrive in this depraved bully-infested world.

Pamela: Wow! Kachi, that is insightful!

The Three-Fold Cord

Kachi: Pamela, the most important thing is that we are not going to be alone to handle our eclectic challenges all by ourselves. No, my dear Pamela. One more person is going to be with us to make us a three-fold cord. When that happens, our union will be forever strong.

Pamela: Really? Kachi, I didn't know you have a child. When can I meet him or her?

Kachi: Pamela, I do not have a child neither am I referring to one.

Pamela: Then what are you talking about Kachi?

Kachi:	Pamela, before I met you, it was all about you and your feelings. Now, it's about you and I, only by the grace of God. Pamela, that is the only way our union can have real meaning.
Pamela:	Seriously?
Kachi:	Yes, seriously my dear lady. Pamela, one of the things you may have noticed about me is that I take the relationship with my God very seriously. In fact, the foundation of my faith stands solid upon the agonizing ransom sacrificial death of Jesus Christ. I will never have to carry a burden on my shoulders, for the shoulders of my lord Jesus Christ are with me.
Pamela:	Kachi, please tell me more.
Kachi:	Pamela, you and I form two cords. Three is better than two; when we let God be the center of our lives, we will have a strong center and become a three-fold cord which is stronger than two. Do you believe that?
Pamela:	With all my heart. Kachi, with all my heart.
Kachi:	That is excellent, my dear one. That is excellent. In fact, his words in the Bible book of Psalms 71:20 is worthy of our attention.
Pamela:	Kachi, I have the Bible on my mobile telephone, would you like me to read it out loud?
Kachi:	Please do.
Pamela:	Psalms 71:20,21 says "Though you have made me experience much distress and calamity, revive me again; Bring me up from the depths of the earth. May you increase my greatness and surround and comfort me."

Kachi: Pamela, what is your take on these two verses?

Pamela: Well, my take is that although God did not cause our distress, he allows us to go through it and as we rely completely on him, he comforts us and makes us great again.

Kachi: I could not have said it any better. You see my dear girl, our complete reliance on the Highest of the Highest, yes, the Almighty God[29] will make us successful.

Pamela: But Kachi, I cannot understand why he had to allow my Uncle and his psycho friends to rape me.

Kachi: Pammy my Darlene, I am sure by now you know that I share your pain and can say with certainty that I will do the very best to understand what you are going through to be a great help to you. And I am so sorry that you had to go through it. In fact, no one should have to go through what you have gone through as a child and a youngster. Let's look at your teenage ordeal in a different way, shall we?

Pamela: What? There is a different way to look at it? My Uncle and his friends are evil!

Kachi: Granted. They are evildoers. But for your sake, let's look at it this way. Consider someone who has never raised a chicken in his life let alone raised a child, come to admonish you on how to raise your children. When you ask him how many children he had raised, he tells you none! Now you wonder where he got his child-rearing knowledge from. He tells you "it's in the book."

Pamela: That is not going to work.

Kachi: Not only that, he a l s o lacks the ability to fathom the fact that ***there is a thick line between theory and practice***. In a nutshell, what may be plausible in theory may not be plausible in practice without the necessary and satisfying maneuverings.

Pamela: I totally agree with you on that because I can relate to that fact. When it comes to child- rearing, it is not always black and white as you see in books. In most cases, you have to do some maneuvering to synchronize your practice with your known theory. Or even more so, you may have to relearn what you think you know a priori. What you think you know may not be applicable to what you are dealing with during child-rearing.

Kachi: True.

Pamela: I believe that years of such practical maneuvering will compel you to share the belief that there is a fine thick line between theory and practice. Now, don't get me wrong Kachi. Having a theoretical knowledge about something that you want to do is a good start as it helps you to map out your strategies, but it's not everything.

Kachi: It is common knowledge that the way you raise a girl differs from the way you raise a boy.

Pamela: Yes, it differs.

Kachi: So, if one had never raised a girl before, even if he had raised many boys…

Pamela: …he still will not be in a proper position to advise you on how to raise your daughters since he lacks the practical knowledge.

Kachi:	Now, does it mean that a person lacking practical knowledge about child-rearing cannot give advice on the subject?
Pamela:	No. Of course, he can give advice on the subject. However, if the person he had advised chose not to accept his admonition because it's not applicable to the needs at hand, then he should not take offence so as not to make it personal. Giving advice must not be personal.
Kachi:	Yes. Making it personal may defeat the purpose of trying to help in the first place, since each one of us is unique and may have unique situations.
Pamela:	Kachi, that is so right.
Kachi:	Pamela, can you imagine the number of people who may have suffered the same ordeal as you did that may be fortunate enough to come your way for help? When such people do come your way for help, would you not be in a better position to help them?
Pamela:	I believe I would.
Kachi:	Me too. I believe you would. Do you know why?
Pamela:	I have a firsthand knowledge on the subject.
Kachi:	Exactly! I believe that you'll be well qualified to help them because not only do you have the theoretical knowledge of being a rape victim, even more importantly, you also have the practical knowledge of it.
Pamela:	Wow! That is so true.
Kachi:	When such ones relate their problems, you can vividly understand them as much as they too can

vividly understand your counsel and appreciate it. You can relate to them, and they too can relate to you. You will be helping them to build a new future devoid of victimization.

Pamela: Wow! Why don't I think of that?

Kachi: The most important point is that the Almighty God allows you to go through that ordeal just so you can learn to trust in him and rely on him completely without reservation. He also wants you to help those who have inhale the same bad breath as you have done; teach them how to exhale and keep that horrible breath out of their system forever.

Pamela: Kachi, thank you for being my comfort.

Kachi: No, no, no, no. Pamela, I need you to let the almighty God be your comfort as he is mine. I need you to rely completely on him as I have. Imperfect man may fail you, but He will never fail you especially if you trust Him completely. What is more, at Psalms 51:17, our heavenly father is ever ready to help those whose hearts are broken and crushed.

Pamela: Kachi, like mine?

Kachi: Precisely. Pamela my baby girl, like yours. You must trust that he will help you completely. Yes, he will rebuild you with a new heart and spirit. What is more, at Isaiah 48:18 our heavenly father does not force us but persuades us, kind of like he practically begs us to pay attention to his commandments because if we do, then our peace would become just like a river and our righteousness like the waves of the sea. In a nutshell, our blessings will be great if we pay attention to his commandments.

Pamela: Is that why he sent you to me?

Kachi: You can ask that question and I can answer yes. But I'm sure you do remember that you actually came to me and so, it is safe to say that he sent you to me.

Pamela: I am so fortunate to be clothe by someone so insightful as you.

Kachi: Pamela my baby girl, I am the fortunate one.

Pamela: Then we are both fortunate. We found each other.

Kachi: Girl, you can say that again. Do you know what we should do?

Pamela: No, what?

Kachi: Do you think we should let our parents and friends know that we are going steady?

Pamela: Yes, I think we should. I'm not afraid anymore. Let's do it!

Kachi: All right, my love.

Pamela: Now, you can say that again!

Kachi: Yes, my love. I said it again.

Pamela: Great! I am your love and you are mine. Don't you forget that!

Kachi: Baby girl, I'll try to.

Pamela: What?

Kachi: Oh, no. I'm just kidding. I won't forget, my sweet baby girl.

Kachi and Pamela hug each other with tender kisses. Pamela lays her head on Kachi's laps. As they continue to enjoy each other's company, making plans for their future and enjoying the view of the starry heavens, Pamela throws an unexpected question at Kachi. It may not be the one you may be thinking about considering the circumstances in which they are at the moment. Let's eavesdrop on their conversation. Shall we?

Pamela: Kachi, have you ever wondered why people in this universe feel the urge to worship someone or something that they might refer to as god and most of them may not know why they are worshipping that deity?

Kachi: Yes, my dear lady. I have wondered about it for quite a while and I've found an answer.

Pamela: Really? Kachi, can you share your answer with me, please?

Kachi: Sure, my dear. I certainly will. Pamela, my thought is that respecting humans, the worship of one's creator is embedded in the equation (or DNA) that constitute that creature. Because one is given the "free will"[23] or the choice to worship or not to worship one's creator, it is possible to replace that part of the equation with the worship of something other than the worship of one's creator.

Pamela: What replacements could that be?

Kachi: The replacements could be the worship of self, wealth, spirits, calved images or lifeless objects which are viewed as gods.

Pamela: Kachi, that makes sense because some rich people I know seem not to have time for anything else but self.

Kachi: Thanks. Pamela, the direction that I'm going can well be explain with the theory of "balancing an equation" in Chemistry.

Pamela: Really?

Kachi: When you remove or replace a key component of a balanced equation with something that vaguely resembles that key component without the necessary manipulations, the equation will no longer be balanced.

Pamela: That is correct.

Kachi: In the same line of thought, when one replaces the creator's worship with the worship of something else, the balanced view of life respecting such one, will be distorted – unbalanced.

Pamela: Unbalanced?

Kachi: Yes, unbalanced. Pamela, there is little or no wonder that in this universe, regardless of peoples' standard of living (whether under-poor, poor or rich) some are balance though materially poor hence, happy and yet, some are not balance though materially rich hence, unhappy.

Pamela: O, I get it. So, to worship something or someone is inherent in us. That is, the practice to worship someone or something is an integral part of us as humans. But whom we choose to worship is up to us so long as we know that our happiness depends on whether or not we are balanced, which in turn depends on whom we chose to worship.

Kachi: Yes, Pamela you are getting it.

Pamela: Let me sight an example to see if I get it. A young girl is balanced and happy when she has no opinion on who to serve but her creator before she becomes an adult. If she decides not to serve her creator during her adulthood on the "assumption that she knows who her creator is and the proper way to serve him,"[24] then her happiness could be short-lived, the result of losing her balance.

Kachi: Once again, Pamela, you have a sound reasoning prowess. Yes, you have the reasoning of a queen that forces my knees to the ground and thank my heavenly father that I'm the man you have chosen.

Pamela: Thanks, Kachi and you are a fine teacher. I can relate to all that you have said. Some of my friends from filthy rich families are not happy and so they norm themselves with hard drugs so as not to feel the pain. They are hooked on concealed substances like cocaine, heroin, or opiate. On the other hand, my other friends from family that are struggling materially, they are happy and are not using any of the concealed substances. So, you see Kachi, I can relate to your teachings.

Kachi: I appreciate that, Pamela. You are a fine student and a great listener.

Pamela: Thanks, Kachi.

Kachi: You are welcome, my dear love.

Extramarital Affair Is A Bully

The evening continues with Kachi and Pamela appreciating the nature's beauty, the gift of life and its wonderful provisions. Many vows are made to honor each other and never to take one's love for granted come what may. Let's drop in on one of their conversations.

Pamela: I do appreciate the way our parents do express emotional feelings to each other without reservation and not taking each other for granted, the reason for their enduring relationship and they are very happy with each other. I would like us to be that way.

Kachi: Pammy-Pam baby girl, we will be that way and even more.

Pamela: Kachi my love, I am serious because there are too many marital breakups and I don't want us to be part of that statistics. I mean, can you believe a married woman having affair with one of her co-workers? That her employer tolerates that horrible behavior at the place of work that supposed to be a haven for the employees most of whom do have families is, indeed, appalling!

Kachi: Yes, I can imagine. Some employers frown at that behavior as they can see the coming of trouble which could affect job performances. It's a simple fact that you are bound to develop emotional attraction with an opposite sex or in some cases the same sex with whom you spent a lot of quality time on a daily basis. Interestingly, that same quality time may be a luxury to him and his wife as he spends countless of those times with someone else in the name of "it is my job," "someone's got to pull the weight around here." Sometimes it forces you to think that such ones are the only ones who seem to have to work and who are actually working.

Pamela: Isn't that something?

Kachi: The thing is, while there may be something peculiarly appealing to you about this coworker that you spend countless of quality time with and go home to make trouble with your spouse just so you can have reason to jump out again to be with "your lover," sooner or later, reality will hit the fan. As the table turns, you may find yourself extremely backed into a corner with no way out. Before you know it, it will be like you are hooked on hard drugs with no remedy in sight.

Pamela: Kachi, you got that right. What a quandary that would be and what follows next would be the many excuses he or she would be making to his or her spouse respecting why he or she got to be at work very early in the morning or why he or she got to stay at work very late into the night or even go back to work in the middle of the night after just getting back from work. Some may even bring their works home because the time they ought to have spent working on their assigned duties at work, guess what they spent it on?

Kachi: Yes, they probably spent it on their own selfish affairs and if their spouses do not know any better, their thought would be:" I am so fortunate to have such an industrious person for a spouse." It's good to know that some people reject that kind of lifestyle.

Pamela: That is why some employers frown at their employees having romantic affairs with each other at work because such ones are actually stealing from their employers. Some are however, smart at what they do, such that their dishonesty may not affect their overall output at work.

Kachi: Well, some of the so-called smart ones may be one of those taking their work home to cheat their spouses out of their quality time.

Pamela: Kachi, not just that, the woman that I'm talking about was actually ridiculing her husband to her coworker whom she calls her lover!

Kachi: What do you know, she might be in a cult where she receives drug to ingest before she gets home to her husband to whom she tells all the lame stories in the world as to why she's taking ill and needed to sleep immediately. Because her husband loves her dearly, he buys that lame stories and let her sleep comfortably.

Pamela: So, she has her coworker to be her real lover while she turns her husband into the unfortunate house doctor who gets nothing but a heavy heart for an unloving wife. She got it all figure out, didn't she? Like a flying Eagle she stays alive and active for her lover out there, but like a dead Sparrow she plays ill and in constant pain to her unfortunate husband whose mistake was carrying out the thought that he could actually make a great family with her. That is so sad.

Kachi: It may look like that, but her day of reckoning is in sight even for someone that ruthlessly clever and elusive. I mean if you don't love someone why marry him? If you love him, why can't you lovingly and respectfully work it out with him? How did she ridicule her husband?

Pamela: Well, let's hear it from the horse's mouth. Shall we?

Kachi: Sure.

The setting here is that Downey and Syretha are on a date and are done sharing a gourmet dinner in a nice restaurant after work. Downey is a single nice looking athletic young man. Syretha is married to someone else and here she's having an affair with Downey. Both Downey and Syretha are emotionally involved and intimate with each other, holding and robbing hands together.

Syretha: Hey honey, you know I never look straight into my husband's eyes the way I look into yours, because I love you. The love I have for you is real, babe.

Back to Kachi and Pamela:

Pamela: When I heard her say that I was upset and I wished I knew her husband, I would have told on her.

Kachi: I am sure that made the man, I mean her lover felt great about himself. Didn't he?

Pamela: Kachi, you are never going to believe this. Her lover actually said something that made me think that it is good to know that there are still some decent men out there. He wasn't a home wrecker after all, I guess some men can relate to others or put themselves in the shoes of their fellowmen.

Kachi: What did the man say to her?

Pamela: Why don't we hear it from his mouth?

Kachi: Sure. Let's do that.

[Back to Downey and Syretha]

Downey: Woman, the reason why you cannot look at your husband in a sensual and emotional way like you do to me is quite simple. Your husband made the worse mistake of his life. He actually considers you as a decent person, he loves you, he cares for you and actually married you! Because of your terrible heart condition, you deliberately equate his wanting you to better yourself and be successful as judging you. See, I don't care about you. I don't care for you! I just want to fool around with you and no strings attached! I guess that is what you want. Who knows, that may be the reason why you can look straight into my eyes in a sensual way like I own you. That is the way you ought to be looking at your husband.

Syretha: Downey, but why are you saying that to me? Why are you treating me like this?

At this point, your guess is as good as mine – they are not holding hands any longer.

Downey: What assurance do I have that you will not end up treating me in the same terrible way that you are treating your husband now, who probably think you are still at work?

Syretha: Downey my love, I will never treat you like that because I love you.

Downey: Seriously? Did you say that to your husband to convince him that marrying you will be in his best interest? You considered your husband to be a fool, you purposely failed to be intimate with him and bragged about that horrible behavior to me. If you don't love the man and you are not going to be faithful to him, why did you marry him? Just to use him? What a bully! Yes, you are a bully!

Back to Kachi and Pamela:

Kachi: Wow! He told her straight!

Pamela: Kachi, the man isn't through yet.

Kachi:

But he raises good questions for the prudent to digest.

Pamela:

Kachi, be patient, let's listen, there is more Back to Downey and Syretha:

Syretha:

I thought I love my husband at first, but things change and so, are my needs and priorities. I finally noticed that the only thing that I love about him is his money. When I'm with you however, I feel the difference between being alive and actually living and kicking.

Downey:

Really? For the past three weeks we didn't see each other because you were taking ill, who took care of you until you get better?

Syretha:

My husband. So? He enjoys taking care of me. What is the big deal?

Downey:

Yet, here you are with me. The moment he nursed you back to health you come to me for love, and that does not bother you at all.

Syretha:

What do you care? Does it have to? I mean why should it bother me? The man enjoys taking care of me and I let him. What is wrong with that?

Downey:

But you don't love him. You are just using him. The man is taking care of you because he thought that you love him and he is the only man in your life and you are the only woman in his.

Syretha:

Hello, in what universe are you living? Who says I have to love a man for him to take good care of me? If a man wants to be treated like a fool, well, you treat him as such. There is no law against that, is there? Besides, I did not come here for you to judge me, OK?

Downey: Guess what? Your day of reckoning is fast approaching when the table will turn on you, we'll see how well you'll fare. Woman, I rather not be a fool.

Syretha: O yes, you are! Saying no to all these beauties that I'm offering to you with no strings attached makes you a fool.

Downey: Yes, that may be true in the mind of a psycho. However, it is for your own good that I'll suggest you go back to your husband, confess to him from the bottom of your unloving heart and start treating him like a king if he chooses to forgive you.

Syretha: What! Treat him like a king? In what universe?

Downey: I tell you woman, for him to have married someone like you and stay faithful, he deserves a crown! After all, they say "heavy is the head that wears a crown." The man is already carrying a heavy load on his shoulder caring for an unfaithful wife you turn out to be. He might as well wear the crown! Stop biting the hands that feeds you, woman!

Syretha: The hands that feed me? Am I not working?

Downey: Does the fact that you are working gives you the passport to cheat on your marriage?

Syretha: So, what are you saying? What about us? You knew I was married yesterday afternoon and you did all that without complaining. Did you not?

Downey: Well, you weren't bragging about your infidelity, making your husband a fool and a sore loser, which got me thinking, today it is your husband that this terrible betrayal is happening to. Tomorrow, it could be me if I don't do something about it right now. So, I must stop this immediately. I suggest you do the same, if it is not too late for you.

Syretha: Look who is talking.

Downey: Syretha, marriage is supposed to be a beautiful thing, but people like you give it a bad rap! That is why I have made up my mind not to get married in this crazy world. If I need to fool around, it is good to know as well as it is a shame that people like you do exist. Yes, people who pay no reverence to something as holy as marriage ought to be. So, what about us you ask?

Syretha: Yes, where does our affair stands?

Downey: Woman, I am dumping you because you lack finesse and human decency. You are not even remorseful of your terrible actions. What a shame! What a shame! Oh, what a shame!

Back to Kachi and Pamela:

Kachi: That is so amazing!

Pamela: After dumping Syretha, Downey walked away. Syretha was left distraught and could not believe what had just happened to her. It took her a while before she realized that she had just been dumped.

Kachi: This is not something you hear on a daily basis. Now, when she finds out that she's been dumped, what would her next line of action be?

Pamela: This is funny, Kachi. She did not know that people are watching her. So, she dipped her right hand into her purse and brought out her wedding ring and drove it into her finger where it belongs.

When we saw her wear her wedding ring, you can hear the applaud a mile away. An elderly woman kindly said to her, "woman, go back to your husband while you still can, and mend it with him. Would you?" She was so embarrassed!

Kachi: I can imagine. Downey is right when he said, "heavy is the head that wears a crown." Her husband trusted that she is at work doing her job to help earn a living for the family, only to find out that she was doing more than just her job - the price he paid for having a spouse that must work out there in the world, mingle and make friends with different people that he does not know. Spouses are usually the last to find out about marital infidelity and when they do, what a headache it fetches for the family!

Pamela: Kachi, I do not want us to have a boring marriage. I want our marriage to be exciting and fulfilling. I want our marriage to be better than fine wine, that is, the older it gets the better it is. Like making fine wine that takes time and effort, we will work hard to make our marriage a success. If we have to work for someone else other than our family business, may we always remember the reason we choose to do that – because we have deep respect and undying deep love for each other. And if all else fail, may we never nourish the idea of making out with someone that we are not married to, but have the courage and dignity to discuss it openly with each other and seek spiritual guidance immediately.

Kachi: Pamela my girl, you have spoken well. But don't worry, we will be all right because we are going to be truthful and loving to each other regardless of our selfish inclinations, which we will do well to curb. Remember, it is about you, me, our families and most of all, the Almighty God. Not just you alone and not just me alone. It is about both of us now.

Pamela: Indeed, it is about both of us now. Of course, it will help a great deal to flee from such act and eradicate every little circumstance that may lead to such flirty conception effective immediately. Is it usually the responsibility of a carcass laying bare on the street to rid the street of itself?

Kachi: No, Pamela it is the responsibility of the living.

Pamela: Kachi, during our marriage would you please let me know if and when I'm falling short of giving you emotional love, support and affection? Because I don't want you to get them from someone else. I want to be your only source and you be my mine and together we let the Almighty God to be our only source for comfort.

Kachi: Pamela, I agree with you totally and I will let you know as you have asked. Years into our married life, Pamela I will appreciate it if you treat me right like your lover and your boyfriend just as we are to each other now and I will treat you right like my girlfriend and lover.

Pamela: Kachi, I will always remember this day and our promises to each other. I promise that I will always treat you right as my only lover and boyfriend. I promise, Kachi.

Kachi: Great! Pamela, I live to enjoy your love.

Pamela: I can learn, and I'll surely do my best to please you well. When you bring up something that I'm doing wrong, I will try not to be defensive and miss the point, rather, with a good heart I'll pay attention with a view to correcting the problem so we can continue to be happy together. Please try the best you could not to read negative meanings to what I do or say. I'll prefer that you ask constructive questions instead. I truly believe that when we see each other as lovers though married for years, can our marriage and friendship withstand fiery challenges and thus, stand solid forever.

Kachi: I will surely do that for us. It is so sad to see spouses who always find something positive or at least make one up for statements bearing negative connotations made by someone out there, but lack the moral fiber and the heart to do the same or even more for their spouses as negative connotations are rendered to sayings that command positive vibes when the proper perception is applied with a loving heart.

Do Everything Together As A Family Bonded with affectionate love

Pamela: The bottom line is, when we start to look outside of the marriage for emotional love, emotional comfort and emotional support, that will be the beginning of the end to that marital relationship.

Kachi: That is correct.

Pamela: Kachi, I love you so much and I don't want our marriage to end. I don't want our marriage to be anything but excitingly clothe with immense love. May we never find ourselves thinking we have no choice but to live in misery. We do have choices. The best choice would be to do everything we can to be happy together as a family and have our family bonded together with affectionate love.

Kachi: Oh, Pamela, Pamela, Pamela. Oh, Pamela my baby girl, saying that means a lot to me. I hope you'll do the same for me too. Because we are imperfect people, sometimes we may have differences which may appear to be irreconcilable. But if we rely completely on the Highest of the highest, I believe we will succeed.

Pamela: I believe so too.

Kachi: If we find ourselves drifting, we will do well to get external help from spiritually mature men and women with practical experiences immediately.

Pamela: I agree with you Kachi.

Kachi: I love you so dearly and I want us to have an endless marriage that commands the deep love that is deeper than the abyss and deep respect that is mutual to both of us.

Pamela: Yes, our purpose for seeking external help will not be to disgrace one another and reduce each other's standards to the lowest ebb. No! Rather, it will be to glorify our God and each other with a view to making our relationship ever stronger and each other looking more attractive than we ever are.

Kachi: Excellent! That is a beautiful and positive way to see it.

Pamela: Kachi. I want us to have a happy and positive family life. I want to be a flying eagle when I'm with you and certainly not a dead sparrow. I'll rather prefer us to agree to disagree or disagree to agree when we come across an irreconcilable issue and then seek help on that issue. In no way would I want to disrespect you by playing a dead sparrow or a sick bird when I'm with you. I will never entertain an attitude of me not wanting to do something on the grounds that it will benefit you. I mean, that thought itself is evil. I want you to see me for who I am, a righteous person.

Kachi: Girl, you read my mind! Indeed, you read my mind baby girl. I will do the same, which will help us a great deal from being a cold and heartless couple. I am sure that you know that I'll be there for you when you take ill. In fact, if there is nothing left, girl, I'll be with you.

Pamela: Kachi, please, don't you ever stop being my knight in shining armor. But why are you smiling like that?

Kachi: You said, "disagree to agree." You ought to see your beautiful face saying it like that. You look so pretty.

Pamela: I just put that in because nobody ever says it like that. Yes, I know that it means the same as "agree to disagree." Ennm, I just want to be funny a little.

Kachi: Girl, you are hilarious!

Pamela: Yes, you are just saying that because you love me, and I appreciate it.

Kachi: I am serious though, you are truly funny and yes, I love you.

Pamela: Thanks, Kachi. I love you too. Hey Kachi, what is your take on a man who is blessed with a family but pretends he has none by playing computer games all alone for hours. Now, don't get me wrong, Kachi I am not saying that is wrong I'm just saying that while he feels he needed to be alone, his family may bid the difference as they may be dying for his affection and to show them that they are wanted and needed in his life.

Kachi: Pamela, thanks for expressing one of the cons of computer technologies. Gone are those days, it seems, when a game must be played by more than one person. During that period of time, members in a family are closer to each other and so are people in general.

Pamela: Yes, during that period of time, I do recall that only those with mental illness, those without family or friends and the incarcerated people seemed to enjoy playing games in solitary.

Kachi: That is correct. Pamela, because people are so busy trying to make a living, it appears that they have little time to spare for families and friends. So, these people make way for self-amusements and entertainments, yes, games that require only one person to play alone, hence, solitary.

Pamela: The problem with that is that we see married couples distancing each other even though they are right there with each other. It would be like they were never there for each other and so, you'll hear a wife complain that she is lonely though her husband is right there besides her.

Kachi: Well, it may be that they have nothing in common or something with which to entertain each other. I can understand that to be the case in a pre-arranged marriage. But in a marriage that is preceded by months of dating and courting, it is difficult to imagine that married couple not to have something with which to entertain each other with a view to strengthening their bond of love. Yes, I know things do change from time to time, people say things they have no business saying and do things they have no business doing, most of which they cannot take back once said and done. But still, first on their list of priority should be strengthening their relationship and not making being together a boring thing.

Pamela: Kachi, I concur with you. I do not believe that married couples should run out of something with which to spice up each other even when things change or as you may say a change in situation. I mean, there is the Bible, there are countless story books they can read together. Yes, things do change, but is it impossible to change that "changed things" back to something that will help rather than hurt the relationship?

Kachi: I do not think it is impossible. They just have to be willing to do it together.

Pamela: Instead of a husband or wife to play that game alone on a mobile or desktop computer, why not play the game together with your spouse? Who is right, wrong or cheat on the game should not be a matter of concern, but togetherness or spending quality time together should be the mainstay?

Kachi: Baby girl, I agree with you.

Pamela: It is possible for the husband to run out of jokes. When that Happens, his wife should be able to help. She can be funny too. Or is there a law that says a wife cannot be funny and that it's got to be the husband that must come up with something funny with which the family can be entertained?

Kachi:	Pamela my baby girl, I am so glad that you feel that way. It is indeed, a relief to know that the burden of entertaining us as a family will not be place on my shoulder alone. It will be a shared effort. It is good to know.
Pamela:	Of course, Kachi, it has to be a shared effort. Like you said no man is an Island even in entertainment.
Kachi:	[coming across a beautiful rose bush] Pamela, don't you just like these flowers that reminds me of your beauty?
Pamela:	O yes, Kachi, they are so beautiful.
Kachi:	My dear Pamela, these flowers are a representation of your beauty but none of them is as gloriously beautiful as you are.
Pamela:	Oh, Kachi my dearest one, my heart has engulfed the whole of you and leaves no space for someone else.
Kachi:	Really?
Pamela:	Yes, really. Kachi. Why did you do this to me? Why did you take the whole of me? Why did you take all of my heart?
Kachi:	Because I love you more than anything in the world. Pamela my Darlene, I love you more than life itself and King Solomon of ancient Israel can't do a thing about it.
Pamela:	Kill me with love, baby, kill me with love.

As the love birds discuss the number of children they'll have, we see them go through a little hiccup. Let's observe, shall we?

Kachi: Pamela my love, you know you owe me twelve children who would look as beautiful as you do and I always collect.

Pamela: Kachi, did you say twelve children?

Kachi: Yes, I surely did.

Pamela: What! Are you out of your mind? Are you trying to kill me? Twelve Children? What on God's glorious Earth are you trying to build, a football team?

Kachi seems to be having the time of his life as he bursts into catchy laughs. His laugh is so catchy that it compels Pamela to laugh out loud. As the two love birds are laughing profusely Kachi says:

Kachi: Pamela my dear, you should have seen your face. I am just kidding. How many kids would you suggest we have?

Pamela: I always wanted a family of seven. That is, five children, you, and I.

Kachi: I can live with that.

Pamela: Tiger, you better, because that's all you are getting from this body of mine!

You Owe Each Other The Truth And Nothing But The Truth

Kachi: My dear Lady Pamela, I got you babe, I got you.

Pamela: Hey Kachi, you look like there is something on your mind bothering you. What is it?

Kachi: One of my friends have been trying the best he could to convince his wife that he has not been having affair neither has the thought of having an affair come to his mind. But it doesn't seem that his wife believes him for some reasons that are best known to her.

Pamela: Ouch! That's not good.

Kachi: But she's not giving these reasons to her husband and that has put a bottleneck on their marriage. They are not happy, or at least she is not happy with the relationship. I don't know how to help them. I can understand her reasoning for not telling her husband why she feels that way.

Pamela: What was her reasoning?

Kachi: She once asked: "Does a fisherman describes the tricks and lures he uses to the fish he caught after which he let go of the fish? If no, then she does not have any reason telling her husband how she come across the feelings she has.

Pamela: She's obviously a smart woman. Kachi, has your friend cheated on her before?

Kachi: Not that I know of.

Pamela: Has he been caught in several lies before?

Kachi: I mean; the man is not a saint. He is as imperfect as any one of us is. So, I won't be too judgmental about that.

Pamela: Then it is the job of your friend to convince his wife that he is neither cheating nor flirting when he goes to work or when he's out of her environment. If he truly loves her then he would want to convince her in words and in deeds beyond the iota of doubt.

Kachi: Pamela, what do you mean by the words "in deeds?"

Pamela: I mean he should take her to his usual places where he hangs out, like his place of work even if he works in a secured environment where key cards are used. He should trust her well enough to give her full access to his office just so she can show up whenever she pleases. He can also introduce her to his colleagues be they married or single, male, or female. Both of them should share an email address. Or, he should give her access to his email, mobile telephone, and any other means through which he communicates with the world out there.

Kachi: Isn't that rather too extreme?

Pamela: Hello, he wants to convince her, right?

Kachi: Yes, he does.

Pamela: Then that is what he must do. I mean, if he has nothing to hide giving his wife full access to his office shouldn't be a difficult thing to do. Otherwise, he should quit that job and look for one that promotes transparency. I know of many couples who are doing just that already. They understand that we live in a world that is controlled by wicked spirits27 and these wicked spirits do not want to see married couples succeed in their relationships and live happily ever after.

Kachi: That may not be that easy to do at least from my friend's standpoint.

Pamela: Yes, Kachi, it may seem formidable to accomplish but if you think about the alternatives, you'll realize that it is way better for your friend to give his wife the full access including his telephones, emails and everything that has to do with his communicating with the outside world. That may give both of them the needed peace of mind.

Kachi: What is the alternative?

Pamela: The alternative is for your friend to be in a relationship with serious trust issues even if he is not cheating! Can you imagine the damage it will do to his marriage if the problem is not address immediately and effectively?

Kachi: Are you serious?

Pamela: Yes, I'm serious Kachi. The thought of your friend having an affair from his wife's perspective even if he isn't will yield the same consequences as if he is actually having extra marital affair. He must, therefore, vigorously prove to his wife that he isn't having any extra marital affair.

Kachi: Really?

Pamela: Yes, really. Kachi, if due to your friend's behavior, his wife develops an idea or somehow believes but not entirely convinced that her husband is doing something that will endanger their relationship, it is the job of your friend to completely convince his wife of the truth leaving no stone unturned; an absence of which the results or the consequences thereof will be the same as if he is truly guilty as charged.

Kachi: Now that I've given it some thoughts, Pamela my baby girl, I agree with you. Yes, with everything he has, my friend needs to convince his wife of his innocence.

Pamela: Now, do not get me wrong, Kachi, it goes both ways. The same standards must be set for both mates. Taking each other for granted must be one of the behaviors that they as married couple must forgo. Both must treat their marital relationship very sacred, eliminating anything that resembles bullying.

Kachi: My beautiful princess, that is logical. Indeed, it makes sense.

Pamela: Thanks, Kachi.

Sky Diving In San Francisco

Next, we see Kachi and Pamela on a date two days later. This time they are in San Francisco sky diving after an adventurous snorkel. While Kachi is a good sky diver, Pamela has never been in a plane before let alone jump off from one. Kachi assures Pamela that there is nothing to jumping off the plane from a high elevation – it's thrilling. Kachi and Pamela are in the plane all geared up to jump out. Pamela who has been enjoying the plane ride faces a deciding moment as they jump out of the plane. Pamela screams as Kachi lifts her up and jumps out of the plane. In the air, when Pamela observes that she is in good hands she relaxes, stop screaming and enjoys the ride.

Pamela: Kachi, this is beautiful. I've never experienced something as beautiful as this. Look, we are flying in the midheavens without a plane and I am not afraid. This is great!

Kachi: Pamela, that is the idea. Now, are you ready for this?

Pamela: Am I ready for what?

Kachi: For this. [Kachi opens the parachute which is blissful though scary at the same time as far as Pamela is concerned]

Pamela: O, this is nice. I love it. I love it. I love it.

Kachi: I'm glad you do.

Pamela: This is what little Joseph needs to get rid of his fears.

Kachi: Little Joseph? Who on earth is Little Joseph?

Pamela: Oh, are we getting jealous here?

Kachi: Baby, for you, I'll get jealous anytime, anywhere!

Pamela: Kachi my love, there's no need for that. My heart has engulfed you, lock itself up, and throw the key away such that there is no room for someone else. Little Joseph is my neighbor's kid in the tenth grade who lets everyone jump on him and he would not defend himself.

Kachi: Really, why won't a boy want to defend himself? Pamela: His parents taught him not to fight because as Christians, a slave of the Lord does not need to fight but should depend on the Lord for vengeance. The boy remembers his father's teachings about Christ's sayings[37] respecting turning the other cheek when slapped.

Kachi: I can understand that. Still, he should learn to defend himself as we live in a system of things that is rule by the wicked one. What is more, Christ's sayings of turning the other cheek is about appreciating the value of endurance and reliance on our heavenly Father[47] to be our vengeance. As Christians, we'll do well to endure every persecution that comes our way because of our faith in Christ, what he stands for and our God can deliver us from the hands of the oppressor. Other than that, we have every right as anyone else to defend ourselves when our rights are encroached upon.

Pamela: I agree with you Kachi. Maybe his parents did not make that clear to him. His parents recently found out that he has been an object of ridicule at school by his peers who are bullies and that has been going on for years.

Kachi: And his parents just find out about it now?

Pamela: The boy is a quiet type, almost like you when we first met.

Kachi: So, how did his parents find out?

Pamela: His parents were called into the principal's office where the boy was detained for nearly killing one of his bullies. So, he told his parents and the principal that the bullying has been going on since the seventh grade and that he taught that since his parents are moving to a different city he will have to change school too and that will solve the problem. Besides, the boy is afraid of what his parents might do to the school when they find out about the daily threat he faces at school.

Kachi: Pamela, can give an instance of how he was bullied at school?

Pamela: Well, when he was using the boys' restroom, some bullies gathered by the open window taunting and threatening him from using the restroom comfortably.

Kachi: How did the boy handled that situation?

Pamela: The boy said that he had to ignore them because he got to go.

Kachi: Isn't that rather too much for the poor boy to handle?

Pamela: Yes, Kachi it certainly is. But how would you have handled it, Kachi?

Kachi: You know when I was in the seventh grade, none of those bullies could mess with me.

Pamela: Really?

Kachi: Yes, really. In fact, they thought I was insane, and nobody can mess with someone insane. To answer your question however, I would ignore them like the boy did as long as those bullies do not touch me. If they touch me, then they will pick up a healthy chicken.

Pamela: Kachi?

Kachi: Yes, my dear.

Pamela: Are you crazy?

Kachi: Yes, I am crazy for your love, baby girl.

Pamela: Hey Kachi, don't change the topic. Ignoring those bullies is one way to go. Another way would be to report them to the school's principal

Kachi: So, are the boy's parents helping the boy with counselling?

Pamela: Yes, they are. They also place the boy in a youth program where they learn to do things together as a team.

Kachi: How is that working out for the boy?

Pamela: Not too well.

Kachi: Hey Pamela, has the youth program tried to practice the Robber's cave experiment50 which was carried out in 1950s by Social Psychologist Muzaffer Sherif et al?

Pamela: No, Kachi. I don't think that the youth program knows anything about the Robber's cave experiment, neither do I know what it is and what it's supposed to do. Do you?

Kachi: Yes, I surely do. Oh, I forgot that you are in medical school studying to become a psychiatrist. Well, they make us take some classes in psychology. That's how I know about the Robber's cave experiment.

Pamela: Seriously?

Kachi: Yes, seriously.

Pamela: I thought your major is Computer Science?

Kachi: Yes, it is. I guess if you want to be a roboticist, you have to take some classes in psychology.

Pamela: Oh, now I get it. If you want a robot to behave like humans, then you need to take some classes in psychology. I see. So, what is the Robber's cave experiment?

Kachi: The Robber's cave experiment is a classic study of intergroup conflict and cooperation demonstrating how groups strongly favor their own members (ingroup bias), and how intergroup conflict can be resolved by these different groups working together on a common task that neither group can complete without the help of the other group. The experiment can reduce the polarization that exists between groups.

Pamela: Really? Kachi, you mean the Robber's cave experiment can unite polarized groups?

Kachi: Yes, it can. Well, maybe I should rephrase that. Pamela what I mean is that if the experiment is carried out the proper way, then it can reduce the polarization that exist between groups and possibly bring them together.

Pamela: Kachi, you got me curious. What is the experiment and how does it work? Tell me, tell me, tell me, Kachi would you?

Kachi: All right, all right, I'll tell you now. Be patient, patience is a virtue.

Pamela: Okay, I'll be patient. So, what is the Robber's cave experiment?

Kachi: Well, The Robber's Cave experiment is one of the most famous Social Psychology experiments carried out in 1950s by Social Psychologist Muzaffer Sherif et al solving the question: "what is it exactly about groups that make for such tension between them and what can be done to reduce that tension?"

Pamela: The question sounds interesting. Kachi: It certainly does.

Pamela: So, Muzaffer Sherif et al (or Muzaffer Sherif and his research team) want to know why there is such a huge polarization between different groups. That is, Sherif et al want to know why opposition is deeply rooted between different groups.

Kachi: Yes, Pamela my girl, and what we can do to reduce the tension or the deeply rooted opposition between those opposing or polarized groups.

Pamela: Kachi, that is quite interesting and very important in modern world.

Kachi: Sure Pamela, it is important. Sherif et al created an artificial situation that mimicked the real world using adolescent boys who are between the ages of 11 and 12 years old inclusively. There are three stages in the experiment.

Pamela: Really? Three stages?

Kachi: Yes, three stages. In Stage 1: The in-group formation stage where forty (40) boys were divided into two different groups of 20 boys per group and per camp. That is, there were two camps, each camp housed one group of 20 boys only, such that each group has no idea of the existence of the other group. Each group focused on group bonding.

Pamela: What is the second stage?

Kachi: In Stage 2: The competition stage where the researchers introduced the two groups to each other, and they created competition for resources where only one winner can exist and there must be one loser.

Pamela: So, for the two groups there must be no draw?

Kachi: No. There must be one winner and there must be one looser.

Pamela: I see. That is tight!

Kachi: Yes, it is tight. What is interesting about this is that there were no prizes for second place, no consolation prizes.

Pamela: Really? No prizes for the second place? That is hard. It's as if the second place would be competing for nothing.

Kachi: That is correct. As expected, this kind of competition created a whole lot of tension between the two groups because as you rightly said, no one wants to compete for nothing. So, both groups were scrambling for the first place.

Pamela: I can imagine that would create a lot of tension.

Kachi: Yes, Pamela that did create tension. First, there was verbal name-calling between the two groups and then they proceeded to vandalism and theft, and even physical violence to the point where the researchers had to physically separate the boys.

Pamela: I said it once and I'll say it again, I can imagine that will create opposition between the two groups.

Kachi: It surely did. Stage 3: This is the integration stage where the researchers created fake situations in which the two groups must work together to solve a common problem. That is, the two groups will work together on a common problem that neither group can complete without the help of the other group.

Pamela: Dependency! That is so clever. So, the two groups are forced to depend on each other to solve the problem that is common to both groups. Amazing!

Kachi: It surely is. In the first task, the water for the camp was shut off by the researchers in such a way that both groups thought that the vandals must have done it.

Pamela: So, the common problem that affected both groups is the lack of water for the camp since there will be no water for any of the groups to utilize. That is smart.

Kachi: So, all the boys in both groups, forty of them, must work together to figure out this problem and resolve it.

Pamela: That is so cool.

Kachi: There are many such similar team building activities between both groups. At the end of the third stage, they found out that the boys wanted each other much more because of these teambuilding activities.

Pamela: I can imagine.

Kachi: At first, there were very strong in-group bias within the team members just associated with other team members. But after these team building events where the groups got together to solve a common problem that neither group can complete without the help of the other group, they found out that they really liked each other a lot more than before.

Pamela: Wow! That is amazingly cool.

Kachi: The Robber's cave experiment was a confirmation of Muzaffer Sherif's Realistic Conflict Theory, which states that when there's competition for resources, negative feelings will arise. When there is competition, there is hostility. Therefore, one of the best ways to reduce this kind of group bias, prejudice, and discrimination that we have for other groups is to socialize with the other groups and work together to solve problems that are of

	high importance to both groups, that neither group can complete without the help of the other group.
Pamela:	This can really help the youth program with the current problems it faces.
Kachi:	Pamela my lady, remember now, I said earlier the concerned parties must be willing to carry out the experiment the right way for it to work.
Pamela:	Yes, Kachi I remember. I think the organizer of the youth program can pull it off.
Kachi:	I really hope so, my lady. Are you going to let them know about the Robbers Cave experiment[50]?
Pamela:	Yes, Kachi. I certainly will because I feel it will help the group to alleviate whatever differences that may exist between them.
Kachi:	Pamela my lady, I think so too.
Pamela:	That's cool, Kachi.
Kachi:	Thanks, Pamela. I appreciate that.
Pamela:	Kachi, you are welcome.

The Robbers Cave experiment mimics the kind of conflict that plagues people all over the world. Studies show that the simplest explanation for this conflict is competition. Divide strangers into groups, throw the groups into competition, stir the pot, and soon there is conflict.[50] Decades of research show that when people compete for scarce resources like employment, housing, land use, and other livelihood, the level of hostility between groups usually rises.[50] In times of high unemployment, for example, the level of racism is usually on the rise among different races like Caucasian Americans who may believe that African Americans and people migrating from other countries are taking their jobs.

Gone are those days, it seems, when a United states citizen automatically becomes a citizen of the world. That is, this American can travel to wherever he wants around the world and enjoys the world's encouragement. Today, however, the advent of corona virus or COVID-19 pandemic and its mismanagement have halted that privilege because the current COVID-19 statistics[53] reveal that the United States had more than 159,000 deaths, over 4.85 Million confirmed COVID-19 cases at the time of writing, and remains among the hardest-hit countries on the planet. As such, Americans are denied entrance to many countries like most of Asia, all of Europe and all of Oceania according to the news[54] media. Concerning his successor's handling of the COVID-19 pandemic, the forty-fourth President of the United States of America Barack Obama says: "More than anything, this pandemic has fully, finally torn back the curtain on the idea that so many of the folks in charge know what they're doing. A lot of them aren't even pretending to be in charge." What the forty-fourth President is saying about his successor, the forty-fifth President and his cabinet is that they are not even pretending to be leading as the leaders are pointing fingers and assigning blame to those they are supposed to be leading - their delegates. What these leaders fail to understand is that delegating responsibility and power to others does not alleviate you from the responsibility of making sure that your delegates are carrying out their duties as assigned. That is, the leaders ought to have complete oversight on their delegates. As such, the failure of your delegates is your failure.

During Joe Biden's largest fundraiser on June 24, 2020 President Obama accuses his successor, President Trump, of 'actively promoting division'52 among American people. According to the media,51 President Trump has done the country a disservice by promoting racial division among American people that he governs, leading to devastating riots like the one in Charlotte, North Carolina in 2017, nationwide civil unrest that began on May 26, 2020 due to the heinous act against George Floyd, a Black American. The killing of George Floyd55 has brought worldwide attention of the brutal racial injustice that black people and other people of color are experiencing in America.

The Robbers Cave experiment was a field experiment having real world application. The experiment may help mitigate the impact that bullying exerts on the general population. We can have these different dichotomous groups socialize and work together to solve a common problem that is of great importance to both groups such that, neither group can solve the problem without the help of the other group under supervision and longitudinally. While competition makes employees work harder against each other, it alleviates cooperative spirit which is necessary for balance in the industrial world. For a change, lets divide these employees into groups and have them socialize and work together to solve a common problem that neither group can complete without the help of the other group toward a common cause under supervision and longitudinally, or amount of time needed to reach the desired goal.

The experiment is not an impossible task to do as some companies in the United States like Google, Microsoft, Intel, and other notable companies are already applying what was learned from the Robber's Cave Experiment, bringing them greater benefits respecting productivity and profit. Yes, applying the experiment on a national level to dichotomous groups may help to reduce groups polarization and mitigate the tyranny of bullies.

Homeschooling

Kachi: Pamela my dear, speaking of homeschooling where parents send their children to school at home so they can have control over their children's education and daily happenings. I do understand that one of the reasons parents have for homeschooling their children is that of safety from bullies. So, homeschooling becomes a valid alternative to private and public schools.

Pamela: Yes, Kachi. While that may be an alternative, there is a major concern with that line of action.

Kachi: Really? What is the concern?

Pamela: The concern is that when these children graduate from high school through homeschooling and they want to work; would they have their own private businesses where they will not need to deal with the outside world that their parents have tried so hard to shield them from?

Kachi: At some point in time, they are going to have to deal with the world.

Pamela: If that is the case, when they are done with home schooling, the parents should spend at least one year teaching their children how to stand their grounds when dealing with the world. Yes, teaching them how to say no bravely and boldly without regrets, if they really mean to say no. Otherwise; it will be like sending out their children as sheep to the wolves.

Kachi: Yes, their children will be devoured. Children need social skills too. You know?

Pamela: Yes! Children need social skills. You probably know of someone who are fine during home schooling and when they get a job working out there, they start having many problems like unwanted pregnancies that they are not prepared for.

Kachi: That is so true. So, the earlier these parents prepare their children for the world the better success they will have with their children making it out there.

Pamela:	That is correct, Kachi. Attending school with other children out there is not all that bad if the problems of bullying are eliminated from the school system to where children feel safe to learn without being ridiculed and threatened.
Kachi:	I agree with you my dear. Speaking from personal experience, from the time I started kindergarten up until now, my parents, especially my Mom always ask me questions about my day at school. It's like they make me trace my activities from the time I leave their presence to the time that I get back to their presence.
Pamela:	Really? Isn't that too protective?
Kachi:	My parents make the process so funny that I don't feel like they are too protective. When my parents feel like I've been a victim of bully from what I told them, they both dramatize to me how I should handle bullies the next time around. I guess it pays to be a parent first before becoming the child's friend.
Pamela:	That is so cool. I guess it is a good practice to first commend your children about the way they've handled a situation before counselling them on how they ought to have handle it preferably through dramatization or role play since that will give the children a vivid mental picture on what to do the next time around.

Children are precious gift, yes, a divine inheritance.[38] Buy the time out of no time, to lovingly communicate with them about their wellbeing from the time they leave your presence to the time they come back to your presence. By doing so, you are not being overprotective, but being loving parents to your precious children. Thinking about it some more, you may realize that the words "over protection" should not apply to caring for your children in this day and age. Your children deserve all the protection you can give them just so they can go through the stages of child development[38] without the problems that bullying poses.

Not long, Kachi and Pamela land on the shore of an estuary in the city of Alameda. Pamela is ecstatic and asks for them to do it again. Kachi says another day and time would suffice. Several hours later, Kachi and Pamela are in a dance club dancing. Pamela discovers that when it comes to dancing, Kachi her man, lacks rhythm. Kachi isn't too proud to let Pamela show him some moves. Gradually, Pamela teaches Kachi how to dance. He enjoys it. They both enjoy dancing together and Kachi is relieved of his timid behavior since he can now dance publicly. Thanks to Pamela.

Abusing Family's Resouces Without Accountability Is Nothing Short Of A Bully!

The term firstborn son is an important concept in Judaism. In ancient Israel, the firstborn son is the one who inherits his father's position as head of the family. Inheriting the father's position does not automatically make the firstborn son the owner of the father's estate, thus making his siblings, his father's children, slaves undeserving of father's inheritance as some abusers who are firstborn sons mistakenly viewed it. Inheriting his father's position as firstborn son means handling his father's responsibility of caring for his father's children like his father would have done. A perfect example of how firstborn sons should view their position in the family arrangement and treat their siblings was demonstrated by Jesus Christ whose disciples addressed as "master." What if Jesus had addressed his disciples and treated them as slaves? He would have been right as he had the authority to do so as the master. Instead, Jesus Christ treated his disciples with deep respect and called them "my brothers" (Matthew 12:49, John 20:17). As a firstborn son, when you treat your siblings as inferiors, when you abuse the family's resources without accountability because you can and will, you are nothing short of a bully! May you imitate the examples of Jesus Christ and have deep respect for your siblings.

Alfred Adler (1870 – 1937) was the second-born child and being unhealthy child, Adler found competition with his older healthy brother and rejection by his mother to be difficult. He felt eclipsed by his model older brother and resented his favored status in the family. Adler strove to change his poor academic abilities at the bottom of the class and was able to rise to the top. With this ability to rise through persistence and dedication, he was able to overcome his inferiority and handicaps paving the way to an early example of his theory of the necessity of compensating for one's weaknesses. (Burger pg. 84). One of the theories that was developed from Alfred Adler's experiences as a child was "birth order." Adler was the first theorist to include all members of the child's family to have early influences on the child. Adler's birth order theory states that "the order in which children are born influences their attitudes and outlook on their life…" A first-born child receives all of attention from the mother and father all to themselves. This helps shape the attitude that they are the most important and if they are the only child, they continue receiving all the attention until another child is born, then the attention shifts, and competition begins. In some cases, the first child and the last child have a special place in the parents' hearts but not the middle child who is left to scramble for a special place with the parents as just another child. Studies show that while an odd number is ideal to form an effective group or team (Myers and Twenge 2015)[42], an even number for the number of children to have as a couple may be ideal. It would alleviate scrambling for a special place with the parents.

While Birth order does not predict how people will score on personality measures, the observation that Adler made about the effects of birth order on personality is such that middle-born children are the most well-adjusted and the highest achievers. I can attest to Adler's birth order observation as a middle-born child. I am always one of the hardest working persons in my department as an Information Technology Enthusiast for the United States government. Initially, I thought my working so hard to climb the corporate ladder was because I am the only African American male employee in my department of over three hundred employees, and to represent my African American people, I must go far up the corporate ladder. As I climb the corporate ladder however, I always seems to find someone in the department who is doing a little bit better than I am. So, I'll work harder with a view to surpassing this person. Now I understand that according to Adler, being a middle-born child is the reason for my striving for superiority and thus, one of the highest achievers. Siblings should have deep love and deep respect for each other regardless of age difference. Doing so, will unite the family.

Your Best Friend's Spouse Must Be Beyond Your Reach, Else, You Are A Bully!

A dictionary defines the term best friend as your "closest friend; someone you trust, and someone in whom you confide..." Your best friend is someone who has your back, someone who protects your interests at all costs especially in troublesome time. Among your many interests, your spouse is your chief interest that must be protected from intruders both foreign and domestic, at all costs. Domestic protection includes protection from you, the best friend. Your best friend's spouse must be out of your reach especially if you are assigned a protector of your best friend's estate or interests. There is an example found in the Bible at Genesis 39 verse 4 where Joseph was put in charge of Potiphar's household because Joseph had earned his trust. Potiphar was at the time Pharaoh's court official and Chief of the guard. Joseph was a well- built and handsome young man and in verse 7, Potiphar's wife enticed Joseph, practically begging him to lie down with her. What would you have done if you were in Joseph's shoes? Well, with every vibe of his body, Joseph refused the wife of Potiphar's proposition to lie down or fornicate with her!

Joseph explained to her that while her husband, Potiphar, left him in charge of all his belongings, or made him a trustee of his estate, she, the wife, is off limits. That is, the wife belongs solely to her husband, Potiphar, not to be touched by any other man including and especially him Joseph. How did Potiphar's wife take the rejection? In verses 12 to 20, she lied against Joseph and have her husband, Potiphar, threw him in prison. You may think that being trustworthy and truthful ended badly for Joseph. But in Genesis chapter 41, Joseph became the second most powerful man in Egypt, next to Pharaoh. Yes, it pays to be trustworthy!

You may have heard or experienced people running away with their best friend's spouse. Usually, such ones run to exotic part of the country, like Florida, Hawaii, etcetera. While the concept of best friend is an interesting phenomenon and a beautiful thing, having affairs with your best friend's spouse is however, a despicable act of evil. It is also a cowardly move because if your best friends had not let you in on their business where you have access to their homes and affairs and observed the gullibility or the wicked hearts of their spouses, you would not have had the confidence to hit on their spouses or encourage their spouses hitting on you. When it comes to romance and relationships, women are very powerful and are trailblazers in their own rights. They have the power to resurrect an almost dead relationship, and they have the power to make or break up beautiful homes, if they want to. Yes, if they want to stop a terrible thing from happening to their relationships, they can do it. The reverse is also true.

Being romantic and being romanced is the opium of a healthy marital relationship regardless of the couple's age. If you observe that your relationship is lacking romance, it is incumbent on you as husbands and wives to resurrect your romantic life, so you can feel young and alive again as a married couple. It is erroneous to think that the expression of romance should fall solely on your spouse's shoulders. No, since "it takes two to tango" in most cases, the responsibility of being romantic as a couple falls on both of your shoulders. Trust and trustworthiness are vital to a healthy relationship. If you have affair with your best friend's spouse, you will deny them the right to a healthy relationship, which may someday come back and bite you where it will hurt you the most. I had the opportunity to interview an older man who had experience in this situation. While he had given me the permission to share the interview with you, for the sake of privacy, I changed his name and those of his family. There are two interviews.

A CASE STUDY ON SAMUEL FURONTAO

FIRST INTERVIEW

Personal Turning Points / Milestones for Samuel Furontao

Turning Points	Social	Emotional	Cognitive	Physical
Prenatal (Before Samuel's Birth)	Parents were friendly with the community. No children.	Parents sometimes happy, sometimes unhappy	Parents thought pregnancy was mother getting overweighed	Baby Samuel was however, growing fine in the Womb
Infancy (~0- to 2-year-old)	Friendly, no sibling	Happy, seldom cried only when parental attention is needed	Understands and speaks mother's tongue fluently. Object observance in cadre	Crawling, walking, strong

Turning Points	Social	Emotional	Cognitive	Physical
Early Childhood (~3 to 5-year-old)	Friendly at home, community and preschool	Happy	Learning appropriate with age.	Physically strong, growing above average
Middle Childhood (~6 to 12-year-old)	Friendly at home, community and at school	Happy, jovial	Had no problem with learning, was given triple promotion at school	Physically strong, growing above average
Adolescence (~13 to 17-year-old)	Friendly, dating, have best friends	Happy, jovial	Highschool Graduate at age fourteen and Full Scholarship to Rice University	Physically strong, growing above average – 6ft. tall
Early Adulthood (~18 to 35-year-old)	Friendly, married to best friend and high school sweetheart	Happy, jovial	Delayed Full Scholarship to Rice University to wait for his best friend to catch up	Physically strong, healthy and handsome.
Middle Adulthood (~36 to 65-year-old)	Friendly	Happy, sad, frustrated	MSc. Accountancy and Successful Bank manager	Physically strong, healthy and handsome.
Late-life (~66 to ??-year-old)	Lonely, introvert	Semi happy, Sad and frustrated	Retired Bank Manager	Fairly healthy, but heart broken.

Samuel Furontao
Life Milestone with Turning Points

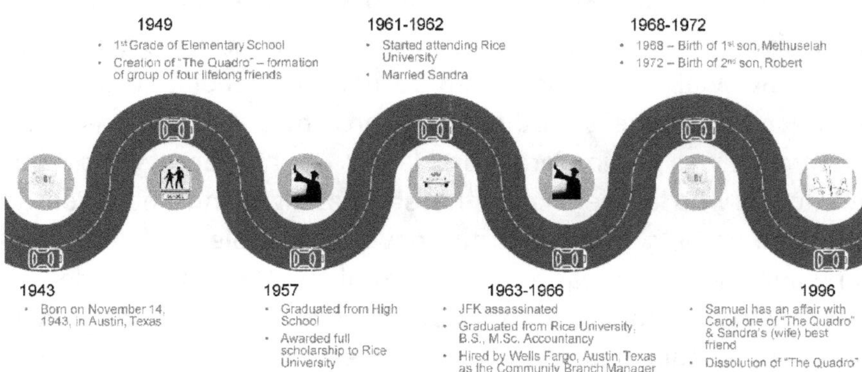

Samuel Furontao
Life Milestone with Turning Points

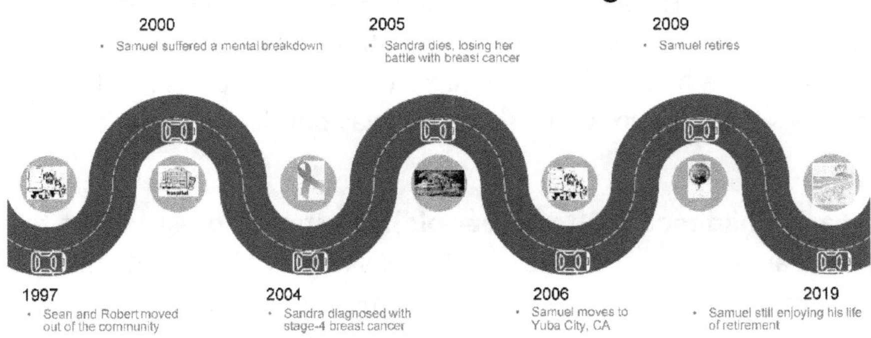

Prenatal (Before Samuel's Birth): The name of my subject is Samuel Furontao, a seventy-six-year-old Caucasian American who was born and raised in Austin, Texas. The circumstances surrounding his birth as the only child was quite interesting. His parents for twenty years prior to having him have no children though in dial need of one. During his conception, his father thought that his mother was putting on excessive weight and did not appreciate that, leading to constant daily quarrels. Samuel's mother was exercising but to no avail since her stomach was getting larger and larger. So, his parents decide to see a doctor who let them know that she was eight and a half months along. The parents who found the news impossible to digest were happy and the father was apologetic to his mother who decided to name the baby Samuel is he's a boy, or Abigale if she's a girl. Well, he's a boy, Samuel says. Hence, the name Samuel from the Bible as his mother felt like Hannah who for long seeks a child. Why Abigale if a girl? Samuel says no idea.

Infancy (~0- to 2-year-old): As an infant, Samuel said he was a happy baby who only cries in times of needs as far as is parents are concerned. He had a normal growth and loves to play even when alone in his crib. His secure base wasn't threatened since him mother was always around. He never had a babysitter because his mother was a full-time housewife taking care of him. So, you can call him a mamma's boy he said with a smile. He was physically strong and ate a lot.

Early Childhood (~3 to 5-year-old): He started preschool at the age 3 years and was very friendly. He was told by his parents that his Aunt likes to come around to teach him phonetics since she was a kindergarten teacher. She and his Mother loved each other dearly and that though they were sisters, they are best friends. The help he got from his mother and Aunt helped him sail through preschool and kindergarten. Samuel is taller than his age group and intelligent which he said he had his mother and Aunt to thank for.

Middle Childhood (~6 to 12-year-old): Samuel started his first grade at age six and was one of the smartest pupils in the class.

Samuel always attributes his success in school to his Mother and Aunt and because of his brilliance, he had a lot of friends who needed him to help with their homework. He was physically strong and tall. His friends called him "LB" for ladies' boy. He was quite a handsome boy Samuel says and hospitable. No wonder, the many friends. Samuel was given triple promotion from the first grade to the fourth grade. His father was against the jump in grades, but later settled with it as mother and teachers convinced him that it was a good jump. Samuel was in the fourth grade at the age of seven. He had three best friends, a seven- year-old boy and two six-year-old girls. Four of them usually walked to school together. The name of the elementary school was Jacksonville Elementary school which Samuel said it's no longer in existence. Samuel was given another double promotion when he was eight years old from the fifth grade to the seventh grade and was in the tenth grade at the age of twelve.

Adolescence (~13 to 17-year-old): Samuel was growing fast and had reached six feet in height at age thirteen in the eleventh grade. Samuel said he was embarrassed to be the tallest person in the class. I let him know that being tall is nothing to be ashamed of, to which he said he know that now. One of his best friends named Sandra agreed to be his girlfriend though she was in the seventh grade as a twelve-year old pretty girl, said Samuel. The other two best friends agreed to go steady as boyfriend and girlfriend. The four best friends were known to the community as "Quadro" because when you see one of them, in no time, you'll see the others. Samuel finished high school at the age of fourteen. He was given a full scholarship to Rice University in Texas but delayed going so as to wait for his friends who are in the tenth grade at the time. So, in the interim, Samuel got a job as a Teller with Margo bank. The Quadro made a pass not to break up the team regardless of situations and circumstances.

Early Adulthood (~18 to 35-year-old): Samuel married Sandra at the age of nineteen as soon as Sandra turns eighteen since they are from the old school Samuel said. They had a great community wedding and everyone they knew showed up. Interestingly, his two other best friends got married some three years later. Samuel and his wife had their first son named Methuselah when he was twenty-five years old. The couple were so happy for quite a while for having a happy baby boy. Four years later when Samuel was twenty-nine, they had another boy named Robert. Samuel said they were on fire with joy. Things were going great with Samuel, his family, and his best friends. In a nutshell, the Quadro were having a blast as the other two friends are out of high school and married. The Quadro did went to the Rice University as planned and had their dream jobs in Austin, Texas. Samuel was the bank manager of the only Margo bank in his community which he got when graduated with honors Master of Science in Accountancy and the other three were medical doctors. Things were going quite well with the Quadro, and their children are like siblings to each other.

Middle Adulthood (~36 to 65-year-old): Samuel was fifty-two years old when he had affair with Carol, his best friend's wife and one of the Quadro which understandably broke up the group. The community were devastated to see the breakup of the legendary Quadro and according to Samuel, he was severely blamed for having affair with his best friend's wife and thus, causing the breakup. His children faced public humiliation from peers on account of their father's deed. His wife was constantly bombarded by her friends and other members of the community to divorce Samuel, all of which fell on deaf ears as she constantly proclaimed her love for Samuel and will never dream of deserting him. Samuel suffered a severe breakdown not for having the affair but for the trouble his family had to suffer from the only community they knew. His two sons moved out of that community to one that is far away from it but still in Austin. Occasionally, Samuel's children would run into people that once knew them and as far as Samuel was concerned, you cannot imagine the pain that inflicted on his sons. His wife later lost her life to cervical cancer at the age of fifty- nine. Thereafter, Samuel moved to Yuba City, California. Since his two kids are grown and married, they refused to go with him. When I asked how his two sons are doing, Samuel said that he has not heard from them and that he lost contact with them after the adulterous incident. Samuel said that with the affair, he had lost more than he had bargained for. I asked why can't he contact his sons for reunion and that I'm sure they must have forgiven him? He said the affair he had ruined trust as well as family ties and so his children didn't want anything to do with him.

Late Life (~66 to ??-year-old): Samuel is seventy-six years old and said all he wants to do is to enjoy his retirement as a single man and never want to remarry. His thought is that not being married is keeping him out of trouble and doesn't have to answer to anyone. When I said everyone need someone sometimes, Samuel said his needs have been taken care of and that he has friends who are not judgmental but letting him be himself. He also said that he's been very careful not to break peoples' homes.

Second Interview

Cultural/Socioeconomic lens: The second interview had begun with my subject Samuel Furontao, a seventy-six-year-old Caucasian American who was born and raised in Austin, Texas. As explained in the first interview, the circumstances surrounding Samuel's birth as the only child was quite interesting. His parents for twenty years prior to having him have no children, though in dial need for them according to Samuel. They were middle-class, well to do couple. Samuel's parents placed great importance on SES (Socioeconomic Status) as they both have college degree, and his father was an Electric Engineer at a time and want the same career for his son. Samuel was born on March 14, 1943, and as an infant, Samuel said he was a happy baby who only cries in times of needs as far as is parents are concerned. He had a normal growth, loves to play even when alone in his crib. His secure base wasn't threatened since his mother was always around and they are well to do. He never had a babysitter because his mother was a full-time housewife taking care of him as both parents agreed since his father's salary was more than enough to maintain their socioeconomic status as well to do family. I asked if Samuel could remember messages about values and expectations that he gets from family & culture? Samuel asked: "You mean as an infant?" I answered yes, as an infant. I cannot remember that far long, Samuel replied. I may be able to remember from age six and up, certainly not a single thing before then, Samuel concluded. Samuel started preschool when he was three years old and was very friendly. He was told by his parents that his Aunt likes to come around to teach him phonetics since she was a kindergarten teacher. I asked Samuel how he felt about Mom and Aunt's help in his early childhood education? He said he was very grateful about it because he had a great start in life because of their help. Samuel started his first grade at age six and was one of the smartest pupils in the class. Samuel always attributes his success in school to his Mother and Aunt and because of his brilliance, he had a lot of friends who needed him to help with their homework. He was physically strong and tall. His friends called him "LB" for ladies' boy. I asked Samuel how he felt about his nickname, he said it felt good to be the ladies' boy and it made him feel better not being called a different name like "goofy" but just ladies' boy. So, he was happy about it. Samuel was given triple promotion from the first grade to the fourth grade. Then I asked how Samuel feels about the triple promotion he had received in his first grade. In one-word Samuel says, "elated. I was very happy because in the fourth grade, I am still the tallest in the class. So, I don't feel like I don't belong even if I'm the youngest." His father was against the jump in grades, but later according to Samuel, his father settled with it as mother and teachers convinced him that it was a good jump. Samuel was in the fourth grade at the age of seven. He had three best friends, a seven-year-old boy and two six-year-old girls. I asked Samuel why he felt those were his best friends, he said because he never felt threatened or controlled when with them, vice-versa and they protected each other, and they usually walked to school together.

Samuel was given another double promotion when he was eight years old from the fifth grade to the seventh grade and was in the tenth grade at the age of twelve. I asked how he felt about the second double promotion, to which Samuel said, he was happy for the promotion as it surely feels good to finish school before time. I asked if the promotions affected his friends, that is, were they jealous that you are leaving them behind? Samuel emphatically answered no! In fact, he continued, they were happy for him. He then concluded that it could be the case that they are too young to have or display any sense of jealousy. Whatever the case may be, he continued, their friendship stayed ever stronger. Then I said, good for you, Samuel, good for you. What is your take on poverty? Is that something you appreciate? I asked. Samuel said, if it is up to him, everybody would be rich such that there would be no class division. He hates to see people suffer because of being poor, hence, his family take education very seriously as a means of climbing the socioeconomic ladder. Then I asked, "what did your family and culture teach you about education, career, money, savings?" Samuel laughed and said that he was taught that education is everything. If you want to be somebody and go places in this world, you must have education without which you'll be a nobody and will be poor without money. You won't be able to get a decent job without education. Then I asked, so education is important to you? Samuel exclaimed: "Education is everything, son! Don't you get it? Without education you can't get a decent job, without a decent job, you can't get a good salary, and without a good salary, you can't get a decent savings for the future, for your family and retirement!" I got it, I said. Do you? Samuel replied. Yes, I did, I said. We both laughed out aloud. I asked how old he was and what he was doing when the former President John F. Kennedy was assassinated on November 22, 1963? After sighing heavily, Samuel says, "I was 20 years old getting my bachelor's degree at Rice University. It devastated us the Quadro such that we fasted for two days, I'm talking about no food, no drink, no romance." Really? No romance? I asked. Samuel said yes, it was that bad. The entire country was in disarray and in a state of chuck and disbelieve. Samuel was ready, he said, but his wife wasn't. So, Samuel had to console her.

Romance lens: The interview became more serious when I asked Samuel to forget about how young he may have been at the time and tell me what messages about values and expectations he got from his family & culture? Specifically, I asked "what were you taught marriage to be?" Samuel said he was brought up in a Christian home and was taught to believed that God instituted the first marriage to be between the man called Adam and the woman called Eve, and both became husband and wife and so whatever God has yoked together, let no man put asunder. So, Samuel continued, marriage is a solemn bond of love between a man and his wife, and he strongly believe so. Samuel said he strongly believe so because nowadays, people are turning marriage to what it's not supposed to be. Hence, the many problems facing the institution of marriage. If man and woman operate marriage like it was supposed to, Samuel continued, all the marital problems you see today, would not have come to light. It seems that there is an invisible force that is making humans do wrong. Otherwise, marriage was intended to be a beautiful thing and a gift to man. His parents showed him how marriage is supposed to be because they were together for better and for worse, through thick and thin until death. I believed that to be the case Samuel said, I nodded affirmatively. How do you feel about crushes? I asked. Crushes are a natural phenomenon between opposite sex that attract, Samuel says, and it is important as it sometimes leads to the formation of a new family. I remembered that was how I met my wife. We met when we were very young and didn't get married until we're 19 years old.

Spiritual lens: I asked Samuel what his family and culture taught him about religion? Samuel said that he believes in the existence of one true God, was raised a Christian and preferred to keep his denomination to himself as he would not want that to change anything between us. I understand, I said. Then I asked, "what did your parents taught you about gender roles and what are your current views on gender roles?" Samuel said that he came from the old school where he believed that if you are biologically born as a boy with penis between your thighs, you'll grow up to be a man; and if you are biologically born as a girl with vagina between your thighs, you'll grow up to be a woman. I don't care what people are saying today, he continued, gender is binary, a man and a woman, period! Samuel emphasized. Then I asked, " what did your family and culture teach you about divorce?" Samuel replied that divorce is not a good thing and so they believed that divorce is a last resort after everything and every help have been exhausted to no avail, then and only then, can he consider divorce. Furthermore, he continued, God hates a divorcing, so does his family. So, I asked, your family and culture must have placed much importance on spirituality, is that so?" Samuel faintly but enthusiastically says "yes we do! So much that it is our lifeline."

Scholastic lens: We moved on to other turning points in Samuel's life and so I asked Samuel to tell me how he felt when he finished high school at the age of fourteen. Samuel says he was very happy, felt he was a genius, though when you go a block further, you'll see another one. However, it made him happy and accomplished especially with the full scholarship to Rice University, what else can a young man asked for? He asked. I asked, in our last interview, you delayed going, to wait for your friends who are in the tenth grade at the time, why and how did that made you feel? Samuel says, "well, they are my best friends and we've been doing things together and I don't want to break us up as the Quadro team, so I figured that I could use that time to earn some money, which wasn't bad at all. In fact, I was a rich kid when I got to Rise University because I worked and that went into my resume too. It's kind of killing two birds with one stone." That's nice, I said. When Sandra, one of your best friends agreed to go steady with you as your girlfriend, how did you feel? Very happy, Samuel said, "especially when I proposed to her and she says yes, of course, I will marry you. I feel like an emperor." I was your wedding? I asked. It was wonderful, Samuel said. "The entire community attended what they called the "Quadro wedding of the decade." When you and your wife Sandra had your first son Methuselah, what changes do you have to make in your lives to accommodate him? Samuel answered, "not much of changes because we were ready for him. In fact, we planned and prayed for him to come. However, we used to go to the gym and walk around as the Quadro, that kind of changed a little because, Sandra was tired from nursing my baby boy.

The Quadro understood that, so instead of walking the blocks, we go dancing and sometimes we just stay home and reminisce on the past and the future. I stop working overtime to be home on time with my family, play with them and watch my boy crawl, walk, and run." The couple were so happy for quite a while for having a happy baby boy which turns out to be another turning point that effect some changes in the couple's life. Samuel's wife being a medical doctor decided to change her hours to part time to give the boy all the support he needed for proper development. However, Samuel continued with his full-time job coming home straight from work to be with the new family. Things were going well, and Methuselah is as intelligent as his parents with normal development. Four years later when Samuel was twenty-nine, they had another boy named Robert. Samuel said they were on fire with joy. Things were going great for Samuel, his family, and his best friends. In a nutshell, the Quadro were having a blast as the other two friends are out of high school and married. The Quadro did went to the Rice University as planned and had their dream jobs in Austin, Texas. I asked Samuel how it felt to have the Quadro at Rice University? Samuel replied that the Quadro felt very joyful, and they help each other out with schoolwork and projects. In short, Samuel says, life at school couldn't be better. Samuel also said that their popularity as the Quadro extend to the university such that there are those who wanted to join our circle at school, we refused because we'll no longer be the Quadro. We are family. How did it feel to be the bank manager of the only Margo bank in your community? Samuel said that although a lot of work was involved, but it surely pays well and it felt great to be the only bank manager – the fame by itself, is amazing. Things were going quite well with the Quadro, and their children are like siblings to each other.

Health lens: There are no health issues with Samuel and his family earlier on. Samuel was fifty-two years old when he had affair with Carol, his best friend's wife and one of the Quadro which understandably broke up the group. I asked Samuel what that affair meant to him? Samuel said that he was as devastated as the community was, to see the breakup of the legendary Quadro and according to Samuel, he was severely blamed for having affair with his best friend's wife and thus, causing the breakup. His children faced public humiliation from peers on account of their father's deed. His wife was constantly bombarded by her friends and other members of the community to divorce Samuel, all of which fell on deaf ears as she constantly proclaimed her love for Samuel and will never dreamt of deserting him. Samuel suffered a severe breakdown not for having the affair but for the trouble his family had to suffer from the only community they knew. His two sons moved out of that community to one that is far away from it but still in Austin. Occasionally, Samuel's children would run into people that once knew them and as far as Samuel was concerned, you cannot imagine the pain that inflicted on his sons. His wife later lost her life to cervical cancer at the age of fifty-nine. Thereafter, Samuel moved to Yuba City, California. Since his two kids are grown and married, they refused to go with him. When I asked how his two sons are doing, Samuel said that he has not heard from them and that he lost contact with them after the adulterous incident. Samuel said that with the affair, he had lost more than he had bargained for. I asked why can't he contact his sons for reunion and that they may have forgiven him? He said the affair he had ruined trust as well as family ties and so his children didn't want nothing to do with him. I asked What did it mean for Samuel to move to Yuba City, California? Samuel said for him, it was a new start as a single person without his wife. He wanted to move away from the pain that the memory of the Quadro and the community deserting his family after the affair. Working for Margo Bank helped him tremendously for the new start not to be overly downhearted.

Retirement lens: Samuel is seventy-six years old and said all he wants to do with this turning point is to enjoy his retirement as a single man and never want to remarry. His thought was that not being married is keeping him out of trouble and doesn't have to answer to anyone. When I said everyone need someone sometimes, Samuel said his needs have been taken care of and that he has friends who are not judgmental but letting him be himself. He also said that he's been very careful not to break peoples' home or let a woman come between him and his friends. Samuel was grateful for the interview as he was sent back on the memory lane. He's now making effort to resume contact with his two sons and according to Samuel, this interview convinced him to regain contact and trust with his family. I asked what did you most want your children to learn? After taking a deep breath, Samuel answered, "I want my kids to understand that marriage is solely between a man and a woman. I want them to have a strong marital value, to view family as authentic as the creator sees it. I don't want them to be like me — breaking people's home. As Christians, we raised our kids in a Christian way. So, I want my kids to have a self- sacrificing spirit as did Jesus Christ. If I'll do it again, I will never break my wife's heart as that's the most regretful thing I've ever done. I wish that my sons will not copy that. I want them to be faithful to their wives and under no circumstances should they break their wives' heart. I want my kids to put God first in their lives as that is the opium of survival. Life is too short to be in pain due to animosity." We ended the interview on that note.

It is interesting to know that Samuel now understands that behavior in life is not just about him claiming "it's my life, I'll do what I want to do. Yes, I'll do whatever pleases me!" Samuel now understands that there are sacrifices we must make for the benefit of those we care about like our children, our spouses, our friends, and even those that we share the same community with. The African saying that "it takes a village to raise a child" simply mean that there is a shared interest among the villagers— the success of the child. Members of the community see each other as a family and what you do with your life as an individual matters to the community, who would let you know that while it may be "your life," it is indeed, a shared life with the community. That is, a collective culture. Collectivist culture is doing things in group like in Africa where group-esteem is promoted, and success is identified by group doing well and things are about "ours" or "theirs." On the other hand, an individualistic culture is doing things individually like in the United States where self-esteem is promoted, and success is identified by personal achievement and things are about "mine" or "yours" and vice- versa. Faced with the same situation, people in a collectivist culture would feel and act differently from those who are raised in individualistic cultures. While it may be easy for someone raised in a collectivist culture to migrate into an individualist culture, it can extremely be difficult for that same person, after getting used to or settling down in an individualist culture to emigrate back into a collectivist culture. Our culture helps define our situations (Myers and Twenge 2015) an example of which are our standards regarding promptness, frankness, clothing and even dancing which vary with our culture. Yes, culture and people shape our sense of self, and the relation between personality and culture is such that people and their personalities exist within a cultural context be it individualistic or collectivist. When we take a closer look at the reactions of people to the same situation, that characteristic differences between people will become obvious. The more closely we look at the characteristic ways people deal with emotional situations, the more we see that people are not alike. Personality is defined as "consistent behavior patterns and intrapersonal processes originating within the individual (Jerry M. Burger: Personality 10th Edition 2017). Personality makes us who we are. It influences nearly every aspect of our lives, including what we choose to do for a living, how we interact with our families, others, and whom we choose to spend eternity with.

Samuel had a healthy and beautiful childhood and adult life until he decided to sleep with his best friend's wife. Thereafter, life has not been a bed of roses for Samuel, it is full of thorns and thistles as he lost the trust of his children, the trust of his wife, the trust of his best friends, and the trust of his community. At some point in time, you will stop to wonder, does it really, worth all those consequences? Samuel answered No! It doesn't! You know the adage: "Prevention is better than cure" is true in my case, because if I had prevented that awful behavior from happening, Samuel argued, I would not have to look for the cure that in most cases or at least in my case, it is just not there! What a pity! I thought. I wish that Samuel's family can forgive him so he would not die of loneliness. I'll be checking up on Samuel on a timely basis to curb his loneliness. If you observe that your best friend's spouse is confusing you for a certified marriage counselor, direct that spouse to a certified marriage counselor for the needed therapy. It is certainly not your place to split them up regardless of their insurmountable marital issues. Be what you claim you are to them by helping to unite them.

11

HOW POWERFUL CAN THE POWERLESS BE WHEN THEY DECIDE TO FIGHT BACK?

Shine the light on the Slow Loris family. Rindi is Papa Slow Loris and Gunmi is Mama Slow Loris. They have three children. Juba is the first son, Motepori is the second son, and Motayori is the only daughter and the last born. Rindi calls the family together so as to teach them a lesson on respecting other animals regardless of the size and strength of that animal bearing in mind that survival skills are encoded in the minds of all wild animals. No creature appreciates any form of incarceration, slavery, or threat to his appreciated freedom. When the life of an animal, a Porcupine for instance that supposed to run freely in the wild is threatened by other vicious and powerful animals, this animal does its best to hide away from such danger. But what if there is no place the animal could run to for refuge? In most cases, that animal gets devoured. This vicious cycle will continue until the living Porcupines however little they may be, develop a defensive mechanism to repudiate their oppressors with a view to staying free in the wild.

Oteetota The Porcupine Fights Back Against Jeunkoku The Tiger

Rindi, Papa Slow Loris, settles down with his family and he asks them to open their books titled "Is Silence Really Golden?" by Elijah Mekwunye to chapter eleven where they will read about instances of how the powerless are empowering themselves even in the universe of the powerful. Look no further because you are holding the same book and on the same page as do the Slow Lorises. You can follow along as Rindi reads.

Rindi: I can see that you are all ready for the family story time. So, let's begin, shall we? Gunmi and the children answer yes, we should Dad.

Rindi: This story is about how the Porcupine's family gained their freedom in the wild through the bravery of one of their own going by the name Oteetota. One day, Oteetota was minding his business looking for food like grasses, fruits, or vegetation. As he walks through the jungle, an angry Tiger going by the name Jeunkoku catches sight with him and attacks the poor little Porcupine.

Gunmi: Oh, no. What happens to Oteetota the poor little Porcupine, is he ok, is he ok?

Juba: Yes, Dad is Oteetota all right?

Rindi: Now, hold on my love ones. Be patient. Patience is a virtue. Don't jump the gun and we'll get to where we are going.

Motepori: All right Dad, we'll wait.

Rindi: Great! Can you imagine this five hundred pounds Tiger that Jeunkoku is, attacking a less than thirty pounds Porcupine that Oteetota is?

Motayori: No Dad, that is unimaginable! Gunmi: Indeed, it is unimaginable.

Rindi: During the attack, several things come to light. Oteetota realizes that he has a defensive mechanism but do not have a clue or the trust that the mechanism can actually word off an animal so large and vicious as the Tiger is. Let's listen in on their row[30].

Gunmi: Sure, sweetheart.

Here we see Jeunkoku trying to grab Oteetota by the neck just so as to strangle him, but that effort is yet to be successful as Oteetota makes it difficult, shooting his little but dangerous quills at Jeunkoku. Oteetota tries his best possible to avoid confrontation with Jeunkoku a priori, but to no avail as Oteetota seems to find himself cornered and in a round box. Does he give up and lay down like a dead Partridge at the mercy of Jeunkoku? Let's find out, shall we?

Jeunkoku: Oteetota, why can't you just let me grab under your neck, I promise I'll be nice?

Oteetota: [Oteetota is naturally a very quiet animal who chooses to be silence and irresponsive to Jeunkoku's question at this point. He, however, continues to fire his quills at Jeunkoku and doing his very best to protect his neck from Jeunkoku's vicious jaws]

Jeunkoku: Come on now, are you going to bow down there forever? You going to have to breathe somehow, and I promise I won't hurt you. Please let me caress your neck, would you? I promise you will enjoy the massage.

Oteetota: Yes, why don't you go caress your wife's neck crazy psycho? I'm sure she'll enjoy it, you overgrown bully!

Jeunkoku: What! Oh, it's on now. You surely are going to get it.

Oteetota: What are you talking about "it's on now?" What have you been doing to me all this time, playing with me? You overgrown psycho.

Jeunkoku: If I can't get to you through your neck I can certainly get to you through your rear. I'm going to break your legs to get to your rear. Believe me Oteetota, you don't want me to do that. So, I'm going to give you one more chance to let me grab your neck.

Oteetota: In your dreams. Tell me, how does this feel?

Jeunkoku: How does what feel?

Oteetota: Here, break these! [Oteetota fires his quills right through Jeunkoku's chest, thus piercing his heart and causing cardiac tamponade. He says] The pangs of sorrow will rain down upon you; overgrown bully, get behind me! The pangs of distress will rain down upon you, overgrown bully, get your mouth off my business!

Jeunkoku: I believe that I should be the one asking you how does this feel?

[Jeunkoku picks up Oteetota by his buttocks, hit his head on the ground and asks.] I asked you a question and I know that you know that my question is not rhetorical. So, I ask again, how does that feel?

Oteetota: [At this point, Oteetota is condition is fatal and yes, you are right, he is half dead. But he manages to say the following to Jeunkoku before drawing his breath.] Hey Jeunkoku, mark my words today. You may have won the battle but not the war. Enjoy your last dinner and few minutes in the jungle. [Sadly, Oteetota dies.]

Jeunkoku: Now, where are we? I am going to enjoy every parts of you, you little stone. Ah! You may be little but you are surely a handful, a force to reckon with. [Jeunkoku devours Oteetota and continues.] I cannot believe that something so small can be so powerful. I feel like I've just fought with many lions. You taste good though. But I will certainly not want to mess with your kind again! It is not worth the effort. For some reason, I am not feeling too well. I wonder what is happening to me. I better go lay down for now. I wonder what he meant by I "may have won the battle but not the war." Oh well, who cares?

Kotito: [A Tigress, catches sight with Jeunkoku who is obviously in an excruciating pain] Jeunkoku, what happen, why are you in pain?

Jeunkoku: Where are the rest of my family gathered? Can you fetch them for me?

Kotito calls for the rest of Jeunkoku's family and before you know it, they are all around him wondering what had happened to the powerful Jeunkoku such that he is groaning in severe pain. Jeunkoku begins to tell his family why he is in such a terrible pain.

Jeunkoku: My fellow family members, I want to thank you so much for coming. I am in severe pain as you can see, and I am dying.

Kotito: What? Who did this to you? Who did you fight with? Tell us, tell us so that we can go and devour him!

Jeunkoku: No. we are not going to do that, and I'll tell you why in a minute. I attacked Oteetota a Porcupine because I was famished.

Family: Oteetota, a Porcupine did this?

Jeunkoku: I was surprised too. In fact, I was amazed not just about the fact that the little Porcupine put up a defense, but that he put up an effective defense and fatal offence. I cannot imagine such an enormous power coming from something so small as Oteetota.

Kotito: I cannot believe that Oteetota did this.

Jeunkoku: Yes, Oteetota did it and him and his kind have earned my respect. Oteetota's determination to fight back when he realized that I was not going to let him go is unique and worthy of emulation and deep respect. As such, I want all of you to promise me today that you will not go and bother Oteetota's family or his kind. Even if you have to, protect them from the other viciously powerful animals. They deserve the freedom to be who they want to be and live freely in the wild. I need you to promise me now.

Family: We promise to protect Oteetota's family or his kind. Yes, we do Jeunkoku.

Jeunkoku: [with his last breath he says] Thank you my family. [Jeunkoku dies]

Family: [morns Jeunkoku's untimely death.]

There are of course few animals like Leopard, weasels, Lions, and other Porcupines around in the thick forest. Some few minutes later they witness the death of Jeunkoku. The news of Oteetota killing Jeunkoku get to every nook and corner of the jungle. Such that none of all the animals in the jungle wants to mess with any of the Porcupines, let alone try to fight with him. Maybe you want to hold on to that thought for a moment because about two hours after the forest has been saturated with the surprising news of Oteetota killing Jeunkoku, a group consisting of twelve Lionesses gang up against another little Porcupine going by the name Pamimpao weighing about thirty-four pounds.

Pamimpao remembers the brevity of his diseased brother Oteetota, summons the courage and boldness to fight back after several attempts to get away safe are futile. Let's listen, shall we?

Pamimpao: Why you all want to eat me? Don't you think that I am too small for the twelve of you to consume? Why don't you just leave me alone and let me be? After all, the jungle is huge enough for us all, won't you say? Please let me go, I promise I won't come this way again.

Mokere: [one of the lionesses] We just want you to show us how your brother Oteetota was able to kill Jeunkoku, one of the Tigers. You may have gained your freedom from the Tigers but not from us and yes, we want to eat you.

Pamimpao: But it is just one of me against twelve of you. I don't think that is fair, would you agree?

Mokere: Look around you Pamimpao, is there anything fair in the jungle?

Pamimpao: I don't think that is my problem. I just want to live my life without your troubles.

Magun: [one of the lionesses] Pamimpao, are you saying we are trouble?

Pamimpao: Well, you are trying to eat me, are you not?

Magun: Of course, we are. You are not making it and you know resisting will not benefit you.

Pamimpao: killing me would?

Magun: who are you to question us like that? Get over and stop resisting!

As the lionesses get closer to grab Pamimpao, Pamimpao fires his quills at them scaring them away. This goes on for about an hour before the lionesses finally give up without hurting Pamimpao.

Mokere: Family, I don't think trying to kill Pamimpao worth the effort. First, he's way too little for all of us to share even if we are able to kill him. What is more, he is firing those dangerous quills at us and none of us wants to be the unfortunate one to have it pierce her heart. Remember Jeunkoku? Yes, he killed Oteetota, but where is he today?

Jeunyo: [one of the lionesses] So, are you saying we should let her go?

Mokere: I am not hearing a better choice. Do we have any other choice that is better than not devouring Pamimpao?

Jeunyo: No.

Mokere: That is my thought exactly. [turning to Pamimpao] Pamimpao, you are fortunate today because we are releasing you unharmed and we'll not bother you again. Go!

[back to the Slow Lorises]

Rindi: What a victory for the powerless in the jungle of the viciously powerful animals. The news of the Porcupines standing up for themselves against the viciously powerful ones and the sacrifices they made to achieve that freedom travel far and wide to all other jungles in the world. That is why the only creature that can be a threat to the Porcupines is the intelligent man.

Do Not Sacrifice Your Long Term Benefits
For Your Temporary Pleasure

Juba: Papa, what does Oteetota mean when he says "you may have won the battle but not the war?"

Gunmi:	I can answer that.
Rindi:	Go ahead brown sugar.
Gunmi:	Thanks sweetheart. Juba, you know how Jeunkoku died some few minutes after eating Oteetota?
Juba:	Yes, Mamma. Jeunkoku died of internal bleeding due to Oteetota's quills piercing his heart.
Gunmi:	That is correct my son. Since Jeunkoku wasn't alive after killing Oteetota, we can call it a draw because they both kill each other. Yes, while Jeunkoku succeeded in killing Oteetota hence winning the battle, Jeunkoku end up losing his life and thus, losing everything. Yes, he lost the war.
Rindi:	That is a very good explanation sugar. Another way to look at it is what mankind's economists will call the "opportunity cost." That is, the real cost that has to be forgone in order to get something that may or may not be of value to you. So, it is the valuable thing that you have to give so as to get something back.
Motepori:	Papa, you know how you and Mamma always rob our bodies with the oil from your elbows and you tell us that it is for our protection?
Rindi:	Yes, Motepori my son. That is a very good example. I want to protect you from the viciously powerful animals out there and so I have to buy your protection. By taking that oil from our elbows and robbing it on you the children, your Mama and I are paying for your protection because when you come across vicious animals and these animals perceive the odor from the oil on your bodies, they will leave you alone and not bother you.

Motayori: But Papa, what if they bother with us?

Gunmi: Motayori my daughter, they dare not bother with you because they know that the oil on your body can kill them if they ingest it. So, they'll leave you alone unharmed.

Juba: So, Papa, Mamma, what it really cost you to protect us is the value of the oil from your elbow.

Rindi: Yes, my son.

Juba: But you have a lot of them.

Rindi: Son, I rather keep my oil because it protects me too. So, I cannot have enough of it.

Gunmi: You see son, sharing our oil with you is the sacrifice we have to make for your protection. What does that tell you?

Motepori: Mamma, that tells us that you love us so dearly. Gunmi: Excellent! Don't you forget that, children?

Juba: We surely won't, Mamma.

Rindi: Now, let us get back to Oteetota. Would you say had won the war even though he lost the battle?

Motayori: Papa, I will say yes, Oteetota won the war because he made a lot of painful sacrifices and the greatest sacrifice he made was the loss of his life. All his sacrifices paid off when his relatives gain their worldwide freedom from oppression due to his exemplary bravery.

Gunmi: My daughter Motayori, that is excellent! Oteetota realized that the long term benefits for him and his family is the global freedom from oppression of any kind and he will not sacrifice that for his temporary benefit of staying alive at the mercy of his oppressors. Hence, he bravely fought to his death.

Rindi: Consider the freedom he bought for his people with his life. His family now know that they do not have to live in fear of the oppressors. They too can bravely fight back to thwart the machinations of the oppressors. Their victory will worth every sacrifice they make.

Gunmi: So, children, don't sacrifice your long term benefits for your temporary enjoyment and comfort. Be your brothers' keeper and your brothers will be your keeper. Take this to heart children, do not make yourselves a victim to anyone. You are made to be free. Stay free at all costs.

Rindi: Freedom or death? Children always choose freedom. On that note, we'll end our family story time. Your Mamma and I appreciate making yourselves available for this family story time. Thank you folks.

Juba, Motepori, Motayori answer thanks Papa and thanks Mamma.

Rindi and Gunmi answer you are welcome children.

Gunmi: Thanks sweetheart for your expression of love towards me and the children. That was a good story and a great lesson learnt. We appreciate your effort a lot. Thank you very much my love.

Rindi: My brown sugar, you are very much welcome. I couldn't have done it without you. Thank you, my love. We are blessed with beautiful and brave children that are bound to be successful in life. We are fortunate. Thanks, my love.

Gunmi: It's my pleasure sweetie.

Be Your Brothers' Keeper – Help The Powerless To Be Strong

Originally, all animals are created equal with survival instincts to live free in the wild and eat only vegetation.[31] Sets of rules are embedded as part of their instincts to deal with each other with mutual respect. Along the way, things changed and so is the diet of all the animals. Every sort of animals now has the urge to rule the jungle, promoting his race or kind while demoting and degrading the rest of the wild populace as outcasts, unfits, or serve as food. Yes, the dawn of the carnivores.

Since freedom is so important to all living organism including wild animals, however things may have changed, the notion of incarceration on their chosen way of life so long as it does not infringe on the others' rights, becomes poisonous to their minds. As such, they are willing to fight till death to live freely as it was originally intended than to live in captivity at the mercy of their oppressors.

The survival instincts given to these animals however little they may be in size and might, motivate them to come up with different mechanisms to defend themselves, to protect their kinds and to fend for themselves. The mutual respect that once existed among the wild animals which allowed them to live freely and in unity no longer exist. The result, every animal seems to be on its own. Whoever has the stronger power to kill, seems to survive the wild, while the powerless is left to wither away. No wonder the coined name "survival of the fittest," living no chance for neighborhood care.

May we do the best we can as humans to act as good neighbors to the wildlife, especially to those facing extinction while protecting the human race. Protect the powerless against bullies. Just as a hunter who learns the ways of her preys, turns around and use the knowledge against her preys, you too can learn the ways of your bully and use the knowledge to protect yourself against his or her machinations. Yes, help the powerless ones to feel powerful.

12

ARMED ROBBERY IS A BULLY

The weekend is here. It is Saturday. Chiyem calls his family together for lunch. As they do, the news is on that a bank robbery is going on a real time. Normally you would think that it is just a regular bank robbery in today's society. However, this bank robbery is significant to the Chiyem's family because Pamela's friend is among those taken as hostages according to the news. While the bank robbers are wearing masks, they allow news reporters to come in with their cameras as they make their demands and reveal the hostages. As the hostages are reveal, Pamela catches sight on Kachi among the hostages and she yells

Pamela: Oh my God! That is Kachi! Oh my God! That is Kachi! Oh my God! Oh my God! Oh my God! Oh my God! Oh my God!

She becomes hysterically distraught. Her parents are seriously concern as they wonder who Kachi is, what is he to their daughter and why is he being one of the hostages is of serious concern to their daughter to the point of making her ill. To end her parents' bewilderment, Pamela makes the following statement with a thin voice that is filled with pain.

Pamela: Mom, Dad? Kachi is my boyfriend. No, he is more than my boyfriend. Kachi is my fiancé. We got engaged yesterday and planned to tell our parents this evening during dinner.

Chiyem: What! Florence, do you know about that?

Florence: This is news to me too. I did not know that Pamela has a boyfriend let alone a fiancé.

Lizzy: Pamela, you have been a bad girl. You've been keeping secrets from Mom and Dad.

Pamela: No, Lizzy it's not like that. Dad, Mom, I want to be sure that our dating and courting would lead to somewhere good before telling you about it. I do not want to tell you about it, and we break up the next day, that would be hard on me. I am so sorry that you have to find out this way. Please, I am terribly sorry.

Chiyem: [hugs his daughter] That is all right my dear little girl. You did quite well. Now, let's go get your man.

Pamela: Thanks, Dad.

Lizzy: Pamela has a boyfriend, Pamela has a boyfriend, Pamela has a fiancé that Daddy doesn't know about.

Pamela: Mom, would you please make Lizzy stop?

Florence: Lizzy, stop teasing your sister. Show compassion, would you?

Lizzy: I better not be in trouble if I follow her footsteps.

Florence: You better not try it. Besides, you are way too young to be thinking about that now. Girl, you still have a long way to go.

Lizzy: Mom, there is a long division and there is a short division. I prefer the short division to the long one.

Florence: I know you do. Let's follow your Dad to the bank. Shall we?

Pamela & Lizzy: Yes, Mom.

Chiyem: Great! Let's go.

Many spectators, well-wishers and concern citizens gather outside the bank. The presence of ambulance, firefighters and the Police Officers with their trucks are seen outside the bank figuring out how to curb the tension. The negotiator is able to convince the gang leader to release the hostages by giving the robbers half of what they are demanding. Little does the negotiator know that the robbers have a different plan of escape. The plan of escape is that as they release half of the hostages, half of the robbers will take millions of dollars through an unknown underground tunnel to another street where their getaway van is situated. The underground tunnel is known only to the robbers and the few who help built it. At the release of the last badge of hostages, the robbers are nowhere to be found. They are gone with millions of dollars, diamonds, and bearer bonds.

It's interesting that the gang leader claims to be on a job working as if they are working on a job that they are legally employed to do. How can taking something that doesn't belong to you be considered as working or being on a job? For instance, your acquaintance stops to ask you hey, what do you do for a living? Would your reply be "I am in the armed robbery business?" Maybe such ones are expected to sugar quote the reply they give based on the definition of work found in any physics book or tell their acquaintances to mind their own business. Whatever the case may be, robbing banks and people are not and should not be considered as a job or working for a living. The Bible at Ephesians 4:28 says "Let the one who steals steal no more; rather, let him do hard work, doing good work with his hands, so that he may have something to share with someone in need."

Kachi And Pamela Meet Their Soon To Become In-Laws

Pamela introduces Kachi to her family. Kachi also introduces Pamela to his family and apologizes meeting them under the present circumstances and hope that they have met under a more conducive circumstance, one that does not involve hostage take over. Pamela's Dad, Chiyem invites Kachi and his family to join his family for dinner to get to know each other a little better. Kachi and his parents accept the invitation. The two families hug each other and part ways until dinner time. The Police Officers canvas the area for days looking for clues to capture the robbers, but to no avail. However, they are able to discover the tunnel to their amazement and make plans to close it off. In closing off the tunnel, other discoveries such as criminals hide out during police chase come to light. These hideouts have made catching the criminals a profoundly dAunting tasks if not impossible. With these discoveries, the city officials do not count prevention of the bank robbery as an all lost endeavor. The Mayor of the city gives an ordinance to go through all banks in the city making sure that no such criminal hideouts and tunnels exist underneath the banks. If any exists, close it up.

The evening is here. It is dinner time with Chiyem's family. Kachi's family arrives on time with flowers for the ladies and everyone is having a great time getting to know one another. Chiyem brings out kola-nut[15] to share with his guest. While Pamela is spending time with Kachi's family, Kachi is equally spending time with Pamela's parents. One of the questions that Chiyem throws at Kachi is about intentions. Let's join in.

Chiyem: Kachi my dear one, what are your intentions for my little princess?

Kachi: Sir, do you mean apart from making her the most beautiful wife the world has ever seen?

Chiyem: Hmmm. [Affirmative nodding]

Kachi: Well, I need you to pay attention to something.

At this point Pamela is having a wonderful time with her soon to become parents-in-law some few yards away. So, after apologizing to his parents asking Pamela to be excuse for a moment, Kachi calls for Pamela asking her to walk to where him and her parents are standing.

As she does, Kachi asks Chiyem and Florence, Pamela's parents to pay attention to how she walks. When Pamela gets to where Kachi and Pamela's parents are standing, Kachi expresses his gratitude for her obedience and asks her to walk back to his parents in the fashion. Pamela does so but wonders what all that is about and leaves it alone. As Pamela walks back to where his parents are standing, Kachi pelts a question to Chiyem and Florence.

Kachi (continues): My dear people, do you see how Pamela walks as if she never uses the bathroom and that everything about her is perfect, and nothing impure can come out of her?

Pamela's parents remain silent wondering where Kachi is going with that line of questioning. Florence however, does have an idea where Kachi is going with the question but wonders whether he could pull through successfully.

Kachi (cont.): By the time I make a beautiful mother out her, she may have to rethink the way she walks. And you know how Pamela is the quiet type of a lady, she barely talks; when she starts raising little Kachis, she will sing soprano!

Chiyem: Kachi, are you out of your God given mind? Are you on drugs? That is my daughter, my little Princess you are talking about!

Kachi: Sir, I do not mean any disrespect. With all due respect to you sir, you asked me a question that I considered ridiculous, the result of which I thought you are being humorous and so, I decide to reciprocate with a ridiculous answer.

Doubtlessly, you can imagine Florence's uncontrollable laugh that makes Chiyem to wonder whose side she's on. Facing her, Chiyem asks.

Chiyem:	How is my question humorous? I just want to know his intentions for my daughter. Is that so wrong?
Florence:	Chiyem my dear one, that is not what I am laughing at. Please forgive me my dear. The way Kachi acted out his answer to your question is not only insightful but enormously humorous. And you should have seen your face at that point in time, it is priceless!
Chiyem:	Yeah, that's why I asked if he's on drugs.
Kachi:	As far as I am concern, with all due respect, Pamela is not some properties that I have intentions for. She is a beautiful lady that will grace my future with beauty and splendor. To those who do not understand my language, Pamela is my present and my future. I love that girl; she is my life!
Florence:	No wonder every time Pamela comes home there is this glow to her eyes and on her face as if she has seen an angel. I could not bring myself to ask her whether or not she has been with a man because of how we raised her, and we trust her judgement. Now, we can see clearly, and we understand.
Chiyem:	Yes, indeed we trust her judgement. She has obviously chosen you, who are we to stop it even if we want to?
Florence:	Kachi, what my lovely husband is saying is that with open arms we welcome you to our family.
Kachi:	Thank you very much Dad and Mom. O, can I call you Dad and Mom now?
Chiyem:	Hey, I'm not that old. [Three of them are laughing]
Florence:	Yes, of course Kachi, you can call us Mom and Dad.

Chiyem:	[talking to Florence alone] My blood?
Florence:	Yes, my heart.
Chiyem:	This guy you call Kachi is crazy and I am very much concerned about the fact that he is dating our daughter.
Florence:	But why are you concerned about that, my love?
Chiyem:	Well, I am concerned because if Kachi is behaving this way, so crazy before he marries my daughter, how would he behave after the wedding?
Florence:	[finds it difficult to stop laughing because of the serious face that husband has on and the nature of his concerns. She says] My love, you have nothing to worry about. Kachi is just funning with you. I like his sense of humor. I think he's good for our daughter.
Chiyem:	All right my blood, I'll take your word for it and I better not be disappointed.
Florence:	Believe me my heart, you will not be disappointed. The parties reunite and Pamela asks her Mom why she won't stop laughing, her Mom replies that "Pamela my girl, I think your choice is right." Pamela decides to leave it alone even though she does not get the sense of what her Mom is talking about. The evening ends blissfully.
Pamela:	Kachi my love. now I feel like I can ask you any question without Upsetting you.
Kachi:	Pamela my baby angel, if you have any question to ask even if you think I'll get upset, I'll be offended if you choose not to ask.

Pamela:	Well, since you put it that way I might as well ask you this one question that has been on my mind ever since we met.
Kachi:	Really? What is it?
Pamela:	Kachi, promise me that you won't get upset?
Kachi:	Ah! With a pretty face like that, who would get upset?
Pamela:	OK, then. Why are your father's hands in constant motion, shivering as if he is afraid of something or under severe stress?
Kachi:	Well, my father's doctors have a name for his condition. They call it dystonia – an involuntary upper body movement. The result of a breech presentation his mother had while giving birth to him.
Pamela:	Really?
Kachi:	Yes, really. The doctors said that because he was declared dead on arrival, they felt that his brain was deprived of the needed oxygen. Hence, the neurological problem.
Pamela:	Wow! Kachi, do you know that your father is a miracle baby?
Kachi:	My Mom still feels that way.
Pamela:	I feel that way too. I cannot believe that I am in love with the son of a miracle baby.
Kachi:	Well, treat me right and do you right baby.
Pamela:	Kachi, could you please tell me more about it?

Kachi:	Patience. Patience is a virtue. In time. In time my little angel I'll tell you everything about it. In fact, my Dad have the saga all written down in a book entitled "Conquering the Stigma of Cerebral Palsy," which will soon hit the store.
Pamela:	Kachi, that is amazing! I cannot wait to read it.
Kachi:	Be patient. My angel, be patient.
Pamela:	I'll try for you my love, I'll try. Kachi, you mention "cerebral palsy" earlier. Does your Dad have cerebral palsy?
Kachi:	Yes, he does.
Pamela:	But he doesn't show it.
Kachi:	He's fortunate about that. However, when you draw close to him, with time you'll see it.
Pamela:	Awesome!

Things Are Going As Planned For Kachi And Pamela

The love birds set a date in which they will marry. Kachi and Pamela want to wait until they graduate from college and get their careers going. On their wedding day the love birds are successful in carrying out their wedding plans. They are both fortunate because they do what they set their minds on. That is, Kachi is now a software Engineer with a hi-tech company, while Pamela is a Pediatric Psychiatrist with a major conglomerate medical corporation. Kachi and Pamela live happily ever after with little Kachis. What about their parents? They too are having a blast with the union, especially with their grandchildren, the little Kachis. Four little Kachis. Chima is their six-year old boy, Ada is their four-year old girl, Ama is their two-year old boy and Dimka, their one-year old boy. Kachi's children are adorable, smart, and well behaved. They are the kind of children you'll hope to have when starting your family. They are a blast.

Kachi and Pamela reminisce on how faithful they have been when they were dating and courting each other. They both strongly believe that romantic love or intercourse should be practiced only by married couple. That they were able to stay chase despite their unbearable urge of romantic attraction that existed between the two love birds prior to marriage, is not only worthy of emulation but also a tremendous cause for joy and deep respect for each other.

The Information Technology Enthusiasts - Victims Of Gang Robbery

On a sunny Tuesday Afternoon, five Information Technology Enthusiasts (ITE - which is a little higher that Information Technology Specialists) are in a luxurious car driving to a rural area with a view to establish an internet presence. As the ITE proceed through a dirt road that is surrounded by mild bushes, they come to a halt. They are ambush by three-gunmen. The three gunmen ordered the ITE to come out of the car with their hands up. The gunmen rob the ITE to their last penny. The gun men even have the ITE to take off their shoes and walk away bare footed. One of the ITE plead for the shoes since it is sunny and the ground is scorching hot, but to no avail. The gunmen drive away with the luxurious car and the stolen goods leaving the ITE in a state of quandary. What do you know? It's like three miles to the next public telephone since all their mobile telephones have been stolen, that is how long the ITE will have to walk to get help. You can imagine the ITE without shoes hopping on their feet to where they can find help.

It is interesting that the gunmen do not get far enough before they too were robbed at gunpoint. The way it happens is that a mile from where the first robbery took place is another ambush that is unknown to the first gunmen. The first armed robbers are really having fun reminiscing on their last robbery and how their victims were hopping along the dirt road barefooted. Before they know it, the three gunmen suffer the same fate as did their victims. The six gunmen that ambush the three robbers order the three robbers to take off their shoes and everything they have including their guns and pants.

One of the three armed robbers that is being rob asks the six gunmen "why are you robbing us?" The head of the six gunmen says because we want to. But it's not fair that you rob us says one of the three gunmen. "Why isn't it fair for us to rob you when you have just robbed someone else?" The head of the six gunmen asks. "Because it is not righteous." Answers one of the three armed robbers. "Oh, so it is righteous for you to rob someone else and it is not righteous for me to rob you, is that your stance?" Asks the head of the six-armed robbers. But our guns are not loaded. Answers one of the three armed robbers. I got news for you pal, our guns are not loaded either! The head of the six gunmen says. As they are all laughing, the head of the six gunmen says: "but we are more and stronger than the three of you. So, our leverage is greater than yours." Then the six gunmen drive away with the newly acquired luxury car as they watch the three robbers hop on their bare feet in search of help.

The three-armed men are no longer armed. As they hop through the dirt road, it is like they are not hopping fast enough to where they could find help because their victims catch up with them. Guess what happens next. The five victims fearlessly go up against the three robbers in battle. Yes, hand to hand combat. Several offensive words are exchange during the battle. In the end, the five victims emancipate themselves and are no longer victims as they beat up the three robbers and have them thrown in jail by the police officers. The Police Officers get a kick when they find out that the three robbers were equally robbed in the same way they had robbed the five ITE. Laughing his heart out, one of the Officers says: "there are no honor among thieves."

Mr. Monroe's Ordeal

The fun does not seem to be over yet as the Police Officer receives a call involving a domestic dispute. The caller, Mr. Monroe reports that his ex-wife is having a quarrel with his wife because she wants to come back to claim her right, that is, to be the new Mrs. Monroe again. The two ladies are throwing things at each other and breaking stuffs, the reporter continues can please hurry before they kill each other? OK, OK, OK. Calm down Mr. Monroe, we will be there before you know it says the Officer. Are you in a safe location? The Officer asks. I think so, Mr. Monroe replies. At Mr. Monroe's residence, three Officers have to literally pull the two fighting ladies apart. Mr. Monroe's ex-wife Michal, reports that her ex-husband isn't supposed to be happy while she is miserable. Mr. Monroe yells out "but you were the one who left me for that woman. O, things are not working out for the both of you and you think that should be my problem? In what universe will that happen? I've moved on with a real lady, obviously you don't want that either. So, everyone should be as miserable as you are, and we call it the signs of the time? Would that make you happy? Why can't you just live us alone?"

Can't you get it that I can't live without you? Asks Michal. Yes, I was fooled by that woman at a time of my identity crises, but I know now with all certainty that you are my compass and without you in my life the North star is no different from the rest of the stars; Michal pours out her heart with tears. Mr. Monroe says that we both know that love has nothing to do with your remorse but your abject failure in your evil plight against me which seems to have backfired at you. Mr. Monroe continues, you have tried your new love but failed woefully, why can't you just let me have mine and stop your unwholesome jealousy? After all, we are divorced. Now you want me to let you come back just so you can finish what you started? You had the Police arrested and charged me with crimes I did not commit just so I can have a bad record, be placed on probation so you can have me under you spell forever? Look Michal, I have a good thing going on for me now.

A woman who loves me with all her heart and who I can count on without disappointments. Why can't you just let me have that and let me go? Mr. Monroe asks in desperation. Michal says she rather be miserable in Mr. Monroe's universe than to share a Kingdom with someone else. Dana, the current Mrs. Monroe says woman, you should have thought about that before you left him for that whore! You damaged the man completely, Dana continues. Now that I fixed him up, you want him back? That is just not going to happen! You can count on that, missy! Dana concludes.

It is obvious that Michal is the perpetrator and since there isn't any reason for an arrest, Michal is asked to leave Mr. Monroe's residence and never come back again. Michal is advised that should she have any legal course against Mr. Monroe, taking it up with the court would be in her best interest. Mr. Monroe and Dana his wife are left alone to go about their business. The Officers advise Mr. Monroe to file a restraining order against Michal if she does not desist from her obsessive jealousy.

Michal does not take the admonitions too kindly as she intensifies the harassments which forces Mr. Monroe to file a restraining order against her. Filing a restraining order against Michal doesn't seem to help the situation either because six months have elapsed since the restraining order is in effect and nothing about the harassments have changed. Mr. Monroe asks, where were all these energy and tenacity Michal is now displaying when she was married to me? I guess she solved her sexuality issues with woman and finally understands that she wants you. It's too late now, Dana replies. Angel, you can say that again, says Mr. Monroe whose pity for Michal's condition prevented him from filing a harassments complaint against Michal whom he ones loved so dearly. Mr. Monroe and his wife decide to ignore Michal's harassments by making a mockery of them. What do you know? The couple find the exercise amusing. As it is, the law soon catches up with Michal for something that does not relate to the harassments and she is soon placed under arrest. Guess who are there to help her out? Yes, the Monroes.

The Monroes are at the correctional facility to bail Michal who is charged with the possession of narcotics with intent to distribute. As they are handling their business, the Monroes hear a commotion going on in the visiting room where a man, Jake, is paying a visit to his son Ethan who is serving a two-year prison sentence for robbery. Ethan tells his father that he committed the crime on purpose so as to have them lock him up just so he will not have to listen to his father's self-righteous mouth. Jake, who is a developmental Psychologist, says that he has done his best raising Ethan up from infancy, asking Ethan his son, where did he go wrong as a father? I gave you everything a person could ever want; at school you were an A-Student, and I was there with you all the way. Where did I go wrong with you, son? Jake asks with a heavy heart.

Ethan stands up calling on the guards saying to them that this man's visit with him is over. As he walks away with the guards, he said these words to his Dad: "You are so selfish. Why do you always think that everything is about you, Dad? Guess what Dad, this is not about you. I'm doing this for me! For the first time in my life I want to experience how it feels to be a failure since you won't let me. It may not feel good but at least, it is a decision that I made all by myself! And Daddy, grandpa and grandma didn't help!" You are killing your mother you know? Jake asks. Well, she'll get over it someday. Ethan replies as he walks off into the thin air.

Mr. Monroe and his wife decide to step over with a view to console the heavy-hearted Jake. Mrs. Monroe asks Jake; how may we address you sir? I am Dr. Jake Samuelson, but you can call me Jake. Hello Jake, I am Dana, and this is my husband, David. We are the Monroe. Thanks for stopping by, says Jake. We could not help but overheard the discussion between you and your son, says David. Well, that seems to be a loss cause, Jake replies. I won't call it a loss cause because listening to your son, I believe he wants you to stop shielding him and let him make the decisions concerning his future whether good or bad, says Dana. But how can a young adult make decisions concerning his future when he lacks the skill and the tools to do so? Jake asks. David says well, you can guide him from behind or even side by side making sure that the decisions made are his decisions and should he fail, be there to encourage him not to give up as failure only helps him to appreciate success when he works smarter next time. Jake expresses his gratitude to David and Dana for their consolation, kind gestures and admonitions.

I hope you guys are not going to forget me here. Michal yells. No, we won't, we'll be right there Michal; Dana replies. David tells Jake that they have to go finish bailing out Michal before she breaks down the wall. The meeting is over, and Michal is out on a hundred thousand (USD) dollars' bail.

13

STAND UP AGAINST THE TYRANNY OF A BULLY

Kachi's in-law, the Chizom family have been planning a family reunion party at the beginning of the year. The reunion will happen when the school is out for the summer. All the relatives of Chiyem and Florence are invited to this family reunion party. Of course, Kachi, his wife Pamela and their four children will be there. Preparations are made to have the party in one of the top restaurants in San Francisco. Mr. and Mrs. Chizom - Chiyem and Florence will host some of their out-of-state relatives in their seven- bedroom resident. Among these out-of-state relatives are Pamela's Uncles, nieces, nephews, and cousins. A total number of twenty will be sharing this seven-bedroom and four-bathroom single family home for four days.

The time has come for the family reunion party and relatives from out of town are starting to flock in as expected. Kachi and his family will be coming tomorrow since they are living about five miles away from the in-laws. The party will happen in two days and everyone is ready for it. The next day is here and the Chizom family is excited to host the reunion party. Here comes the Kachis. You can imagine the joy of seeing relatives you've not seen in a long while. They are all happy reminiscing about the good old days. Pamela introduces Kachi and her children to her Uncles, nieces, nephews and cousins. What a great time they are all having.

Kachi And Pamela Confront Her Abusive Uncle

Suddenly, the sunny day turns gloomy when one of Pamela's Uncle, her father's younger brother and yes, her childhood victimizer going by the name Chika asks to be alone with Pamela. Chika is thirty-four years old and Chiyem is six years older. Pamela had already told her husband Kachi about Chika, her childhood rapist and will definitely not want to be alone with him again. The conversations go this way.

Chika: Hey Kachi and Pamela, you both are a wonderful match for each other.

Pamela: Oh, thank you very much Uncle Chika.

Kachi: Yes, we appreciate that, Uncle Chika.

Chika: Hey Kachi, can I borrow your wife for a minute? When Chika asks that question, Pamela squeezes Kachi's hand letting him know not to honor Chika's request. Did Kachi get the signal? Let's find out.

Kachi: There is no way in Ge-hen'na that I will let you spend a Nano second alone with my lovely wife. You are a sick pathetic psycho!

Chika: What! Why are you talking to me like that? Kachi, why are you insulting me?

Kachi: I know what you did to my wife when she was a child. Now, you want me to leave the two of you alone so you can continue from where you stopped? That is not going to happen! You victimized her when nobody was there to protect her from your vicious acts. Guess what? I am here now. Believe me, you do not want to mess with me.

Chika: What are you talking about? I don't want to pick up a healthy chicken here. Pamela, what lies have you been telling about me?

Kachi: Oh, now you want to play dumb huh? Coming from someone like you, that is too low. You have already pick up a healthy chicken a long time ago. As a matter of fact, you have dipped a leaf into your mouth right in the presence of the mute when decide to harm your little niece. The least you can do is to accept your responsibility for what you have done! Believe this, that may be the beginning of the cure to your pathetic psychosis.

Chika: All this accusation? I did not touch your wife when she was a Child! I never touched her like that!

Pamela: Yes, you did Uncle Chika! You raped me! You invited your friends to rape me and threatened me not to tell anyone. Now, you going to deny it?

Chika: I don't know what you are talking about. I didn't do such a thing! Of course, by now the everyone is aroused concerning this revelation and want to give Chika the benefit of doubt as he comes out of the closet unwillingly. Pamela's father Chiyem, hears the row, runs to the scene in disgust and asks:

Chiyem: What is going on here?

Kachi: Why don't you ask your brother Uncle Chika?

Chiyem: Ask my brother what?

Kachi: Ask your brother what he did to your daughter when she was a child?

Chiyem: What? Chika, what is he talking about?

Chika: Diokpara[32], I do not know what he is talking about.

Pamela: Dad, my Uncle Chika raped me when I was a child and he threatened to kill me if I tell you and my Mom about it. That is why I did not tell you guys about it. I am so sorry Dad.

Chiyem: Chika, you hurt my little girl like that?

Chika: No, Diokpara I did not touch her. She came on me and entice me.

Chiyem: What! She came on to you? She was just a little girl!

Chika: But she came on to me! I told her no. But she won't take no for an answer and so, I gave in.

Chiyem: She was just a child that trusted you to protect her.

Chika: I tried to stop her but she won't let me, threatening that she will tell on me that I raped her if I don't do what she wanted.

Kachi: What about your friends?

Chika: Yes, what about my friends?

Kachi: did little girl Pamela came on to them too?

Chika: She might have, I don't know.

Chiyem: You mean you raped my daughter and you invited your friends to rape her too?

Chika: But she came on to me, diokpara.

Chiyem: She was just a little girl. You are supposed to protect her.

Chika: She wasn't that little when she was coming on to me?

At this point Chiyem and Chika engage in fist fighting. Their relatives split them up from the fight and Chiyem sent his brother packing.

Chiyem: Get out of my house and don't you ever come back. As far as I am concerned, you are no longer

<table>
<tr><td></td><td>my brother! It is a disgrace that we both come from the same parents.</td></tr>
<tr><td>Chika:</td><td>Yes, I am glad that we finally come to that understanding, diokpara! It's not like you have ever done anything to help me out when I needed your help anyway. So, what is the big deal? And the rest of you, why don't you try comparing my circumstances to yours, see if you would have done any better before ridiculing and revealing my failures to the enemies of progress?</td></tr>
</table>

Chika leaves with his seven months' pregnant wife and a four-year old daughter who has been asking her Aunt Florence the question "why is my Uncle Chiyem fighting with my Dad?" The four-year old little girl isn't able to get a satisfying answer. However, she observes with intense curiosity as her Dad picks her up to leave. Children feel unease when the parents are not at peace. As they are living, Lizzy stops Chika's wife and says if I were you, I will investigate to make sure that my four-year old daughter has not been abused and keep her away from that man you call her father. Guess what, Lizzy! You are not me, are you? Certainly, I'm not you, am I? Chika's wife replies and walks away.

<table>
<tr><td>Kachi:</td><td>Dad?</td></tr>
<tr><td>Chiyem:</td><td>Yes, son.</td></tr>
<tr><td>Kachi:</td><td>I am so sorry that you have to go through that. Disowning your brother, however, is not the answer. Yes, you can stop associating with him for what he did to Pamela and thus breaking your bond of trust, but he's still your brother. Don't write him off as dead because doing so, will be grieving your parents. I am sure that you would not want to do that to them.</td></tr>
</table>

Chiyem:	Kachi, you are a true son in-law, thank you. Son, how long have you known about your wife's abuse?
Kachi:	Pamela told me when we were dating.
Chiyem:	Wow! She must have trusted you more than she trusted us, her parents.
Kachi:	Dad, it is not like that. Do not look at it that way. Do you know what would have happened if my baby girl had told you back then? You probably may not have believed that your brother Chika have it in him to do harm to her like that.
Chiyem:	That is plausible.
Kachi:	What if she had told you back then and you didn't believe her and her Uncle found out that she had told you about it and you just did not believe her. What do you think would have happened to your daughter?
Chiyem:	She would have been in more danger than she has.
Kachi:	Exactly! Since you have to work to make a living for your family you certainly cannot guarantee to be with Pamela all the time so as to protect her from Chika and his friends. You see, Dad, the Bible says there is time for everything[49] under the sun. Maybe that wasn't the right time to let you in on your daughter's ordeal at least for her safety. Now is the time. Dad?
Chiyem:	Yes, son. Thank you for everything and for looking out for my little girl.
Kachi:	Dad, you have to realize that my wife, your little girl is a brilliantly Beautiful and smart woman. I guarantee you that we will be successful

regardless of the terrible things that your brother did to her.

Chiyem:	Kachi, I am a fortunate man. Do you know why? Kachi: No, Dad I don't know why.
Chiyem:	I am a fortunate man because you are my son in-law. I love you son.
Kachi:	I love you too, Dad.

Florence and Pamela have been a source of encouragement to each other, they rejoin Chiyem and Kachi who have been having a private discussion.

Chiyem:	Pamela, I am so sorry for what your Uncle and his friend did to you. I am even more sorry that your Mom and I did not assure you well enough to make you know that you can come to us with anything that bothers you. My dear son, Kachi, made me understand why you did not tell us when it happened and I am so sorry not to have been there for you.
Pamela:	That is all right Dad. Don't worry. I am fine now. What is more, I have Kachi and my God with me. We'll always be successful. I am happy now, Dad.
Chiyem:	Yes, you still have your sister Lizzy, your Mom and I too you know?
Pamela:	Yes, I do, and I am very proud of all of you my family.
Chiyem:	Please, give us peace of mind that transcends all thoughts, oh sovereign Lord of the universe.

Chiyem, Florence, Lizzy, Pamela and Kachi hug and kiss each other with heavy hearts.

Chika And Janice In Family Feud

Chika and his wife have been having unbelievable arguments on their way back to the airport going home but they forget their daughter's book at Chiyem's resident and so they have to go back and get it. Chika goes in first to look for the bag but to no avail. He goes back to the car letting his wife to that he couldn't find the bag. So his wife goes in the house to look for the bag and find it where she had told her husband to look. She goes back to the car with the bag and there is silence. No one speaks for quite a while. Chika decides to break the silence by asking his wife Janice where she had found the bag. Let's join them, shall we?

Chika:	Janice, I looked everywhere for the bag and could not find it. Where was it?
Janice:	The same place I told you to look. But I guess you are busy looking at all the wrong places.
Chika:	Woman! How did you think I found you? By looking at all the right places? Hardly. If I had looked at all the right places, I guarantee you woman, you would not have been one of my choices, let alone the one I chose.
Janice:	That is not what I mean.
Chika:	Yes, I know what you mean, and you better be glad that I looked at all the wrong places. It should not have been you.
Janice:	Like I said, I don't mean it like that. It just came out the wrong way.

What is evil is evil, what is righteous is righteous and yes, what is holy is holy. A criminal may not have the heart to sleep at all if judgement day is in sight. Chika is currently in that situation and he is desperate to get out of it at all cost. It's kind of having the thought that money gives all the courage in the world that you need to do evil. So, this may not be the right time for his wife to be unkind to him in words and deeds. After all, she is all that Chika has at the moment. The Bible book of Ecclesiastes 3:1-8 tell us that "there is an appointed time for everything. A time for every activity under the heavens…" So, Chika's wife, Janice, must be discerning both in words and in deeds during this trying time that her family is currently going through. This is certainly not the time for Janice to use Chika's trouble and their inability to reconcile their irreconcilable issues against him and thus gain the upper hand as it might backfire at Janice. Besides, there are few people that may have the right to press charges against Chika for rape, Janice is not one of them.

The couple are at the beginning of the end of their relationship because of the many irreconcilable differences they've been dealing with leaving no room for compassion and empathy. In spite of what had transpired, Janice reassures Chika of her undying love for him and want their marriage to work by working out their many differences. Janice have Chika promise that when they get home, they will make appointment with a marriage counselor who could help them to address their irreconcilable issues. Chika's argument is that the marriage counselor had better not be one that will blame the cause of all their issues on him because however bad of a man he may have been, he is certainly not the cause of all the world's problems. So, they agree to look for an impartial marriage counselor.

Implicit Division of Guests Into Discussion Groups

Back to Chiyem's home where the shock of Pamela's child abuse is still on the minds of many. Interestingly, the guests implicitly split themselves into groups of male and female with each discussing family problems and how solutions can be realized. The first group has cousins Janet and L'Oréal discussing about Janet's daughter going out to search for her long- lost father. The second group has cousins Jacob and Levi sharing their view on the problems that the lack of quality time poses on modern families. Other guests are passive participants. Let's listen to a couple of such discussion. Shall we?

Janet: Have you ever wondered why some children look for their long lost fathers and when they find these men, regardless of what they may have done and why they left in the first place, the children who are now young adults want them back in their lives as if nothing has happened? Whereas the fathers who have stayed to lovingly raise them up gets the boot later in life when the children are grown. What is up with that?

L'Oréal: Well, Janet I have also thought about that and come to a conclusion that the world is just not fair.

Janet: Yes, yes, yes. L'Oréal I know that some teenagers for example, may spend all year long hating their fathers who may be the family's disciplinarian and hence, authority figure but it poses a problem if fathers are too hard on these teenagers.

L'Oréal: Janet, what if mothers are using these children as tools against their husbands or fathers of these children, won't that aggravate matters further thus, causing these children to have developmental hatred against their fathers who have been doing the best to lovingly raise them up from infancy?

Janet: Yes, I agree that no parent should be using the children against the other parent. The children should be made to love both parents equally. After all, it takes two to make them, it should take two to love and raise them too.

Rae: [a female cousin] You know they say you don't miss what you have until it's gone. Years of missing their fathers in their lives creates a void in them, which they probably will do the best they can to fill some days. When they finally find their long-lost fathers, the thought of finally closing that void comes with ecstasy of joy, such that nothing else would matter.

Janet: My twenty-year old daughter is out there alone searching for her father who had left us ever since she was two years old. Can you imagine my daughter whom I raised up alone, now a young lady, tells me that there is a huge void in her life and her father is the only one who can fill it? What am I supposed to do, lock her up?

L'Oréal: No, my cousin Janet. You are doing exactly what you ought to be doing for your daughter. Letting her go and search for her father is one of the best things you can do for her. The alternative, she may resent you. I am so sorry my dear cousin to be compelled to raise her alone. She turns out to be a fine young lady with a college degree. Not everybody can say that. Janet, you are a successful parent. Don't let anyone take that away from you.

Rae: Janet, your daughter is an adult now. She needs her space. So, if she wants her father back in her life, help her to achieve that goal. Let this be about her and you will not regret it.

L'Oréal: If you had obviously not raised her to disrespect her father, you'll have nothing of concern. Some people usually forget that when they raised their children to disrespect their father, they are inadvertently raising those children to disrespect them as mothers someday. The question is, who'll save them when these same children start to disrespect them? Would it be time to call the police on them? Only if they can fathom the fact that they are actually reaping the benefits of their labor.

Janet: No, I did not raise her to disrespect her father. I have never badmouthed her father in her presence.

The conversation continues but let's listen to the second group with Jacob and Levi.

Jacob: Hey Levi, don't fall for any woman who tells you that she does not have any career in mind and that her career is to support your career for you are the reason why she is placed on this earth. In most cases, she lies. She just wants to get you to marry her.

Levi: Seriously?

Jacob: Yes, seriously. When you fall for it and you marry her, she'll suddenly becomes a career woman under your nose; one that you barely can reason with henceforth. Look at my wife for example, who would ever believe she'll be a career woman? Look at her now. We barely can see eye to eye now, let alone deeply look at each other's eyes heartwarmingly. It's all a mess!

Levi: But she's helping out with the family. Isn't she? I mean, if looking into her eyes is the problem, just sit her down for ten minutes and stir into her eyes. If you have a specific goal in mind, then continue to stir into her eyes until you achieve your goal.

Jacob: Don't get me wrong Levi. I do appreciate the fact that my wife has a career. It's just that we don't have time for each other like we used to. I missed that part.

Levi: I understand. You know Jacob, you can come to an agreement with your wife on how to buy quality time out of no time so that you can have more quality time to share together.

Jacob: Yes, Levi we are working on that.

Levi: Great. Keep working on it. I promise, you will not regret it.

Jacob: Thanks man.

Levi: You are welcome, Jacob. Hey Jacob, what is the story about the famous actor being accused of sexual misconduct and now, they are threatening to retract his PHD degree. Can they really do that?

Jacob: Yes, Levi the school that conferred the degree on him as a gift can retract it for improprieties.

Levi: Really? I thought the degree is the actor's once it has been conferred upon him.

Jacob: Yes, that is true Levi, only if you actually do the work to earn the degree.

Levi: Jacob, what do you mean do the work? I thought they will not have conferred the degree upon him if he had not done the work.

Jacob: You know he dropped out of college in his sophomore year to pursue his acting career. Now that he is a successful actor, especially acting as a doctor on sitcom and movies, encouraging youngsters to go to college and stay in school, the university he once attended decides to give him a PHD degree as a gift to show appreciation for his successful acting career and role model.

Levi: So, you are saying because he did not stay in school to finish his course work and actually graduates from a PHD program, the degree that was conferred upon him was not earned.

Jacob: Exactly! Levi, I know you will catch up. The actor did not do the actual work. He did not enroll into any PHD program and actually finish the training. So, the degree conferred upon him was not earned, hence, it is a gift that can be taken away from him anytime by the same body that gave it to him.

Levi: Jacob, isn't gift something that you cannot take back?

Jacob: Yes, that is according to the economists. Maybe it depends on the kind of gift. Or it could be the case that the gift emanating from an institution of higher learning is not in that category. Who knows? I guess the actor may have a legitimate right to fight that in court.

Levi: Thanks Jacob for clearing up the air of the difference between earning a degree and having it as a gift. When you earn a degree, it cannot be taken away from you. An incarcerated criminal for example, can earn a PHD degree and still be addressed as a doctor because he earned it. However, if the degree is conferred upon you without the benefit of earning it, like that actor, it can be taken away from you.

The discussion continues. Let's snick up on a third group as it discusses the problems that culture poses on marital life, which one of the cousins who is married into a different culture experience.

Latifa: I love my husband but I just don't appreciate when he's speaking to me in a loud voice as if he's upset at me, but he's not. And his seventy- seven years old Mother always gets on my last nerve when she comes to visit us. After we finished eaten, she'll volunteer to do the dish which is fine by me. But she passes dirty pots and plates for clean ones! When I try to explain to her how I want my dishes to be washed, she thinks that I am insulting her. When she gets upset, she just leaves. Before she leaves, she tells me and I quote "young lady, you do not have the apparatus to argue with me!" That gets on me so much that I want to scream EEEJIGIJIGIJIGI!

Joy: Calm down. Calm down. Calm down. Would you? Let me get this straight Latifa. Are you saying that although your man yells when he talks to you; he is not mad at you at all?

Latifa: Yes, that is what I'm saying, Joy. He wasn't upset at me at all. In fact, he was making jokes with me. It's just that, if you don't understand him, you'll think he is shouting to disrespect you.

Joy: But he's not. Is he?

Latifa: No, he's not. In fact, his heart is as beautiful as beautiful can be. That's just how his people talk. If you see him with his brothers and sisters talking, you will think that they are upset at each other and about to go to war, even though they are just having fun.

Joy: So, what is the problem? Because you are sounding like a wife who deliberately forgets the lastname she has had for years in a divorce case just to show the court how much she despises her soon to become ex-husband.

Latifa: No, Joy. There's no problem except that when people see us together talking, they always think he's mad at me and that he might beat me up. So, I always have to explain to those people that we are not fighting, my husband is not upset at me, and that is just how he expresses himself. I am just tired of having to explain to people about it every time we go out.

Amaka: Latifa my cousin, I believe you are turning other peoples' problems into yours. If you understand and believe that your husband is only expressing himself when he talks loud at you and not that he's disrespecting or upset with you, who cares what people think about it?

Joy: Sure! It's none of their business that your husband yells when he talks. if you understand that's how he expresses himself and you know that before you marry him, trying to change him now will be doing both of you a great disservice, which may end up hurting you really bad. Besides, is that not one of the qualities that pulled him to you?

Amaka: So, if you want to be a successful spouse to your man, won't you think it wise to understand him first that he doesn't mean any disrespect when he talks to you with a loud voice, and that is just how he was raised? Or would you rather want to use the fact that he talks loud against him just so as to color him bad or even control him to your vantage?

Latifa: No, I will not do that to him. I love him too much not to do that to him.

Joy: Good, because it's your responsibility to protect him from those who choose not to want to understand his culture as much as it is his responsibility to protect you from those who choose not to want to understand your culture.

Amaka: Latifa, just as the pursuit of wealth reveals the essence of a man, the essence of a woman is about her beauty, her presence, her trustworthiness and yes, her dignity. If her beauty is found in the way of righteousness, good for her as it is to the glory of her God and her husband. On the other hand, if her beauty is found in the way of unrighteousness, not even her will appreciate the degree of her glory.

Joy: Yes, when you protect each other from the outside world, you will have the peace that transcends all thoughts. About his Mom, always remember that she is living her time, which you may not understand right now until you get to be her age. Always treat her with deep respect. Yes, Latifa always have genuine respect for her. Remember, without her, there will not be your husband with whom you are in love.

Amaka: Yes, Latifa think about your mother in-law as you some forty years from now. How would you like your son or daughter in-law to treat you?

Latifa: Thank you ministers. I will protect my man from the outside world. [Together, they all laugh out loud]

Joy: On a serious note though. What is wrong with men anyway?

Latifa: What do you mean, Joy?

Joy:

When I ask my husband to repeat himself because I did not hear what he was saying he would not want to repeat himself. In most cases, he changes the subject by saying something different from what he had said before that I really want him to repeat.

Amaka:

Joy, have you ever wonder whether or not you are getting older and it's affecting your hearings?

Latifa:

The question that is raised by Amaka is very important because sometimes we forget that as we get older our ability to function the way we used to, or even our acumen may reduce implicitly. So, we just have to do some personal examinations to test our current functionalities and abilities.

Joy:

I know for a fact that I am not going deaf. I just could not hear and understand what he was saying. Besides, it should not be a problem for him to repeat what he had said if I want him to. After all, I'm his wife and as far as I know, his only love.

Amaka:

Sometimes it can be a problem if the speaker exerts more than the usual power to speak clearly, something that we take for granted. Joy, what you could do next time is to ask him nicely by first placing your hand on him just so he can feel that you do not mean any harm or insult, then ask him to repeat his statement. I believe that will go well.

Joy:

Even when I ask him nicely, he tells me that I may need to consult with my doctor since my not hearing him clearly may mean an early stage of hearing loss.

Latifa:

He says that?

Joy:	Yes, he surely did. That upsets me so much that I said at one time that the only reason why I could not understand what he says is because he slurs his words.
Amaka:	You said it like that?
Joy:	O, I surely did.
Amaka:	O really? How does he feel about that?
Joy:	O, my cousins, that upsets him so much that he reminds me of the number of years that we have been married without the insults of how he speaks. And that I knew how he speaks before I married him and yet, that did not stop me from marrying him. He wonders why the ways he speaks now suddenly becomes a problem.
Latifa:	What did you tell him in reply because I think he's got a point.
Joy:	I was upset because he was upset. So, I went into my silent mode. Then he said something that further upset me.
Latifa:	What was it?
Amaka:	Yes, what did your husband say?
Joy:	He says that I must have been so desperate to have married him considering his speech problem. As such, I ought to be grateful that he did me the favor to marry me and that I ought to be treating him like a king.
Amaka:	Yes, maybe you should treat him like a king. As a matter of fact, married couples ought to be treating each other like Kings and Queens. Who

knows, marital problems may be abated by doing so.

Joy: The thing is, I really do treat him like a king should be treated. I love that man like crazy.

Latifa: Yes, you may love him like crazy, but do you make him feel that love?

Amaka: That is a good question you know? Because a lot of time we claim that we love someone, but the way we treat them may bid otherwise. Especially, when we think we know what they need and never bother to ask them just so they can tell how they want us to love them. Interestingly, we want them to ask us how we want to be loved, why can't we just ask them how they want to be loved too?

Latifa: Maybe when they tell us, we probably take them for granted just as we feel that they are taking us for granted.

Joy: Well, I don't think marriage is about "tit for tat." Misunderstanding maybe one of the reasons for marital problems.

Amaka: Hey Joy, if you feel that way, why can't you just explain it to your husband that you mean no harm and that you just want to have a clearer understanding of what he was saying, hence, the need for the repeat request?

Joy: I tried to. But, once one of us gets upset it becomes like that is the end of the road for that line of communication. I hate it when it gets to that point.

Latifa: Then don't let it get to that point. I am sure that you know how to make your man happy if you want to as much as he knows how to make you happy if he wants to. Do you remember your advice to me? About how it is my job to protect my husband as much as it his job to protect me? However hard to the hearings that advice may have been, it is the fundamental truth in marriage. Protect each other internally and externally. Protect each other domestically and internationally. That simply means, protect him from your upsets and anger as much as you would want him to protect you from his upsets and anger. That protection should extend outside the walls of your home.

Amaka: I appreciate Latifa's reasoning although I am sure she does not mean to see things in a military way. But the truth is, upsets and anger are like war zone that we all (including our men) need protection from. I am sure that our marital problems would abate if we put that idea into practice unselfishly.

Joy: Girls, I appreciate your admonitions and I will try to implement them with my man.

Amaka: One of the few problems that I'm having with my husband is that he wants twelve children, but I only want five.

Latifa: He wants twelve children? What are you, a child-rearing factory? Can you even afford twelve children mentally and especially, financially?

Amaka: Financially, yes, we can afford twelve children. But mentally, that is yet to be determined. I've let him know that currently we have four children, when we hit the fifth child, my child-rearing factory will be closed.

Joy: How does he feel about that?

Amaka: Not happy of course. He tells me every day that if it is God's will that we have twelve children, who are we to change that? Then I said we'll see about that when the time comes and so, there is no need to fight about that now.

Latifa: That is a calm and better way to handle that.

Amaka: Thanks.

The Coronation Of Kachi And Pamela At The Reunion Party

The discussion continues as we exit the day. The next day is here and the reunion party is on in a top five-star restaurant with a hired disco jamboree to handle the music. The dinner is great since everyone present enjoys every bit of it. With all that had happened yesterday, all the families decide to make Pamela the star of the reunion party by crowning her as the family queen of the year which automatically makes her husband Kachi, the family king of the year. "The family king of the year" and "The family queen of the year" is a yearly contest that the Chizom's immediate and extended families hold during the family reunion party. The winner of the crown is someone who has gone through a severe traumatic experience and come out victorious for the benefit of the family. The traumatic experience can include overcoming insurmountable obstacles, again, the family is the beneficiary.

Does this mean that a single person male or female cannot win the crowns? No, it doesn't. When a single person wins the family queen of the year for example, she is given the choice to choose who her king will be. Her chosen king may be her fiancé or someone that she is dating unofficially and uses that occasion to announce that she is going steady with the man and are now engaged. In a nutshell, the victorious single male or female may turn the coronation party to include an engagement party.

All the families agree that Pamela and Kachi will hold the crown for five years uncontested. This means that for the next five years, the family reunion party will hold the contest, and the king and queen crowns of the year will automatically be presented to Kachi and Pamela with all the rights. Using the language of the dignified Queen Pamela, the elephant has finally climbed out of her quandary. Yes, Pamela's fears created by her childhood trauma are completely laid to rest. Thanks to the support of her loving husband, Kachi. They both enjoy the poetry recital uniquely meant for the victors for the next five years. What a joyful occasion the reunion is.

In Your Expressions of Kindness Do Not Let The Wicked Take Away Your Joy

Ruth is a close friend of Pamela since college. Ruth has a son as old as Kachi's first son. Pamela and Ruth's friendship soar over the years and the boys are fond of each other, such that seeing the two boys playing together, you'll think they are actually brothers of the same parents. Not long, Ruth finds herself in a family quandary respecting her husband ending up with what you will call an irreconcilable issue. Thus, leaving Ruth in a marital state of divorce. Part of the irreconcilable issue that Ruth's marriage suffered has to do with trust and trustworthiness. Doubtlessly, being trusting and be trustworthy are two of the fundamental keys to running a successful marital relationship. If those two are lacking in a given marital relationship or threaten in any way fathomable and the resolution to such problems are not in sight, that may be the beginning of the end to that marital relationship. It will take an unbelievable amount of work on the part of the couple to resuscitate from that marital epileptic downturn. There is no wonder that most marital couples take the easy way out especially if there is little or no property at stake.

The court grants double custody of the son to both Ruth and her ex-husband, Rogers. Sadly, that ends that twenty-year marital relationship. The divorced couple has two sons, Josiah and Asap. The first son, Josiah is a twenty-two-year-old United States Marine captain stationed overseas. While Kachi and Pamela agree to help Ruth until she gets back on her feet, Ruth's ex-husband however, has nowhere to go because he had spent the past twenty-three years grooming and raising his family. Hence, there was no time for him to make trustworthy friends who would have been there for him in times like this until he gets back on his feet with his dignity intact. Momentarily, he lives in a hotel until he's able to figure out his new path.

Ruth's ex-husband, Rogers believes in the institution of marriage as the foundation of a new family, and he had accepted Ruth as his lifelong family member come what may. So, the notion of divorce never occurred in his mind until it happened. There is no wonder that Rogers took the entire divorce proceeding a little harder than Ruth. Rogers' denial of reality was the reason for his siblings to find out about the divorce only after it had occurred. Rogers's siblings are obviously upset for finding out about the divorce after it had occurred because as far as they are concerned, they probably would have been able to help and thus, prevent the divorce from happening.

Rogers is a dignified hospitable man who feels that it is his duty to help people and not the other way around. You can imagine how difficult it has been for Rogers to receive help from his siblings or from others who have been recipients of his undeserved kindness. Interestingly, the God of mercy does not abandon those who are kind and merciful at heart to totter. Rogers gets all the help he needs from people he never thought could have the means to help let alone the acumen to help protect his dignity while helping.

Rogers is one of the few who believe that storing treasures in heaven[36] where no thief can get to is paramount to human existence. One of the ways to store these treasures is by being kind and merciful to others without the expectation of receiving something in return from such ones. In a nutshell, being your neighbors' keeper may come with rewards that are of divine descent.

Think about it, there is a fine line separating the rich from the poor in the sense that any wrong investment or financial decision made by someone wealthy may plunge such one into financial instability which could lead to a situation such as filing for bankruptcy. Thus, shifting the wheel of categories from being wealthy to poverty. In the same line of thought, it is possible for someone who is currently in the poverty category to fortunately make a wise financial decision or just simply be fortunate to pounce on wealth and thus, changing the wheel of categories from poverty to wealth. Therefore, being insanely wealthy should not give you the passport to contemptuously look down upon those who are unfortunately suffering from the effects of poverty. Rather, may you tap into the original heart with which you were created to be kind and generous to those who are not as fortunate as you.

The original heart you were created with can best be explain with the birth of a child whose heart is simply pure. This child does not know evil until it is taught to him. The infant can even nurse from a woman who is not his biological mother without trouble. As far as the infant is concerned, everything in the world is simply good. During the infant's stages of development however, so many things including the practice of evil are taught to him. Before you know it, the once an infant with a pure heart that knows nothing but goodness, now becomes a young man with a heart to kill. So, the original heart he once had has been replaced with another one that is polluted with the evil things of this world which convince him to be unkind to others. However, the original heart can be recall to take effect over the corrupted one, which usually happens when that young man displays kindness, generosity and hospitality to others.

Ruth is naturally a nice woman whose short coming lies on her pliability as well as her ability to want to please everyone. She may have not heard or read about one of the popular stories concerning "the man, his son and his donkey." which you can type into one of your favorite internet search engines without the quotes for the full story, if you want to. While there are many versions to the story, the moral of that story remains the same across the aisle. That is, if you set out on pleasing everyone, you will end up pleasing no one. "Robbing Peter to pay Paul" is usually not a fair thing to do, is it? What Ruth ought to have done is to figure out those she's directly responsible for or legally bonded to. She can be kind to everyone else in general but not under obligation to please them even if it is within her prowess and power to do so without compromising or even endangering the rights of those she is directly responsible for.

There is no that the only person you have the power to change is you. However, it should not escape our minds that there are necessary and satisfying conditions that must take place to make the change effective. The change can be easier for a single person to make than it would be for someone who is married in the sense that a single person has only self to deal with, whereas a married person has more than self to deal with in making the said change. Since there is no guarantee that in an imperfect world a given marriage will be perfect, the future of such marital relationship gives room for some necessary improvement and character adjustments in the interest of justice, equity and good conscience.

You may agree with me that making such improvement or change in one's life without the support of one's spouse can be very difficult, if not impossible. You may have heard someone who is going through some marital problems state the following: "yes, yes, yes, I know, I know, I know! I have to make the change for me because I can only change me and not my spouse. I've been working on me for quite a while now and I'm going to keep on working on me. That is all I need to do." While there may be an element of seriousness and sincerity on the part of the speaker, asking the speaker how well that has been working out may reaffirm that in a sane world, "it takes two to tango" and regardless to the scientific experiments on the creation of life regarding humans, it takes a pair of opposite sex to make a newborn.

Yes, it is a good start to realize and acknowledge that you personally need to make some changes and improvements as a married person. However, making such changes may not be as effective without the involvement of your better half. It makes it easier when the married couple work together to make the said improvement effective regardless of who actually needs to make the change. After all, they both need the improvement for a brighter future. They must, therefore, unite in providing the necessary and satisfying conditions to making it happen.

Pamela's initial thought is that since she and Ruth have been such great friends for a long time, living together now will be a piece of cake and an easier way to be her friend's keeper. Well, Pamela finds out soon enough that you may not fully know someone until you actually live with that person. Even so, you still cannot know everything about that person hence, the English words: "Benefit of doubt, compromise, faith, tolerance and acceptance." Pamela observes that Ruth always call her twenty-two-year old son who is serving his country in an oversee country to badmouth his father. While Pamela is trying the best she can to advise Ruth of the danger of badmouthing her ex-husband and the father of her sons, little does she know that Ruth is working on Kachi.

When you have a loving relationship with your spouse that resembles perfection in an imperfect world, there is nothing like it. Unknown to Ruth, that is what Kachi and Pamela have. Here is the thing, Ruth was brought into Pamela's home to receive the needed help that will get her back on her feet and certainly not for her to become a sharp two-edged dividing sword between Pamela and her husband, Kachi.

Kachi had complain several times earlier to Pamela of Ruth's breaking their rule of keeping nude only in the room of the person who chooses to be in nude. Whenever Pamela takes the complains to Ruth, Ruth expresses her apologies to both Kachi and Pamela who then let it go. This time however, Ruth accuses Kachi of coming on or hitting on her. This accusations and sexual traps against Kachi went on for quite a while. Pamela's belief that her husband is not like that and will never go that way is well founded because Ruth's heart is filled with jealousy as she reasons: "why should Pamela be in a happy relationship when I'm not? Besides, all men are the same. Once I show them my nakedness, they want to do something, married or not it doesn't matter. Some of them I handled in the same way I did my ex-husband when we were married: going to bed with him in lingerie with no action intended. I just want to have Pamela to myself just so we can do things together traveling all over the places. Is that so bad to desire?" But all of Ruth's seductive attempts on Kachi have been futile. You can imagine her frustration. She was so frustrated that she actually voices out her reasoning to Pamela and Kachi in the exact way that is stated above. What a revelation to Kachi and Pamela who finally make the difficult decision to let Ruth go at least for the sake of their sanity and peace of mind.

You may wonder whether or not that horrible experience on the expression of hospitality that Kachi and Pamela have just gone through would stop the married couple from further helping those in need. Not in a long shot. The couple set out to buy a home about a mile from where they currently live to help those in need. They've been doing it for quite a while with lots of blessings. Therefore, do not let any horrible experience you may have had as a result of your expression of kindness debar you from being who you truly are – a kind and generous person.

Abusing The Disabled Community Is A Despicable Act Of A Bully

Chika and his wife Janice are back home in Parkin, Arkansas. As promised, Chika and his wife are going through marriage counselling to work out their marital issues. Things appear to be working out for the married couple in the time being and bearing in mind that "Rome was not built in a day" no one expects their problems to disappear or even dissipate at any time soon. The important thing is for Chika and Janice to lovingly and respectfully work together at solving their problems without demeaning each other.

The city of Parkin is in Cross County, Arkansas. According to the United States Census Bureau, the population of the city was 1,105 in the year 2010 which was a drop down from 1,602 in the year 2000. You can tell that with these not so huge population, everyone knows everyone. The County of Cross has been going through a major crisis emanating from Parkin's city before Chika and his family travel out for the family reunion. Part of the crisis is about a young homeless woman going by the name Rosanna, who is homeless of Parkin's city due to her mental illness. Despite all the available help at her disposal, Rosanna prefers the streets for reasons that are best known to her. Who dare to ask Rosanna why she prefer the streets to shelter? It would be like a trap maker who ensnares himself with his own trap and don't know how to get out of it. My guess would be that Rosanna probably wants to live freely like everyone else and she is free to do so, as long as she is neither hurting herself nor someone else.

The major crisis is about Rosanna's miraculous pregnancies which she carries to term. At one time, people will see her with a newborn baby and shower her with gifts. The next time however, the baby disappears leaving the people to wonder where the baby is or who might have taken the baby. Asking Rosanna about the whereabouts of her newborn baby will understandably be futile as she is severely mentally ill. This is not the first nor the second time that Rosanna's babies have been abducted some few days after delivery. The pattern has been going on for quite a while with no solution in sight.

The mind bubbling questions are, who is the father of these babies? Who has been impregnating this mentally ill woman and leaving her to dry? If we can find this person who has no respect for humanity, chances are that we will equally find the abductor of the babies. This is so because all of the adoption agencies and shelters in the area and beyond have been contacted in search of the babies, but to no avail. Cross County put out a Countywide hunt for this man or these men impregnating and abducting Rosanna's babies.

The Countywide hunt in no time becomes a statewide hunt, which inadvertently becomes a national media frenzy. Such that the County of Cross and the city of Parkin that were once quiet and unpopular, suddenly become the national focus. In the search, Cross County and Parkin city get more than they can chew respecting help coming from both the State and Federal government as well as concerned citizens.

The Cross County's residents and authority are convinced that Rosanna must have vividly known the perpetrator(s) for the pregnancies to have occurred in the first place. Some argue that for the perpetrator(s) to have impregnated Rosanna and then come back to abduct her infant without Rosanna's putting up a formidable fight, demonstrates Rosanna's emotional affection for the abductors regardless of her mental illness. However, due to Rosanna's mental state, it becomes impossible for her to be of any help locating her infants and her runaway heart(s).

The hunt is on. One way in which the detectives plan on getting the perpetrators is to interview any man they see around Rosanna at any given time, day or night, it doesn't matter. Months have passed and the police have no suspect in custody. The heat is on. However, the perpetrator can feel it since he hasn't show up to see Rosanna for months. I am thinking that you probably could help Parkin city and Cross County solve their crisis since you may have met the perpetrator in the preceding chapter. If your guess is on Chika, then your guess is right.

Chika who had done a lot of soul searching trying to figure out how to get out of the mess in which he had placed himself but to no avail, now considers turning himself in to the law. He later changes his mind on that decision because as far as he is concerned, the public humiliation alone will be too great for him to handle. So, he decides to commit suicide. His decision on suicide isn't originally an option, but when the number of infant skeletons he had buried beneath the basement of his home is up to five, the decision to commit suicide becomes appealing. Chika leaves two suicide notes before hanging himself in his basement. The first suicide note goes to his wife and daughter, and the second suicide note goes to Cross County. In both notes, Chika tenders his apologies, blaming the whole ordeal on the devil that possessed his soul and controls his actions. Again, we have us a national media Frenzy covering Chika's death and suicide letters.

Chika's wife, Janice and the entire County of Cross find themselves in two states: They are relieved that the crisis is over and the perpetrator is no longer at large. Although her distraught neighbors do not hold Janice responsible for her husband's horrific behavior, Janice no longer feels comfortable living in that neighborhood. Thus, Janice and her daughter move out of Parkin, Arkansas right after she buried her husband. They moved to Fresno, California.

Cross County decides to help Rosanna by treating her as an award of the state. Though under surveillance for her protection, Rosanna is free to go wherever she wants. Some months have passed since Rosanna is going through a County sponsored group therapy for the mentally challenged. Rosanna meets someone with similar condition and before you know it, they become best friends. One might argue that Rosanna does not have the acumen to date anyone considering her condition. While that argument may be plausible, no one should forget the fact that Rosanna is a human being with desires that are peculiar to humans regardless of her disabilities.

Rosanna invites her male friend to her place of residence. Up until now, Rosanna is unaware that the County's eyes are upon her for her own safety. Before she knows it, couple of detectives come asking about this male person that Rosanna seems to be chatting with in a rather comfortable manner. Rosanna introduces her male friend as "Daniel my therapeutic body whom I met at the training." Yes, you guessed right. Rosanna thought she is going through a job training. The detectives understand that she meant group therapy. Through investigation, Rosanna's story checks out and the friendship is allowed to continue. Cross County does not leave the matter as it is as Rosanna and her new friend are subjected to relationship counseling fully paid for by Cross County.

Can anyone really be denied the right to get married based on mental illness especially if such one is fortunate to find someone comparable? There are those who may rightly argue that if such ones are incapable of the union due to the low level of their mental capacity, then the union should not be allowed to form, let alone exist as it may do more harm than good. Some may even add; can you give a marriage license to a couple of seven- year old just because they express their desire to marry? With such an argument, you may wonder why the so-called normal people have the right to divorce if their union happens to be doing more harm than good while on the other hand, the disabled should not even think about the formation of the union in the first place.

Rosanna is pregnant with Daniel's baby and at the verge of delivery. Like normal people, Rosanna and Daniel who are now living together as friends with benefit since they've been denied the right to marry, now prepare for their baby's arrival. Remember, they are under the County's surveillance and with a one-bedroom apartment on the County's tab, one can only imagine how much Rosanna and Daniel could accomplish with the baby's crib. But they are trying the very best considering the condition in which the two friends find themselves. As far as the County is concerned, the support for the preparation of the baby's arrival isn't there. Or at least it seems.

The baby has arrived. The baby's arrival opens a new can of worms as the County prepares to put up the newborn for adoption with a "normal family." The County would not let Rosanna leave the hospital with the baby. Although they understand the compelling reasons behind the County's decision to put up the Baby boy for adoption, Rosanna's neighbors however, find that decision to be appalling, barbaric, and against everything that is good about humanity. So, the neighbors put up the funds to help Rosanna and Daniel to fight against the County's decision through the legal system.

Cross County Court House, Arkansas

Rosanna's neighbors hired an Attorney who filed the case in the Cross County courthouse and in a short time, the court is in session.

The Cross County Judge Zedichaiah R. Whisky presides on the case. The court's preference is to decide the case privately without media frenzy as the last occurrence is still fresh in everyone's mind. It happens that the court does not get its wish this time because for some miraculous way, the news of the case hit the media nationwide. Cross County is once again a national focus. While many are those whose wishes are that Rosanna and Daniel win the case against Cross county and thus, be allowed to raise their son like everyone else and be given a marriage license if they so wish, there are those who bit the difference.

The Cross County Judge Z. R. Whisky is among those who do not agree that Rosanna and Daniel should be allowed to form a marital union and raise a mouse, let alone a son. The obvious reason for his stance is that Rosanna and Daniel are not in tune with reality considering their obvious mental state. The judge continues by saying that placing an infant with Rosanna and Daniel considering their condition will not be in the interest of justice as the couple may mistake the infant for a racoon. When that happens, the judge continues, it will be like sending the boy to his early grave and the couple would be incapable of recognizing the gravity of their errors. As such, Judge Z.R. Whisky rules for the county of Cross to go ahead as planned. That is, take the infant away and plan to give him up for adoption.

The judgement raises a national brow. Well, Rosanna's neighbors are out of funds. Interestingly, a californial law firm, "The Law Offices of Margret S. Alwellbrown and Associates" agrees to represent Rosanna and Daniel on a "pro bono publico." This simply means that Rosanna and Daniel will be represented on a free of charge basis. Remember, the case is in the nation's focus and enjoying media frenzy. While Rosanna and Daniel as well as their neighbors are happy for the legal offer, the California law firm is equally happy that winning the case will place it on the national map as a hotshot law firm. Then the real money will come.

The first order of business that the California law firm put in place is to file an injunction to vacate the Cross County Court Judge

Z. R. Whisky's rulings which automatically stops the county of Cross from pursuing its plan to take the infant from his rightful parents and give him up for adoption. The high level of national awareness for this case, qualifies it for the Supreme Court of Arkansas. Before you know it, the battle is on. All eyes are on the highest court of the land – Arkansas Supreme Court.

The Supreme Court Of Arkansas Has The Ball

The Arkansas Supreme Court has three Justices, Chief Justice Mark J. Templeton, Associate Justice Stewart P. Goldwell and Associate Justice Mariam T. Codwell. The presiding Justice of the Supreme Court of Arkansas Chief Justice Mark J. Templeton, patiently listens to both sides of the aisle as they vigorously argue their cases. Mr. Felix O. Albright, the lead counsel for the defense - Cross County, opens up the floor for the closing argument. He argues that their "decision to put up the plaintiff's baby for adoption is based solely on the fact that both parents of the baby Rosanna and Daniel, are mentally challenged and thus incapable of raising a child. Besides," the counsel continues, "Rosanna had gone through some traumatic experiences in which all five of her infants were abducted and assassinated by their biological father, and up until now Rosanna is yet to display any emotional pain if at all she is capable of doing so.

Mr. Albright continues, "If Rosanna is incognizance of the disappearances of her five infants nor does she have any emotional connections with the babies she had lost, how could she develop any emotional bond for her newborn? What is more, your honors, the plaintiff Rosanna and Daniel do not have any clue why they are here in court in the first place. So, they may not feel it when the baby is given up for adoption. How did we get here? The plaintiff's neighbors sue the County on the plaintiff's behalf; an absence of which this court will not have convened for this case. Therefore, your honor, it will be in the interest of justice to rule against the plaintiff. Your honor, the defense rests." Aren't those reasons compelling enough to win the case?

The plaintiff's counsel Mrs. Margret S. Alwellbrown takes the floor and argues that the "inception of emotional bonding between mother and child is at the conception stage regardless of the mother's mental state. According to our expert witness, the display of emotions can be categorized as explosive/explode or implosive/implode. Explosive emotion is an outward burst of anger or emotions that you can see when the bearer displays it. It is kind of like you'll see a bomb when it explodes half a mile away from you. On the other hand, an implode or implosive emotion is an inward burst of anger or emotions that explodes inwardly or inside of the bearer which cannot be seen even by those closest. An implosive emotion is likening to a molten lava inside of a volcano. When it finally explodes, it destroys everything with which it comes in contact."

Mrs. Alwellbrown continues by saying that "while the County's counsels are used to people with exploded display of emotions, they lack the advanced training and hence, the acumen to decipher the necessary and satisfying conditions of an imploded display of emotions. With all due respect to the opposing counsels, had they received the proper training, they would have recognized my client to be someone who displays her painful emotions implosively. Your honor, for the sake of this argument let's assume for a moment that my client displays her emotions explosively as the opposing counsels would have preferred, who would have listened considering the fact that my client is mentally challenged when she lost her infants? The trained and experienced onlookers were the ones who raised the awareness that my client had lost her infants. That awareness led to the County's involvement in my client's affairs so as to help her, which is well appreciated. However, the County does not have the legal right to put up my clients' baby for adoption without my clients' legal aided expressed written consent regardless of the proclaimed extenuating circumstances respecting mental illness."

"Furthermore," Mrs. Alwellbrown continues, "we have heard

from witnesses that the group and relationship therapies that the County ordered for my clients are really helping them. They have been functioning as a couple for quite a while and with the help of a trained counselor, they too can cope with all the problems that reside in the territory of a marital relationship. Think about it your honors, why should the experiences derived from the good, the bad and the ugly of a marital relationship be confined only to 'normal people'? If it is the court's concern that the experiences that are confined only to marital relationship will turn my clients insane, hello, your honor, my clients are way ahead of you and have put your worries to rest! What is more, my clients' neighbors hiring an Attorney to represent my clients in the first lawsuit against the County can only mean one thing your honor. Simply put, it shows that my clients are well loved and respected by their neighbors. Thus, these neighbors seek justice for my clients."

Mrs. Alwellbrown continues, "in deliberating on this case with a view to rendering its ultimate decision, we respectfully urge the court to consider the admonitions given by the expert witnesses to offer my clients some aides that will help them raise their infant in a dignified manner. You don't have to take the baby away from my clients, because if you do your honor, that established emotional bond that exists between the infant and his parents will be broken. Your honor, we both know that will only happen in the absence of justice as it will not be in the infant's interest nor will it be in the parents' interest to have a broken parent-child emotional bonding. Instead, we respectfully urge the court to grant my clients their divine parental rights of keeping the infant and provide them with a specialized nurse to go in and monitor the infant's bathing, nursing, sleeping, and other activities on a daily basis until the infant becomes a young fellow able to care for himself."

Mrs. Alwellbrown asks for the court's indulgence to drink water, walks to her table, picks up a glass of water, drinks some water and continues. "Your honor, by providing my clients with livelihood, group and relationship therapies, Cross County is up to a good start.

We need the County to continue on that path by helping my clients to keep their baby. After all, the County already has my clients on surveillance. We beg the court's indulgence to give my clients a chance to prove themselves for it will be in the interest of justice, equity, good conscience and above all, it will be in the interest of humanity." Mrs. Alwellbrown rests her case.

Chief Justice Templeton's Ruling

All eyes are now on Justice Templeton to deliver his judicial decision on this nationally publicized case involving two disabled parents going head-to-head against the county of Cross. The tension concerning who will be on the winning end of the Justice' gavel is very high. The several interviews that was conducted by the media show that majority of the populace wish that the "disabled parents win the case just so they can raise their son like every other couples. Afterall, they brought the boy into this world. Let them raise him; crazy or not it shouldn't matter." Others are, however, worried about flaws in the parents' judgement of confusing their son for racoon and thus endanger the infant. What do you think?

The only view that matters at this point is the Justice' view who has begun his ruling. Let's listen. "...After much deliberation on this case and carefully considered the arguments presented by both sides of the aisle, the court has reached its decision in favor of the plaintiffs. This favorable decision for the plaintiffs is partly based on the tremendous respect and love that the plaintiffs enjoy in their neighborhood. Since the plaintiffs have demonstrated over the years that with therapy, they can co-exist with the so-called normal people, the court is convinced beyond the iota of doubt that the plaintiffs are capable of raising their own son with little help. Therefore, it is the order of this court that Cross County continue to provide livelihood, group counseling and relationship counseling as it has been doing."

Justice Templeton continues: "Now that an infant is involved, the court order Cross County to provide three specialized nurses working around the clock for the plaintiffs indefinitely for the sole purpose of helping the plaintiffs with their infant's bathing, nursing, sleeping, and other activities that the plaintiffs cannot handle without supervision. There will be three 8-hour shifts for the three specialized nurses. The timetable for the shifts is 7:30 AM to 3:30 PM, 3:30 PM to 11:30 PM, 11:30 PM to 7:30 AM."

Justice Templeton takes a sip of water and continues. "Respecting marriage, the court believes that marriage is a fundamental right of the plaintiffs and since the constitution does not place any stipulation or restrictions to such right, this court is not about to change the law. As such, it will be in the interest of justice to grant the plaintiffs the right to marry, if they so wish. As a matter of fact, the court will do something it has not done in a long while by asking the plaintiffs whether or not they want to marry."

Justice Templeton turns to the plaintiffs Rosanna and Daniel asking them the question of whether they would like to marry now. The plaintiffs answer yes, they'll love to. Then Justice Templeton performs the marriage ceremony, issues the marriage certificate to them, and continues: "The court congratulates you, the newlyweds wishing you success in your endeavors..." The Arkansas Supreme Court's decision sits well with many, such that they all feel like winners as they fill the nation with a joyful uproar. The impassioned populace yells out the slogan: "Victory for the disabled is victory for all!" The disabled community is certainly grateful for the support.

Although the plaintiffs' counsels are prepared to take the fight all the way to the United States Supreme Court, the highest court of the nation, the counsels and the Disabled Community are exceedingly grateful that it doesn't have to go that far.

The last time we check on the married couple, Daniel and Rosanna as well as their son named Victor, are unbelievably doing very well. Like you and I, all that Daniel and Rosanna need is a little help and the opportunity to thrive in a bully infested world.

Gold-Digging Spouses Are Bullies

In its most basic term, community property refers to property owned jointly by married couple excluding properties owned by individuals prior to marriage. A classic example of community property includes items acquired during the marriage, such as wages or salaries earned by either spouse during the marriage, home, vehicle, business, computer, furniture, and others. In the United States, the states having community property system are Louisiana, Arizona, California, Texas, Washington, Idaho, Nevada, New Mexico, and Wisconsin at the time of writing. Community property states follow the rule that all assets and liabilities acquired during the marriage are considered "community property." This, according to Stacy Rocheleau the founder and managing partner of Right Lawyers in Las Vegas, Nevada USA, means that the court will divide all assets and liabilities, or debts incurred during marriage equally or 50% to 50% among the couple in a divorce proceeding. The spirit behind community property in my view is that of equalization, which means that regardless to who the breadwinner is in the relationship, the couple will each have equal assets and liabilities to move past the woes that the divorce may present. As it is, there are those who have chosen to abuse the provision of the community property. The prevalent of such abusers is so high that there is a global name for them, the gold-diggers.

The Oxford Learner's dictionary defines gold-digger as "a person who uses the fact that he or she is attractive to get money from a relationship with somebody..." I am here referring to the relationship of a married couple in a community property system. Usually, a gold-digger can occur when someone with a pure heart enters a relationship with someone that has criminal mind and evil heart. The one with the pure heart have all the good intentions to have a happy and successful relationship, working smart and hard to prove that there exist the understanding that for the relationship to be successful, there are necessary and satisfying conditions that must happen, part of which is the daily contribution to the joy of the spouse. On the other hand, the spouse with the criminal mind and evil heart has hidden intention which is to enter the relationship as the cleaner – that is, to clean out the spouse for everything that has been worked for and owned long before the marital relationship began and even during the relationship. The victim of that abuse is left with a deeply broken heart and with the broken heart searches for someone kind enough to help mend the broken heart. So, this abused person with heavy heart travels around the world in search of someone to mend the broken heart.

Through a mutual friend, this abused person with broken heart was introduced to someone from one the third world countries, specifically China or Nicaragua, who later become his spouse. A word of caution to the wise, if you do not have the intension of living in the country that your proposed spouse is from originally, then do not marry someone from that country. The advantages of living in the country that your spouse came from is that of maintenance and association. By maintenance I mean that since you appreciate your spouse's beliefs, values and attitudes already, living among the people and customs that imbued those beliefs, values and attitudes that you so appreciate will maintain or guarantee continuance of such behavior. But if you move her to your country, then you will make her learn cultures that are completely foreign to her. She may end up appreciating that culture. It should not come as a surprise to you however, when she starts to behave like the women in the new culture you've introduced her to, women whose behavior, values, attitudes, and beliefs are not attractive to you. Afterall, she is bound to have new friends and associates from that culture whose attitudes, values, beliefs, and behavior she may love to imitate, especially if she is gullible. If that happens, would she continue to be pleasing to you? Or, would she become a stranger that is so unlikeable to you such that you would wish you had never met her? You should understand that association is very important in each society. So, if you appreciate your wife's current behavior, values, attitudes, and beliefs; then strive to keep her within that society, custom and association to foster continuity of what you love about her. As discussed above, a change in the current society and customs may be detrimental to your relationship.

It may have come to your attention that there are some group of women from the third world countries who marry Americans so as to get a free pass to the United States, become citizens and after having one or two children with these Americans, they become unfaithful and plan to divorce their American spouses with a view to claiming at least half of the properties that their spouses have worked for years prior to the inception of their fraudulent marriage. Unless these victimized Americans hire good lawyers to protect their interests, the court may end up giving the fraudulent soon to become ex-spouses everything they ask for using the little children as leverage. What a disgusting bully they are! You probably may allude to several cases like the above where people from different countries come in to abuse the big and kind heart of American society. Imagine a woman from a third world country for example, who understands that the United States have a tender heart for rape victims and protect them at all costs. She has never been raped a day in her life, but because she is dying to come to the United States at all costs, she hires someone to beat her up pretty bad, then she runs to the United States Embassy in her country asking for asylum on the grounds that she has been raped. In most cases, this fraudulent woman will be given visas to the United States for asylum. These criminal acts continue until someone leaks the evil plight to the United States Embassy. The help that the American society provides to protect rape victims is strictly designed to help people who are truly really raped and certainly not for fraudulent acts. When people start to abuse the privileges that are meant to help rape victims, they will not only be robbing the true rape victims of these privileges, but also be bullying them.

The good news is that the American government through its embassies and immigrations worldwide is doing its very best to protect American people from foreign scavengers pretending to be loving spouses so as to gain the trust of their American husbands and thereafter, suck them up mercilessly, for everything they have. As the American government is doing its best to protect American people from scavengers, American people have a shared responsibility to protect themselves from scavengers pretending to be loving to them. You do not have to put their names on the properties you owned before you met and marry them. You could also put in place a sound prenuptial agreement which legalzoom.com defines as "the agreement entered into before marriage. This agreement can set forth what will happen to your and your spouse's assets and income in the unfortunate event of divorce, separation, or death. Most importantly, a prenuptial agreement can preserve the nature of property in the event the marriage ends..." By a sound prenuptial agreement, I mean an agreement that is duly signed by you, your soon to become spouse, and your Attorneys. Yes, one that will stand the test of time of not being tossed aside for lack of clarity and proper signatories. The American government have also put in place the protection of all those true raped victims against faked rape victims. It is only a matter of time before all those faked rape victims and scavengers pretending to be loving spouses will be brought to justice. What a bully such ones are! Yes, gold- diggers are bullies and to them I say, when palm fruits land on the ground for a while they will scatter. Yes, your evil plans will never come together, they will scatter!

Chuwawa And Her Chicks Fight Back Against Sassy And Her Sons

Shine the light on Sassy, Zach and Sean at Chuwawa's den. Yes, I am sure that those fellows are still on your mind.

Chuwawa: You folks are back again to get another whopping defeat like you did last time, don't you? You sore looser!

Sassy: You won't be saying that when we are through with you.

Zach: Let's get her Mom?

Sean: Yes. Let's get her.

Sassy: You boys get her Chicks, leave Chuwawa for me to deal with.

Chuwawa: Oh no missy! You know that I know that you know you can't get me. Hey, chicks let's have a little fun with these goons, shall we?

[Chuwawa calls on to her little ones to come together instead of taking cover for their dear lives.]

Chuwawa: In one word, what would you call an unpleasant person doing unpleasant things?

Chicks: Abomination!

Chuwawa: In one word, what would you call a mentally unstable hater with loaded assault rifle at his disposal?

Chicks: Abomination!

Chuwawa: In one word. What would you call the Fox family threatening to turn the Chicken family into dinner?

Chicks: Abomination!

[Sassy takes a leap on Chuwawa but misses]

Chuwawa: Oh no missy! You know that I know that you can't get me!

Sassy: Oh Yes, I can, you little hamster. You call me a goat; we'll see who the goat is soon enough. Now where are the humans to save you from my claws?

Chuwawa: That is a good question. Hey Fuzza, take Osan and Mel with you. Get me some humans to come and help us get rid of these hooligans who enjoy reaping where they did not sow. Go quickly, would you?

Fuzza: Yes, Mom. We will.

[Fuzza leaves with Osan and Mel.]

Chuwawa is tap dancing at this point, hopping everywhere in her attempt to avoid and escape Sassy's devouring claws and sharp scary teeth. There she goes again rapping with those words in a hysterical manner.

Chuwawa: I told you once, I told you twice and I will tell it to you again because I know that you know that I know you are way too slow to learn; you sniffling no good for nothing Mamma Fox.

Sassy: I am sniffling no good for nothing Mamma?

Sassy takes couple of swings at Chuwawa and misses. She continues to figure out ways to get Chuwawa who is so hysterical that she and her chicks are hopping, running helter-skelter, and flapping their wings with a view to flying away but could not.

Chuwawa: Oh no you can't get me with your ragged teeth and smelling little nose. I told you before, you are way too slow for me. O yes. I'm going to tell you what time it is because if I didn't tell you, then another Mamma would. Perm on her hair with them slick looking scary curl, what you doing? You been sharking all them sweet a-pop-a licking all them sweet a-pop-a sweet a--sweet a--sweet a-pop-a pop-a-sweet a--sweet a-pop-a. Hey boys, I told you once, didn't I? What you call that hair dude on your knuckled heads, Jerry curl? That's not jerry curl, that's scary curl!

Zach: Ah! Mom, you see she said it again.

Sassy:	I heard her. Do not worry about a thing son, because we are about to get Chuwawa and her chicks. Let's just hope that those humans do not get here to prevent us from devouring them.
Chuwawa:	Ah! You can't catch me! Somebody help! These crazy fools are about to get me! They are about to make a nice tasty feast out of my gut! Please come and rescue us from them!

Zach and Sean are after Chuwawa's chicks when mankind shows up. Sean chases Nebum while Zach goes after Ikem.

Sean:	Now, who is your daddy? [Wait a little while and said] I can't hear you. O, you are so dead!
Nebum:	In your dream! You surely will try, but it won't do you any good because I'm too fast for you. What is more, I am wiser than you'll ever be.
Sean:	We will see about that, won't we?

Nebum is fast, acrobatic, and tricky. He dribbles very well too, the reason why Sean is having a hard time catching up with him. Before you know it, Nebum is on top of a tree. What do you know, Sean climbs up the tree going after Nebum. Relentlessly, Sean continues to climb the tree and at the same time Nebum fearlessly torments him.

Nebum:	Evildoer, desist from your evil practices. Hater, stop your evil thoughts. Yes, stop hating! What benefits do you derive from your evil thoughts and hatred?
Sean:	[Gasping for air, Sean stops to take in a deep breath. While panting, Sean says] I will let you know when I catch up with you. Like a weasel you are going to beg for your life when I catch you, you little hamster!

Nebum:	you are such an implacable being.
Sean:	What! Implacable?
Nebum:	Yes, implacable! Haven't you heard? An implacable creature is a source of trouble; a pliable creature is sure to suffer. That is what you are, and you are about to suffer defeat.
Sean:	Who do you think you are? Talking to me in riddles. When I catch up with you, I will enjoy giving you a slow and painful death.
Nebum:	Again, not even in your dreams will that ever happen. A very clever animal is caught in a trap; how difficult would it be for a very stupid animal to be caught with the same trap?
Sean:	Are you calling me stupid? I didn't call you names; why are you calling me names?
Nebum:	You are planning on eating me aren't you?
Sean:	You can count on that!
Nebum:	The dashiki that I have on, I passed through the thistle thorn bushes unharmed. The radiantly explosive red garment that I have on, I passed through the thistle thorn bushes unharmed with my garment intact. That brilliantly white garment that you see on me, I passed through dirt and crude oil untouched. A stern warning to you bullies, desist from threatening me! A stern warning to all the intensified bullies out there, desist from your evil thoughts!
Sean:	I do not understand your language. I'm not sure if that is English language or what?
Nebum:	Yet, they call you Sean the soothsayer. What

I said simply mean you can't touch me! A butterfly attempting to quench an open flame lamp with its wings will end up destroying itself. Let all of you with heads on your shoulders, hold on tight to your heads, and you with a body, hold on tight to your body! The ride is about to get bumpy! For we are not gullible, we are exercising one of our enduring virtues, patience.

Sean: We'll see about that!

Ikem: Hey Nebum, don't you dare let that crazy Sean catch up with you.

Nebum: I won't and you better believe that! How are you doing with your pet?

Ikem: O, I am taking Zach to school. He has never been schooled before. He is learning a great deal of lesson here.

Zach: Yes, you keep talking. You can run all you want, but you surely will soon run into my mouth.

Ikem: Keep dreaming. The lack of connivance increases the load of the unwise in multiple.

Zach: Why can't you speak English?

Ikem: Yes, my point exactly. Whosoever plucks a leaf and deep it in his mouth seeks to be an adversary to the mute!

Zach: What? The mute? I never deal with a mute one in my life. What language are you speaking anyway?

Ikem: Let me be merciful to you and speak in your language Oh, lay man. The mouse becomes the landlord only when the cat is out of the house. Guess what?

Zach: What?

Ikem: Look behind you.

Zach looks behind him and behold the coming of mankind.

Ikem: Here comes the cat.

Zach: Save by mankind again! Man! One of these days Ikem, you would not be so fortunate!

Ikem: Until then, bye you little scavenger.

Zach: Sean let's go, mankind is approaching. We going to save getting these weasels for another day when no mankind would be around to save them.

Chuwawa: Thank goodness, here comes mankind. O what a beautiful day this day has become. Alas! We are not going to be eaten today!

Sassy: What? Not a gain! Save by mankind again! Hey Chuwawa, you are not off the hook yet and you better believe that! We'll catch you another day! Those crazy mankind always take our food away from us. One of these days we going to have to stand up against them!

Chuwawa: Yes, you and what army? Behold the enemies of progress are hoping, wishing, and expecting us to fall flat on our stomach, where on Earth do you place the outworking of the Father of celestial lights? Where in your lives do you place the outworking of the owner of the universe? Shame unto bullies. Yes, shame unto ridiculers. O, what a shame!

Kolokolo: One of these days, we will have our day, Chuwawa.

Chuwawa: Kolokolo, there is nothing wrong in dreaming, so, keep dreaming. Mel, Nebum, Ikem, Fuzza, Osan come on up here and join me in our victory song against the scavengers.

As they all gather, Chuwawa and her chicks start singing antiphonally.

Chuwawa: What are the bullies saying?

Chicks: Let it break! Let it break!

Chuwawa: I can't hear you.

Chicks: Let it break! Let it break!

Chuwawa: What are the scavengers saying? Chicks: Let it fall! Let it fall!

Chuwawa: Say what?

Chicks: Let it fall! Let it fall!

Chuwawa: What are the ridiculers saying? Chicks: Let it fail! Let it fail!

Chuwawa: Ahan! Ahan!

Chicks: Let it fail! Let it fail!

Chuwawa: What are the bullies saying?

Chicks: Let it break! Let it break!

Chuwawa: Tell it to me children.

Chicks: Let it break! Let it break!

Chuwawa: Ah! The Baobab tree no longer falls, shame unto bullies. What a pity! What are the ridiculers saying?

Chicks: Let it fail! Let it fail!

Chuwawa: Ahan! Ahan!

Chicks:	Let it fail! Let it fail!
Chuwawa:	What are the bullies saying?
Chicks:	Let it break! Let it break!
Chuwawa:	Tell it to me children.
Chicks:	Let it break! Let it break!
Chuwawa:	Ah! Behold the desert Acacia tree no longer falls. Behold the Kapok[28] tree yes, the Baobab tree no longer falls. Shame unto ridiculers. Yes, shame unto bullies. O, what a pity!

Chuwawa and her chicks continue to sing and dance. Black out on Chuwawa's den and it shines on Sassy, Zach, and Sean on their way home.

Sassy:	[breathing deep and fast like a warrior who had just lost a devastating battle] Well, boys Chuwawa is save by the bell again. One thing for sure, she and her chicks will not mess with us again.
Sean:	Mom, although we didn't get them because mankind came to their rescue, but I don't think any of Chuwawa's descendants for generations to come will dare mess with us again.
Zach:	You better believe that Sean. They surely won't have the guts to call us names like knuckle heads with scary curls anymore.

Cassandra's Silence Is Golden

Sassy and her little ones are not having a good day. But how is that Cassandra's problem? Cassandra does not intend on making Sassy's problem respecting starvation to be any of her business. Besides, she despises bullies like Sassy and does her very best to avoid the likes of Sassy. That you are hiding from trouble does not mean that trouble won't find you, how you handle that trouble when it finds you matters a whole lot. Let's see how Cassandra handles the trouble that comes her way. Shall we?

Sassy:	[Coming towards Cassandra, Mamma Duck] Look who we have here, our dear friend with a long beak that's not made for talking. [At this point, Sassy is trying very hard to provoke Cassandra but to no avail. Cassandra quacks without saying a word. Yes, that saves the day.]
Sean:	See Mom, Cassandra is not saying a word and so, we don't know what she's thinking.
Sassy:	[Remembering her encounter with the quiet Akala, she says] Yes. I can see that. I'll tell you what we are going to do. We are going to leave Cassandra and her ducklings alone. I'll be very much concerned about the quiet ones; you don't know what they have cooked up in their minds. Let's keep stepping!

So, they leave Cassandra alone and unharmed. Cassandra and her ducklings are so happy that they break into singing and dancing to the song "Stop Bullying."

Stop Bullying

O father of celestial lights, grant me success over the insolent bullies.

O king of eternity, protector of the righteous protect my offspring from the tyranny of bullies.

The intensified bullies are seeking to shame me; as long as the holy angels that have my back will never suffer shame certainly, I too will never suffer shame.

The Devil beans that get from behind the river

O bullies. O bullies. O bullies, get from behind me.

The Velvet beans that get from behind the river Unfortunate happenings get from behind me.

Behold the Deer-eye beans that get from behind the river Unfortunate wicked minds get from behind me.

The dead fronds that get off the neck of palm trees O bullies. O bullies. O bullies, get off my back.

The dead fronds that get off the neck of palm trees Intensified character assassins get off my back.

The dead fronds get off the neck of palm trees Incorrigibly unmanageable children get off my back Behold the incorrigible bullies.

They bullied themselves to Ge-hen'na O what a deceitful way to go! Behold the incorrigible bullies, they bullied themselves to Ge-hen'na. O what a joy to rid our communities of those incorrigible bullies alas

Look upon those incorrigible bullies wishing to see me fall, but I've been firmly established by the supreme ruler of the whole universe.

Before the entrance of the intensified char.acter assassins; I've been crowned with glory by the king of eternity in the presence of the intensified bullies.

The king of eternity dignifies and elevates me.

Behold the community of character assassins wailing in distress Their enormous falsehoods finally catch up with them.

May it not be late for the bully's community to reject the road to Ge hen'na.

May the intensified bullies accept divine help for a renewed mind and heart.

May the sovereign Lord of the heavens change their minds for the better.

The intensified bullies are wailing in distress

May it not be late for them to reject the way to Ge-hen'na.

May it not be late for bullies to accept help for a renewed mind and heart.

For the incorrigible bullies have no place in my affairs.

On my behalf, the sovereign ruler will handle their affairs.

I will never suffer shame for the King of eternity is my protector.

Like the shame of a thief when he is caught, so shall the incorrigible bullies experience in disgrace

In the king of eternity, I have taken refuge.

The intensified bullies are seeking to shame me, as long as the holy angels that have my back will never suffer shame; certainly, I too will never suffer shame.

The Devil beans that get from behind the river, O bullies. O bullies. O bullies, get from behind me

Behold the velvet beans that get from behind the river Unfortunate happenings get from behind me.

The Mucuna pruriens that get from behind the river Unfortunate wicked minds get from behind me.

The dead fronds that get from behind the neck of palm trees O bullies. O bullies. O bullies, get from behind me.

The dead fronds that get from behind the neck of palm trees Intensified character assassins get from behind me.

The dead fronds that get from behind the neck of palm trees Incorrigibly unmanageable children get from behind me.

Join hands together and protect my children from those incorrigible bullies.

Join hands together against the machinations of those incorrigible bullies.

Join hands together yes, run those incorrigible bullies out of town. That majestic Dashiki I have on, through the bush of thistle thorns, I passed unharmed.

That radiantly explosive red garment I have on, through the bush of thistle thorns, I passed untouched.

That brilliantly white garment I have on, through muddy, muddy, muddy oily dirt, I passed untouched.

Persuade the bully community to stop bullying.

Persuade the bully community, bullying is a friend to none. Persuade the bully community, it pays to stop bullying.

In the interest of justice, practice righteousness. In the interest of equity, practice kindness.

In the interest of good conscience, be merciful. Yes, be an oasis in a hot dessert to the powerless.

Self-Advocacy

Self-Advocacy simply means standing up or speaking up for yourself. To a layman, self-advocacy means self-defense - the ability to protect yourself from bullies and intruders.

There are five steps to self-advocacy, and they are:

Step 1: Identify and Clarify ➜ First, you must know the problem that you need help with. What is the problem? You must be clear and specific about what you need and be clear about how to express yourself so that your listener can understand perfectly what you are asking.

Step 2: Reach Out ➜ Choose someone you trust to ask for help; or someone you think might be able to help. Even if this person is not able, she might know someone whom she trusts can help. Then she will create a plan with that trusted person to help solve your problem.

Step 3: Have Courage ➜ A dictionary defines courage as doing the right thing in the presence of danger. It is not easy to ask for help, is it? So, you need courage to ask for help. You must believe in you. You must believe that you are worth it. Take one step at a time. Practice what you're going to say and be prepared that you may not always get what you want. You must understand that when asking for help, you will either win when the answer is 'yes,' or you will learn when the answer is 'no,' but you will never loose. When the answer is 'no,' you could When the answer

When the answer is 'no,' you could go back and ask: "Sir, earlier I came asking for help but you refused to help me. What can I do next time to merit your help?" You will learn from the given answer.

Step 4: Speak up ➜ Speak to the person whom you feel can help you solve the problem. Choose the right time and place. Be specific and maintain respect for both of you during the conversation.

Step 5: Reflect ➜ This is like you are looking at a mirror of what you have done thus far, or recap of your steps from step 1 to step 4. You check- in with yourself and asking yourself: What have you learned from Step 1 to Step 4? What can you do next time to improve? Are there next steps?

Parents, kindly find time to teach your children the beauty of self-advocacy. Self-advocacy is to stand up or speak up for yourself. But how can children self-advocate if they lack the ability to do so? Another phrase for self-advocacy is self-defense. How can children defend themselves if they do not know how to do so? At the onset of this book, the definition of bully was given as someone who enjoys running down the vulnerable, or the gullible. One way to avoid being gullible or vulnerable is to learn how to fight to stand up for yourself. Yes, to speak up for yourself calls for prior knowledge of self-defense, an absence of which could render you vulnerable to bullies. Children, pay attention to the ways of bullies and learn about their weaknesses. Yes, learn about their vulnerability and use it against them. Your parents and siblings could be the best people to teach you how to defend yourself and as discussed above, you need to have the courage and humility to ask them to teach you how to fight. You may have to convince them that you're wanting to learn how to fight is not to be a troublemaker, or a bully, but to be prepared when trouble finds you. You may have to role- play with your dad in the following way. You'll play the role of Uzoh, while your father plays the role of dad.

Uzoh: Hi dad. Could you please teach me how to fight?

Dad: Son, why do you want to learn how to fight?

Uzoh: I want to learn how to fight to defend myself. Yes, to advocate or speak up for me.

Dad: What do you mean, son?

Uzoh: I want to be able to advocate of speak up to defend myself.

Dad: Really?

Uzoh: Yes, really, dad. How can I defend myself if I don't know how to fight?

Dad: Do you want to learn how to fight to bully people around and start trouble?

Uzoh: No, dad. I don't want to bully people or start trouble. I don't like bullies and I don't like trouble. Dad, I want to learn how to fight to be able to defend myself when trouble finds me. Believe me dad, in this crazy world, trouble may find me someday. I just want to be prepared when it does. Moreover, learning how to fight may help me to be in control of my emotions.

Dad: Then I guess I'll have to teach you how to fight. But I don't have the time, son.

Uzoh: Dad, if you don't have time to teach me, can you send me to a self-defense training school where they can teach me how to defend myself?

Dad: Sure, son. I can do that.

Uzoh: Thanks, dad.

Dad: You are welcome, son.

You may need to have a clear image of the big picture in your mind to know where each piece of the puzzle goes. So, you need to figure out the best way to convince your father that you really need this self- defense training which will help you reach the goal of self-advocacy.

Parents, Teach Your Children To Utilize Self-Management Strategies

Self-Management

Self-management is a personal application of behavior-change tactics that produces a desired change in behavior. You teach yourself to despise the maladaptive behavior that prevents you from exhibiting preferred behavior. For someone who desires to quit smoking for example, preferred behavior would be "quit smoking," and maladaptive behavior would be "hanging around bad associates who are recreational smokers and hardcore smokers." For someone serious about quitting smoking, it will behue you to discard your bad associates that glamourize smoking and make new friends that despise smoking. In previous chapters, I explained maladaptive behavior as observance of those factors preventing you from exhibiting the preferred or target behavior. So, you must first despise the maladaptive behavior as something totally wrong for you, an absence of which would make it near impossible, if not impossible to redirect your steps to see the glamour of the preferred behavior. In a nutshell, an evidence-based program to quit smoking, alcoholism, or weight loss can work if and only if, you have the discipline to make it work for you. The discipline will make you stay on course and not relapse even for a moment, as relapsing for a second would render the program futile and you would have proven false to the program. Therefore, stay on course, do not deviate from your chosen evidence-based program.

Self-monitoring is a procedure whereby a person observes her behavior systematically and records the occurrence or nonoccurrence of the target behavior. For someone desiring to quit smoking, you want to record the number of times you give in to or not give in to maladaptive behaviors per day, per month, or per year. Yes, you will observe your own behavior and honestly grade your progress.

Self-recording is a comparison of the individual's performance with a predetermined goal or standard. You have a set goal which may be to quit smoking, you want to compare where you were last month with where you are now, figure out if there is progress in your performance thus far, and adjust for the better.

Pivotal Behavior or Skill

- An application where the individual keeps track of his or her own behavior
- Self-management transfers the control from the adult to the child
- Self-management can be taught to students with varying ability
- Self-management can be used to teach a variety of skills

Two Components of Pivotal Behavior

Controlled Response: the target behavior that a person wants to change.

Controlling Response: self-management behavior emitted to control the target behavior.

Self-Management Tips for Children Under Five Years

Use pictures instead of words - Some children under five years often may not be able to read, so picture-based systems would be more appropriate. Thus, use of pictures instead of words is appropriate for children under five years old[59]

Develop & complete an activity schedule – You could come up with a schedule for the family to engage in some activities like camping, building camps together, drawing, fishing, and the likes.

Use Visual schedules – Set up a visual schedule and place it where all can see. It can be a colorful but not an expensive one. Plan on designing the schedule with your children with ASD asking for their input.

The If-Then Contingencies – This Premack principle is predicated upon encouraging your children to engage in a more challenging activity first, then they can handle the less challenging one. If, for example, your child asks to play with his preferred toys, and you need her to clean up her room, which is a chore that she finds very challenging to do, you could tell her to first clean up her room, then she can play with her preferred toys.

Self-Management Tips for Children Under Twelve Years

Chore charts ➔ Children under twelve can design a chore chart which they can place on a refrigerator for their pride and joy. A sample of chore charts is on the internet which you can find by typing "chore charts" on your favorite search engine.

Brief task analysis like morning routine ➔ Task analysis is the process of breaking down a complex task or chore into smaller and more manageable steps. It should be stated however, that for some individuals on the autism spectrum, even simple tasks can present complex challenges. Therefore, you want to break those simple tasks into simpler tasks for such ones. You can describe the step you'll take to accomplish your morning routine. For example, Step 1. Make the bed. Step 2. Brush your teeth. Step 3. Get ready for school. Step 4. Eat breakfast. Step 5. Go to school.

Delayed reinforcement through token economy systems ➜ The token economy system is a system in which targeted behaviors are reinforced with tokens and later (delayed) exchanged for rewards. The reward is not immediate, the collected tokens will be exchanged for a reward at a later time. Unlike money, tokens are secondary reinforcers (reward involves learning delayed gratification) which children can earn for good behavior, and you, the parents make the rules regarding the number of tokens that can be exchange for specific rewards which are primary reinforcers (reward does not involve learning) like candies, play time, drink juice, etc.; they are things you already know how to do without having to learn how to do them. For example, you know how to eat candy, you know how to play and drink juice.

Benefits of Self-Management Strategies for Children with ASD

The American Psychiatric Association[41] defines Autism Spectrum Disorders (ASD) as "persistent deficits in social communication and social interaction across multiple contexts, as manifested by the deficits in social-emotional reciprocity, deficits in nonverbal communicative behaviors used for social interaction, deficits in developing, maintaining, and understanding relationships such as difficulties adjusting behavior to suit various social contexts and the lack of interest in making friends..." In a nutshell, ASD is a complex developmental condition[60] that involves persistent challenges in social interaction, speech, nonverbal communication, and restricted/repetitive behaviors[61]. The effects of ASD and the severity of symptoms are different in each person[62]. An estimated 5,437,988 (2.21%) adults in the United States have ASD. The prevalence of US adults with ASD ranged from a low of 1.97% in Louisiana to a high of 2.42% in Massachusetts[63]. In a study conducted in 2020 by the

Centers for Disease Control and prevention (CDC), estimated that 1 in 59 children in the U.S. has autism. The prevalence is four times higher among boys than among girls.

The CDC found that children with autism spectrum disorder (ASD) were significantly more likely to wander than children in other study groups. The study revealed that among children with confirmed ASD, more than half, or about 60%, were reported to wander compared to children with a previous but unconfirmed ASD diagnosis, about 41% were reported to wander; compared to children with other developmental disabilities, about 22% were reported to wander; and compared to children in the general population, about 13% were reported to wander. This issue of wandering among people with ASD may be curb via self-management strategies.

The benefits of self-management strategies for children with ASD include self-management helps children and adults with self-regulation, and through self-management, people learn rules and norms for acting appropriately in different situations[64]. Included in self-management strategies are self-monitoring and self- reflection[65]. Self-management also can transfer or generalize to other behaviors and skills across environments and settings, including school, home, and the community.

Self-Management Tips for Teens

Behavioral contacts to earn allowance – Teens can plan to earn more allowance by asking parents what they as teens could do to earn more allowance. Teens can also be their own rewarders by setting reachable goals and rewarding themselves when those set goals are reached.

More advanced task analysis – Task analysis for teens should be more advanced than that of those children under twelve years old. Apart from your morning routine, your task analysis can be made to include the sequence of steps of what you would do at school, after school, at home when you are back from school, before dinner, and before bedtime.

Homework checklists – After putting together a list of your work at home, prioritize and number those tasks in order of importance. Then place a check mark on the ones you have completed until the list is exhausted.

Self-Management Tips for Adults

Task management apps - like "Google Keep." Learn how google keep operates by typing "google keep" on your favorite search engine.

Workplace applications of task analysis - Task analysis is the process of breaking down a complex task, or chore into smaller and more manageable steps. Breaking down your complex task into a sequence of smaller steps, simpler, and more manageable tasks at work ensures that products and services are designed to support those goals efficiently and appropriately. A Work Task Analysis identifies the physical sequence of steps of a specific job with a view to create the right fit between an employee and the job. In a nutshell, an analysis will provide the exact requirements necessary to perform a job safely and efficiently.

Future steps should include programming for maintenance of skills where children with ASD use their self-management skills across settings (school, home, playground, or environment), and time - that is, own these skills forever. Practice makes room for improvement. So, the more these children with ASD practice, the better they will become in managing their own affairs especially during social engagements.

The End

NARRATOR'S CORNER

The moral of this story is that silence can indeed be golden in a case involving an irate opponent who may even be a bully or someone acting unwisely. Silence is simply the best answer for the unwise. This, in a layman's terminology can be said as "silence is the best answer for a fool...." You don't have to give a reply to an irate person with unkind words as it may place you in the same cadre as that irate person and make the situation worse; or as some may prefer, "worsen the situation..." Take for instance, if you suddenly see two people running together and going in the same direction and someone tells you that one of those two runners is mentally challenged or mentally ill and asks you to pick him out. Would you be able to decipher or pick out the mentally challenged runner from the two runners if the similarities are overwhelming? Chances are, you may pick out the wrong one. In the same line of thought, while you may feel that you have to make a point in a given situation, in other situations however, you do not need to. Your silence may be the best answer you could ever give at that point in time to simmer the boiling situation and separate you from the irate one.

Casandra's or Mamma Duck's silence kept her family safe from being harassed or even devoured. We certainly cannot say the same for Chuwawa or Mamma Chicken as her inability to be silent at that trying time made up Mamma Fox's mind to want to turn both Mamma Chicken and her little chicks into dinner. Thanks to mankind, that plight was abated. We need to give it up to Mamma Chicken for yelling out for help when she observed that she was in a situation where all things are no longer equal. When dealing with bullies and you find yourself in a situation where all things are no longer equal, like Mamma Chicken, yell! Yell! Yell out for help! Yes, like a crazy chicken, yell! Yell! Yell out for help! Keep on yelling out for help until it arrives. Behold the things that are falling apart are now coming back together to form a strong whole. Yes, in most cases, silence can indeed, be golden.

A Note To The Bully Community

O, you bullies and those who love the works of darkness, do not endanger the moon; for just as the works of the earth are resident to the earth, the works of the moon are resident to the moon. Does darkness disturb or endanger anyone? No, darkness does not disturb or endanger anyone, except the evildoers. The behavior of an evildoer will not stop the works of righteousness neither can it stop the earth from revolving on its axis around the sun. Compare to the galaxy in which the earth resides, the earth is infinitesimally small. No wonder the greatest man that ever walk on the face of the earth, Jesus Christ, advised that even the most accomplished men on earth should consider themselves as "good for nothing slaves or unprofitable servants"[25] because what they have done is what they ought to have done. Besides, your physical accomplishments as a lone star are resident only to the earth, not recognized outside of the earth's perimeter. And if you want people to believe that you are indeed smart, that knowledge should give you the mindset to be modest with a view to promoting good conscience, character, equity, natural justice, and yes, the general duty to act fairly guided by the wholesome fear of the Highest supremacy.[29]

Come to think of it, the world is like a marketplace. There are buyers and there are sellers. These buyers and sellers exchange goods and services for money or for other goods and services. If you accept gifts of any kind that's worth a fortune in secret, you might become a slave to the donor in secret.

Today, the richest people in the world are fortunate sellers whose services are well paid for by the buyers. If the services of these richest people are no longer required by the buyers, it will only be a matter of time for these richest people to go bankrupt. The direction that I am going with this line of reasoning is that in a marketplace that this world is, both buyers and sellers dearly need each other for thriving. Should one (let's say the buyers) go on strike, the other (the sellers) will be in trouble and vice versa. As the world becomes smaller and smaller by the minute and as time becomes more critical in fulfilment of the Biblical prophecy at 1 Timothy 3:1-5 marking an abrupt end of this abject wicked system of things, "no man will be an Island." Yes, the one you bully today may be in a position to protect and save you tomorrow.

O bully! O bully! O, bully! Always remember Chuwawa's sayings: "whosoever picks up a healthy chicken will pick up a whole lot of insolent complaints." Yes, when bullying someone, you may pick up a whole lot of trouble including one that you probably are not equipped to deal with. "Whosoever plucks a leaf and deep it in his mouth in the presence of a mute, is seeking to be an adversary to the mute." Silence does not equate powerless. It takes strength and deep understanding to exercise the right to be silence especially in a terrible situation. Just because a person is quiet does not and will not make her powerless. Sassy found that out in a way she had never thought she would when she bullied the quiet Akala. What is more, as the condition of this world deteriorates and the intensified remedy to such deterioration is not in sight, the ***eventual ultimatum*** befalls mankind where all things including your plans for the next day suddenly stop at death. As such, being nice to your fellow beings will be in the interest of justice, equity, good conscience and humanity. Be like an oasis in a hot desert to someone, would you? Yes, you can help to mitigate the problems of bullying, if you want to.

Think about it, if a very clever animal is caught in a trap; how difficult would it be for a very stupid animal to be caught with the same trap? There is no doubt in someone's mind that the chief bully, the wicked one, Satan the Devil[33] is a master at setting traps and one of his lures is the "glamour of bully." But this chief bully is already caught in a trap himself and he's doomed for destruction. Why follow him? Kindly help to mitigate the problems of bullying.

I trust that you can do it. Together, may we look forward to the day when our communities will be free of bullies and bully-like challenges.[35]

A Little Bite for Counselors, Therapists, and Teachers to Chew

Do you remember when in training you were taught not to take things personal when giving advice to your clients or students when things are just not going the way you had intended? Or simply, your clients disagreed with your counsel for reasons that are best known to them. One of which may be that your counsel is not beneficial to them. Or that the template you have applied was one that did not fit their situations. Would you lose your cool, or temper, and become belligerent on your clients that you are supposed to be helping and even blame them for your belligerent attitude, accusing them of lacking the spirit of humility? The teachings of not taking things personal because they are not about you, but about the ones you are seeking to help do have Biblical backings at Galatians 6:1. Using the Amplified Bible, it says: "Brothers, if anyone is caught in any sin, you who are spiritual [that is, you who are responsive to the guidance of the Spirit] are to restore such a person in a spirit of gentleness [not with a sense of superiority or self- righteousness], keeping a watchful eye on yourself, so that you are not tempted as well." The Apostle Paul was talking to those with spiritual qualification (which in this case are the Counselors, advisors, therapists, or teachers) about the person who is inadvertently going astray before he knows it (which in this case are the clients or students). Counselors should do the restoration or readjustment with the spirit of gentleness. This means that in counseling clients, Counselors must not be egotistic, must not be puffed up with pride believing that because they are always right, disagreeing with them will be futile with severe consequence. The spirit of gentleness will help Counselors not to have a sense of superiority, or self-righteousness over clients who they seek to help. Having the spirit of gentleness will help Counselors not to become belligerent when clients disagree with them, understanding that clients may be going through situations that are beyond the templates and thoughts of the Counselors.

There are those who have the mistaken view that clients must also have the spirit of gentleness. While all are encouraged to develop the spirit of gentleness, the person who is already going astray may have lost that spirit, hence, going astray. So, this person needs someone who has both the qualification and the spirit of gentleness to readjust him back to the way.

Have you ever heard the notion that "it really does not matter how a counselor counsels the clients"? Hearing that statement makes you wonder whether the bearer of the statement is a well-trained duly certified counselor, or a complete phony. If duly certified counselors, such ones may have proved false to the power of their training as well- trained counselors. All those years spent in college with all the many classes taken emphasizing the importance of expressing empathy to your clients and not taking things personal as it is not about you if your clients are not seeing things your way, seemed to have fallen on deaf ears.

Doubtlessly, some clients can be noncompliant. But you have been trained to handle such cases appropriately using evidence-based behavior reduction procedures like extinction burst that utilizes the power of ignoration. Your clients tremendously need your help in finding their way because they are lost. So, they would do things they have no business doing, and say things they have no business saying. So long as you have it in you that your clients' maladaptive behavior has nothing to do with you and hence, not about you, the counselor, that should give you the spirit of mildness or of gentleness not to be belligerent but to keep your cool as you counsel your noncompliant clients. Do not underestimate the power of extinction procedure or extinction burst which refers to a time when problematic behaviors get worse before they get better. When problematic behavior get worst, that will place your power of ignoration into serious test, in which you must ignore that problematic behavior until your noncompliant client put on the preferred behavior. When the preferred behavior is on, then you can resume giving your attention to your client. When you dance to the music that your noncompliant client is playing for you, you will be reinforcing or rewarding the behavior which will encourage your client to intensify that behavior. If you know that the goal of your noncompliant client is to upset you, you will be reinforcing his behavior if you show her that you are upset.

Therefore, even if the behavior upsets you, you must hide that emotion from your noncompliant client by ignoring that behavior or removing your attention from that behavior. Do not give in regardless to the intensity of that maladaptive behavior. Keep your cool remembering that it is not about you, and things will get back to how you want them. Extinction burst is an evidenced-based procedure that helps keep your cool or your spirit of mildness or of gentleness when dealing with noncompliant clients. Be mild. Be gentle.

May the dusk be more favorable to us than the dawn, O, Father of celestial lights. We are in the beginning of our creative writings, may we never come up short and empty. May our creative writings find favor in the minds and hearts of all the young ones and all the forever young at heart. To such ones we say, we deeply respect and love you dearly. Stay safe and be happy.

The Author: Elijah N. Mekwunye

ENDNOTES

1. August: inspiring reverence or admiration; of supreme dignity or grandeur; majestic. When use as an adjective like in the phrase "August Visitor," it simply means a supremely dignified visitor.

2. Stump: to walk heavily and often angrily.

3. Quench: put out a fire.

4. Debris: the broken pieces that are left when something large has been destroyed, especially by an explosion, fire, or accident.

5. Suffocate: to die from lack of air or kill somebody by stopping him or her from breathing.

6. Trample: to put your feet down on someone or something in a heavy way that causes injury or damage.

7. Incur: to experience something unpleasant as a result of something that you have done.

8. Caliber: somebody's ability, intelligence, or character

9. Goose-years/Human-years

Criteria	Goose-Years	Dog-Years	Human-Years
Puberty Or Adulthood	Most African geese reach puberty in a little over 2 years and will start to look for a mate for life	Most dogs reach puberty between 5 and 12 months old[16].	Most people reach puberty between the ages of 11 and 16[18].
Exceptions To The Above	A different breed of goose may start laying eggs earlier than one-year-old.	Some dogs hit puberty earlier than 5 month-old[16]	Some people reach puberty between the ages of 6 and 10[18].
Ratio in Years	1 year	1 year	8 years

Criteria	Horse-Years	Cat-Years	Human-Years
Puberty OR Adulthood	Most horses reach puberty in a little over 12 to 18 months old[17].	Most cats reach puberty between 5 and 6 months old[16].	Most people reach puberty between the ages of 11 and 16[18].
Exception To The Above	A different breed of horse may reach puberty earlier than 1-year-old[17].	Some cats can breed earlier than 5 months in some cases if they reach 80% of their adult age[16].	Some people reach puberty between the ages of 6 and 10[18].
Ratio in Years	1 year	0.5 year	8 years

In general, one (1) Goose-year is equivalent to eight (8) Human-years. An example is, a 2-year-old goose will be 2 X 8 = 16 years. So, we say that the goose is 16 years old in human-years.

A 3-year old dog will be 24 years old in human-years since one (1) dog-year equals eight (8) human-years (3 x 8 = 24).

A 4-year old horse will be 4 x 8 = 32. So we say that the horse is 32 years old in human years.

A 2-year old cat will be (2 / 0.5) X 8 = 32 years old in human years.

10. Slang: To attack (someone) using abusive language

11. Challenger Deep: The deepest part of the ocean is called the Challenger Deep and is located beneath the western Pacific Ocean in the southern end of the Mariana Trench, which runs several hundred kilometers southwest of the U.S. territorial island of Guam. Challenger Deep is **approximately 36,200 feet deep**. [Wikipedia, the free encyclopedia]

12. The easiest way is to get on the internet and type in "the great turtle myth" without the quotes.

13. Fifth Amendment (U.S. Constitution): "No person shall be held to answer for a capital, or otherwise infamous crime, unless on a presentment or indictment of a Grand Jury, except in cases arising in the land or naval forces, or in the Militia, when in actual service in time of War or public danger; nor shall any person be subject for the same offence to be twice put in jeopardy of life or limb, nor shall be compelled in any criminal case to be a witness against himself, nor be deprived of life, liberty, or property, without due process of law; nor shall private property be taken for public use without just compensation." Whenever you do not feel like answering a question that you think might incriminate you in the United States, you can invoke or use the fifth amendment as a leverage. That means, you do not have to

answer that question.

14. Matthew 7:12 - The Holy Scriptures

15. Kola-nut: Every country and culture have their own version of kola-nut. In the western hemisphere for example, kola- nut can be an alcoholic beverages or drinks such as wine or gin that one serves his guest with. Kola-nut can also mean the real seed of the kola or cola tree that some traditional Africans serve to their guest to be chewed sometimes with alligator pepper or pepper corn. This seed can also be made into a drink like wine.

16. Article on "Age of Sexual Maturity in Dogs", "Age of Sexual Maturity in Cats" by Dr. Foster & Dr. Smith – Educational Staff of Pet education. Article on "Feline Puberty Arrives | Animal Planet" by Naomi Millburn, Demand Media 1997

17. Article on "Horse Breeding Behavior" by Ashley Griffin, University of Kentucky. "Equine Reproductive Maturity in Mares and Stallions" Submitted by EquiMed Staff on Sat, 03/13/2010

18. "Puberty" - Wikipedia, the free encyclopedia. "The Beginning and End of Reproductive Life: Pubertal and Midlife Changes" by Kirtly Parker Jones, M.D. Associate Professor Department of OB/GYN University of Utah College of Medicine, 1997.

19. The publication of Hannah Arendt's 1963 book Eichmann in Jerusalem: A Report on the Banality of Evil.

20. Genesis 4:8,9 - The Holy Scriptures

21. Ecclesiastes 3:11 - The Holy Scriptures

22. Genesis 6:4,5;7:1-8 Numbers 13:33 – Revised Standard Version

23. Joshua 24:15; Deuteronomy 30:15,19 - The Holy Scriptures

24. John 4:24; 8:32; 17:3 - American Standard Version

25. Luke 17:10 - The Holy Scriptures

26. A-Student: A student who gets a letter grade of "A" in all of the classes taken per semester/quarter system.

27. The Holy Scriptures at Ephesians 6:4; 2 Corinthians 4:4; Acts 19:12-16; Luke 7:21

28. Kindly type the name exactly as you see it in this book onto your preferred internet search engine or browser to see a clear image of the object. We may also put some on the
https://msurecords.com/animal-characters-in-the-book-is-silence-really-golden/

Small birds like the red and blue cardinals, the blue Grosbeak, are fantastic singers and when you are in a jungle like bush; you will hear their beautiful voices but may need a set of binoculars or good eye sights to see them. When you do, colors become an integral part of your appreciation of these little fellows. There are differences between a Cattle-Egret and a Great-Egret. They both look alike in that they are white feathered birds. As the name implied, the Cattle-Egret is usually found mingling with cattle and has short thick necks in comparison to the Great- Egret. The Great-Egret on the other hand, is long necked not usually found among cattle but in swampy bush or forest and it is superstitiously believed by some that its bones must not be broken. If it does, you do not want to be around to witness the adverse effects it will have on the believers of that superstition. It makes you wonder, if the Great- Egret is edible, how does believers of the superstition prepare it if its bones are not to be broken? I'll let you think about that as a puzzle.

29. Exodus 6:2-3; Psalms 83:18 - The King James Version

30. Row: pronounced raou - means a noisy argument or dispute.

31. Genesis 1:30 - New World Translation of The Holy Scriptures

32. Diokpara:this is used to address the eldest or the first son in a Family circle as a sign of respect.

33. Revelation 12:9, 12 - New World Translation of The Holy

Scriptures

34. Job 26:7; Isaiah 40:22 - New World Translation of The Holy Scriptures

35. Psalms 37:9-11,29; Revelation 21:3,4 NewWorld Translation of The Holy Scriptures

36. Matthew 6:19-20 - King James Version

37. Matthew 5:39 - Revised Standard Version

38. The Holy Scriptures Psalms 127:3 - King James Version

39. Kindly type the words "child development stages" into your preffered internet search engine.

40. Sigmund (Sigismund) Schlomo Freud: The Ego and the id (German: Das Ich und das Es) 1923

41. Jerry M. Burger: Personality – 10th Edition 2017

42. American Psychiatric Association (APA): Diagnostic and Statistical Manual of Mental Disorders—DSM-5 2013

43. David G. Myers & Jean M. Twenge: Social Psychology – 12th Edition 2016

44. Proverbs 22:3 - New World Translation of The Holy Scriptures

45. Matthew 7: 24 – 27 - New World Translation of The Holy Scriptures

46. Genesis 1:26,27 - New World Translation of The Holy Scriptures

47. Adrian Raine: Psychopathy: An Introduction to Biological Findings and Their Implications (Psychology and Crime) 2014

48. 1 John 5:14; Hebrews 2:4; John 9:31 – The Holy Scriptures

49. Philemon 14; Leviticus 1:3; Hosea 14:4 – King James Version

50. Ecclesiates 3:1,2- Revised Standard Version

51. Cynthia Lightfoot, Michael Cole, et al: The Development of Children May 4, 2012

52. https://www.npr.org/2020/07/08/888539083/trumps- drive-on-division-and-fear-may-not-be-a-winning-strategy- come-november - July 8, 2020

53. https://cnnphilippines.com/world/2020/6/24/barack- obama-accuses-donald-trump-actively-promoting- division.html - By MJ Lee, Dan Merica and Sarah Mucha, CNN. Published Jun 24, 2020 11:29:38 AM

54. Corona Virus or COVID-19 Statistics https://www.bing.com/search?q=current+number+of+infected+ with+coronavirus&form=EDNTHT&refig=a52f96bf95f84 c5c959ae8f9aa568aec&mkt=en-us&msnews=1&PC=HCTS&sp=2&ghc=1&qs=SC&pq=current+nu mber+of+affected+&sk=PRES1SC1&sc=3-27&cvid=a52f96bf95f84c5c959ae8f9aa568aec&cc=US&setla ng=en-US

55. https://thepointsguy.com/guide/places-americans-can- travel-internationally/

56. The New York Times on brutal racial injustice in America – https://www.nytimes.com/video/us/100000007159353/geo rge-floyd-arrest-death-video.html

57. Revelation 21:3,4 - King James Version

58. Romans 1:19,20; Colossians 1:15,16; Hebrews 11:27; 1 Timothy 1:17 – Revised Standard Version

59. Judith A. Lewis, Robert Q. Dana, Gregory A. Blevins –

60. Substance Abuse counseling sixth edition AC Stahmer, L Schreibman (1992): Teaching children with autism appropriate play in unsupervised environments using a self-management treatment package - Journal of Applied Behavior

61. LK Koegel, MN Park, RL Koegel (2014): Using self-management to improve the reciprocal social conversation of children with autism spectrum disorder - … of autism and developmental disorders- Springer

62. L Schreibman, RL Koegel (1996): Fostering self-management: Parent-delivered pivotal response training for children with autistic disorder - psycnet.apa.org

63. KL Pierce, L Schreibman (1994): Teaching daily living skills to children with autism in unsupervised settings through pictorial self-management - Journal of applied behavior analysis - Wiley Online Library

64. Lisa D Wiggins, Carolyn DiGuiseppi, Laura Schieve, Eric Moody, Gnakub Soke, Ellen Giarelli, Susan Levy (2020): Wandering Among Preschool Children with and Without Autism Spectrum Disorder

65. K Callahan, JA Rademacher (1999): Using self-management strategies to increase the on-task behavior of a student with autism - Journal of Positive Behavior …,- journals.sagepub.com

66. LK Koegel, MN Park, RL Koegel (2014): Using self-management to improve the reciprocal social conversation of children with autism spectrum disorder - … of autism and developmental disorders- Springer